Lagrange Rising

A Cuss Abbott Novel

Doug J. Cooper

Also by Doug J. Cooper

Crystal Deception (Book 1)
Crystal Conquest (Book 2)
Crystal Rebellion (Book 3)
Crystal Escape (Book 4)
Crystal Horizon (Short prequel & sampler)

Bump Time Origin (Book 1)
Bump Time Meridian (Book 2)
Bump Time Terminus (Book 3)

For info and updates, please visit: crystalseries.com

Published by: Douglas Cooper Consulting

Beta reviewer: Mark Mesler
Book editor: Tammy Salyer
Cover design: Damonza

ISBN-13: 978-1-7337801-7-9

Author website: www.crystalseries.com

For Jim, with love

Chapter 1

Floating over to the makeshift operating table, the doctor hooked his toes into stirrups on the floor, securing himself in the weightless environment. His patient—a man in his nineties—lay face down, strapped to the table, unmoving from a drug-induced coma. His shirt had been removed but nothing else.

The doctor studied the tired skin on the elder man's neck and back, a wrinkled canvas below thinning gray hair. Typical of the aged, he had a few skin tags, a small cyst near his right shoulder, and a scatter of brown blemishes, bigger than freckles but similar in appearance, as if someone had dripped brown paint on him from a foot or so up.

The doctor didn't need to disinfect the back of the old man's neck because the guy wouldn't live long enough for an infection to take hold. But he cleaned it anyway, a habit ingrained from his years of practice. He lowered magnifying glasses over his eyes and adjusted the overhead light to provide maximum illumination to his work area.

Using an index finger, the doctor traced a line from the bottom of the man's skull, down the cervical vertebrae of his neck, stopping an inch or so onto his torso. He selected the self-cauterizing scalpel from his minimalist tool set, carefully pressed the blade against the skin at the base of the skull, and repeated that same trail, this time using the instrument to make a shallow, six-inch incision, drawing the blade through the skin, stopping his cut where the thoracic vertebrae started.

He exchanged the scalpel for a sickle probe, teased open the layers of skin, and fished around until he found the fine coated wire buried inside. Ever so gently, he tugged the wire up, working it out of its narrow channel, moving it gingerly so as not to disturb the connection near the skull. The tail end of the wire resisted his efforts, and he used the scalpel to widen the opening, worrying it until the wire came free.

Holding the short wire up from the old man's body with his left hand, he used his right to fit a white adhesive bandage over the wound to seal it, careful not to pull on the end of the wire still buried. He lay the wire on top of the dressing and placed a strip of medical tape near the buried end to ensure it didn't move.

Blowing through pursed lips, he exhaled in relief. The hard part was done. Though it was cold in the room, he wiped sweat from his brow using a sleeve of his dress shirt—the doctor wasn't wearing sterile medical scrubs the way he would in his regular practice.

A small electronic appliance was fastened to a table next to him, coils of cable floating loosely above it. From among the coils, he located the connector on the end, snaked it over to the wire on the man's neck, and clipped the two together. He watched the display on the box, and when it registered the name of the patient, Robert Garrison Moore, he allowed himself a smile.

He spoke to his employer, who was in an adjacent

room. "It's done. Can you see it?"

His employer reviewed the doctor's work using his own equipment. "How much time do we have?" he asked.

The doctor checked Moore's vital signs. "He's in good shape. Keep him hydrated, and he should last five days. I'd even bet on a week."

Betting is what put the doctor in this position in the first place.

"Good. Top off the drip feed and you can go."

"Confirm my balance?" he asked as he transferred clear liquid into the reservoir.

"This brings your debt down to a hundred grand. I've logged it for you."

The doctor earned twenty-five thousand common for each case. When they'd given him the choice of either this or dying, he'd owed them a hundred and seventy-five thousand with no hope of paying it off. He'd have to do this four more times to bring his debt to zero.

Assuming he didn't get caught. And that he didn't lose any more money to them from his gambling addiction.

Chapter 2

C uss Abbott drained his coffee and tried to catch Hatha's eye. He wanted another cup, but she was chatting up a customer on his way out the door. Sinking back into the chair, he watched the foot traffic outside and waited his turn. With food kiosks located throughout the city and plentiful seating near them, he went to cafés for the same reason everyone else did: human interaction and personal attention.

The place—Nature's Nook Café—was cozy enough, with red and yellow blossoms on foliage hanging from the ceiling, trailing down the walls to the floor. But given that plants were everywhere in Hermes—oxygen sources were vital to a space habitat—it wasn't the floral display that brought him in.

He was here because he found Hatha alluring. Mid-thirties, petite, orange-red hair that hung to her shoulders, hazel eyes, cleft on her chin with matching dimples, strongish nose that worked with everything else. She wore a simple pink shift draped in front with a smock-style white lace apron, a chaste uniform that inexplicably stirred his imagination. He could be patient.

Nature's Nook had six tables, three on either side of the door. Made of metal lattice glazed in white enamel, they were lined up in front of big windows looking out onto the main thoroughfare. He sat to the right, at the table farthest from the door, his chair the one that put his back to the wall so he faced out to see the room. He was the only customer on his side of the entrance.

Across the way, two women were seated at the table nearest the door. They were chatting about something that seemed outlandish to one, an older woman who, as she listened to her companion, brought a hand to her throat, then covered her mouth, then sat back in her chair, mouth agape, hand back at her throat.

Hatha had finished with the departing customer and was starting toward Cuss when a punk entered the café. The guy loped across the white-tiled floor in the long strides of someone comfortable in a low-gravity environment.

From that first instant, Cuss disliked the guy. It was primal. Visceral. He'd dealt with his share of toughs in his forty-one years, and this one was stereotypical of the lot. Average height, square face, muscular in the chest, arms a little too long for his body. Arrogant sneer. He wore black pants, black shirt, black jacket, and black shoes, strutting like King Shit on parade in clothes that looked expensive but didn't quite fit the way expensive clothes should.

The King squared up in front of Hatha, feet apart, elbows out.

The interruption meant Cuss would have to wait longer for service. And the guy's attitude bothered him. Using his lens—an inconspicuous contact lens packed with ultra-high-tech capabilities that enhanced both sight and sound—he listened to the exchange.

The tough tilted his head forward and looked under

his heavy brow. "I've been nice to you, and you avoid me."

"You shouldn't bother me at work," she said in a firm tone. "I have customers." She tilted her head toward Cuss, bringing him into it.

"Agree to have dinner with me and I'll leave." The punk clenched and unclenched his fists. Fast. Nervous. Like he was using imaginary squeeze balls to strengthen his grip.

"I'm asking you to leave."

Cuss pushed his chair back, his mind calculating angles and distance, accounting for obstacles, giving the floor a quick scan for stray liquids. This was Luna level, so the gravity was one-sixth that of Earth, just like the Moon.

While he waited to see if the thug would cross a line, he lifted up on the edge of his table, confirming it was fastened in place, a practice that made it available as a handhold, a courtesy for those accustomed to Earth gravity who needed places to grab to keep themselves upright as they navigated their day.

It also meant he could use it as a launchpad, pushing against it with his feet, propelling himself in the weak gravity across the room like a human missile. Given their positions, he felt confident he could put his shoulder into the punk's right knee before the guy even knew he was on his way.

A blow like that, delivered by a six-foot one-inch tall, two-hundred-twenty-pound projectile, would cave the joint and disable the guy. That would give Cuss time to right himself—something that took longer in weak gravity—and get control of the situation. And while seemingly dramatic, it would save him from having to explain why he drew a weapon inside the city.

But then Hatha shifted one foot back and lowered her body, centering herself over bent knees, chin up, hands in front of her, loose, not in fists, facing the punk square on, unflinching in the face of intimidation.

Cuss's lust turned to love.

The punk, lost in his personal drama, didn't seem to notice her shift to a ready stance. But he did realize he was drawing unwanted attention, because he looked around the room, saw Cuss glaring at him, and stepped back from Hatha.

"Another time." He gave her a curt nod, then turned and made for the exit. He swiveled his head toward Cuss on the way out the door, challenging him with a cold stare, looking him up and down like he was cataloging him for later.

Cuss used his lens to ID the guy: Stanislav Shevchenko, thirty-six years old, here in the city on a visa from Earth.

Cuss called to his partner, Ygo, who monitored everything he did using the multitude of sensor feeds from throughout Hermes. "Profile that asshole. Both directions." By that he meant for Ygo to search back in time to learn Shevchenko's history. And track him forward, documenting the full who, what, when, where, how, and why of his life until they understood who he was.

"Only if you pitch her." When Ygo spoke, Cuss heard him inside his head, a private communication no others could hear.

But Cuss had to speak aloud for Ygo to hear him. "Please don't lose him." He leaned forward to watch Shevchenko through the window. The punk was cutting across pedestrian traffic, taking bounding strides to the pod station across the way.

"She knows you're interested," said Ygo. "Why else would you go there three days in a row and stare at her? If you don't ask her out pretty soon, she'll move you from admirer to creep."

Hatha walked in his direction carrying a coffee carafe, dancing on her toes to keep the steps small, her swaying hips stoking Cuss's overactive imagination.

He stood as she approached, smiling to reassure her, his Greek and Italian heritage combining to give him a certain charm and appeal. He'd learned early on that women were attracted to him, praising him in the past with labels as flattering as Greek god. One had told him he was as handsome as a Praetorian guardsman, which he took as a compliment, though he wasn't really sure what image the term conjured for her.

"Refill?" Her smile showed her dimples. "Cops eat free."

"Ouch." He looked down to recall what he was wearing. It was pretty much what he wore every day: sturdy black pants, blue collared shirt, gray blazer.

"Sorry." She shrugged. "Your whole outfit screams 'cop,' but those shoes are a dead giveaway."

His shoes were Vela ShapeShifters. Ugly as hell, but popular with working stiffs because they were still comfortable after a long day of standing and walking. Plus, they had adaptive contours that automatically adjusted foot position as gravity changed, valuable if your day took you across the decks of the city.

Nature's Nook Café was located in Hermes, one of four cities comprising Lagrange. Each of the cities was contained within its own thirty-kilometer-long, five-kilometer-wide cylindrical structure floating in permanent station between Earth and the Moon. Two million residents called the four immense city-tubes of Lagrange home.

"Hey." She tilted her head to catch his eye. "Looking like a cop isn't a bad thing. Not to me. I worked Community Patrol for four years before I opened this place."

Cuss acknowledged her words by removing his badge from his inside jacket pocket and holding it up for her to see—a gold, six-pointed star in a brown wallet, emblazoned with the title: Interworld Marshal.

He waited for her reaction, knowing that local cops, though usually their detectives, saw marshals as a threat. For them, it was all about who got the credit for closing a case, who could list the success on their record. Credit was important currency in their world because it bought the next raise or promotion. Or perhaps paid for the unfortunate, "We'll overlook your fuck-up…this time."

"A roamer," she said. "Impressive. I didn't realize I was in the presence of Mister Fancy Pants."

The countries of Earth, Nova Terra on the Moon, Lagrange, and Utopia on Mars were sovereign nations. With independent governments, each decided their own policing priorities. But with different cultures, their priorities didn't always align. Mars in particular wanted to attract settlers and wasn't picky about the quality of their immigrants. And all three non-Earth worlds were reluctant to commit precious resources to solve a rich neighbor's problem.

Sophisticated criminals began exploiting the differences, seeking to escape justice by fleeing to the world where their transgression wasn't an enforcement priority. Eventually, all the worlds got dinged enough times that it drove them to agree on a common solution: forty interworld marshals with the authority to investigate major crimes and pursue suspects if the offense crossed world boundaries. The authority to pursue led to the "roamer" label.

Cuss put a leg forward to model his pants, teasing her with a straight face, "They're not *that* fancy." Then he adopted a serious demeanor. "Was that guy bothering you?"

"Why, are you my knight in shining armor?"

He shrugged. "If he's a problem, I can talk to him."

She studied him. Like she was deciding. "You *are* hot for me." He was about to speak when she said, "I can handle Stan. But let me add that you don't hide your lust very well, Mr. Pants. You've been undressing me with your eyes for days. It's both embarrassing and intimidating."

Cuss's face turned bright red. He considered himself a smooth operator. "I'm Cuss."

"What?"

"Cuss."

"Okay. Dammit to hell." With an impish grin, she

winked. "I see your name when you pay. I've been hoping you'd come back just so I could use that line." A chime sounded, and she looked toward the door, saw a couple entering, and said, "Gotta get back to it."

"I'd like to get to know you better." He spoke in a rush before she got too far away. He normally suggested coffee as a first date, which is what he hoped this would be, though he'd never say that out loud. But since Hatha worked the business, he went for something different. "Would you like to visit a park with me? Go for a walk?"

She looked back over her shoulder but kept moving. "I'll be at Lobo Park tomorrow after lunch service. I'd love it if you stopped by."

. . .

Hatha's enthusiastic reply put Cuss on top of the world. But the euphoric feeling was short-lived. On his way out of the café, Ygo called.

"We caught a case."

"Let's hear it," he said as he crossed the pedestrian thoroughfare that ran in front of Nature's Nook and the neighboring shops.

There were no private conveyances in the city—no cars, carts, or scooters—though there were the occasional utility lorries moving merchandise, equipment, and the like. For shorter distances, people traveled by foot, moving along the lanes of a road that looked something like the straightaway of a running track.

The surface of the thoroughfare was a brown rubbery

material that provided a firm grip while at the same time easing the impact of each step. The roadbed itself was divided in two by a narrow median that separated people moving in opposite directions. Each side was divided again to provide a fast lane for those moving quickly in the low gravity and a slow lane for those taking their time. But like Cuss and his jaywalking, few residents worried about staying in their proper lanes.

Traffic was light, and he made it across in five easy hop-steps. On the other side, he headed for the pod station: public transit that made cars and scooters unnecessary. It was the same station that Stan the Punk had used.

"Janice Wallingford claims that her father, Franklin Wallingford, has been kidnapped from his home in Armstrong," said Ygo. "Ms. Wallingford made enough noise for an investigation, and Detective Darlena Washington—remember her?—has uncovered evidence that supports the kidnapping claim. Darlena believes Mr. Wallingford is being held here in Lagrange."

Did he remember Darlena? Cuss couldn't forget her. A full-figured black woman with big hair and big opinions, Darlena was hardworking and competent at her job. He'd helped her solve a case last year that had started on Earth and ended in Armstrong, the capital city of the lunar nation of Nova Terra. She'd warned him when they first met that he should stay out of her way, claiming that interworld marshals were showboaters who hogged the spotlight but contributed little. She never apologized for the snark, even after he'd located and captured the suspect, then given her credit for the bust.

"What's her evidence?" he asked Ygo.

"A sensor feed showing Mr. Wallingford being escorted from his apartment by an unidentified man. A later feed shows the pair boarding a private ship at Port Collins. That ship was tracked here. I have a record of the ship's arrival six hours later."

Cuss approached the pod concourse, an entryway that merged everyone into a single line to feed the loading platform. There, in the same way that a ski lift stages gondolas for skiers to board, this system presented much smaller travel pods for people to ride in. Each pod could seat four in a compact open-air cabin, whisking passengers along special lanes to any location in the city.

He entered the queue and, channeled by shiny chrome guardrails, made his way up the ramp to a loading platform. The walls on either side of the entryway were covered in decorative, oxygen-producing plants, interspersed at regular intervals with informative signs, a combination of loading and travel information for newbies, and adverts for a variety of goods and services available in the city.

A soft voice issued a warning: "Please be ready to step forward when it's your turn."

The line moved quickly, his brain subconsciously matching the people ahead of him with the queue of pods. He'd get the unadorned yellow one seven cars back.

But he was wrong, which annoyed the detective in him. Two of the passengers ahead of him, clearly a couple, were going to different destinations, so they took separate pods. That meant he'd get the one after the yellow one, a pod painted with a colorful theme of Poetry Power, decorated and signed by the students from Ross Elementary.

"Who was Mr. Wallingford's escort?" asked Cuss, moving to the edge of the platform. He was next.

"The person used a data mask, so we don't know. But mask usage reinforces the claim of nefarious activity. Normal people can't get them."

In Ygo's lexicon, "normal people" were law-abiding citizens.

Cuss stepped into the pod, a small box with brown padded seats facing each other, the seats wide enough for two passengers and close enough that if people were sitting on either side, their knees would be just inches apart. Unlike a ski lift, the pod didn't hang from a cable but had its own self-contained drive system that moved it along dedicated lanes.

He folded himself into the forward-facing seat, muscled arms stretched along the top of the surround, huge hands draped back inside. The pod started moving. The next person in line stepped forward to the edge of the platform.

"Is the ship still here?" he asked Ygo.

"It is."

"Anyone get off?"

"Two people, but with the data mask, I can't really be certain who they were."

"Any freight removed?"

"The usual. Nothing unusual, anyway."

"Has anyone searched the ship?"

"The pilot let a couple of Community Patrol officers on board to look around. He didn't insist on a warrant, which in retrospect was a clever move. He was in their face the whole time, protesting his innocence and outrage, so they hurried, which kept the search superficial. In any case, they didn't find the old man. I've poked around the ship myself and couldn't find him either, but that doesn't mean much, because most of their internal sensors are either broken or disabled."

"If he's not on board, then where is he?"

"That's the thing. He's disappeared. I can't locate him in any of the cities."

"*You* can't?"

Ygo was an enhanced human, so hearing him say he couldn't do something as simple as locating a person known to be somewhere in Lagrange didn't make sense. An interworld marshal himself, Ygo resided in his own private den in the lower hold of *Nelly Marie*, the Marshals Service space cruiser he shared with Cuss. The den was his permanent home, where he lived in solitude, never emerging, a hermit in his lair. He supported Cuss electronically, using an AI network integrated into his brain, dedicating the resource to give his partner unparalleled access to information.

Though Cuss considered Ygo a close and trusted friend, they had met only once in their six-year partnership, the day Ygo moved into the ship's hold.

"Has Darlena sent along the interview with the daughter? What was her name again?"

"Janice Wallingford. I have the interview. But she's here in Lagrange. She came to agitate the locals into helping. I thought you'd want to speak with her yourself before viewing Darlena's work."

"She's here? Where?"

"Deck 6. She's staying downtown at the Braxis Inn."

"Let me guess. She's from Earth. She traveled to Nova Terra fairly recently because of her father. She's staying middeck here to keep her sea legs no matter which world she goes to next."

"And that's why they made you a marshal."

While Ygo was often sarcastic, Cuss liked that he was always loyal and supportive.

"Another guess. This pod isn't headed for *Nelly Marie*. I'm on my way to Deck 6."

"They should make you director."

The fact that the pod was ascending was a pretty big clue.

He could feel his weight increasing as he rode up the interdeck shaft, pods ahead and behind him, decorative lights and omnipresent foliage along the rise making the ride cheery. He popped out on Deck 6, putting him in a gravity that was halfway between Earth and the Moon. Downtown was three kilometers away, and as the pod started in that direction, he sat back and enjoyed the view.

The middle levels of the city, Decks 3 through 10, were the working-class neighborhoods, where rent was more reasonable, amenities fewer, and the ceilings lower. In the middecks, the "sky," the floor of the deck above, was a hundred meters up. High enough for a thirty-story building. High enough to project a credible sun sweeping across a sea of blue, one you could feel the heat from, with clouds of different types on different days. High enough for a star-filled sky at night with the Moon passing through its phases over the course of a month.

But it was nothing like the three-hundred-meter skies of Terra or Luna, the so-called premier decks, where the virtual presentation seemed so real that if you'd magically arrived there blindfolded, you might be fooled in the first minutes.

The pod tooled along its dedicated lane toward downtown, located near the center of the thirty-kilometer expanse. Like all decks, population density peaked in the middle, decreasing toward the suburbs located near the ends of the cylindrical structure.

Property was incredibly expensive in the tube city, so it never got close to rural in the suburbs. But there were parks in the outskirts. And neighborhoods with individual houses. The homes in the upscale neighborhoods even had tiny front yards, often demarcated with a narrow hedge to contain a societal indulgence, perhaps a sculpture or a bench, a luxury because it was a decoration not producing oxygen.

The pod jogged left and, after a bit, turned north on Strip S-9 toward downtown.

"Don't let the ship leave until I can look myself."

"Easy enough."

"And do your best to get an inventory of everything that's been removed."

Below and to his left, a group of teenagers moved toward the city center on the pedestrian thoroughfare, laughing, talking loudly, one doing acrobatics made possible by the weaker gravity. Buildings lined both sides of the roadway, four- and five-story constructions, each one pressed against the next to ensure there was no wasted space.

The structures were formed from condensate—composite material derived from asteroids from the belt—lending a certain sameness to their appearance. The similarity was reinforced in that the bottom floor of each building was devoted to commerce: a store, restaurant, or office. The floors above were all homes and apartments, living space for those who used the shops below.

But the presentation was by no means dreary. Contrast was created by tinting each building with a different pastel color—pale reds, yellows, greens, blues—with a varying selection of foliage covering the front. The result was a stunning display when viewed from afar.

About halfway to his destination, he passed the Olde New England Glass Museum, its façade constructed to look like an old-time glassworks. He wondered if it might be a place to take Hatha should tomorrow's walk in the park work out. He viewed their offerings on his lens and discovered they had a resident glass blower who used a brick furnace to demonstrate the craft.

Four buildings down from the museum, he passed the Fisherman's Wharf Seafood Restaurant and Pub. He learned they had a nice beer selection and offered a virtual whale-watching adventure as well. Together the venues sounded like a fun evening. He logged the information for later.

He reached downtown soon after. The buildings there were similar to the ones farther out, but here they climbed to eight and ten stories. And the shops at street level were upscale venues—clothes, shoes, furnishings, jewelry, electronics—placed in the city center where crowds gathered.

The pod stopped at a platform two blocks from the Braxis Inn. Cuss stepped out and walked the last bit. It was still a good hour before lunchtime, but Cuss's stomach growled anyway, a seemingly permanent condition. He eyed a delight of pastries in the window of a store at the pod station exit, decided he wanted something more substantial, and grabbed a sandwich wrap from a shop three doors down, perfect for eating on the go.

"Janice is quite effective at agitating for her dad," said Ygo. "If you're conciliatory up front, it will lessen the drama."

Scarfing his food, Cuss didn't respond, finishing just as a modest marquee on the front of a building announced it as the Braxis Inn. He disposed of his lunch waste in a city trash chute and entered through broad glass doors adorned with stylized black *Welcome Home* decals painted on the front.

The lobby of the Braxis Inn, a small open concourse with a floor of commercial-grade mosaic tile, was unremarkable. A light fixture designed to look like an old-style candle chandelier hung from a white-painted ceiling overhead. A gift shop cubby with touristy souvenirs was positioned to the right. A cloth-covered couch and matching chairs to the left, with stock prints in simple frames hanging behind. And at the back, a huge clock built into the wall stared at him from behind the registration desk, telling him it was 11:16. The desk itself was made of faux oak stained a mahogany red with a white marble top. And unlike Earth with its ubiquitous androids, there was an actual person, a middle-aged man, standing behind it.

"Welcome home," said the man with forced enthusiasm. "Will it be just one today?"

Cuss shook his head as he showed his badge. The man stiffened, something Cuss was used to.

"You have a guest named Janice Wallingford." He said it as a statement. Ygo was never wrong about that sort of thing. "Is she in?" He knew she was. Ygo again. "Could you ask her to come down to the lobby? Tell her that Marshal Abbott is here to speak with her."

Cuss didn't want to call the woman himself, because people tended to ask questions before assenting to the meet: Who are you? What's this about? Should I have a lawyer? He'd learned it was better to start the conversation when they were face-to-face.

He also didn't want to invade the woman's privacy. The rooms here were certainly tiny. She'd have her personal effects spread out in the limited space. And they'd need to either stand in the cramped room or sit on the bed, a setting unfavorable to a productive interview.

The clerk looked at a display on the desk behind the countertop, confirmed Cuss's statements, and nodded.

"I'll be over there." Cuss poked a thumb over his shoulder at the couch, then moved there to wait.

The doors to the lift were adjacent to the registration desk. When they opened, the clock on the wall showed 11:22. Janice stepped out, scanned the lobby, saw Cuss looking back at her, and then looked at the counter clerk for confirmation. The man nodded. She strode in his direction, arms folded in front of her.

Cuss waited, letting her come to him, mostly so they would have distance from the clerk, but also so they could sit in the lobby chairs.

As she approached, Cuss saw a well-kept woman in her late sixties, which meant the missing father was likely in his late eighties or early nineties. She wore a cream-colored sweater and gray slacks. At five foot one, she was a full foot shorter than Cuss. She looked tired.

Cuss took out his badge wallet and showed his credentials. "I'm Marshal Abbott." He motioned to a chair and then turned the adjacent one to face hers. After sitting, he leaned forward, resting his arms on his knees, trying to show engagement and interest. She sat upright and stiff, perched on the edge of her seat. "I understand you're worried about your dad."

"He's been kidnapped and is being held here in Lagrange," she replied without preamble. "Have you spoken with Detective Washington? She led the investigation in Armstrong. She documented his movements."

"My partner is in contact with her, but I need to work through it with you myself. I know that's frustrating, but it's my process. It'll help me move quicker."

She started to speak and then stopped and nodded.

"First you. Where do you live?"

He walked her through the basics. Janice was an only child, born and raised in Cleveland, now living in

Lakewood, Colorado. She was sixty-six, divorced, and childless. Her mother had passed ten years earlier. Her missing father was ninety-six and had lived outside Golden, Colorado, until fourteen months ago. His frailties were impacting his quality of life, so he'd moved to Armstrong, where the weak gravity restored his mobility.

"Did you visit him in Armstrong?"

"I came with him when he moved, but I couldn't stay. I need sun and love the mountains, and I'm not comfortable in low gravity."

"She also has a boyfriend in Lakewood," Ygo told him. "Teddy Edgar. They've been an item for three years."

Cuss let the omission slide for now but noted that she was editing her story. "Does he live in a senior facility?"

She shook her head. "His mind is sharp. It's his mobility limiting him. That's why he moved to Armstrong. He lived in a house in Colorado but moved to an apartment in Nova Terra so he wouldn't have to worry about maintenance."

"Do you visit him?"

"I accompanied him on his move and then visited twice more, once for his birthday, and again at Thanksgiving. The trip is so expensive, though, that I couldn't make a regular thing out of it."

"She's upper-middle-class," said Ygo. "But her dad is loaded and generous to her. It wasn't the money keeping her away."

"Tell me about his disappearance. Take me through the sequence of when you became concerned about him, traveled to Armstrong, and then came here."

"Dad and I talk daily. Not long conversations. But long enough for him to know I'm okay, and me, him. Five days ago…" She paused, calculating in her head. "…yeah, Saturday, he didn't answer. I tried a half-dozen times over the morning and early afternoon. Then I called his neighbor, Lisa Derrick, who knocked on his door but couldn't rouse him. She has a key and reported that he wasn't home. She said a chair was tipped over, and a plate of food—she thought it looked like dinner from the night before—was still on the kitchen table, uneaten."

Janice began wringing her hands. "I contacted the Armstrong police, but they were dismissive. I raised hell but they wouldn't budge, saying to give it time. He was still missing on Sunday. Panicked, I booked an express flight and spent the ride calling everyone who would listen. Turns out the only ones even a little bit interested were the people at Lewiston-Mark, his financial advisors." She caught Cuss's eye and shrugged. "Dad's an important client to them. Anyway, they used their muscle to get the cops moving. I met with Detective Washington on Monday afternoon. By Tuesday morning, the detective had established that he'd accompanied a man here to Lagrange." She pointed at the floor. "Now here I am, anxious for your help."

Cuss asked a series of clarifying questions, pinning down the timeline, refining his understanding of the other players she'd mentioned, all while Ygo checked through her story, confirming flights, contacts, and the like.

Then Cuss moved to the difficult part. "Have the kidnappers contacted you?"

She shook her head slowly, like she hadn't thought much about that part.

"Kidnappers have a goal. Ransom. Retribution. Something that justifies the risk." He let that marinate for a moment, then asked his favorite question. "Who would do this to him?"

She slumped back in her chair and looked into the distance, eyes unfocused. He sat back himself and waited.

"He doesn't have enemies that I know of. Not this kind anyway. I guess that leaves someone who wants his money."

"Does he have a lot?"

She nodded. "Somewhere in the neighborhood of thirty million common. He had a great run in real estate when he was younger and then got lucky with some long-shot mining investments after that."

Cuss rubbed his cheek, momentarily surprised by the clean-shaven feel of his face. He never wore a mustache or beard, but he usually had a few days' growth. He'd forgotten that he'd upped his grooming habits while trying to gain Hatha's attention.

"Are you and your father close?"

"Of course." Irritation crept into her voice. "I wouldn't be doing all this if I didn't care."

Cuss considered how to phrase the next question but then just asked it. "Rich people don't stay on the middecks. Why aren't you staying on Luna or Terra?"

She nodded to signal her understanding. "Wealth separates you from the masses. I'm one of those rare birds who actually likes people. I know that sounds dumb, but it's true. To have them as friends, you need to live like them. When he passes, I inherit it all and will donate the bulk to charity."

After a bit more back and forth, Cuss took her through the process of a police investigation, assuring her that they were searching all four cities from top to bottom. "If he's here in Lagrange, we'll find him."

"Where else could he be?"

That's what Cuss wanted to know.

Chapter 3

After giving Janice his contact information with instructions to call him with any new developments, Cuss made for the local Community Patrol station—police headquarters for the deck—while Ygo arranged for a confab with their senior detective, Juan Luisa. Cuss would have been happy with a virtual meeting, but after hearing a brief of the case, Detective Luisa had insisted on doing it in person. He was out in the neighborhoods finishing up on a call and would be back at the station inside an hour.

Walking across a small courtyard adorned with flowering bushes, Cuss approached the handsome building, a gray edifice with lots of shiny chrome, clear glass, and sharp angles. He entered through double doors set in the middle of a line of floor-to-ceiling windows running across the front. Inside, uncomfortable-looking benches, the seats sloping downward ever so slightly, were lined in a row in the middle of a gray-tiled floor. Cuss figured they were designed that way to ensure that those waiting were committed to their cause.

To the left, a Heroes Wall listed the names of the fallen, a short list because the controlled environment of Lagrange didn't offer much opportunity for violence. A bronze-colored statue of an officer down on one knee, his hand on the shoulder of a child, stood in front of the wall, promoting the image of caring and service.

To the right, a community display had information about upcoming events: a 5K fun run, a swap meet, a cooking competition, an advert for a neighborhood block party that had happened the week before. Ahead, a clear barrier separated the lobby from the rest of the building. An officer in uniform, likely selected for his patience, sat behind a service window, dealing with a small line of people there on business.

Cuss used his badge at an entryway in the barrier down from the service window, stepping through the clear wall into the inner workings of the station.

His badge triggered an alert—the locals wanted to know when an interloper was in their midst. He waited less than a minute before a lieutenant in a smart uniform exited yet another door and called to him.

"This way, Marshal. I'm Adele Laurent. How may we help you today?"

Cuss introduced himself and explained that Detective Luisa was on his way in. "I wonder if I can sit somewhere while I wait. I have background material to review." He wanted to watch Darlena Washington's interview with Janice Wallingford.

"Of course." She held the door and then led him into the complex, turning left and right down narrow, brightly lit hallways, stopping at the first of a row of doors. "If you need privacy, all we have is an interview room. Is that okay?"

He nodded his assent. "Will I be locked in?" He asked it with a smile, but it had happened to him before, once when he'd needed to move in a hurry. Ygo had broken into the building systems to free him that time, causing an unfortunate brouhaha with the staff.

She tapped a panel next to the door and said, "Your badge is registered. You have free access."

He thanked her, adding, "I'd appreciate it if you'd let Detective Luisa know I'm here."

Interview rooms hadn't changed in forever. This one was a small box, every surface painted an off-white, with nothing visible on the walls or ceiling, though he knew sensors recorded everything inside. A small drab-green table sat in the middle of the room with two hard-back free-standing chairs on one side, across from a similar one bolted to the floor. Metal loops were affixed to the table on that side for prisoners who needed to be controlled. Even those who didn't were certainly intimidated by the presence of the shackles.

He sat in one of the free-moving chairs, wishing he'd asked about coffee.

"Can you show me Darlena's interview?" he all but whispered as if he was muttering to himself.

Ygo fed it to his lens. He sat back and watched.

Detective Washington had done a thorough job debriefing Janice Wallingford, challenging the woman at every juncture, an adversarial approach that had yielded extra tidbits. She'd weaseled out the existence of the boyfriend. She'd also gotten Janice to acknowledge why she didn't visit more often: she found the flights from the Earth to the Moon physically difficult. The express flights took only sixteen hours from Earth, but the aggressive thrust of the rocket was hard on her body. The regular flights were more physically tolerable in that sense but required that passengers be cooped up in a small cabin for over thirty hours, a different kind of stress. Other than that, the facts were the same.

Cuss was contemplating the father's disappearance when a man opened the door and poked his head in. "Hey, Marshal. Juan Luisa. Glad you're here. Let's move someplace more comfortable."

When they shook hands, Detective Luisa made full eye contact, shook with a firm grip, and radiated a friendly demeanor. He was a small wiry guy in his early fifties with a neatly trimmed mustache; short, curly hair; and quick-moving eyes that Cuss guessed didn't miss much. He liked him right from the start.

They swung by the kitchen for coffee, and Cuss gave him even more points. Juan gestured at a box of doughnuts. Cuss declined, Juan took one, and they moved down the hall to the detectives bullpen, a room with no windows, four old desks, extra chairs, and no one else.

They sat and sipped while Cuss took Juan through the case, taking care to reinforce the interworld nature of the abduction, justifying his involvement.

Juan listened, interrupting only once to learn more about the use of the data mask. When Cuss finished his monologue, Juan asked, "Would you mind if I interviewed the daughter myself?"

"Have at it." Cuss didn't have the authority to stop him but liked that he asked. "I'm going to need to poke around pretty much everywhere while we try to find Mr.

Wallingford. It'll carry across decks and possibly across the cities. I'll need a liaison."

Juan sat up, his excitement showing. "I'm the man for the job. Especially given the case I'm on now."

Interworld marshals were normally teamed with a high-profile local detective who, because of their status, tended to be stationed on the Luna or Terra Decks. In spite of the outward posturing between services, the hotshots clamored to be involved for a list of reasons. It let them draw on resources that otherwise required exasperating layers of approval. They could travel a broader range in the course of the investigation without question. It bestowed a certain freedom for them to set their own schedule. And perhaps most important: their boss's boss would be paying attention, giving them a chance to make even bigger names for themselves.

If Cuss pulled some strings, Juan had a chance at the brass ring because Janice Wallingford had chosen to slum it on the middecks.

"Tell me."

"I just got back from an interview with Claude and Helena Moore. Claude's father, Robert Garrison Moore, was abducted yesterday. He's rich too, like fifteen or twenty million. The man who took him used a data mask, just like your case. And as of this moment, we can't locate the guy." Juan mimicked an explosion with his hands. "Poof. He's vanished."

Cuss felt his face tingle.

"Uh-oh," Ygo said in his ear. "I'm on it."

The second abduction changed everything. The two

cases were linked, at least on the surface, which meant a coordinated investigation. Since one case crossed world boundaries and the other didn't, the local brass would likely go full-on bureaucracy, with meeting schedules, task-force assignments, and everything else that hampered progress.

Fortunately, Ygo was a master at dealing with the nonsense, freeing Cuss to focus on what he did best: catching criminals.

Cuss had worked with a number of Lagrange detectives in the past, some quite talented. But they always ended up resenting him for one reason or another: his irascible nature, his tendency to ignore protocol and annoy leadership, his willingness to reason with his fists if the situation devolved, his success at closing cases in spite of it all.

His initial impression of Juan was favorable, and he wondered if the detective might be a good choice as liaison.

Ygo was ahead of him. "Detective Luisa won't be their first choice. Their second, either. He's horrible at politics, and that's reflected in his annual reviews. They ding him repeatedly for not being a team player, even though his clearance rate is better than most. His partner, Debra Gosling, is better at placating the brass, but she's been a detective for just three years."

Cuss was starting to really like the guy. "Have you had lunch? I think better on a full stomach." He made a show of looking around the empty room. "Can your partner join us?"

"She's down the hall, studying vids. Her name is Debra, by the way. Good cop, but young. Idealistic. She has this theory that she can follow the data mask by focusing on the absence of information, like tracking a shadow. Or a ghost."

"Love the idea," said Ygo privately. "Already tried it. The tracking works until they enter someplace dark and poorly monitored. Then I lose them."

Cuss wanted to meet Debra before deciding if Ygo should work his magic and have them assigned as liaisons. He stood, eager to get moving. "Maybe I can introduce myself on our way out?"

. . .

Debra Gosling, a gawky redhead with a longish face full of freckles, was a couple of inches taller than Juan and a couple of inches shorter than Cuss. Like Juan, she wore civilian clothes. But unlike him, hers fit well and were freshly pressed. Her hair was bunched in a loose bun with strands poking out. Her posture was impeccable. Cuss could feel her inexperience.

She lit up when she saw him. A classic brown-noser, she called him "sir," and said "good thought" and "nice observation" in the first minutes of conversation. Then she upped the ante.

"We studied the Klingenberg case in the Patrol Academy. Great work."

Klingenberg was a pedophile with horrifying predilections. After a brutal weeks-long chase four years ago to rescue a nine-year-old girl, Cuss had guessed the guy's next move and cornered him. The slimeball had attacked, and Cuss hadn't held back, delivering a beating so thorough the asshole had died soon after. Multiple reviews concluded that Cuss had acted in self-defense. Of course, Ygo wouldn't have allowed a different outcome.

"What did you learn from that case?" he asked.

"Excellent question." Her brow furrowed as she thought. "An officer's instincts can be the difference between success and failure. Instinct can be developed with practice. Successful officers work to develop theirs from their first days."

It sounded like she was answering a question on the Academy exit exam.

While Cuss prided himself on his insight, having Ygo in his ear made him seem larger than life to everyone else. In spite of her naïve enthusiasm, Cuss was starting to like her, too.

He gave her a thumbnail sketch of the Wallingford abduction, highlighting the similarity of using a difficult-to-obtain data mask to hide their movements.

"Was any of it caught in the sensor dump?" she asked. "I'd love to compare the two and test my tracking method."

"I just sent her everything we have," Ygo told him.

Acting as if casting a spell, Cuss gripped his right hand into a fist, moved it in a circle near his chest, and then pushed his hand out, splaying his fingers, directing the thrust toward the display Debra had been using.

"Access granted."

She turned to the display to confirm his claim. "Holy shit. How did you do that?"

He shrugged. "Juan and I are on our way to lunch.

Care to join us?"

He could see she was conflicted, wanting to brown-nose some more but anxious to resume her analysis. He gave her an out. "Or we could bring something back for you."

She said to Juan. "A slice of pepperoni pizza from that kiosk near Donny's Crafts." Then to Cuss, "Stop by later. I may have something to show you." Then back to her partner, "We want this one, Juan. Don't fuck it up."

Juan blushed. Cuss laughed. He was sold.

He and Juan decided to have pizza as well, grabbing slices from the food kiosk Debra had suggested. Sitting on a bench along the pedestrian thoroughfare, they chatted while they ate, focusing on what they'd learned from their morning interviews.

Both agreed the similarities pointed to a common culprit. Neither believed the family was involved, but they were keeping open minds. They concluded that case records going back several years needed to be reviewed, both in Lagrange and Nova Terra, to see if there were other abductions that fit the pattern of a rich, elderly person being taken by someone with a data mask.

"It will take a while," Ygo said in his ear. "I'll let you know."

They agreed to switch interviews. Juan would talk with Janice Wallingford. Cuss would visit Claude and Helena Moore.

As Juan grabbed a fresh slice to bring back to his partner, he made his pitch. "Debra and I would be good liaisons. The commander will likely have a different opinion, though. If you're interested, you'd have to make the ask."

Cuss was honest. "I can promise you'll be part of the task force. But if a related case pops where the assigned detectives are making good progress, that will complicate the decision."

His disappointment apparent, Juan forced a smile. "Let's finish our interviews and then meet with Debra to compare notes." He checked the time. "Aim for sixteen hundred?"

Cuss agreed, shook Juan's hand, and made for the pod station.

. . .

Robert Moore lived in the suburbs on Deck 8. He had a gorgeous house on a tiny plot in a neighborhood reflecting significant prosperity. Ygo confirmed that Moore's son and daughter-in-law were at the home. Cuss didn't call ahead, wanting to catch them unprepared.

The door chimed as he approached. A man in his forties answered, appearing tired, acting impatient.

"What?" he demanded, looking Cuss up and down.

"That's the grandson, Thomas," said Ygo.

Cuss took out his badge wallet and showed his credentials.

"You found him? Mom! Dad! The police are here with some news!"

Cuss waited for Claude and Helena to come to the door before popping their bubble. "We haven't found him, but we're sparing no effort in the hunt. I'm following up on my partner's visit this morning." There was no benefit in distinguishing Juan's role from his. Families wanted answers, not organizational charts. "May I come in?"

Thomas moved back from the door, and Cuss stepped into a smaller version of a grand foyer, a showpiece in spite of its size. Marble tile on the floor, ornate crystal chandelier overhead, a worn but beautiful oriental rug toward the back beneath a grandfather clock and an antique pedestal table holding a vase of flowers. An oak staircase looped up behind the clock and table. And on either side of the entry, archways trimmed with matching molding led into other rooms.

"Please," said Helena, motioning to the archway on her right. "Let's sit in the living room."

Cuss followed them into a room where the expensive furnishings continued. Oak floors covered with more carpets. Floor-to-ceiling shelves along the back wall filled with knickknacks, family pictures, and old books. Paintings that didn't look like copies.

The family sank into a grandma couch: an overstuffed sofa with generous cushions covered in rich cloth, made elaborate with intricate needlework. The men sat at each end, Helena in the middle. Cuss sat in a matching armchair, facing them across a glass-topped coffee table.

"Can I get you something to drink, Marshal?" asked Helena.

She and Claude were dressed formally like they'd come from an event, perhaps a church social. Thomas wore jeans and a T-shirt.

"Thanks. I'm fine." He saw expectation on their faces and knew he was about to disappoint them further. He delivered the lines he'd said so many times before. "I know you've already answered questions from my partner, but I need to work through it myself. I appreciate that it's frustrating, but it's my process. It'll help me move quicker."

As expected, their faces fell, then Thomas started in with objections. Cuss weathered the storm and began his questioning. Claude answered the bulk of his inquiries, with Thomas interrupting to add details he felt his father had missed.

Robert was Claude's father, Thomas's grandfather, Helena's father-in-law. He owned the house they were in and lived alone. Claude, Helena, and Thomas lived together in a home on Deck 9. Robert's wife had passed four years earlier. Louise, Claude's sister, lived outside Paris toward Versailles. Thomas was single and dating.

They'd all moved to Lagrange a decade ago because Earth was in chaos. Drought, wildfires, hurricanes, crime, disease, angry people, shortages of goods and services, androids everywhere. The Moon's gravity didn't work for any of them. The calm, predictable, human-centered society of Lagrange had been a perfect match.

That was, until yesterday.

When Robert hadn't responded to several calls, Helena had come to check on him, only to find the house empty. Sensors had captured it all: someone leading Robert out of the house and toward downtown. He appeared to be accompanying the person voluntarily, but they couldn't identify the escort. Whoever it was showed as a blur. The security service had checked the system and couldn't find any malfunctions. There hadn't been any contact or demands for his return. They were in a panic.

"Can you think of anyone who would do this to him?"

They looked at each other, then returned their gazes to Cuss, shaking their heads.

"He has a beautiful home. He lives here alone?"

"He loves his privacy," said Claude.

"Do you think they're after his money?"

"If that was it, wouldn't they have asked for ransom by now?" Thomas responded, clearly frustrated with Cuss's methodical style.

Cuss ignored him. "How much is he worth, ballpark?"

"Dad is very secretive about his wealth," said Claude. "He doesn't share much. But piecing together bits and pieces over the years, I'm guessing it's somewhere close to twenty million common. His investment advisors are at Lewiston-Mark. They'd have exact figures and information about where it's all stashed."

"Did you catch that?" asked Ygo.

Cuss had. Lewiston-Mark was the same firm Janice Wallingford had mentioned. He didn't believe in coincidence, but then again, that firm was among the biggest players in wealth management. Their client list likely had tens of thousands of very rich people.

"You don't have access to it? Or see any reports?"

Claude shook his head. "Dad is very generous, but private."

"So you wouldn't know if he was moving funds yesterday or today?"

Claude bit his lip, looked at his wife, and shook his head again.

Chapter 4

Yuri Melnikov swooped a finger, initiating the liquidation of Robert Moore's investment in a real estate partnership in Sedona, Arizona. He'd already swept the cash, sold the stocks and bonds, and was down to transactions that would require days to complete, more than two-thirds of the portfolio in Moore's case. He'd have time to get some of it. How much depended on how long the old man lived.

He looked over when the door opened. His second in command, Stan Shevchenko, floated in, dragging a crewman by the collar. The man's face was puffy and purple, his nose at an odd angle. One of his arms stretched out in an unnatural position, broken during the beating when Stan had learned of his actions.

They floated across the room, Stan grabbing the edge of a storage locker so they hovered in front of Melnikov. His grip on the crewman remained firm.

Melnikov stayed strapped to his seat, eyeing them both. "This is the asshole?"

Stan nodded, trying to show bravado but looking more like he was hiding his apprehension.

Melnikov stared hard at Stan. Stan had recruited the guy. He'd vouched for him. That meant they shared sins. And associated penalties.

Then he looked at the broken crewman, glad he was hurt, hoping he was in pain. If his stupidity brought it all down, no amount of suffering would be enough.

"You left a body on the farm?" he all but shouted. "How did that make sense? And what were you even doing there?"

"Sorry, boss," said Rex Luskin. His broken mouth made it sound like he had a speech impediment. "It wasn't my fault. I swear. The bitch was way more athletic than the guy. She broke out, and I had to stop her before she sounded the alarm."

They'd snuck Robert Moore off right away, but then the cops showed up to search the ship. They'd had no choice but to hide the woman until things cooled down. The plan had been to move her off tomorrow.

Melnikov watched blood and saliva float out of the whimpering man's mouth. Disgusted, he pulled a dirty rag from a bottom desk drawer and flicked it toward Stan. "Clean that up, for God's sake." Back to Rex, "Whose fault was it that she escaped? And why in hell did you just leave her there?"

"I didn't have time to think." Rex started to sob. "It happened so fast I just reacted."

"You didn't have time to think," Melnikov mocked with contempt. Then he slammed his fist on the desk, the force lifting him from his chair, the strap preventing him from drifting upward. To Stan, "This is what you call a solid recruit?"

Stan remained silent, wise enough to know that no words would placate his boss, not when he was in a mood.

"Dump him into the feed port. Let his atoms become part of the next build."

Rex began to struggle. Stan grabbed his head in an armlock, spun him to the left in the weightless environment, then in a quick motion, fought the momentum of his rotating body by twisting hard to the right. The action produced a sickening *crunch*. The man went limp.

As Stan floated Rex from the room, Melnikov gave him his one hope. "Put a lid on this disaster, Stan. Fuck it up and I'll dump you in the feed port myself."

Chapter 5

On his way out of the neighborhood, Cuss visited more than a dozen homes along the path to the pedestrian thoroughfare, hoping to find someone who'd seen Robert Moore and his escort. Witness descriptions were rarely worth much, but it was basic police work, it had to be done.

While he knocked on doors, Ygo performed a sweep of the community sensors along the route, gathering data from the previous day to see if they got lucky. Neither effort yielded anything useful, though no one answered the door at half the homes Cuss checked.

He returned to the Deck 6 station, reaching it at the appointed hour. Juan met him in the lobby. As they made their way into the bowels of the building, Juan impressed Cuss by confiding that he'd learned that both missing men had used Lewiston-Mark as their financial advisors.

"They have a regional office on Luna Deck," said Juan. "I want to pay them a visit. If you join me, I can skip the interdeck politics."

"Absolutely," said Cuss. "But first let's finish the interviews along the route from Robert Moore's place while memories are fresh. Could you and Debra follow up on that?"

Juan nodded. "It's on our list already. We're targeting

dinnertime to improve chances that folks are home."

Cuss thought about Hatha's invitation to meet her on Luna Deck after lunch the next day and wanted to be in the neighborhood when she was visiting the park. "Let's visit Lewiston-Mark tomorrow during business hours, maybe just before noon?"

"Works for me."

"And I want to look inside that ship. I'll have the warrant by tomorrow morning and could use your help."

Juan punched the air in excitement. Like he'd scored a goal. Or won the lottery. "Deal."

When they reached the cubby where Debra Gosling had been analyzing data, they found her slumped in her chair, feet up, staring at the wall, deep in thought. She had grown frustrated trying to track shadows, concluded it was a red herring, and was ready to return to traditional detective work.

They briefed her on what they'd learned and fleshed out a schedule for tomorrow. After a few minutes of unrelated chitchat, Cuss excused himself and made for Hermes' passenger port and the *Nelly Marie*.

To him, investigations were like chess games, a contest of tactics and strategies. That meant reading the board. Observing. Planning. Short-term actions feeding longer-term goals. He'd learned early in his career that rushing things rarely paid dividends. He needed downtime to think things through.

Getting to the passenger port and his ship was a bit convoluted because of how the city was constructed. To picture it, imagine twelve metal cans with top and bottom lids removed, all the same height, each a different diameter, lined up in a row from wide to narrow. Put one can inside the next, like Russian nesting dolls, so when looking at it from the top, you see a dozen concentric circles, something like the shape of a target. Or maybe the ripples running out after dropping a pebble into water.

Fix the cans in place so they hold perfect spacing. Then expand everything so the assembly is thirty kilometers long, and the outside can is five kilometers across. Put caps on each end and fill it with air. Create gravity by gently spinning the massive structure along its length. Not too fast, about half the speed of a second hand moving around the face of a clock.

The spinning creates artificial gravity the same way that swinging a pail of water over your head in a smooth circle does. Move the pail around fast enough, and centrifugal force will push the water against the bottom, preventing it from spilling out. Inside the spinning tube city, water, people, animals, buildings, equipment, plants, rocks, dust, *everything* gets pushed out against the walls by centrifugal force.

The gravity is greatest on the outside cylinder—the one with the largest diameter—because the centrifugal force is greatest. When turning at about half the speed of a second hand, the five-kilometer-wide cylinder will generate a force equal to Earth's gravity. That's Terra Deck.

The gravity on the next cylinder inward will be slightly less because it's not as far from the center of rotation. Less again on the next one in. Keep going, and by the twelfth cylinder, if they're spaced correctly, gravity will be one-sixth that of Terra Deck. That's Luna Deck, with a gravity the same as the Moon.

Now give the whole thing an axle down the center, like one last can, but this one is narrow, a hollow tube, more like a drinking straw. And it doesn't turn, instead staying in a fixed position while the cylinders of the city spin around it in their lazy rotation.

Make the axle huge like everything else, a thirty-kilometer-long tube with a diameter of just half a kilometer. Cover its outside surface, about five thousand hectares, with farmland. Fill its inside with equipment to clean the air, purify water, process nutrients, regulate temperature, control air pressure, distribute power, store harvest, and everything else required to keep the crops growing and a city of half a million people alive.

At each end of the giant axle—again, a narrow tube that isn't spinning—construct spaceports where ships can land and take off. Give one of the spaceports extra amenities and use it for passenger craft. Let the one on the other end be less refined, more industrial, and use it for loading and unloading cargo ships.

Now build four of these immense cylinder cities, populate them with two million residents, and you have Lagrange.

The *Nelly Marie* was docked in Hermes' passenger spaceport. To get from the gently turning cylinders down to the stationary axle, Cuss needed to ride a shuttle, like a big enclosed pod, with small thrusters that could overcome the rotation, stabilize the tiny craft, and guide it on the short flight to the port's flight deck.

In contrast to prevalent pod stations, there were only a handful of shuttle stations, all on Luna Deck, all located in the outskirts. Cuss got in line, allowing himself to be channeled by guardrails, following the ramp up to the loading platform. The line moved slower than at a pod station because the people boarding a shuttle often carried suitcases and packages and pets in carry cases, bags with food and gifts, and all the other stuff they felt they needed for a journey to one of the other worlds.

Each shuttle had seating for ten people arranged in a circle around the inside of the craft. Big windows behind the seats let passengers see out during the ten-minute journey to the port.

Cuss was paired with two families, parents with children, and either an aunt—that was his guess—or possibly a family friend. He waited patiently while they stowed their carry-on luggage, and then he took his seat, smiling and nodding politely to his fellow passengers.

The door hissed shut. His ears adjusted as the tiny craft pressurized. It moved forward, sliding down a dark ramp. Then, like someone spitting out a watermelon seed back when watermelons still had seeds, the shuttle popped out into open space.

Everyone oohed and ahhed. Cuss almost joined them, even though he'd ridden shuttles like this more times than he could count. The view was beyond spectacular.

The four cities of Lagrange—Hermes, Athena, Demeter, and Apollo—floated side by side in open space, massive cylinders oriented lengthwise so one end pointed toward Earth, the other at the Moon.

The namesake of the microworld was Joseph-Louis Lagrange, an Italian mathematician and astronomer born Giuseppe Luigi Lagrangia. Lagrange had determined back in the 1800s that there was a sweet spot between a planet and its satellite, a specific point where the gravitational pull of each exactly balanced. An object placed in this sweet spot would stay there forever, needing minimal energy to correct for drift and maintain its position. The tube cities were placed where Lagrange had predicted, a spot much closer to the Moon where its feeble gravity would exactly counteract the mighty tug of Earth.

When the shuttle burst into space, the looming structure of Hermes dominated, with sheets of iridescent photovoltaic material covering its curved surface, and seams and ridges forming crisscross patterns where pieces joined. At seemingly random intervals, fixtures and assemblies poked upward like blemishes on smooth skin.

As the craft drifted, passengers caught a glimpse of the other cities, amazing constructions, smooth from a distance, floating like shimmering logs on calm waters, hovering against all odds. Then the Earth and the Moon came into view, brilliant disks in a star-filled sky, appearing to be the same size because that was where Lagrange had predicted the sweet spot would be.

The thrusters kicked on, correcting for the spin they'd inherited from Luna Deck's rotation, moving the vessel in an efficient fashion toward the end of the enormous cylinder and the passenger spaceport inside. As they passed through the entryway, mechanisms captured the shuttle and guided them into a chute. Muscular gray metal doors with latches and guide pins slid closed behind them, holding in the air, protecting the deck from the cold vacuum of space. Matching doors opened in front of them. A jerk and a bump, and the shuttle was locked into position at the passenger port's loading platform.

The shuttle door opened, and Cuss moved quickly to be the first one out, leaving the families to gather their belongings. Because the center tube wasn't spinning, there was no centrifugal force to create artificial gravity. Cuss floated into an unadorned off-white gangway that directed passengers to the left. Handholds along the way were positioned so people could propel themselves along, but a steady flow of air blew through the corridor, moving everyone forward like the current of a river, relieving passengers of the need to bother.

Cuss turned off the main drag, using handholds to fight the current and direct himself down a short branch to the right. A security door at the end—steel gray with bright-red signs warning passengers not to proceed, telling them that the door led to a restricted area—responded to his credentials, putting him inside the cavernous spaceport.

He moved out into a huge open area, a broad flight deck holding dozens of spaceships of different shapes and sizes, with room for dozens more. Bright lights among the girders high overhead lit the place like the sun. The sounds of machines echoed from every direction. A mélange of smells—exhaust, lubricant, burnt rubber—filled his nose. Painted lines on the floor showed where it was safe to move and boundaries not to cross.

Fuel trucks, utility lorries, and service vehicles, all held to the floor by magnetic fields, whizzed back and forth, delivering fuel, carrying cargo, and servicing ships. Warning beeps cautioned workers as a tug pulled a large white passenger ship into position for launch. Cuss figured it was the craft his shuttle mates were here to board.

He faced the *Nelly Marie*, off to the side near the front of the deck, kept there for easy access and rapid departure. Bunching his legs, he floated up and positioned his feet against the wall near the security door, preparing to push off and fly across the flight deck, something the deck master frowned upon, though regulars did it anyway.

Then he paused, taking a moment to scan the ships, looking for the private craft that had carried Franklin Wallingford here from Armstrong.

It was easy to eliminate the bigger ships with windows along their length and colorful logos on the tail fins. The smaller corporate craft, all painted and clean, weren't likely candidates either. As he viewed the craft, he could identify at least four that looked ratty enough to have broken sensors inside, and sinister enough that they could carry abducted humans.

Still in a crouch against the wall, he asked Ygo, "Which one is it?"

"See the blue luxury liner with the red fins?"

Cuss didn't see it immediately.

"To your right, about halfway across the deck toward the back."

He found the craft Ygo mentioned. Next to it, his lens highlighted a small silver-gray craft on tripod legs near the rear wall. "The shitbox with the dent on its nose?"

"That's the one. It's called *Yankee Spirit*."

He studied the ship as he contemplated searching it. The task was on his list, and after seeing it, he felt the urge to advance their schedule. "Any chance you can wrangle the warrant tonight?"

"The judge is on a dinner date, but I think I can get him to sign off after dessert."

Then almost immediately, the tone of Ygo's voice changed. "A farmer just reported a body. He describes her as really old, says she isn't moving, and looks dead. She's up on the farm, lying in the soybeans. It's not far from where you are."

Cuss pulled his feet off the wall as he pondered how to get there from here. He knew the farm was on the outside of the axle tube he was now in. But he'd never been out there and didn't know the way.

"I'll bet it's Agnes Ming," Ygo continued. "I've discovered that she went missing from Armstrong a few hours before Wallingford was taken. Similar MO. If they brought one of them here, it wouldn't surprise me if they'd brought the other as well."

"Christ, Ygo. Why didn't you tell me that you'd found related cases?"

"I'm down to a handful of possibles and still sorting through the details. It's an educated guess until I'm done."

"How do I get to her?"

"Hold on." A pause. "Well, there you go. There's an access door right behind *Yankee Spirit*. It's not twenty meters from the ship to the door. Now I say it's Agnes Ming for sure."

"I'll check it out. Will you contact Juan and Debra and have them join me as soon as they can?" He didn't wait for a reply. Ygo would get it done. Again tucking his legs against the wall, he adjusted his aim to target the *Yankee Spirit* and pushed off, sailing head first across the port, the flight deck scrolling past below him.

His trajectory carried him at an upward angle, an unintended result of rushing his launch. But he got lucky on the other end, where he was able to stretch out a hand and grab one of *Yankee Spirit*'s tripod legs as he floated by, spinning him around but stopping his flight before he banged into the wall.

Hanging onto the landing strut, he took a moment to study the ship's main hatch. He was anxious to look inside, warrant or no. But an hour wouldn't change much, and having help would make the search more effective. So he pulled himself hand-over-hand down the landing leg, fighting annoyance when he realized the shabby craft was covered in grime, and now, so were his hands.

When he reached the deck, he pushed off and floated to the door in the wall. Signs warned that it led to emergency rally points—safe havens should there be a breach or other failure—and that alarms would sound if the door was opened.

"Can you kill the alarm?" he asked Ygo, waiting maybe five seconds before proceeding. No alarms sounded that he could hear.

Chapter 6

C uss floated into a wide hallway distinguished by an excess of handholds, an emergency lighting system, and placards telling people what to do in the event of an emergency. As he moved down its length, he passed a door labeled *Rally Point I*, followed ten meters along with a door labeled *Utilities*, and a little farther, *Rally Point II*. A door at the end of the corridor was labeled *Surface Access*. He opened it and floated through.

Someone in the room screamed and dove behind a low cabinet, a blue box filled with rows of drawers. Cuss had caught the motion in his peripheral vision, so he knew the person was wearing oversized bright-orange coveralls and had long locks of brown hair.

Already on edge, he pulled his gun with his right hand, his thumb moving the weapon from safety to drop, while his left hand searched for something to steady his drift.

"Don't shoot!" cried the man, peeking out from around the cabinet. "It's me!"

"Me" turned out to be Beckman Thicke, the farmer who'd found the body. He'd panicked because he thought Cuss was the killer.

"What is this place?" asked Cuss after he'd holstered his weapon and shown his badge.

His first impression was a fire station for the flight

deck. It was a large room, bright but a little dirty, with a row of orange gravity suits hanging along the back wall. A variety of hand tools—spades, rakes, trowels, hoes—were clipped in place along the wall to the left. A dressing area with showers, benches, and lockers was tucked to the right. A portion of the ceiling was a void, rising like a tunnel, open as far as he could see, a shaft disappearing into the distance.

Standing, Beckman Thicke—fortyish with a full beard and hair to his shoulders—explained that the room was a staging area for farmers, a place to prepare before heading up to the land and its crops.

Cuss was confused. "You come through the flight deck to get here?"

Thicke pointed toward the locker room. "We come in that way. The common hallway is because we share the rally rooms with the flight deck." He looked both ways, like he was checking to see if someone was listening. "Want to know what sucks?"

Cuss didn't answer, taking in the scene, trying to understand the movements of Agnes Ming.

"That door marked Utility in the hall? That's really an upscale rally room for rich and connected passengers. Better food. Nicer amenities. Carpeting. It's bullshit."

If true, Cuss couldn't disagree. He also didn't care. "Let's get to the woman and help her if she's alive."

Beckman's attitude changed, as if in the excitement he'd momentarily forgotten about the body in the soybeans.

"First you need to put on a grav suit." He motioned to the row of orange coveralls hanging behind him.

"Otherwise, when we get up there, you'll float away."

Cuss had worn gravity suits in the past, and while he didn't understand the physics, he recognized the benefit. Thicke pulled one off the rack and held it out. After stepping into it, Cuss moved his gun from his shoulder holster to an outside pocket. If a murderer was on the loose, he wanted to be ready.

He sealed the suit's front seam, and his feet settled to the floor. Bending his arms and lifting his knees, he tested the fit. The suit was light and flexible in spite of its ungainly appearance.

"This way," said Thicke, moving toward a gated area against the same wall that held the door to the rally rooms. It turned out to be an open elevator, with a waist-high industrial fence enclosing a space large enough to hold twenty people.

As Cuss followed, he peppered Thicke with questions. Where do you live? How long have you worked here? Who works with you? Is this your regular shift? What are your tasks? Did you see anyone who didn't belong? Did you see the woman anywhere down here before finding her up there? How long did you wait before you contacted the police? Who would do something like this?

Thicke engaged a mechanism as they talked, and the platform began to rise, filling the shaft in the ceiling out to the edges. The ride took most of a minute. The walls moving past were dark and smooth. As the lighting dimmed, Cuss used the infrared capability of his lens to study Beckman's face during questioning.

Halfway to the top, they passed a series of large

compartments built into the forward wall, each holding a farm tractor or other machine that presumably could drive onto the platform for transportation to the surface. Cuss knew words like harvester, baler, combine, and plow, but he couldn't tell what was what or if those words even applied to the equipment he saw.

Cuss didn't slow his queries during the ride, and by the time they reached the top, he'd concluded the man wasn't involved other than being an unlucky farmer who found a body. Ygo agreed.

The elevator came to a stop inside what Thicke called "the barn." When Cuss thought of barns, he thought of wooden structures with hay on the floor, stalls with animals, and tack and tools on the walls. This one was made of molded brown composite instead of wood. It had bare walls and no hay or animals in sight.

It did have a red tractor with spikey tires parked along the back wall, much bigger than a mowing machine you might have at home on Earth, but not nearly as big as the huge equipment he'd seen in the fields when driving through the Midwestern United States. The barn also had sacks of different sizes and colors piled high, with labeling too small for Cuss to read from his vantage point. He guessed they held seed and fertilizer and whatever else farmers spread to produce crops.

"If someone wasn't wearing a suit," he asked Thicke, "could they glide up the chute without much effort?"

"You're talking about the lady? Yeah. It's super dangerous, though." He pointed up. "When you reach here, you'll smack your head on the rafters if you aren't prepared to catch yourself. And when you get outside, one wrong move and you're drifting into the air."

Thicke led the way toward a human-sized door at the front of the barn, placed next to a broad sliding door big enough for the tractor. A low hum filled the air. Cuss looked around for the source as he followed but couldn't place the sound.

When he stepped outside, he stopped in his tracks. The view was beyond spectacular.

In front of him, neat rows of green bushy plants stretched out for as far as he could see. The curvature of the surface was apparent, as the rows to the left and right fell out of sight with the slope of the land. But what made the view so enthralling was above him. Turning slowly overhead was the arched ceiling of Luna Deck. Maybe half a kilometer up, it was the innermost canister in the sequence of twelve.

Luna Deck had huge viewports so people could see the farm. From this side, so far away, the majestic arch and window mosaics evoked the feeling of a European cathedral, with their dramatic vaulted ceilings adorned with stained glass and painted murals. A display of lights high overhead illuminated everything, like the cathedral was decorated for Christmas. Only here the beams provided energy for the plants to grow.

Unlike a cathedral, the stunning presentation stretched out for thirty kilometers, farther than the visual horizon, creating one of the most amazing human-constructed vistas Cuss had ever seen. He stared in awe until he was jolted from his reverie by Thicke.

"This way."

"Stop!" shouted Cuss. "Don't move."

Thicke ducked and covered his head, a whimper escaping his lips.

"I want to preserve evidence. Stay here and guide me to where she is."

Thicke rose, not at all sheepish by his display of fear, and pointed out into the field.

Cuss couldn't see the body. "How far?"

"Maybe ten meters." A pause, then, "Sorry, man. I walked all around here getting my stuff together. I didn't know she was there and didn't find her until I was halfway through collecting my samples."

As Cuss peered into the soybeans, his attention was drawn downward by the incessant hum. He realized it came from a black slotted grating system that ran between each row of plants. His first thought was drainage for excess water. But when he squatted and probed with a hand, he could feel a slight sucking. "Is this a vacuum?"

"It is." Thicke nodded. "We keep the ground moist and use the suction to ensure a constant downward airflow. Otherwise, all this open area would fill in with dust. The suction is what's holding the lady from drifting away."

Cuss studied the ground, saw no footprints to his right, and stepped gingerly from grate to grate, moving parallel to where the body lay, continuing until he was well past the disturbed ground. Then, using the grate as a walkway, he advanced to where Thicke had pointed.

He saw her after a dozen steps and stepped over a row of plants to get closer. Face down, she lay lengthwise on a grate. She wore blue pants and a white blouse that now had a spatter of blood on the back. Her short gray hair was matted with blood from an ugly gash on the back of her head.

Cuss was about to call for paramedics when Ygo said, "She's gone. No pulse, no respiration, and a falling body temperature. Her physical measurements make me confident that it's Ming. I'll need to see her face to get to a hundred percent, though."

Cuss scanned the area for whatever had caused the head wound but couldn't see anything that would produce that kind of trauma.

"Did you pick up any tools or rocks near here?" he called over to Thicke, who was still standing near the barn.

"No. Oh, you want whatever hit her head? If it's not the ceiling of the barn, he either carried it back with him, or it's floating somewhere out there." He waved a hand out into the vast open space between the farm and Luna Deck. "Good luck finding it."

"From the size and placement," said Ygo, "it's consistent with a rafter in the barn ceiling."

Cuss agreed but didn't want to miss anything based on an assumption.

A different kind of hum drew his attention, this one deep, throaty, and growing louder. He turned to the noise and saw a small vehicle flying through the air, descending from high overhead, with lights flashing red and orange, official insignias emblazoned across the side of a blue-and-white exterior. Cuss recognized it as a police Community Patrol craft and hoped it was Juan and Debra.

It slowed to a hover ten meters up and off to the side. Juan opened the door, leaned out, and called, "Where can we land?"

Cuss guided them down to a spot away from the disturbed ground. As it settled, the landing legs of the craft burrowed into the dirt to keep it anchored. The noise faded as the engines wound down.

Debra was out first, followed seconds later by Juan. They both wore bright-blue versions of the orange grav suit Cuss had on, though theirs were emblazoned with the words *Community Patrol* in large white letters across the back. On the front, a gold-embroidered badge sat over their hearts, the design unintentionally providing a target for a sniper, an emblem that said "aim here." At least, that's what Cuss thought whenever he saw it.

He pointed out a path they should take to join him, one that wouldn't disturb the crime scene. When they were together, they studied the body from afar.

"I've confirmed she's dead," Cuss told them.

"Any ideas who it is?" asked Juan.

"I'm guessing Agnes Ming. She disappeared from Armstrong a few hours before Franklin Wallingford was taken. That's two related interworld abductions, putting me squarely in the lead on this mess."

Normally not one to play politics, he worried that local maneuvering would interfere with his progress and wanted to stop any gamesmanship before it started.

They didn't argue with his claim.

"I'll get a crime scene crew down here," said Debra, stepping away to make the call.

Not two minutes later, Cuss's concern played out when a second vehicle, twice the size of Juan and Debra's, rose over the short horizon, a siren whooping as it approached, its light display rivaling that of a trendy nightclub.

"That's the mayor," said Juan with a dejected tone. "I seem to be permanently in the doghouse with her, so I'm done here. It's been nice knowing you."

The noise from the vehicle made it hard to do anything else, so they watched and waited while the mayor's craft landed.

Isabelle Florence, mayor of Hermes, stepped out, resplendent in a golden grav suit that complemented her coloring and matched her hair.

Cuss had dealt with her in the past, and they were on cordial terms.

That was about to change when Barry Malkovich, dressed in blue coveralls that matched Juan's and Debra's, stepped out behind her.

Barry, tall, dark, and homely, was the lead detective on Luna Deck. Cuss had worked with him before, knew him to be a pompous blowhard who hampered more than he helped, and didn't wait for the drama to start.

He turned away just long enough to ask Ygo, "Can you lock down Juan and Debra?"

Ygo answered the way Cuss had hoped. "I thought you'd never ask."

Murders were a big thing in Lagrange because they were so rare. The cities didn't tolerate psychopaths or sociopaths. And with community sensors everywhere, big crimes rarely defied a solution. With outcomes all but certain, ambitious politicians like Isabelle put themselves front and center right from the start, assuming the resolution would provide positive press with few downsides.

Like a little boy hiding behind his mother's skirt, Barry the Blowhard started right in. "Marshal Abbott, why are you at my crime scene?"

Cuss ignored him, pretending to study the footprints on the ground.

"Working as a farmer, I see." The clever remark was directed at his orange coveralls. "I'm glad you found a profession that suits your talents."

The mayor upped the nasty, directing her scorn at Juan and Debra. "Detective Luisa, Detective Gosling, thank you for your service here. I'm sure the middecks have plenty to keep you busy." Then she lifted her head, a tell indicating she was receiving a call. "Yes, Governor," she said as she turned her back to them and walked away for privacy.

Cuss watched her argue, her hands waving as if she were conducting an orchestra.

Governor Belnick had taken the lead in pushing for the Interworld Marshals Service and had supported Cuss and Ygo early on when the worlds were haggling over their nominees. Cuss had worked hard ever since to repay the favor, keeping Belnick in the loop, mentioning his help at the conclusion of every success whether there'd been help or not, and giving him distance in the rare instances when things didn't pan out.

Her face red when she returned, Cuss thought of a pot

about to boil.

"I expect hourly reports, Marshal." Then to Juan and Debra, "You better come out shining, Detectives. Anything less and you'll be solving crimes out at the Factory."

She huffed back to her craft. Barry's gaze shifted from the mayor, to Cuss, to Juan, to Debra, then back to the mayor. He scurried after her.

Juan and Debra looked at each other, confusion on their faces.

Cuss threw them a victory party. "You're my official liaisons. Welcome to the team." Then he got to work. "Debra, would you see if there's any evidence that she hit her head on the ceiling in the barn? Mr. Thicke over there can show you where it would have happened. Then poke through the stuff in there and see if you can find anything that might be the weapon."

As Debra moved toward Thicke and the barn, Cuss used an index finger to draw an imaginary arc out past the body, saying to Juan as he did so, "Could you circle around out there a ways and check for tracks or objects? Step on the grates when you can. Let's pin down our perimeter."

When they were gone, Cuss spoke to Ygo. "Thanks for the save."

"I promised the governor that we'd have progress to report by tomorrow and the killer in custody shortly after."

Cuss thought the timeline overly ambitious but didn't argue. "Do we have feeds showing the attack?"

"We don't. Believe it or not, the farm has fewer sensors than *Yankee Spirit*."

"We'll need to manage his expectations, then. I'm not

getting warm fuzzies from any of this."

The medical examiner's team—two women in white gravity suits—arrived twenty minutes later, followed by the rest of the crime scene crew, who deployed a cloud of microdrones that began documenting everything. Cuss watched from the perimeter until one of the medical examiner turned the head of the body, letting Ygo put the identity of Agnes Ming at one hundred percent.

Debra came out from the barn at that point and called to Cuss. "There's a smear of blood on a beam above the elevator shaft. I didn't touch it but tied a piece of twine near it."

Cuss passed the information along and then got his crew moving. "Let's go check out that ship."

On the ride down the elevator, Ygo reported, "We have the search warrant."

Cuss gave a single nod in acknowledgement.

"And I've scanned back through the sensor feeds for the rally tunnel. While I can't see the attack, I've identified the guy chasing her. I'm gathering background on him now."

This time Cuss smiled.

As they moved through the rally tunnel toward the flight deck, Cuss let Juan and Debra get ahead and then asked Ygo, "Can you open the ship's hatch?"

"No. They've done a good job of stripping the ship of conveniences I could exploit. You'll have to do it the old-fashioned way."

The old-fashioned way meant disassembling the access panel next to the hatch and overriding the electronics to open the door.

It turned out that Debra had some skills in that area. They borrowed the tools she needed from the deck master. With her legs wrapped around one of the landing struts three meters off the ground, she got to work. As she fiddled, Cuss and Juan studied the craft from the deck.

One of the first things Cuss noticed was that the serial numbers on the three landing pads were all different. It wasn't surprising given the age of the craft. But if it were true for other parts of the ship, it meant that tracing the history and ownership would be a hassle.

After working for a good five minutes, Debra announced, "I think I have it." She shifted her position to the front of the hatch.

When she called, Cuss and Juan were on the far side of the ship, looking for tags and insignias they could combine with the serial numbers to lock down ownership. They moved quickly, passing under the craft to join her.

She signaled the hatch to open.

Boom!

A pressure wave, instantaneous, undeniable, overwhelming, smacked Cuss across his body, emptying his lungs, thumping his eardrums, knocking him senseless. The powerful blast tumbled him backward, and he tripped over Juan as he fell to the deck.

Consumed by the maelstrom, he didn't see the explosion peel back the frame of the ship, propelling the hatch like a bullet, the heavy plate hitting Debra with the force of a speeding truck. It launched her from her perch on the ship and smashed her against the wall twenty meters away, right below big letters painted on the wall that said *Rally Point*. Her body crumpled, then slid down the wall to the deck.

Emergency horns blared as echoes of the blast faded. Acrid smoke—black, gray, and white—billowed out from the gaping hole in the side of the craft. Overhead exhaust fans engaged to clear the air. A fire suppression mist worked to contain the flames inside.

Cuss tried to stand, his ears ringing as loud as the alarms. But he couldn't rise higher than his knees.

He crawled past a groaning Juan in an attempt to reach Debra. A crewman beat him to it, joined seconds later by two more.

"She's gone," he heard one say.

In a daze, his mind filled with sadness and fury.

Then he lost consciousness.

Chapter 7

When Roscoe Antonov learned that a booby trap had killed a cop, he wanted to cry. A bloated man in his early fifties with a goatee he grew in an attempt to elongate his round, puffy face, he regretted ever having talked to his uncle. Really regretted it. He'd gained ten pounds since this whole disaster started. The way his belt pinched into his stomach served to highlight the fact.

It had started innocently enough.

Roscoe was head of production at the Factory, the industrial complex floating in space alongside the tube cities of Lagrange. The Factory received regular deliveries of asteroids from the belt, crushed the massive rocks into fine powder, melted that into a goopy slurry, added chemicals and stabilizers to create what Corporate called the "secret sauce," and then formed the mix into massive sheets of condensate composite. The Factory was running at full speed, with current production earmarked for the construction of tube city number five and the buildings inside it.

The asteroids were harvested from the ring out past Mars, where they were deflected onto a trajectory toward Earth, a seven-month journey. Tugs snagged the mountain-size boulders as they neared the Moon and ferried them in, delivering them to the Factory's intake funnel.

Each asteroid was specially selected for its high fraction of condensate base material. With sufficiently high condensate, the rest of the rock could be included in the final composite, like adding aggregate to cement to make concrete, resulting in a strong product with zero waste.

This helped maximize the Factory's production rate. And perhaps more important, it eliminated the need for disposal of unused material. The citizens of Lagrange didn't want clouds of discarded rock floating near the cities. And moving the crushed stone somewhere else—the Moon, Earth, or Sun—was a surprisingly expensive proposition.

Just over a year ago, Roscoe had discovered a way to boost Corporate's profits.

From the time the Factory first began production, everyone knew that the waste blended with the condensate included modest amounts of gemstones and precious metals: diamonds, rubies, and emeralds; and gold, platinum, and silver. In fact, the initial design of the Factory included equipment to recover the valuables for resale.

But prior to construction, the Corporate business team performed an economic analysis on the recovery plant. The analysis considered the purchase and installation of extra equipment to capture the precious material, additional bots to operate it, power to run it, maintenance costs to fix things that broke, and on and on. The amortized costs approached seventy million common per year, which was more than what the valuables would bring on the open market. Given the imbalance, Corporate concluded that recovery wasn't worth the investment.

It was a conclusion that Roscoe viewed as shortsighted. In his spare time, he toyed with alternative designs and discovered something that changed the calculus. The business analysts had costed out a method to collect both gemstones and metals from the rough chunks before turning everything to powder. But if you sacrificed the gemstones, letting them get crushed to fine powder along with everything else, and attacked recovery when the mix was a goopy slurry, it was easy to recover the precious metals using basic mining technology, a simple process that had been around for more than a century.

After spending months refining the details and verifying the economics, he'd sent a report up the chain. He spent the next weeks dreaming of a raise and promotion. Maybe a fat bonus as well.

Perhaps it was the inertia of their long-held positions. Maybe they didn't want to take on anything that added risk to their already-tight deadlines. Whatever the reason, the people in Corporate rejected the plan. The vice president of the company told Roscoe personally that he shouldn't be wasting his time on ideas above his paygrade.

Roscoe was stung by the reprimand, believed it was wildly unfair, and took it hard.

Deciding he needed a break, he used his banked vacation time to spend the holidays with his folks in Trenton, New Jersey. At a family gathering one night, he bragged about his idea, pitching it as a sure thing, lamenting the short-sightedness of his Corporate superiors.

He went so far as to claim that if he just had the money, he could purchase the equipment and have it installed himself. It could be done with very minor modifications to the plant. Then he'd collect the precious metal worth tens of millions common, and since Corporate didn't want it, he'd keep it for himself.

"Corporate wouldn't know?" asked Yuri Melnikov, his uncle on his mother's side, the black sheep of the family who'd stopped by for a meal. A dour man in his mid-sixties, Yuri had a whispered reputation that both fascinated and frightened Roscoe.

Roscoe shook his head. "People from Corporate occasionally tour the Factory. But it's a dangerous place, so they never stay long. And they don't know what they're looking at anyway. It's all just metal housing surrounding big machines. Boring stuff to look at."

"What about the other staff at the Factory?" Yuri pressed. "Surely they'd know."

Fueled by beer, Roscoe continued to puff his ego. But at the same time, he believed his words. "Outside contractors install new equipment. The staff would think it was the next in a never-ending line of projects. And because of the nasty environment, we have enough bots on-site that people wouldn't see any extra workload."

As he was leaving that night, Yuri suggested that he and Roscoe have lunch sometime. Two days later, he invited Roscoe to join him at a private club. Feeling both excitement and trepidation, Roscoe arrived at The Kasha Room, greeting Yuri and meeting his associate, Stan Shevchenko. They quizzed Roscoe, who continued to inflate his self-importance.

"What would it cost to start recovery using your method?" asked Stan. "Purchase, installation, and startup?"

"About forty million, give or take."

"If you pulled the trigger today, how long before you'd start capturing the metals?"

Roscoe shrugged. "Maybe six months. First you need to finalize the design specs, then get bids, then the winner would need a few months to construct the equipment off-site. All that takes the most time. Installation at the Factory would take maybe a month more."

"Any way to speed that up?" asked Yuri.

"Sure, but it would cost. If you skipped the bidding process, you'd save a month, but there's no way you'd get the best price that way. Then you could pay a premium for fast construction. Overtime and all that. That would shave maybe three more weeks."

"How much would it produce? Or more to the point, how long to earn the investment back once it's ready to go?"

"I did my analysis using traditional Corporate methods. That came out to six months for construction and installation and four months to earn it back." Roscoe paused to order another beer before putting the icing on the cake. "After that, it would be pure profit."

Yuri looked at Stan, who gave him a brief nod. "When you get back, send us the details. We'd like to run the numbers ourselves."

"No need to wait." Roscoe tasted his newly-arrived beer. "I'll send it now."

That ill-fated day had changed his life, and not for the better. Quite the opposite. He wished that day had never happened.

. . .

"It was supposed to burn evidence," Yuri growled to Stan. They were meeting in a room in Corridor 62, one of sixty-four habitable spaces inside the Factory. "It was supposed to be flames, not an explosion. And we've killed a cop. They won't stop until they find who's responsible."

The guy who'd rigged the bomb was Rex Luskin, the idiot Stan had recruited, the one who'd been dumped into the feed port. Yuri almost wished he was still alive so he could kill him again.

He tried to comfort himself with the belief that the spacecraft was untraceable. It had been assembled from the parts of more than a dozen wrecked and retired ships scrounged from a private scrapyard outside Armstrong. When police started chasing down the different serial numbers and ident tags, it would send them from Lagrange to the Moon to Earth and back again. They'd be spinning in circles only to find it led nowhere. The ship was literally assembled from a pile of junk.

He hoped that anger and outrage would act like blinders on the investigating detectives. If they wasted enough time tracking ownership of the ship, it would give him the time he needed to scrub their trail and protect the operation from exposure.

The frustrating part was that they were almost done with the cash collection phase. Well, certainly done at this point. Their take was a little low, but he'd try to make it work. Either way, there wouldn't be any more old people disappearing. No more capital felonies to commit.

If the investigation didn't lead back to them in the near term, perhaps it never would.

And phase two, the purchase and installation of the precious-metals recovery equipment, was mostly a civil issue. At worst a corporate crime.

. . .

Roscoe tapped on the door and floated into Yuri's office without waiting for an invitation. He'd been summoned, something that exacerbated his heartburn.

"What's up?" he asked.

"We have a slight issue," said Yuri without preamble.

Roscoe waited.

"We have twenty-seven million. Plus the ten we've already paid in deposit. No more."

"The balance due is thirty common." His stomach turned flipflops. "What are we going to do?"

"Do you think they'll accept less? Twenty-seven is still a nice sum."

"Not a chance." He said it like he was talking to a child, then corrected his tone. "They think they're dealing with Corporate. If we short them, their lawyers will raise holy hell. Corporate will be here asking questions the next day."

"How about if we promise the last three million when we process the first asteroid?"

"Again, that's something Corporate would never do."

His uncle studied him. Roscoe could feel his disappointment.

"Can you delay things somehow? Maybe visit the

contractor, inspect the equipment, and find something wrong that buys us a few weeks? That will give me time to find the last bit."

Roscoe thought for a moment and nodded. Predelivery inspections were not a common practice for Corporate but not unheard of either. It could work, maybe for a week or ten days, but not much longer.

"Take Stan with you. He's good at this sort of thing."

Roscoe tried not to think what "this sort of thing" even meant, but his knees went weak anyway. If they'd been in a gravity environment, he'd have to sit down to keep himself from collapsing.

Chapter 8

C uss surfaced to find himself in a strange bed, one with an angled back and chrome guardrails. An antiseptic smell, penetrating and astringent, filled his nose. A phalanx of electronic equipment was stacked in an instrument rack to his left, black boxes with tiny red power lights, some with dials, others with small displays. Past that was an unoccupied bed like the one he was in. And past that were two doors. He presumed one was to a bathroom and the other led out to the hospital hallway.

On his right, in one of the two visitor chairs, sat Hatha.

"Welcome back," she said.

"She showed up on her own," Ygo told him. "The hospital staff was going to send her home, but I pulled some strings so she could stay. I figured it would cheer you up."

"How long have I been out?" Cuss asked her.

"The explosion happened at twenty-two hundred last night," replied Ygo. "The emergency response crew gave you a sedative on the scene because you wouldn't stay down. Doctors examined you here and got you in bed just before midnight. Physically you're fine. It's now eight in the morning."

"I've been here an hour," said Hatha, rising and approaching the bed. He could tell by the way she moved that they were in the full gravity of Terra Deck. "I'm not sure beyond that." She rested her hands on the bed's guardrail. "Do you want some privacy?"

"No!" His emphatic response caused her to smile. Then more calmly, "Stay. Please." His brow furrowed. "Where am I, and how did you even know I was here?"

"I told you I'd worked patrol. I still have friends on the job." She swirled a hand to indicate their surroundings. "This is Mercy Hospital on Terra."

A man in blue scrubs came through the door. "Good, you're awake. "

He pulled a display from a coat pocket, stretched it open, and looked at information Cuss couldn't see. As he studied it, he said, "I'm Dr. Morrison. How do you feel?" He closed the display, returned it to his pocket, and looked at Cuss expectantly.

"I'm fine. Thanks for caring for me." He pushed on the mattress with his hands, scooting himself up to a sitting position. "I'm ready to check out."

"In vids, the doctor tells the macho cop that he needs to stay in bed longer, and then the guy breaks out or whatever as soon as I leave." Dr. Morrison smiled at Hatha. "I see you have your getaway accomplice with you already." Then he shook his head. "But no concussion. No broken bones. No internal damage. Some bruising, and your ears will be ringing for a while. But physically, that's your only concern."

The doctor took a white disk the size of a coin from a different pocket and held it up. "Would you wear a monitor for a few days? We stick it on your chest, and it will alert us if anything changes."

"Let him do it," said Ygo. "It's the fastest way out."

"Sure." Cuss nodded. "How's Juan Luisa?"

"Your partner? He's down the hall. He's being discharged as well."

"And Debra Gosling?"

The doctor broke eye contact and studied the tiny disk in his hand. "I'm sorry. She didn't make it."

Cuss fell back and closed his eyes.

"She died instantly," said Ygo.

"Do you know where she is?" asked Cuss.

"I'm not sure," said the doctor. "I'll check after we get you connected."

"She's in the morgue in the basement of Saint Luke's Hospital on Luna Deck," said Ygo.

The doctor lowered Cuss's hospital gown so his chest was exposed, stripped the backing off the white disk, and pressed it to smooth skin over his heart. Pulling out his display again, he watched for a moment, and then returned it to his pocket. "You're all set. Do you have any questions for me?"

"No. Thanks again for your diligence."

The doctor nodded at Cuss, gave Hatha a smile, then made for the door. "Good luck catching the bad guys, Marshal. Stop by the desk at the end of the hall. I'll have them locate Ms. Gosling for you." He stepped into the hall and then poked his head back into the room. "Oh, and they're holding your weapon at the security desk." The door closed and he was gone.

Cuss turned his attention back to Hatha, who was

staring at his bare chest, her smile radiant, her dimples adorable. A natural mesomorph, his well-muscled body clearly enthralled her.

"Privacy please," he said with mock sternness. He made no move to cover up.

"I am so not sorry." She turned her back.

Scooting out of bed, he made for an upright cabinet he assumed held his clothes.

"Want any help?" she asked.

"Thank you, but I need proper courting before we get all hot and sweaty."

As he slipped out of his hospital gown, he caught her peeking at his reflection in a mirror on the side wall. He couldn't resist. "Madam, you don't hide your lust very well. It's both embarrassing and intimidating."

She didn't blush a bit.

After dressing, he turned to face her. "I'm glad you came. Waking up to your smile is the best medicine I ever could have hoped for." Using a serious tone, he continued. "But now I need to connect with Juan. And then I need to bring hellfire to the monsters responsible for at least two deaths and, I fear, more."

He stepped to her and gave her a hug. When she hugged him back, he gave her a quick kiss on the lips. She tasted faintly of raspberries, her fragrance a subtle floral. "I'm not sure if I'll make it to the park this afternoon."

She locked eyes with his, connecting in a way that reached his soul. "I walk my pooch there most days after work. If not today, then perhaps another."

. . .

Cuss left Hatha and made for Juan's room. The floor in the hallway was condensate composite dyed to look like Carrara marble, polished smooth, but with an invisible texture of some sort to keep people from slipping. The walls were white and clean, with faux-wood doors evenly spaced on either side. The ceiling glowed uniformly, like the entire surface was one diffuse bulb.

"Did we confirm a cause of death for Agnes Ming?" he asked Ygo as he scanned the doors. Then he interrupted himself. "Which room is it?"

"Two more doors on the left," replied Ygo. "As for the coroner, she's finishing Debra Gosling's autopsy now, and it looks like she'll be doing Agnes right after that."

"Where is she working?"

"The basement of Saint Luke's on Luna Deck. The coroner's office is down the hall from the mortuary."

"Could you ask if she'll meet with Juan and me? We should be there in an hour or so."

"Of course, my liege."

Ignoring the sarcasm, Cuss tapped on the door to Juan's room and entered without waiting for an invitation. The layout was a duplicate of his own.

Juan was getting dressed in front of his locker. He looked pale, and Cuss tried to determine if it was from injuries, the loss of a partner, or both.

His wife was with him, a neat woman almost as tall as Juan but wider and heavier. She had an oval face, black hair with modest curls, and wore a nondescript turquoise top and tan slacks. Her bare feet were shoved into everyday sandals.

Cuss got the sense she was normally jovial: smiling, upbeat, quick to laugh. But today she was as somber as Juan but likely for a different reason. If Debra could die on the job, so could her husband.

Juan introduced them. "Cuss, this is Maria. Maria, Cuss."

Cuss nodded as he shook her hand. She kept her hand limp, staring at him with daggers in her eyes. He was the one who almost got her husband killed. Now he wanted to take him deeper into battle. Cuss wasn't a friend or colleague. He was the enemy.

"I'm going to get a cup of coffee," he told Juan. "Meet me outside the front entrance when you're ready."

He said goodbye to Maria and made his escape.

. . .

While he waited, he bought and drank a coffee, retrieved his gun from the security desk, and bought and ate a fried egg sandwich. He was considering another coffee when Juan walked out the front door of the hospital and joined him by the pedestrian thoroughfare. Maria wasn't with him. Cuss was happy to escape her judgment.

"Did you snag your weapon?" he asked.

"I did," said Juan, opening his coat to show it as if Cuss might not accept his word. He still looked pale.

"Are you all right?"

"I've never lost a partner." He wouldn't meet Cuss's

gaze. "It hurts deeper than I ever imagined."

Cuss put a hand on the man's shoulder and chose his words carefully, wanting to show respect and remain sensitive to his sorrow. "She was a great person. Her absence will be painful. Take some time. Maybe spend a few days with Maria."

Juan shook his head and spoke through clenched teeth, his hands in fists by his side. "I'm too angry to sit at home. I'll mourn after I bury whoever did this to her."

"I support whatever decision you make." In Cuss's experience, fury could give an investigation energy. But it had to be properly channeled because it could just as easily lead to recklessness.

Cuss pointed toward the pod station on the corner and got them walking. "We have a busy morning. First stop is the coroner's office on Luna to learn what we can about Agnes Ming. Then I want to examine that ship. Do you know if a team's been through it?"

"I'm sure they have. Hold on while I see if I can access their report." Juan placed a call and began a conversation.

"They did send a team," Ygo said in his ear. "The explosive used was Thuroxon. It's powerful stuff used mostly for mining. They go through literal tons of it in Nova Terra because creating new caverns for city expansion is a never-ending process. Unfortunately, that means lots of people have had access to it over the years.

"The damage inside the ship was extensive," Ygo continued, "and genetic traces of only two people survived the conflagration: Ivan Kosmin and Rex Luskin. They're two toughs who've had repeated brushes with police on

Earth."

Juan finished his call and gave Cuss a similar report. As they got in line at the pod loading ramp, Juan added, "Don't forget about visiting the Lewiston-Mark office. There's something driving this. It's not about love or jealousy. Revenge and anger and pride don't fit, not on the surface anyway. But money sure does. Especially if Ming used Lewiston-Clark as well."

"She did," said Ygo. "And she was worth upward of ten million common."

"My sources say she did," said Cuss as they climbed into a pod. They sat in facing seats but on opposite sides so they could stretch their legs. "And she was rich."

"Bingo."

As the pod got underway, Juan finally looked Cuss in the eye.

· · ·

The ride from Terra to Saint Luke's took them across all twelve decks and then three kilometers along Luna Deck, a half-hour journey in all. Juan received a call along the way.

"The mayor wants to meet with us," he reported to Cuss. "She suggested lunch, but I don't want to spend that much time with her."

"What's her motive?"

"Her assistant said she wanted to reach out about Debra. Express her sorrow and support. I'm sure there's more to it, though."

"Do I need to be there?"

"She specifically asked for both of us. You don't report to her, so you're free to do whatever. But it would make my life easier if you were there."

"Sure, then. Happy to help. She's up on Terra? Ask if thirteen thirty will work." He lamented privately that being agreeable meant he'd definitely miss Hatha in the park.

Saint Luke's was a stately structure, eight stories tall, the condensate formed to look like blocks of granite, with gardens around it and strips of grass in front that distinguished it from most other buildings on the deck. On one side of the entrance stood a marble-like statue of Hermes, a young man holding a scepter, naked but for a cape hanging from one shoulder. A statue of Saint Luke, a wise old man dressed in robes, stood on the other side.

They climbed the stairway into the lobby, a large space with a dramatic mural depicting a scene with Hippocrates painted on the ceiling. A tiled floor held clusters of faux-wood chairs, the seats polished by thousands of butts sliding across them. A dozen people milled about, some looking for assistance, some awaiting answers, others preparing to finally go home.

"The coroner's office is down the main hall to the left," Ygo told Cuss. "At the end of the hall, take the stairs to the basement, then come back this way three doors."

Cuss was about relay the information, but Juan had already engaged the building's virtual assistant, asking for directions.

"Follow the yellow dot," replied the assistant.

A yellow dot appeared on the floor three meters way, blinking slowly, waiting for them to advance. They walked toward it and it slid ahead, guiding them along the main hall to the left, down a flight of stairs to the basement, then back this way three doors.

The basement was a drabber version of the main level. It had the same tile on the floor, but here it was worn, like it had seen heavier traffic over the years, or perhaps they'd skipped this level during the last refurbishment project. The ceiling was a meter lower, adding to the basement feel.

The door chimed when they stopped in front of it. After a twenty-second wait, it opened.

"Welcome, gents." A stocky woman in blue medical scrubs—medium height, kind face, intelligent eyes—waved them into the room. Her hair was pressed against her head, a little moist from perspiration, as if she'd been wearing a stocking cap and just took it off.

As they introduced themselves, Cuss knew he'd seen her before and struggled to place her.

"I'm Dr. Lewis. Call me Shawna." She led them though a room of tables and benches cluttered with an assortment of glassware, instruments, and devices, chatting excitedly as they walked. "I'm glad you came, because after what I found, I was going to ask you to come down and see for yourselves."

She stopped at a sturdy door made of a silver-colored metal, likely an aluminum alloy but possibly stainless steel. She looked back over her shoulder. "It's cold in there. Grab a coat." She pointed to a row of white coats hanging on hooks to her right.

She put on a coat herself that had been draped over the back of a chair and then snugged a cap on her head that had a light in front, the kind that followed her eyes, illuminating wherever she looked. She flicked the light on.

As Cuss slid into his coat, he snapped his fingers. "You were on the medical examiner's team that processed the crime scene."

"Good for you, Marshal. That was me with Renee." She answered his next question before he asked it. "We don't get much call for either medical examiners or autopsies here in Hermes. Not crime-related autopsies anyway. I like to keep busy."

She opened the door to a sigh of air. They stepped inside, and the cold hit them like a crisp arctic morning.

Cuss scanned the room and saw it was all the same bright, clean metal alloy. On the wall to the left were rows of shiny doors, four across and two high, each big enough to hide a slide-out rack holding a corpse. Somewhere hidden, a compressor hummed as it worked to keep the bodies inside even colder than the room.

A lab bench ran along the wall across from the refrigerated cabinets, the same silver metal, with columns of drawers filling the front. The top of the bench held a sink, a nested stack of plastic tubs, and a number of electronic appliances. Overhead cupboards had transparent doors that revealed a supply of beakers, test tubes, petri dishes, and flasks.

In the center of the room sat an operating table, with hoses and faucets and drains. It had a scale for weighing body parts and, overhead, a light fixture hung on an adjustable arm. A body covered in a thin blue cloth lay on the table.

Shawna moved over to the body and positioned herself on one side. She motioned for them to stand next to her.

"I won't make you look at everything. It's pretty gruesome if you're not used to it." When they were in position, she lifted the edge of the cloth, exposing Agnes Ming's head and neck.

The woman was lying on her stomach with her face turned away from them. Shawna pointed to a fine wire that trailed out from under her skull. The wire was about ten centimeters long. Below it, an incision of the same length ran down the back of Ming's neck.

"Look at that." Shawna stepped back so they could see.

"What is it?" asked Juan.

"I don't know. But as soon as we're done here, I'm going to research it. Check this out." She lifted a flap of skin near the skull and tugged on the wire, pulling it out from the opening. It had a small black chip the size of a fingernail on the other end. She held it up for them to view.

"Dios mio," said Juan, making the sign of the cross.

"That's an identity authentication link," said Ygo. "They were popular thirty years ago when a spate of hacking thefts was plaguing the rich. That device ensured that only they could access and transact with their investment portfolio."

"I think that's a bank link that the super-rich used decades ago," Cuss said. "It's a security thing."

"How come I've never seen one before?" asked Shawna.

"Only a thousand or so were implanted," said Ygo. "Then technology changed. It was replaced by equally secure but noninvasive technology."

Cuss shrugged. "I guess that after a few years, new technology came along that made them obsolete, so there's not that many out there."

He turned to Juan. "I'd be interested to know if Franklin Wallingford and Robert Moore have them. If the kidnappers have figured out a way to access them to take their money, it could explain a whole lot."

Juan spoke softly. "Something tells me that the people at Lewiston-Mark would know."

"This is great stuff, Shawna," said Cuss at the end of her presentation. "Let's keep this as quiet as you're able. Our advantage is greater if the bad guys don't know that we know."

He wanted to get them going before Shawna or Juan suggested viewing Debra. The raw reality of a morgue wasn't the best place to remember someone you cared for. But just as he got Juan moving, he stopped. "What killed her?"

"It was the blow to the head on the ceiling beam in the barn. A cast of the wound matches up with where we found her blood."

"If she was fleeing a kidnapper," said Juan. "It makes him just as responsible as if he'd delivered the blow himself."

Chapter 9

Back on the street, Juan pushed for visiting Lewiston-Mark next.

"C'mon, Detective," Cuss scolded. "All those firms promise their clients confidentiality, and the richer their clientele, the more they protect that right. We need to show up with a warrant. They won't cooperate otherwise, and empty threats won't scare them."

"I know, but I'm worried about the delay. It will take me until tomorrow to get a warrant, and that's if I work at it full time and get lucky. I've started organizing and documenting the background material, but I still need to brief my captain about it, then work with the department's counsel to flesh it out, then deliver it to the court, then sit around while the judge decides."

"I have a few contacts who might be able to move things faster. Give me some privacy while I touch base with them?"

Cuss loped down to a kiosk at the end of the block and bought his third cup of coffee for the day. His left shoulder felt stiff and he rotated it, working out the kinks as he sipped. In the process, he learned that his left elbow was tender, something that had escaped him before now. He was finishing the cup when Ygo said, "The judge is in court and will be breaking for lunch at noon. I have the application ready, but I can't get it in front of him before then."

"Shit. That means we can't go in until after the meeting with the mayor."

"So let's go look through the ship. Lewiston-Mark will still be there this afternoon."

. . .

Cuss borrowed a grav suit and, together with Juan, circled the *Yankee Spirit*. Portable stairs sat nearby, the kind used by tech crew who needed access to different parts of a ship. But before they moved the unit into position, Cuss wanted to learn what they could from the deck.

The body of the craft bulged, misshapen from the powerful blast, blown outward all around like someone had tried to inflate it. They worked in a methodical fashion, studying every piece of the vessel in turn, looking for numbers, tags, or insignias they could trace to understand its history and identify the owner. They'd learned previously that the landing pads were from three different vessels. They repeated that process with the landing struts, the flex hinges, and the bracket system connecting the legs to the body.

The ship was propelled with a Paulson drive, and the four thruster nozzles under the ship, black cones the size of Cuss's torso with ribbing that gave them structural strength, had two different origins, as did the small stabilizing thrusters around the body of the craft.

Juan used a device to record the different identifiers

for later analysis. Cuss let him do so without comment, even though Ygo was grabbing everything using Cuss's lens, organizing the data into tables, and evaluating it all to solve the puzzle on the fly.

When they'd exhausted the external clues, Cuss grabbed the stairway unit and moved it into position so they could repeat the process inside the ship. Juan helped him jockey the steps against the hull where the hatch had been, now with sharp spikes poking out around the opening, jagged daggers of metal that looked like someone had used a giant church key to open an oversized can.

Cuss climbed up first and stepped inside the craft, careful not to snag his suit on the shards around the opening. The craft was a smaller version of the *Nelly Marie* but with the same general layout: three decks and a lower hold inside an egg-shaped hull. He stepped far enough forward for Juan to follow and then paused to assess the scene. The interior was dark, causing lights built into their suits to activate, casting a glow to aid their study of the craft.

The first level was a circle about five meters across. It held the pilot's station in front of an expansive display, with seats for two crew members behind the pilot's chair. Located around the circumference were viewports to be used in the event of a display failure; a panel of hand controls for manual adjustment of air, humidity, and temperature should the environmental system fail; and a battery backup station in case of power generation failure. Directly across from the hatch were steep stairs leading to the second level, almost a ladder but with handrails.

That's what was supposed to be there, anyway. What Cuss saw was an aftermath of that layout. The viewports were blown out. The seats had vaporized, their brackets and supports remaining, still attached to the deck, with a shadow around them like a photonegative of what had once been. The panels and controls around the perimeter were bent and warped. The ladder to the second level was now twisted, as if it were trying to become a spiral staircase.

Cuss made a quick tour so Ygo could capture what he needed. Then he moved to where a trap door in the floor had been, an accessway down to the hold. Like the ship's exterior hatch, it too was gone, leaving a jagged hole in the deck and leading Cuss to believe there had been a second charge detonated below.

He stood on the precipice and peered down into a scene of utter destruction. "Did the cops who searched while the pilot was on board look in the hold?" He asked Juan, who was standing at the base of the twisted ladder, looking up.

"I don't know. Let me check." He placed a call, but when no one answered, he left a message.

"I'm going down." Cuss gauged the opening and then dropped into an area just tall enough for him to walk upright. The damage below was as extensive as that on the first deck. Ygo began logging identifiers while Cuss poked around.

The hold was packed with technology. There was the Paulson drive and its fuel reserves, an environmental system with its stores of air and water, several pieces that comprised waste processing, the navigation computer, and the power generator. Every recess not used for ship's tech was lined and covered with a door or false front for storage of food, drink, clothes, entertainment, tools, medical supplies, pressure suits, and everything else one might need to journey through space. On the larger *Nelly Marie*, this was also where Ygo lived in his private den.

All of it was charred and crushed from the blast. And with everything blown apart, he could see nooks and crannies big enough to hide a person, spaces that would not be obvious in a search. In spite of the destruction, enough identifiers had survived to provide Ygo with the information he needed.

"This ship is a mix and match from more than fifteen different craft," said Ygo. "It seems like a deliberate attempt to create confusion, because if an old ship needs a new drive, or new landing struts, or the seats are too worn, then you'd replace them but keep everything else. For big overhauls, you find a donor craft to combine with the original to make one good one. Maybe you go to a third ship for certain items. But fifteen different craft is over the top."

"Who would do that?"

"All these tags are from old craft from the different worlds. But in the aggregate, they tell a pretty clear story. Someone is trying to hide something. Someone who has access to an inventory of retired vessels stored in a place no one would think unusual."

"Like a spaceship boneyard," said Cuss as he moved a shelf under the hatch so he could climb out. "I'd put my money on Nova Terra. I don't see this piece of shit lifting off from Earth."

"It could," said Ygo. "I mean structurally it's capable. But I wouldn't want to be riding in it."

"How many ship boneyards are there in Nova Terra?"

"Only one that I can find."

"Do you think whoever built it knew what it was going to be used for?"

"They'd at least know *who* they were building it for. Someone paid the invoice. Someone flew it away."

When Cuss emerged from the hold, Juan was nowhere in sight. He climbed the bent stairs to find him on the second level. A circle seven meters across, this was the living area of the ship. The damage here was extensive, but nothing like the first level or the hold, making Cuss think that the victims were kept down where the explosives had been located.

Around the circumference against the wall, he saw a kitchenette, a narrow worktable, an entertainment system, and a row of floor-to-ceiling cabinets. The rest of the area was open and reconfigurable, allowing for lounge chairs, or a dining table, or exercise space, or whatever else the occupants desired.

"I heard back from one of the guys who searched the ship," Juan told him. "He says he went down into the hold and opened some doors but didn't really tear it apart. The pilot was screaming at him, and without a warrant and without seeing anything suspicious, he didn't want to push it too far."

"I wonder where the pilot is now?"

Juan looked around like he'd dropped a coin. "They

didn't find another body. I would have heard if they had."

"I'm betting the guy they're calling the pilot is the same guy who chased Agnes Ming," said Ygo. "I've been trying to track him down in between the thousand other things you've dumped on me. Sensor feeds show him riding a Skeeter out of Hermes, but he doesn't arrive at any of the other cities."

"Maybe he rode a personal craft out of here," Cuss said aloud, "and met up with a larger ship lurking among the city structures."

"If so, then he's long gone," said Juan.

They climbed to the third level, the smallest and least damaged of the lot. About four meters across, it held two unkempt sleeping areas, presumably for Ivan Kosmin and Rex Luskin, the two who'd left genetic material behind. The bedsheets were foul. The clothes on the floor smelled of body odor. The ship's bathroom was filthy. After a cursory inspection, Cuss made for the exit, disgusted by his quarry, glad he'd worn protective gloves, and wishing he'd worn a facemask.

. . .

They ate lunch at a diner on Terra, mentally preparing for the meeting with the mayor. As they chowed on burgers and fries, they discussed next steps in the investigations.

"I think we need to split up for a bit," said Cuss. "I'd like to check out the spaceship boneyard in Armstrong, and you could take the lead hunting down Franklin Wallingford and Robert Moore while they're hopefully still alive."

Juan nodded in agreement. "If they have one of those wire thingies, I wonder if we could use it as a location device."

"Excellent idea," said Ygo, his enthusiasm for the suggestion clear. "I'll look into it. I can tell you up front, though, that if it's possible, we'd need specialized talent to implement the result."

"No idea," said Cuss, "but I love the creativity. Do you know anyone who'd have the juice to figure it out?"

"The department has a consultant who's an electronics engineer. He works as an adjunct professor at Central Tech but builds the cool stuff in his workshop at home." Juan looked into the distance, lost in thought. "He'd need a model to work from, so we'd have to get him that wire and chip that was inside Agnes Ming. But if it's connected to her money, I'm not sure what liability that would open up for the city."

"Is he the type who would get criminally creative?"

"Anyone who becomes an expert at tracking and hacking and eavesdropping is someone who's thought a lot about getting creative. That's my instinct anyway."

"I object, Your Honor," said Ygo. Cuss tried not to grin. Ygo continued. "The chip needs to be adjacent to the cerebellum to execute personal banking functions. We can give it to him without risk of theft."

"Maybe daydreaming is enough for him," said Cuss. "If you think he's the guy, I'll sign out the wire in my name so you and the city are off the hook. But since you have the relationship with him, you should be the one to make the ask."

Juan shook his head in wonder. "I want your job. Mine has rules and procedures and dictates and documentation and reviews and fricking egos that makes community policing a very different game."

"Before you both get too excited," said Ygo, "we need to confirm that Wallingford and Moore have the implants, and that the wire can be used for tracking."

Cuss checked the time. "Let's find out what the mayor wants. The warrant should be ready soon, and then we'll visit Lewiston-Mark and learn about Wallingford and Moore."

.   .   .

City Hall was an impressive structure with lots of glass and a waterfall feature down the front that splashed off architectural outcroppings to generate mist. Special lighting behind the spray created a rainbow effect that arced over the front plaza. Water used in such a fashion was as dramatic as it was rare in the city, drawing a steady stream of tourists who wanted to stand under the spectral arch for a fun vid they could share with the folks back home.

The lobby was equally impressive, with a waterfall of vines hanging from above, covered in blue and white blooms that led into a multicolored flower arch, creating a vegetative interpretation of the waterfall outside.

Cuss and Juan were escorted by the mayor's assistant up to the top floor, where they were instructed to wait outside her office. They sat in chairs against the wall while the assistant ignored them, reminding Cuss of sitting outside the principal's office in grade school. Ten minutes passed before the door opened and they were escorted inside.

Mayor Isabelle Florence, fifty-six years old, dressed in a beige designer suit with a white blouse and red scarf, her hair coifed like she was attending a gala, stood behind her desk, a broad wooden table with no drawers and nothing on top. No family pictures, no cup or glass. Not even a pen. Smiling broadly, she moved around the table to greet them.

"Detective. Marshal. Thank you for coming." She shook hands with both of them, her warm demeanor the exact opposite of the confrontational behavior she'd displayed on the farm, putting Cuss on full alert. "Juan, I'm so sorry about Detective Gosling. She was an asset to the city, a friend to all, and will be deeply missed. I'm so glad you escaped without injury. I'm told the psychological burden of such an event can be tremendous, so I've authorized an extended leave so you may recover and heal."

Cuss's bullshit meter was already at maximum, but the move to shift Juan off the case was too much. He spoke up.

"Thank you for your concern, Isabelle. But Juan and I have discussed it at length, and we're both committed to seeing this to the end."

Juan nodded in agreement.

"Wonderful." She continued to smile, but the edges of her lips twitched, like she'd eaten a spoonful of seafood chowder and was realizing the shrimp had gone bad.

Standing in front of them, her eyes flicked from one to the other. Twenty long seconds passed, and then her attitude changed. She waved a "come here" motion toward the door, and a woman entered, mid-forties, hair in a tight bun, permanent scowl, dressed in severe clothes that showed no joy.

The mayor didn't introduce her. The woman sat on a couch against the wall to the mayor's right.

"The press are all over this." The mayor rested her butt against her desk table and motioned for them to sit in visitor chairs that matched the couch, her perch letting her lord over them. "We have a press conference in forty minutes. Two people have died, one a member of our Community Patrol, and they're clamoring for information."

"Murdered," interrupted Cuss, now understanding the motivation for the meeting.

She glared at him with a stare that could weld metal. "Yes, murdered. I want a complete brief on what happened, where we are, what to expect next, and when this will be wrapped up. Don't leave anything out. Make me look bad, and even the governor won't be able to save you."

The woman on the couch spoke. "The mayor will be at the podium. You will be standing behind her, one on either side. We expect twelve or so reporters. You will not say anything, whisper anything, or make facial expressions of any kind. You will not contradict the mayor in any way. Keep your hands at your sides. When you are introduced, you are to remain in position. Your job is to project confidence and capability. Nothing more. Nothing less."

Cuss felt sorry for Juan because he had to live with this kind of crap every day. He wondered why the commander or deputy chief wasn't present, guessed they'd be blindsided by the press conference, and realized that meant the governor would be as well.

Cuss covered his mouth and coughed. With his hand still up, he whispered to Ygo, "Warn Belnick."

"Did you say something, Marshal?" asked the mayor.

"Just a cough." He smiled and shrugged. "Some water might help."

She ignored him and looked at Juan. "Detective Luisa, you may begin."

With his back straight, Juan slid forward to the edge of his chair, clearing his throat as he did so. "It seems we have multiple crimes that are tied together. Franklin Wallingford and Agnes Ming were taken in separate abductions from Armstrong five days ago. Both were transported here to Hermes on the spaceship *Yankee Spirit*. Well, we know Ming was on the ship. We have sensor feeds that indicate Wallingford was as well, but he's missing, so we can't confirm it with certainty."

The mayor spoke to Juan but looked at the woman on the couch. "This press conference is about murders. Don't complicate it with unrelated issues."

The woman on the couch shrugged and shook her head as if to say she didn't know any more than the mayor.

"Yes, ma'am," said Juan. "We believe these were perpetrated by the same people in a coordinated event. Plus there's the kidnapping of Robert Moore three days ago from Hermes Deck 8, which we suspect is part of it all."

The mayor frowned and folded her arms across her chest. "Is he dead as well?"

"Just missing. But his profile is the same as

Wallingford and Ming."

"What does that mean?"

"All three were very rich and quite elderly."

The mayor shook her head rapidly as if to clear it of confusion. Juan persisted, this time simplifying it to what the mayor seemed to want to hear.

"Agnes Ming was abducted from Armstrong five days ago, transported here to Hermes, and was being held captive on the *Yankee Spirit*. She escaped from the ship and fled her captors. In her panic, she jumped up a farm access shaft and, unfamiliar with its construction, hit her head at the top of the rise with enough force to kill herself. Since she was a victim of a capital crime and was attempting self-rescue, it's classified as murder according to Lagrange law. The body was discovered by a farmer, Mr. Thicke, and we—meaning the marshal, Detective Gosling, and I—investigated. The crime scene team arrived, and while they worked, we departed and approached the *Yankee Spirit*, seeking to gain entry. We had a proper search warrant filed and approved…"

Juan paused and looked at Cuss, who nodded, confirming that a warrant was in place.

He continued. "Detective Gosling was attempting to open the ship's hatch when a bomb exploded inside, killing her instantly and destroying evidence of the crime within."

"Good. So the interworld nature of the crime is why Marshal Abbott is involved."

Cuss answered by smiling. He saw no percentage in engaging with the woman.

"If Ming killed herself at the top of the shaft," asked

the woman on the couch, "how did she get out in the field?"

Cuss had assigned the mystery woman the title of press secretary. It was an insightful question, and he gave her a second look while Juan answered.

"We believe her captor didn't want to carry her back to the ship. Too much exposure. So he delayed her discovery by hiding her among the soybeans. That's the working theory, anyway, supported by the medical examiner and our own investigation."

"No body was found inside the ship," continued the press secretary. "So where's the kidnapper-turned-murderer?"

Another great question, thought Cuss.

"Yes." The mayor retook control of the questioning, her gaze flicking back and forth between Juan and Cuss. "Who is responsible? And how long before they're in custody?"

Since this was a no-win answer, Cuss chose to come to Juan's rescue. "We can't reveal the names of the perpetrators without compromising the investigation. We are closing in and expect them to be in custody in the next few days."

"Do you know who it is?"

Cuss shook his head. "Use that answer. We'll know soon enough."

The mayor's lips pressed together. "The reporters will ask all kinds of questions. Why did they bring her to Hermes? What's their motive? Are the criminals from here or Nova Terra? Are citizens here at risk? It will go on and on."

"All of them have the same response. We can't answer without compromising the investigation. We are closing in and expect them to be in custody in the next few days."

Juan raised his hand to his shoulder to signal he had a question. When the mayor looked his way, he said, "Other questions might be, Will Detective Gosling's name go on the Heroes Wall? Will there be a city remembrance ceremony? Does her estate qualify for KIA benefits?"

The mayor looked at her press secretary, who told her, "I'll generate answers you can use for that line of questions."

"Make it quick," she barked. "We need to head down in a few minutes."

Cuss stood, his six-foot, one-inch frame putting him above the mayor.

The mayor looked him up and down. "In fact, let's go now and get organized."

They crowded into the elevator and rode the eight floors down to the main level in silence. The pressroom was a large conference room in the back of the building, configured with twenty chairs covered in institutional blue fabric, with plastic arms and straight legs that allowed them to be stacked to the side so the room could be used for other purposes. The stage ran the width of the room at the front, a single step up from the carpeted floor, with a podium in the center front.

The press secretary took a roll of black gaffer's tape from a podium shelf, peeled off two short strips, and stuck them onto the stage. "Put your toes there, gentlemen." She checked the time and said to the mayor, "We should let them in."

As she walked to the door at the back of the room, the mayor motioned for Cuss and Juan to follow. "We need to make an entrance." She led them to a door at the side of the stage and into a small waiting room. "Stand on the tape and look confident. Everything will be just fine." She took a deep breath and exhaled.

The press secretary joined them moments later, then peeked out into the room. "Let's give them a few minutes to get seated."

A second door opened at the back of the waiting room, and a distinguished man in his early sixties, with graying hair, wearing a power suit and power tie, as tall as Cuss but not as broad in the shoulders, stepped through and joined them. He winked at Cuss.

"Governor Belnick," said the mayor, her face turning red. "I'm so glad you could make it."

"I'm sure you are, Isabelle," he said in a tone so dry it would parch a desert.

After introducing himself to Juan, he got down to business. "I'll go first to explain the interworld nature of the situation, then I'll pass it to Marshal Abbott to answer specifics of the investigation. Then the mayor can follow and give the city's perspective. Sound good?"

He didn't wait for an answer, instead opening the stage door and striding out to the lectern, the rest of them ragtagging behind.

He stood there looking regal, waiting for the room to quiet. "Hello, everyone. Deaths in our family are always difficult to accept, and senseless deaths caused by criminal behavior are the hardest of all. The loss of Detective Debra Gosling, a brave servant and fine officer, falls into that category. She was a community officer, so in just a moment, I'm going to let Mayor Florence talk about her and answer your questions."

He went on to describe his leadership in creating the Interworld Marshals Service, how it was the proper structure for solving challenging crimes like the abduction and death of Agnes Ming, how in the past, politics made such investigations difficult, and how he was committed to bringing these and all criminals to justice.

"Marshal Cuss Abbott is the man for that job," he finished. "Marshal, come answer the reporters' questions." He turned to Cuss, motioned him forward, and looked back at the reporters. "Thanks, folks, but the legislature is voting on budget amendments today, and if I'm not there keeping an eye on things, they'll cut the programs we love and fund the ones we don't."

The reporters laughed and then started shouting questions. Acting like he didn't hear them, he waved, and in three long strides reached the stage door and was gone.

Cuss introduced himself, then went on to praise the governor, laying it on as thick as he dared. "He is a man of vision, one who saw crimes like the murder of Agnes Ming get mired in interservice rivalries and led the way forward with a solution that works. He's vowed his full support in whatever is necessary to bring to justice those responsible for this heinous crime. And my partner, Community Patrol Detective Juan Luisa, and I intend to do just that."

Questions came fast and furious, and he soon reached the point of replying with, "I can't answer without compromising the investigation. We are closing in on those responsible and expect to place them in custody within the next few days." After the third such response, he introduced the mayor and made for the stage exit. He'd had enough. Juan could fend for himself.

Chapter 10

Forty minutes passed before Juan joined Cuss near the pedestrian thoroughfare outside City Hall. He moved slowly, looking pale and dejected.

"You still have a job?" asked Cuss, only partly in jest.

He gave a shallow shrug. "I didn't know there was something worse than her doghouse, but apparently there is, and I'm definitely in it. She was in a rage after the conference, and I took the full brunt."

"Sorry, partner. It's been a rough couple of days for you. Let's grab a coffee and decompress. Then we'll head for Lewiston-Mark."

They both decided on iced tea and sipped while they walked aimlessly for twenty minutes, lost in their private thoughts. As they approached the fourth pod station of their jaunt, Juan pointed to the entry ramp. "I'm as ready as I'll ever be."

They rode down to Luna Deck, then to the city center and Lewiston-Mark's office. The place had a posh exterior, with a cut-limestone-like entrance, gold-colored embellishments on the windows and door, understated signage in fancy script, and little else to call attention to it. It presented like a private club, very exclusive, which in many ways it was.

Inside it was equally upscale, with lush beige carpet and

two faux-leather armchairs behind a mahogany coffee table. The minimal seating reinforced the notion that this wasn't a place for common folk. Clients didn't wait, at least not out front. Lighting came from an ornate cut-glass fixture that didn't really match an office environment but did fit the message the company seemed to be sending.

A smallish man, somewhere in his fifties, expensively dressed in a gray pinstripe suit, appeared from a door that fit so perfectly into the gorgeous cherrywood walls, Cuss hadn't realized it was there.

"How may I help you, gentlemen?" He spoke with a slight British accent. "I don't have an appointment on my calendar. Have I erred?"

Juan introduced himself and then used a pocket display to show the man the search warrant. "We're here to ask a few questions about three of your clients. Let's talk in your office."

The man took a long time reading the warrant. "May I see badges?" He studied their credentials carefully as well, sighed, and motioned toward the armchairs. "Please. Have a seat. How may I help you?"

"We'll have a seat inside," said Cuss.

The top of the man's head came to Cuss's shoulders, and he looked up at him under bushy eyebrows. "What is this about?" His British accent was gone.

Cuss pointed to where the door had been. "Inside."

"I need to call our attorney."

"You may call your attorney, but then you must cooperate, or we'll need to bring you to the station. This warrant permits forcible entry. If I use a crowbar to peel open that door, your clients will not be impressed."

"Calm down," said the man. "No need for threats." He squared up in front of the door, it slid open, and he led them inside, talking to someone as he did.

"Connie, this is Drake Marisette over at Lewiston-Mark. Two police detectives have served the company with a warrant. Could you come by and make sure everything is proper?"

Cuss didn't hear Connie's reply but said to Juan, "Maybe we should call for backup, get a patrol officer to meet Connie in the lobby and keep her company?"

"Connie's a he," said the man. "And I'm Drake Marisette. What in heaven's name is going on? We're a prestigious firm and are meticulous about obeying the laws on every world we serve. I've worked in this office for eighteen years, and we've never been questioned by the authorities."

Juan ignored him. "Who else is here?"

"It's just me."

The inside was modest in size, with two handsome offices, one on either side of a conference room that could hold eight people comfortably. A short hallway ran in front, with a tiny kitchenette on one end and a bathroom on the other. The rich carpeting continued on this side of the secret door, as did the cherrywood walls. This side also had paintings in expensive-looking frames on the walls.

"Are there any more hidden doors leading anywhere?" asked Juan.

Before Drake could answer, Cuss added, "Your answers are being recorded, and untruthful responses violate the search warrant, which means they carry consequences."

"I'm cooperating, officers." He waved a hand in front of a wall behind them to reveal a modest closet with office supplies—folders, pads, pens, and the like—all with Lewiston-Mark's insignia on the them. "That's it."

He turned and motioned to the office on the right. "This one is mine. The other is Sandy Merced's. She generally works mornings, and I cover afternoons."

Cuss led the way into Drake's office and sank into one of two plush armchairs in front of the desk. Juan sat in the other. Drake moved around the desk, a table similar to the mayor's, though his had family pictures on it. He sat in an ergonomic office chair and looked at them expectantly.

"We'd like to confirm that Franklin Wallingford, Agnes Ming, and Robert Moore are clients, and learn what financial transactions they've made in the last week."

"Oh, my." The color drained from Drake's face. "Confidentiality is a huge part of our business. Violating it is a firing offense, with all sorts of financial penalties on our accumulated bonus account."

"The warrant doesn't give you a choice," said Juan.

"Please," he implored. "Privacy is the core of our business model, that and making piles of money for our clients. If word got out that I talked to you, it could damage the reputation of the firm."

"Our warrant is limited to these three people," said Cuss, "and refusing is not an option. Agnes Ming is dead, and the others may be as well if we don't find them soon. If you don't provide answers, we'll call techs down here to dig it out. Instead of exposing limited information on three clients, you'll be exposing everything about everybody."

"And if you refuse and we learn that they died after this moment," said Juan, "you could be charged as an accessory."

"Good lord." Drake chewed on his thumbnail as he looked from them to his display and back. "How about if I call up their information and you read it from the display? That way I'm not telling you anything."

Cuss looked at Juan, who tilted his head in a shrug.

"I know it's a technicality, but this way I can say that I kept my mouth shut."

"Show us," said Cuss. "Then we'll decide."

"Give me a name from your list."

"Robert Garrison Moore," said Cuss. He gave the man's address and birth date as well.

Drake turned to his display, mumbled words that activated it, and wiggled his fingers in front of it. The display flipped through different screens, stopping on a dense report. Drake adjusted the display so they could see.

"What are we looking at?" asked Cuss.

With his lips pressed together, Drake pointed to the upper corner and the name, Robert Garrison Moore. Then he pointed mid-display. Seven days ago, Moore had a balance of 19,019,267 common. Drake moved his finger down and pointed to a transaction table. Starting four days ago, his account showed a flurry of sell orders, the most recent being yesterday afternoon. In that time, just over eight million common had been cashed out, with more orders pending action.

Juan whistled. "Where's that money now?"

Drake manipulated the display, leaned forward to study the information, and then slumped back. He pointed to the destination: Grand Cayman Bank.

"It's in the Cayman Islands on Earth?"

"I wish," said Drake, shaking his head. "Then we'd have a chance of locating where it is now. GCB is located in Utopia, Mars, and has nothing to do with the islands. They won't cooperate with anyone, and the Utopian government is desperate for business, so it protects them. My guess is that within seconds of landing there, the money was moved to another bank, then moved again, bounced around the different worlds, probably several times. It's gone, officers. Untraceable."

Cuss was mystified. "Why would you let that happen?"

"All our customers have secure identifiers, physical items linked to their person that ensures only they can move their money. If a transaction order is placed and our system has verified it, then we execute it. Mr. Moore placed these orders. I guarantee it. It's not our business to question him."

"What physical security device did Moore use?" asked Cuss.

"What do you mean?"

"We're interested in learning if it was a wire thing implanted in the back of his neck."

Drake made a face. "Eww. I don't think so. I mean, the technology keeps changing and has changed over the years. But I've never heard of anything like that."

"Does your screen show what kind of device he has?"

Drake shook his head and pointed to the upper right corner of the display. The words *Secure Transaction* had a green checkmark next to them. "All I see is that the system has confirmed a secure link."

Ygo asked, "How long has he been a customer of Lewiston-Mark?" Cuss relayed the question.

Drake manipulated the display and pointed. He'd opened the account thirty-one years ago.

"Somewhere in all this," said Cuss, "the system knows exactly what device it's connecting with. Where does that happen?"

"I have no idea. Best guess is that someone in our tech center in Armstrong would know, or know how to find out." He gave a sheepish smile. "My job is to make you feel good about our company so you're comfortable investing."

They repeated the process for Agnes Ming, who hadn't made any transactions in the last week and had been a client for thirty-two years. Franklin Wallingford had been a customer for thirty-two years as well and, in the past days, had moved just over eleven million common to the Grand Cayman Bank in Utopia.

On the way out the door, Ygo told Cuss, "Unfortunately, that banking shuffle means I can't trace the funds either. We've learned when, how, and how much, but we still don't know who is responsible or where they are."

. . .

Seated in the pilot's chair of the *Nelly Marie*, Cuss ran a final check as he prepared to fire the ship's engines. He was headed to Nova Terra and its capital city, Armstrong, with a growing mission list and was antsy to start the five-hour journey. The vessel had been pushed out of Hermes' spaceport and was drifting in space. In another minute he'd have enough clearance to get underway.

"You ready, pal?" he asked Ygo.

"I was born ready."

Cuss smiled, thinking just the opposite.

Ygo had been born horribly disfigured, and as he'd grown up, he'd learned he could minimize his social pain by hiding himself from the world. When he was in his twenties, he'd undergone experimental surgery that let him integrate his brain directly with electronic data feeds. Using that modification, he sought out the most capable AI in the four worlds, duplicated his favorite, and integrated them into his being.

The AI, serving as his interface with the world, gave Ygo amazing insights and capabilities. Now approaching forty, he remained hidden, living in the hold of the *Nelly Marie*, devoting his life in support of the Marshals Service in general and Cuss in particular. His loyalty to his partner and friend was absolute, an honor Cuss didn't fully understand but did not treat lightly.

As a burden of that loyalty, Ygo insisted that Cuss never draw attention to him, never mention his existence. To treat him the way he would a thought in his head. It put Cuss in the awkward position of accepting credit for Ygo's achievements, something he would never do to others and disliked when it was done to him. They'd argued about it early on, with Cuss refusing because it felt dishonest, even immoral. When he understood it was a condition not only of Ygo's participation in the Marshals Service but also of their friendship, he relented, though even after half a decade, it still felt wrong.

Ygo's permanent home, not five meters from where Cuss now sat, had been built to the man's specifications. The *Nelly Marie* was twice the size of the *Yankee Spirit*, and Ygo had assured Cuss that his den was comfortable, that the room provided him with everything he wanted.

"I'm exhausted and want to hit the sack," said Cuss. "You mind keeping watch?"

Ygo answered by firing the ship's engines. The Paulson drives roared to life, pushing the craft forward at a constant one gee, providing Cuss with Earth-level gravity while they were underway. Cuss watched the pilot's display for a few minutes, confirmed that everything was as expected, then stood and stretched.

As near as Cuss could tell, Ygo spent his days in a recliner, wired to the world through his AI, living vicariously through Cuss. It had been an abrupt reality change for Cuss, a man whose hard-won skillset and career success had earned him a spot in the Marshals Service. Serendipity partnered him with Ygo, and the first months were strange indeed. The Service had pioneered lens technology, something that let Ygo ride along as if he were sitting on Cuss's shoulder, or even in his head. Cuss smirked when he thought of the first time he'd used the toilet with Ygo watching. He'd wished it was easy to remove the lens.

But he had gotten used to that and a whole lot more.

Perhaps the culmination of his concern occurred the first time he'd made love to a woman—the gorgeous Yvette Rousseau. Cuss believed Ygo had disconnected and given him privacy. He didn't want to consider the idea that Ygo had watched, using the lens to experience many of the things Cuss was feeling, perhaps second-guessing his choice of partners, maybe even judging his performance.

Cuss had resisted for months, trying to reconcile the new existence with the private individual he'd always been. But over time, he'd learned to accept it, and when he understood that Ygo was gifting him his amazing capabilities, he came to embrace it.

If someone had ever asked him to consider this life up front, explaining to him what it would entail, what he'd become, how his life would change, he would have laughed in their face. But it had happened gradually, bit by bit. Now they were a team in work and life, and Ygo was part of his identity.

· · ·

"Rise and shine."

Cuss's eyes popped open, and he checked the time. Ygo had let him sleep the entire trip. Pre-Ygo, he would set his internal clock, telling himself how long to sleep, his mind being eerily accurate in waking him at the appointed hour. But like so much of his new life, keeping time had become one of Ygo's tasks. Cuss let it happen. He had plenty of other things to worry about.

"Landing sequence starts in thirty minutes."

Ygo was giving him time to shower, dress, grab coffee, and get secured in the pilot's chair before the constant one gee he now experienced transitioned into lunar gravity. And not smoothly but in a series of thumps and bumps as the *Nelly Marie* deorbited and came to rest at a landing gate in Port Collins.

Unlike the disgusting bunks he'd seen on *Yankee Spirit*, he had a private cabin, kept neat and clean by Peanut, the ship's bot. This ship was his home, his bachelor pad, the place he hoped to bring Hatha in the not-too-distant future. He wanted her to look around and feel comfortable, maybe even be a little impressed.

Up on the third level, his bedroom was good-sized for the modest vessel. One wall curved as it traced the hull of the ship, with a viewport built in to provide wondrous views. It had a wide chair with super-soft cushions that swallowed those sitting in it, big enough for two to squeeze in comfortably if they cuddled each other. There was a fold-down desktop, a generous closet, and a first-class entertainment system that Ygo had wrangled for him. The photos on the wall were a combination of his personal life—his parents; his sister, brother-in-law, and nephew; his childhood dog, Johnson, now passed—and a smattering of music posters, bands he'd seen perform at venues across the worlds.

After showering, he dressed in his "uniform": sturdy black pants and a blue collared shirt. He carried his holster and blazer in his hand. He'd put them on when he was leaving the ship.

He collected his gun from its hold in the wall and

performed the ritual of pulling the magazine and verifying it was full—ten bullets—cycling the slide to load one into the chamber, then putting the bullet he'd ejected the night before back into the magazine, giving him eleven in all.

The weapon, a Tosic 325 Hybrid, was a modern combination of an old-style Taser and a regular pistol. The ammunition looked and acted like traditional cartridges. But the slugs would pierce most things until they came in contact with flesh, where they collapsed upon impact, leaving a bruise but not penetrating the skin. In the process of crumpling, they delivered one of three electrical charges depending on the position of the gun's safety selector: stop, drop, or dead.

As part of his routine, he worked the selector, which when pushed with his thumb, moved from safety to stop, then dead, then drop. With the selector on stop, the electric charge from a bullet felt like a hard punch with a fist, good for crowd control or to warn a target of what could come next. Pushing the selector all the way forward set the gun to drop, a position easy to find in a panic and the most useful choice for a cop. Like an old-style Taser, though without wires trailing behind the projectile, the drop selection caused a target's voluntary muscles to seize, dropping them to the ground, disabling them for several minutes. The dead setting was in the middle, a harder position to find in an emergency, requiring a deliberate choice on the part of the shooter. The result was exactly as it sounded.

He climbed down to his living space on the second level. As always, Ygo had started the coffee machine so he had fresh brew. He filled his large coffee cup, the kind with a sealed top so moments of weightlessness didn't create a mess, and scrambled down to the first level, where he snugged himself into the pilot's seat.

"Good morning," he said to Ygo after taking his first sip. He never talked before then.

"De-orbit maneuver in two minutes."

"How did I get so far ahead of schedule?" It was a ritual joke. Cuss was known to slide into the seat with mere seconds left before the ride got too rough to be standing.

Chapter 11

P ort Collins was a vibrant place, with ships of all kinds coming and going throughout the day and night. The port serviced the nation of Nova Terra, which included two major cities: Armstrong and Aldrin, with four million and two million residents, respectively. A dozen townships situated around the perimeter of the two cities provided homes to another million people. Add tourists, part-timers, and visitors on business, and the nation boasted over seven million inhabitants at any one time. Plus a hundred thousand or so bots and droids.

Massive expansion projects were a never-ending fact of life for Nova Terra, with new construction scheduled to add room for two hundred thousand people every year for the next decade. All the living space was carved out of rock, making the cities subterranean in that sense. But high overhead, a clear roof made of structural polymer provided a stunning view of the sky.

Cuss made his way through the port concourse, snugging his blazer as he weaved through the crowds. It was two degrees cooler in Nova Terra compared to the cities of Lagrange. In its first years of existence, the government had kept the city thermostat lower to save energy. The lunar nation was three decades older than the tube cities, and it had faced a host of challenges early on, limited by the technology of the day.

Now that it had the resources to raise the temperature, the citizens had voted to keep the cooler setting, perhaps having adapted to it the way northerners on Earth acclimated to their environment. Or possibly to discourage more people from moving to the crowded world. Or maybe they valued it as a formative tradition, an important part of their history.

He boarded a tram—Nova Terra's public transportation system—and made for the city center. Each tram had seats for twenty passengers, rode on a fixed track, and had stops more widely spaced throughout the cities and towns than Lagrange's pod stations. Unlike the personal delivery that pods offered, getting to different points in Nova Terra often required changing tram lines, though prompt service and convenient timetables made this a straightforward proposition.

The trams had open tops, and Cuss looked up through the transparent polymer roof at the breathtaking view of Earth. The Moon was tidal-locked with Earth, meaning the same face of the Moon pointed toward the planet at all times. Nova Terra was located on that face, so the gorgeous orb of Earth, blue and white and green and brown, always hung in the sky, with the Sun cycling in and out to mark the day.

He searched for a glimpse of Lagrange, always located between Earth and the Moon, even knowing it was all but imperceptible to the naked eye. He couldn't find it and was about to give up when Ygo helped by zooming his lens, focusing on a specific point near Earth's equator. He caught sight of a speck floating in front of Earth and smiled, thinking of Hatha at work serving breakfast in her pink-and-white costume to ungrateful schlubs.

For safety reasons, the port sat most of a kilometer out from the population center, and his view disappeared when the tram entered a tunnel. As the tram emerged two minutes later, the dominant color he saw as he approached Armstrong was olive green, the color of the oxygen-producing plants covering everything. While the strains in Lagrange mixed beauty with functionality, here they continued to use plants from the early days that maximized oxygen production without concern for splendor. Like all plants, they did bloom, but the display was muted, in some ways reflecting the reserved spirit of the people.

His itinerary had three objectives: meet with Armstrong's chief of detectives to get help with a search warrant for the Lewiston-Mark Tech Center, visit the center to learn if Robert Moore and Franklin Wallingford had wire implants in their necks, and visit Johansson's Ship Salvage to see what they knew about the *Yankee Spirit*.

As the tram traveled into Armstrong proper, he contacted Juan for an update on his investigation.

"I checked with Janice Wallingford first," reported Juan. "She's close to her father, and so I thought her the best bet for knowing if her dad had a neck implant."

"Nice idea." Cuss had suggested Juan do this and was pleased to hear he was following through. "Any luck?"

"She has a vague recollection of something along those lines, but it was so long ago for her that the details are foggy. She couldn't say for certain one way or another."

"Did you tell her about the missing money?"

"Heck no. She can't do anything about it, and if she went ballistic and made noise, the mayor would have something more to whip me with. It would move me from investigation to damage control."

"I can see that. What about the Moore family?"

"They don't have a clue. Apparently Dad is a secretive guy."

Cuss waited for Juan to suggest next steps. When he didn't, Cuss prompted him. "What are you going to try next?"

"I have a few ideas, but I'm open to more."

"My instinct would be to get pictures of Moore, Wallingford, and *Yankee Spirit*'s mysterious pilot, visit all the flight decks, and ask everyone if they've seen them. Do it in person so you can watch their faces and body language."

Juan nodded. "That was on my list. I'll do it next."

"I'd check both the passenger ports *and* cargo ports in each city. I know that's a big undertaking, but good old-fashioned police work is how we get lucky."

"You got it. What's up on your end?"

"Not much. I just landed and am on my way to see the chief of detectives for help with a search warrant. I'll let you know if it leads to anything."

As the tram pulled into a station at the edge of the city, he said to Juan, "I've reached my stop." It was still early, and he'd decided to get some exercise and walk from there into downtown. "Catch you later."

. . .

Making his way toward the city center, Cuss walked along a pathway covered in pea stone. The stone—a waste material from city excavation—cupped the foot, letting him push off and take long, easy steps. As he built up speed, he saw a grooming bot up ahead, a machine that looked something like a giant turtle, tasked with keeping the stone surface smooth to prevent injury. Feeling cocky, he launched himself when he neared it, hurdling over the bot in a ten-meter leap, never breaking stride.

About a third of the way along, he reached Founders Park and decided to take a detour. Slowing with short hopping steps, he turned and entered through a welcome arch made of tree branches, looking forward to spending a few minutes viewing the park's collection of dwarf oaks and maples, birch and elm, and mix of firs.

The beauty of the trees and the earthy smell of soil took him back to his youth and memories of hiking through forests on Earth. He'd never gotten used to the lack of trees on Lagrange and considered the park a lifestyle win for the people of Nova Terra. He walked the display loop three times, communing with nature as he recharged his spirit. Then he returned to the pathway and headed for downtown and Government Center.

The foundations of the buildings along the way were carved directly into the bedrock. The structures on top were built from stone blocks mined during excavation, largely basalts with some granites. The stone had a dark hue that, when draped with olive-green vines, created a stark skyline. But just the way people can see beauty in a desert, some described the drab façades as dramatic, commanding, and even striking. In his mind, better words would be "bleak" and "austere."

The city was organized into clusters of apartments, each surrounding its own commercial square. The stores in the different squares, usually mom-and-pop shops, offered items that reflected the tastes of that neighborhood. As Cuss loped along, he observed the different takes on groceries and spirits, eateries and pubs, clothing and shoes, and entertainment venues from racy to staid.

The people he passed in the squares all dressed in colorful garb, much of it styled with dramatic flair, as if compensating for the cheerless buildings around them. He knew that the clothes had nuances that identified the people as belonging to certain groups and neighborhoods. But he wasn't schooled in the differences and, in the end, wasn't curious enough to engage Ygo for help in deciphering the code.

Fifty minutes after leaving the tram, he arrived at Government Center, built around Citizens Square, a tribute to early strife when people confronted the corporations for a say in their future. While corporate influence maintained its hold on government policy even today, the people had demanded and eventually won the right to vote for leaders who represented their values, giving them a say in their future.

Citizens Square was actually more of a circle. Around the perimeter, two-thirds of the frontage was occupied by federal buildings—executive, legislative, judicial, and their purview—while one-third was devoted to municipal structures and city-specific government: mayoral and city council offices, public safety, transportation and housing, public works, health and social services, and parks and tourism. Like every structure in Nova Terra that was more than ten years old, the buildings in the square were constructed of the same dark stone and covered in the omnipresent olive-green foliage.

Armstrong police headquarters was located in the city's public safety building, which shared the space with the parks and tourism departments. Cuss hopped up the dark stone stairs, walked the low-grav shuffle across the dark stone courtyard, and entered the building through clear doors made of the same structural polymer used to construct the city's vast roof.

Public safety, including fire control, law enforcement, and emergency medical services, were on the lower floors of the building. The cops were on the first floor to the right, and Cuss showed his badge to a uniformed officer sitting at a desk. The officer studied it, consulted his display, waved Cuss through an entry, and made a call, all without saying a word.

Toni Carrabelle, chief of detectives, appeared a few minutes later, waved him into the inner sanctum, and led him down a brightly lit hall to his office.

Toni was gender neutral in both clothing and physical characteristics, preferred male pronouns, and today dressed in an outfit swirling with color. Once inside his office, he welcomed Cuss with a big hug. In spite of the affectionate behavior displayed in the heartfelt greeting, Cuss knew Toni was all business and tough as nails. He wouldn't let friendships interfere with his commitment to the law. He wouldn't have the job otherwise.

As a young detective, Toni had watched suspects escape capture by fleeing Nova Terra for other worlds. When the idea of an Interworld Marshals Service was floated as a potential solution, he'd become a vocal cheerleader for the concept, though his lowly position as a street detective meant his endorsement didn't carry much weight.

After years of posturing by the powers that be, the idea became a reality, and Toni had applied for a slot. When he wasn't chosen, he'd been privately angry, even bitter. But a few months later, he was made chief of detectives, perhaps the reason he'd been passed over for the Service. He embraced the opportunity with gusto, his attitude restored.

His office mirrored every other government office in Nova Terra. The local factories had produced the same desks, shelves, chairs, and tables year after year, thousands upon thousands of them, before the nation became established enough that it could afford to broaden the offerings. City and federal employees were expected to use the old standards both as a way of containing costs and as a sign of commitment to the cause.

"You called about following up on an abduction. Robert Moore, was it?" Toni invited Cuss to sit in metal-gray hard-back chair. Seating himself in the chair next to Cuss's, extending the feeling of familiarity, he crossed his legs at the knee and said, "Tell me about it."

"Incoming," warned Ygo.

The office door chimed, and Toni raised a finger.

"Hold on." He waved toward the door, and a woman entered. Her hair coiffed high in a shape reminiscent of a chef's hat, she wore a blue form-fitting jumpsuit with splotches of color all over it, as if someone had squirted her with red and orange and green and yellow paints.

Cuss smiled and nodded to Detective Darlena Washington who, when she saw him, stopped in her tracks, shook her head, and said, "Hell, no."

He frowned, her attitude surprising him.

Then she threw her head back and let loose an open-mouthed guffaw. "I'm just messing with you. Good to see you, Cuss."

She pulled a chair from against the back wall with its display of Toni's numerous framed awards, commendations, and certificates, and placed it so they formed a circle. "Chief, remember I told you how Cuss saved my ass last year with that fuckwad Fletcher?" She shook her head as if she were recalling the affair. "Carl Fletcher. That asswipe's serving twenty thanks to Cuss here." She grinned at him. "Looks like we're going to be teaming up again."

. . .

The detectives bullpen was a windowless room with the same metal-gray furniture as Toni's office. Two men were huddled in a private conference at one end. Darlena led Cuss to a desk at the other, but before they sat, she asked, "You want coffee?"

"I'd love some."

They detoured out to a cubby in the hall and filled cups. Darlena pointed to a box of doughnuts. "Help yourself." Cuss declined. Darlena snagged one and finished it before they'd made it back to her desk.

As they sat, Cuss took a sip and tried not to wince. While Lunar coffee held a good jolt of caffeine, something he appreciated, it had a bitter taste and aroma that made it hard for him to enjoy.

"So what's going on?" asked Darlena.

Cuss took her through the arrival of the *Yankee Spirit* from Port Collins, the disappearance of Robert Moore, and the escape and death of Agnes Ming.

She interrupted him at that point, opening a desk display and paging through some screens. "You should have told us about Ming. We've been spending resources trying to find her."

"She's right," said Ygo. "That fell off the table when you ended up in the hospital."

"It's only been a few days," Cuss told her. "Things have been moving quickly, and I'm here now to make sure we're both up to date."

She didn't seem mollified but kept quiet, letting him continue his story.

He told her about Franklin Wallingford, a case local to Lagrange but with similarities to Moore and Ming.

She interrupted again. "Have you shared those files?" She turned back to her display and started paging again.

"She has them now," said Ygo.

"Here they are." She leaned forward and squinted at the image. "Transmitted two seconds ago. Nice." She leaned back in her chair, folded her arms in front of her, and glared at Cuss.

Cuss felt it getting hot and wondered if the bullpen was kept warmer than the rest of the city. He told her about the secure-link wire implanted in Agnes Ming's neck and how he wanted to follow up with the Lewiston-Mark Tech Center here to see if the others had one as well.

Darlena unfolded her arms and leaned toward him at the revelation. "A wire buried in the back of her neck that fed into the brain?"

Cuss nodded. "Very fine, maybe ten centimeters long, with a tiny chip at the end."

Darlena swiveled toward the two men at the far end of the bullpen. "Hey, Hobby. Marshal Abbott here found a lady with a wire in the back of her neck like that one you found last month. You got a minute?"

Now Cuss sat up.

"I missed it," said Ygo. "I focused on off-world abductions when I searched their records. Damn, I'm sorry."

Ygo rarely cursed, so Cuss could tell he was upset with himself. He wished he could reassure him, but given the circumstances, he kept quiet, making a mental note to follow up when he had a chance.

Hobby Bronson, who had the swagger of someone who might be a criminal if he weren't a cop, sauntered over, leaned his butt on the edge of the neighboring desk, looked at Cuss, and waited.

Since Cuss was the visitor, he took the lead, detailing the different cases and finishing with his desire to get a warrant to learn if the missing men had wire links like Agnes Ming. Then he prompted Hobby. "So you found one, too?"

Hobby wasn't ready to share, first asking a long list of questions centered on means, motive, and opportunity mixed with who, what, when, where, how, why. When he'd drained Cuss of information, Hobby asked Darlena, "Have we been copied on all those records?"

Darlena used the display to look. "We have now." She looked at Cuss. "Better late than never, huh, Marshal?"

"Look," said Cuss, working to calm his annoyance. "Things have been moving fast, and two days ago I was in the hospital after an explosion killed a member of my team. You're fully up to date, so can we get past the pissing contest and focus on catching these guys?"

"Why, so you can be the hero?" sneered Hobby.

Cuss looked at Darlena with raised eyebrows.

"He's not like that asshole Burton. Cuss let me take the credit for Fletcher last year. I trust him. For now."

This was the second time in the past six months that Cuss had heard a complaint from locals about Miles Burton, a fellow marshal and exasperating asshole. Bad behavior made all their jobs more difficult, and he wondered if he should give the director a heads-up, or talk to Burton himself.

The "who gets the credit" issue had been a sticking point foreseen by just about everyone when the structure of the Marshals Service was being finalized. To make it work, they'd adopted a different metric.

"I don't know why Burton acts the way he does. Our

success is measured by whether we can get local cooperation on a case that gets solved. Let me help you catch the bad guys, and you'll get the credit for the bust all the way up your chain. The body of the report should mention that I helped, but your names go in the lead detectives field at the top of the report, mine doesn't."

It was like handing people free money, but because either they or someone they knew had been burned in the past, their understandable response was, "What's the catch?"

"I'm going to refill my coffee." He walked into the hall, giving them a chance to work it out without him sitting there.

As he filled his cup, he said to Ygo, "Don't feel bad about the local case. You've been a miracle worker during an intense few days. I'm ecstatic with your work."

Ignoring the sentiment, Ygo used Cuss's lens to show him the file on Hobby's case. Kaycee Gibbons, ninety-seven years old, had been found in the industrial district. She'd been dumped near the Botanical Fertilizer Plant #2, a largish facility given the amount of vegetation for oxygen and food grown in the city.

Because there weren't personal vehicles in the city to move a body, Cuss's first inclination was that the murder had occurred somewhere very close to the fertilizer plant.

"She weighs just sixteen pounds on the Moon, and she's small in stature," said Ygo. "It's possible they moved her with something as simple as a carry pack. And the industrial district isn't like the city. They use carts for lots of things out there."

A closeup of Kaycee Gibbons on the scene showed her lying face down behind a hedge running next to the fertilizer-plant parking lot. The back of her neck had been bandaged to cover the wound, with the fine wire exposed above the white gauze. It cinched the notion in Cuss's mind that this was the motivation for the crime.

The person dumping the body had used a data mask, leaving him unidentified and pointing to the same group who'd committed the other abductions. Gibbons had been taken five days before the body was dumped, and the coroner's report stated that she'd died half a day before a worker at the plant found her.

"Does she…" Cuss started to ask if she had an account at Lewiston-Mark.

"Yup," said Ygo, his enthusiasm reflecting his return to high spirits. "And she's worth millions. I can't see if her money has been moved, though, so I'll add that to the warrant." A pause. "You can go back in now. Darlena has decided to work with you."

"Someone at Lewiston-Mark has to be involved," said Cuss, pausing at the door to the detectives bullpen. "Either they're stealing the money themselves, or they've sold someone a list of people who have that kind of data link."

"It could also be someone from the link manufacturer, Prairie State Privacy outside of Chicago," said Ygo. "They went out of business fourteen years ago, so it would have to be someone who can access their old records. That can't be a long list."

Back inside, Hobby had returned to the far end of the room, huddled again with the same guy he'd been talking with when Cuss arrived. Cuss retook his seat and looked questioningly at Darlena.

She rested her arms on her desk, leaned forward, and whispered, "Hobby doesn't like marshals. It's nothing personal. He hates all of you. I'm going to take you through the case, and if you have any questions I can't answer, I'll ask Hobby for you." She shrugged. "It's what I can do."

Cuss wanted to sigh and shake his head but instead forced himself to nod and say, "Thanks, Darlena."

By the time she was done, he'd learned a few facts more. Kaycee Gibbons had moved to Armstrong from Earth four years ago to regain mobility in the Moon's low gravity. Her husband had passed a decade earlier, her three grandchildren visited more than her two children. She kept to herself, had everything delivered to her apartment, her neighbors thought she was nice but didn't really know her.

When Darlena finished, Cuss said, "I've worked up a search warrant for the Lewiston-Mark Tech Center. It's to learn if Franklin Wallingford and Robert Moore have secure-link wire implants and seeks a list of everyone who has access to that knowledge. Someone is using the information for themselves or selling it to others to exploit. It also lets us learn if Kaycee Gibbons made any financial transactions after she'd been abducted. If she's like the others, her account was drained between the time she was taken and the day you found her."

He paused to give Darlena a chance to ask questions. She didn't, so he finished. "The Marshals Service will push this through and get a judge to sign off. The judge will want reassurance that a local is partnering with me when the warrant is served. Will you join me? The document is on your display if you want to read it."

She turned to look, skimming through the details. "What about Hobby?"

"Fuck Hobby. Let's stop these assholes before they hurt someone else."

She grinned. "Count me in."

Chapter 12

C uss was anxious to poke around at Johansson's Ship Salvage while they waited for the judge to clear the warrant.

"Would you like to come?" he asked Darlena, knowing he should have someone other than Ygo along as backup. He also saw the offer as a courtesy that would strengthen their relationship.

"I already had a full day planned before you showed up. It'll be hard enough for me to get away to execute the Lewiston-Mark warrant."

They both looked toward Hobby, then back at each other, rejecting the idea at the same time.

"It violates departmental protocol to go alone," she said. "Hold on and let me find a patrol officer to partner with you."

She left the room, and Cuss escaped from Hobby by stepping into the hall and pretending to refill his coffee. Darlena reappeared a few minutes later with a young man in tow.

"Cuss, this is Smitty Shellback. Smitty, this is Marshal Cuss Abbott."

Smitty had light coloring, a slender frame, a smooth face, and looked to be all of twenty-five years old. He wore a blue patrol uniform, giving him an air of authority. But he wasn't carrying a sidearm, which made him of questionable value as a backup partner.

Cuss extended his hand. "Thanks for your help."

"Nice to meet you, Marshal." Smitty's handshake was mushy.

"How about if you call me Cuss and I call you Smitty?"

Smitty nodded.

"I've approved a cart so he can drive you," said Darlena. She made for the bullpen but stopped at the door. "Give me a warning when the judge approves the search so I have time to break free. And please copy me on everything you learn at Johansson's."

She made it sound like a request, but Cuss knew there'd be hell to pay if he didn't.

Smitty led Cuss out the back of the building and into a tight parking lot with a dozen electric carts. A handful of empty spaces hinted that others were out and about.

The vehicles were nothing more than a passenger shell combined with balloon tires that stuck out all around, reminding Cuss of a golf cart crossed with a dune buggy. Emergency flashers were embedded around the perimeter of each roof, and law enforcement insignias were affixed to the front and back fenders, conferring institutional authority. Half the carts had a sturdy wire cage on the back with seating for two prisoners.

Smitty got in the driver's side of a cart without a cage, and Cuss joined him on the passenger side, sinking into a well-padded seat. Safety straps secured him for the bouncy ride, the snug embrace comforting because the cart had no doors. The front dash was smooth and padded, with a tiny display projector barely visible in the center, and an operator's bubble in front of the driver.

Smitty waved a hand in front of the bubble to engage the cart, and it bobbed and bounced on soft suspension as they drove out of the parking lot, up a short dirt trail, and then parallel to tram tracks running behind the building. With a startling jolt that made Cuss grab the overhead handhold, the cart bounded onto the tracks, the tires molding down around the rails.

As the cart accelerated, the display came alive with a map showing them traveling east along tram rails through the city. It also showed the position of tramcars ahead and behind them. The ride on the rails was smooth, except when they changed tracks after a few minutes to head south, causing Cuss to grab the handhold yet again.

"This track brings us to the industrial district," said Smitty, "so it should be smooth sailing until then."

Cuss had a thought. "Could you show the location of the shipyard on the map?"

He'd been making the request to Smitty, but the cart responded on its own by projecting the industrial district on the map, positioned between Port Collins and Armstrong's population center. When he'd taken the tram through the tunnel earlier, he had traveled under it. Johansson's was located on the edge of the industrial district nearest the spaceport, which made sense given the nature of their business.

As if reading his mind, Ygo overlaid the location of Botanical Fertilizer Plant #2 on Cuss's lens. The plant was barely three kilometers from Johansson's Shipyard.

While Cuss digested the tidbit, he engaged Smitty in conversation. "How long have you been on the force?"

"Almost eight months. My probationary period ends on Friday."

"Where's your gun?"

Smitty's hand went down to his hip and he blushed. "I get to wear it on Friday."

"Have you ever worked backup before?"

"Of course. I cover for Sergeant Tanaka all the time." After a pause he added, "She's my training mentor."

Cuss wondered why Darlena made a point of insisting he have backup and then pairing him with someone who was all but useless. Rather than dwell on it, he changed topics. "What do you know about Johansson's Salvage?"

"I know some. They do repair work, and they buy and sell used ships. Most of their inventory is up on the surface because it's way too expensive to house them down inside." Then he became animated. "We had this amazing tour of their boneyard in high school, and back then they had something like forty craft up there. I'll bet it's even more now."

"How do they get ships up and down to work on them?"

"Most of them still fly well enough for a short hop. If they can't, they disassemble them and ferry them down in pieces. They have this huge trawler to move the ships from the port over to their salvage yard."

The cart moved faster than the trams, and one came into view up ahead. The cart slowed to keep pace with it.

"Have you met Johansson? What's he like?"

"I met the father, who died a year or so after our visit. He'd worked as a tug captain before setting up the shop and had great stories to tell from those years of his life. Anders, the son, runs the place now. He's not at all like his dad. He employs some questionable characters. We've been called out a few times for suspicion of theft. A few fights. Stuff like that."

"Theft?"

"There've been claims that he steals parts from unoccupied ships sitting in port and turns around and sells them. We've never been able to prove anything. But the complaints started a few months after his dad died, which seems awfully coincidental, don't you think?"

Cuss didn't respond, but *Yankee Spirit* had been built from a collection of parts, some stolen, so it certainly heightened his interest.

"Don't worry," said Ygo. "He won't get anything off the *Nelly Marie*."

. . .

Anders Johansson's world was becoming complicated very quickly. He'd received a heads-up from Yuri Melnikov, a guy he'd built a ship for a month or so back.

"A marshal is coming to arrest you," Melnikov had told him. "They discovered that the ship you built for me is made from stolen parts, and they've traced it back to your shipyard."

Anders's initial reaction was that Melnikov was full of shit. He was good at muddling ownership. In fact, it was a point of pride for him, something he excelled at.

Melnikov went on to say, "I tried to hide the evidence by having a guy blow up the ship, but he fucked it up and killed a cop. You're on the hook for that, too, because the cop was investigating the stolen parts when she died. If they catch you, they'll hang a murder rap on you along with the larceny charge."

"A bullshitter can smell a bullshitter," Anders said to himself after the call.

A simple merchant, he didn't have the skill or resources to verify Melnikov's claims. But he sensed he was being conned into doing something that would help Melnikov more than himself. So he ignored the issue and continued with business as usual.

His routine was to send out a microdrone every morning to monitor Port Collins, looking for things to steal that night. When the drone showed that a marshal's ship had landed, his attitude about Melnikov's claims waivered.

"There are millions of reasons for a marshal to visit," he said aloud, trying to convince himself.

But to be sure, he directed the tiny drone to follow the marshal, instructing the device to alert him if the marshal headed his direction. Armstrong was a fishbowl, so surveillance wasn't a challenging task.

While he waited to learn the marshal's intent, he brainstormed with Gustav, his chief thief, about what they should do if things went bad.

"A marshal has come to arrest you," he told Gustav, using the same line he'd been fed. "He knows you steal parts from the spaceport. A cop died investigating that ship we finished last month. That means you're on the hook for murder."

Gustav, who wasn't a critical thinker, suggested solutions to the problem that ranged from disturbing to horrifying. Anders didn't take any of them seriously, because he believed Melnikov was jerking him around, though he still didn't know why.

"It's possible the marshal is here for a different reason," he told Gustav, trying to calm him. "So before we do anything, let's watch and see what he does."

But when the drone alerted him that a cop cart carrying the marshal was headed in their direction, he decided to send Gustav out to run interference.

"Take Bundee and block the access road out near the tram track. Keep watch, and if he starts to take the blockade down, call me. It means he's determined to come here, probably just to talk but maybe to make arrests. I'll use the time to destroy what I can. Hopefully I can protect you."

Anders had suggested that Bundee, a mechanic who worked at Johansson's, tag along because he was generally stable and would be a calming influence. If Gustav called to say the marshal was on his way, Anders would purge their records. But a bigger concern was the stolen parts they had lying around the shop. It would take two days of hard work to clear them out.

When the drone signaled that the cart had turned away at the last minute, instead driving the marshal to the place where they'd found a dead body a few weeks back, Anders breathed a sigh of relief. He'd had nothing to do with the murder and wondered if Melnikov did. It would explain the marshal's visit and could be the reason Melnikov was trying to get him to act.

But after the cop viewed the crime scene, he didn't turn back toward the city. Instead, he turned onto the access road leading to the salvage shipyard.

Anders's mind froze as he speculated about the marshal's intent. Chewing his lip in worry, he waited for Gustav's call.

. . .

When the tram ahead of them disappeared into the tunnel leading to Port Collins, Smitty directed the cart to turn off the tracks and follow a packed-dirt road leading into the industrial district.

"Let's swing by the fertilizer plant before heading to Johansson's," said Cuss.

"Which one?"

When Cuss hesitated, Ygo said, "Number Two." Cuss relayed the information.

Smitty moved a hand in front of the dash bubble, and the vehicle turned left at the next intersection. Unlike in the city, carts were everywhere, driving people and product from here to there. Pedestrians, presumably workers, ignored the vehicles as they walked along what continued to be packed-dirt roads. Every now and again, Cuss's body swayed in his seat as their cart swerved to avoid the crowds.

The first buildings they passed appeared to make products destined for the retail outlets inside the city, sometimes with two or three manufacturers in a single structure. Cuss saw signs for kitchen appliances, home furnishings, entertainment systems, women's clothing, personal hygiene products, and alcoholic beverages. After a few blocks, the businesses became more industrial, with signs for pipe and plastics, robot production, modern textiles, pumps and compressors, and fine chemicals.

All the buildings were tall to minimize use of expensive real estate, and all were made from the same dark lunar stone and covered with olive-green vines.

While he'd visited Armstrong and Aldrin many times in the past, he hadn't been to the industrial district in years, and he leaned out of the cart and looked up to get a better view of the skyline. It hit him that there was a rock ceiling overhead, not a clear roof like in the city. It was brightly painted, well lit, a good hundred meters up, but rock nevertheless.

"Why no transparent roof?" he asked Smitty, perturbed that he'd missed something so apparent on his previous tours.

"The polymer roof is super expensive, like three times more than just leaving the rock in place. People don't live out here, so it's not considered a quality-of-life issue."

"So technically we're in a huge cavern."

"Yup."

That's when Cuss saw King Shit coming out of the Pine Industrial Fabrication building. Though he knew viscerally that he recognized the guy, and was certain he didn't like him, he couldn't place him. "Slow down," he said to Smitty. "I've seen that guy somewhere."

Cuss remembered just as Ygo said, "That's Stan

Shevchenko. He was bothering Hatha in her café."

Stan was in an animated discussion with a middle-aged fat man who had what looked like a ferret growing around his mouth and down his chin. Stan seemed to be making a point, moving his hands in broad gestures while the fat man nodded, his double chin bouncing in a way that made it look like the ferret was wagging its tail.

"I wonder what he's doing here?" Cuss asked as they drove past. "And who's he talking to?"

"I didn't see the guy," said Smitty, looking back over his shoulder.

"He's talking to Roscoe Antonov," said Ygo, "head of production at Lagrange's Factory. The industrial fabrication company behind them makes equipment used in the Factory, so Antonov being here is easily explained. It's less obvious why a thug is tagging along. The biggest commonality I can find is that they both were born and raised in Trenton, New Jersey. But their age difference is enough that they wouldn't be school chums." A pause. "It's an unusual pairing."

Cuss mused over the possibilities. Maybe they sat next to each other on the flight up, discovered they had the same home town, and started a game of "do you know so-and-so?" Or maybe their mothers were friends. Or perhaps Roscoe had a daughter that Stan liked.

He toyed with different ideas as they drove a few more blocks, and then his attention was drawn to a bold sign alerting them that they were entering the city's municipal operations sector. It warned of danger ahead and cautioned that the road was a dead end.

While there were a few buildings dotting the landscape in the municipal sector, most of the space was consumed by industrial monstrosities walled off by chain-link fencing. An air purification installation, an eyesore on any world, sat to the left as they drove down the street, with its bristling metal towers, rumbling furnaces, storage cylinders as big as houses, and thrumming pumps, all connected by a tangled maze of pipes. To their right, a similar complex focused on water reclamation. Not only had the buildings all but disappeared but so had the pedestrians and cart traffic, a change that did not escape Cuss's notice.

Their cart slowed and pulled into the packed-dirt parking lot in front of Botanical Fertilizer Plant #2, stopping next to two brown carts with the words *Public Works* decaled on the back. Cuss climbed out and turned slowly, taking in the setting. The drivers of the public works carts were nowhere in sight.

A sturdy gate protected the entrance to the fertilizer facility, bolstered by a red-and-white sign declaring that access was restricted to authorized individuals. Inside, he heard plant equipment humming away but he couldn't see any workers milling about. No staff posted near the fence who might have seen something like a body being dumped.

He walked into the dirt street and looked both ways. A cart approached, similar in appearance to those in the parking lot. He stepped out of the way and waved a hello. The two people riding inside nodded in acknowledgment as they looked him up and down, assessing the stranger among them as they continued past.

The entry gate for the air purification plant across the

street was a hundred meters farther along. Two kids were playing in the road in that direction, taking turns riding some sort of motorized scrambler. He looked back toward the intersection where they'd entered the municipal sector and could just make out the hustle and bustle they'd left behind.

"A perfect spot to dump a body," observed Ygo.

"You read my mind."

The shrubbery he'd seen in the photo ran on both sides of the fertilizer plant parking lot, marking its boundaries. Kaycee Gibbons had been found lying on the far side of the hedge to the right, and he led Smitty around behind it. A ridge of rock about chest high ran parallel to the shrubs, creating a narrow alley of sorts.

Cuss walked up the alleyway, and after a dozen steps, Ygo stopped him. "Right here."

He squatted down and looked. Since there was no wind or rain in Armstrong, the dirt on the ground still showed the impression of the body, plus dozens of footprints, presumably of the criminals, investigators, and workers from the area. The scene had been processed and released, so no barrier cordoned off the site. After a moment, he stood and squeezed around Smitty, who was waiting his turn to squat in the dirt.

Back in the road, he told Ygo, "They drove her here in a cart and dumped her."

"I agree."

"How far did we say it was to Johannsson's?"

"Three kilometers, plus or minus, depending on the route you take."

Smitty came out from behind the hedge, and Cuss asked him, "How common is it to find bodies dumped out here?"

"You mean in the municipal sector?" He thought for a moment and shrugged. "We don't get many bodies dumped anywhere in Armstrong."

Cuss considered the two brown carts in the parking lot, thinking he should talk to the drivers to see what they knew. But a higher priority was the salvage yard, a place he wanted to visit before they served the search warrant at the Lewiston-Mark Tech Center. He pointed down the road to the kids playing in the street. "Let's talk with those two, and then we'll head to Johansson's."

The kids turned out to be brother and sister, ten and twelve years old. They'd gotten the scrambler the week before and had picked this spot to play because of the open roads and lack of traffic. They hadn't come down this way much before that and hadn't seen anything useful to the investigation.

"Looks like fun," Smitty said to them as he started the cart for Johansson's. "Be careful."

Chapter 13

"Let's take the route with the least traffic between here and the salvage yard," Cuss said to Smitty as their cart passed Botanical Fertilizer Plant #2. "One a body dumper might take."

The cart followed a road that bordered the edge of the commercial sector, bounced over the tram tracks, and continued onto a lonely packed-dirt lane along the outskirts of the district. The rocks and boulders that had been cleared to make the quiet road were piled in a series of chest-high mounds on either side of the track, stacked between stone ridges that had been left in place when clearing the massive underground cavern.

"This is a back way," said Smitty as they bounced along.

They drove less than thirty seconds, just far enough to be out of sight from passing trams, when they saw a blockade ahead. Twin piles of rocks stacked in three-foot-high pyramids sat in the road, close enough together that the cart couldn't squeeze between them. And with ridges of rock running parallel to the road on either side at that point, they couldn't drive around.

"That's weird." Smitty bit his lip as he shook his head.

"What do you mean?"

"Maintenance bots travel the roads out here, keeping

the dirt packed and clearing obstructions. Even back roads like this one get visited pretty often. That means someone built this in the last day or two."

"By 'out here' you mean…?"

"The industrial district."

"Does this road lead anywhere besides Johansson's?"

"It runs behind a few businesses along the way, then feeds right into the salvage yard at the end." Smitty stopped the cart at an angle so the driver's side was nearest the piles. "I can clear this pretty fast." He jumped out of the cart.

"Something is off about this," warned Ygo, his tone conveying urgency.

The combination of a recently constructed choke point, Smitty's comment, and Ygo's warning put Cuss on high alert. As he stepped out, he drew his gun, thumbing the selector all the way forward to the drop position.

With the cart parked at a diagonal, it sat between Cuss and the rock pyramids. He hopped into the air to glance over the ridge to his right. Not seeing anything suspicious, he moved around behind the cart to scan the other side for danger.

Boom!

The ground shook as the concussive force of an explosion thumped his body, powerful enough in the low gravity to lift the cart off the ground, propelling it just over his head. He'd instinctively raised his arms to protect himself, and as the cart flipped past, a tire smacked his right hand, knocking the gun from his grip with enough force to topple him to the ground. The cart bounced end over end behind him, coming to rest on its side ten meters down the path.

Cuss's position behind the cart had been fortuitous. The vehicle had absorbed the force of the blast, protecting him from the rock shrapnel. Smitty hadn't been so lucky. He'd taken the full brunt of the explosion, the blast throwing him a good three meters. He lay limp against a rock ridge, his face bloody, his clothes shredded, with ugly cuts and gashes up and down his body.

Rising to his knees, Cuss shook his head to clear the fog. Bits of rock tossed high from the explosion fell around him, and he put his arms above his head to shield it as he cast about for his gun. Between the dust and his mental confusion, he couldn't find it.

"I've contacted emergency services," said Ygo. "They should be there in a few minutes."

Back on his feet, Cuss staggered to help Smitty, dissecting the situation as he did, seeking to make sense of what had happened. He'd taken two steps toward his fallen partner when a small boulder, something that would weigh a hundred pounds on Earth, flew over the ridge and past his head, missing it by inches. The boulder's trajectory told him it was not a projectile from the explosion.

He rushed to the ridge and pressed his body against the rock face near Smitty, seeking protection from any additional projectiles. Two men in canvas overalls, middle-aged, husky, and scowling, appeared on the peak above him. Looking down at him from above, the uglier of the two flashed a gap-toothed sneer, clenching his fists, signaling his intent.

"Watch out!" yelled Ygo, giving Cuss a warning he

didn't need.

Cuss pushed off the rock and backpedaled, scanning them for weapons, relieved that none were in sight. He moved quickly, seeking to create distance if one of them tried to jump him. Moments later, the ugly one did just that, launching himself like he was diving into water, his arm cocked to deliver a flying blow.

Fighting in low gravity was different from fighting on Earth. In both places, the force of a punch was the product of mass times acceleration. The mass of a fist was the same in either world. But the ability to accelerate a punch, to put power behind it, depended very much on gravity.

On Earth, feet stayed firmly planted on the ground, allowing the shifting of hips and shoulders to multiply the mass as a fist moved toward its target. On the Moon, the same style of punch would fail, the light gravity making a different physics more prominent: every action creates an equal and opposite reaction. Such a rotation of weight would drive the person delivering the blow backward before the punch landed, spinning them around, opening them up for a counterstrike.

Knowing this at an intellectual level wasn't enough, because it took practice to learn how to compensate, how to first start the body forward and wait for momentum to develop before moving the fist. Fighters who lived on the Moon had practiced their timing. As a visitor, Cuss had to dredge up occasionally used muscle memory and hope it was enough.

The man who'd launched himself at Cuss was the equivalent of a two-hundred-pound projectile flying through the air. He'd generated plenty of momentum to put behind a blow, but he was now committed to the act, unable to change it no matter how much he might want to.

Cuss couldn't duck in time, because the same slow-falling physics governed both of them. On Earth, if he crouched by swiftly bending his knees and flexing his abdomen, his body would drop in an instant. On the Moon, the same actions would lift his feet off the ground as his body fell in a lazy descent. One of the first principles taught for low-gravity hand-to-hand combat was that ducking was slower than normal. But pushing up was faster and easier.

He waited a split second, watching the man's dive develop, gauging his approach. Then he thrust hard with his legs, launching upward, timing it so his right knee would meet the man's face.

If Cuss missed, his powerful jump, amplified by the adrenaline pouring through his veins, would have sent him four meters into the air. But his knee met its target, crumpling the man's nose, snapping his head back, straining the vertebrae of his neck, while at the same time tempering Cuss's rise.

Pivoting, he grabbed his attacker's shirt as the man's body continued past, using it as a counterweight to pull himself toward the ground and ready himself for an attack by the partner. It didn't come. Instead, the other man disappeared behind the ridge.

Leaping a second time, Cuss landed on the peak of the ridge where the men had been standing, using the height to scout for his quarry. Cuss saw him bounding away, running scared, clearing the area as fast as he could.

Resisting the impulse to give chase, he instead jumped to the ground to confirm that his attacker, now even uglier with a broken, swelling nose, was down, unresponsive to rough jabs. Cuss took a moment to scan for his gun, worried that the man might surface, find it, and turn it on him. He couldn't see it in a quick sweep. Neither could Ygo. So he turned his attention to Smitty while keeping one eye on his assailant.

Sirens wailed in the distance as he viewed his fallen partner. Smitty's face was crushed. Blood seeped from his ears. His neck had a sliver of rock protruding from it. His right hand was missing fingers. His abdomen, peppered with stone fragments, was cut and bleeding. He had no pulse.

As gently as possible, Cuss moved Smitty onto his back on flat ground, hooked a foot under an outcropping for added leverage, and began CPR, suspecting that it wouldn't make a difference but unwilling to make the call, a tribute to his partner, a man doing his best to protect the community.

"Who are they?" he asked Ygo as he pressed rhythmically on Smitty's chest.

"The one on the ground is Gustav Albrecht, a troublemaker with a modest criminal record here in Nova Terra, and an ugly one—grand larceny, aggravated assault, arson—on Earth. He's not an employee at the salvage yard, but he's a known associate of Anders Johansson. The one who ran is Benjamin Bigelow. He goes by Bundee, is a mechanic at the yard, and has no felony convictions here or on Earth."

An ambulance—a white cart with red detailing and a cabin large enough to hold a gurney—came bounding down the lane, siren wailing, lights flashing. As it swayed to a stop, two med techs jumped out.

"I'm Marshal Abbott," called Cuss, pulling out his badge wallet and showing his star.

One med tech led Cuss away from Smitty while his partner unfurled a resuscitation rig and worked to attach it to the fallen man.

"Where are you injured?" the tech asked him.

"I'm fine. Help him." Cuss pointed at Smitty.

As the med techs worked, Cuss heard a groan. His attacker, Gustav Albrecht, rolled on his side and touched his face. Cuss moved over to him, grabbed a wrist, and twisted the arm behind his back, pushing it upward, forcing the man onto his stomach. Resting a knee on Albrecht's back and keeping upward pressure on the arm, he was about to ask the med techs for cord or tape to tie the man's hands when a police cart with two officers arrived on the scene.

He waved "come here" to the nearest cop. "I'm Marshal Abbott. You have cuffs?"

The officer pulled a tie loop from a pouch on her belt and handed it to Cuss, who secured Albrecht's hands behind his back. Standing, he again showed his credentials and let the officer take over.

Cuss noticed the other cop making his way toward what had been the rock pyramids. "I'd stay back from there until an explosives specialist clears them."

The med techs working on Smitty became less frantic

as reality set in. Standing, one said what Cuss had not wanted to concede. "He's gone."

The cops huddled briefly and then called it in, their job now to preserve evidence until the crime scene team arrived. Then they approached Cuss and peppered him with questions: What happened? Why are you here? Where are you headed? Who did this? Where did the other perp go? After Cuss related the details, one of the cops climbed up on the rock ridge to look for Bundee. The other connected with Darlene Washington to verify Cuss's story and schedule a debriefing for him.

With their attention elsewhere, Cuss looked down at Smitty, viewing him with a sense of anger, frustration, and sadness. He didn't know if the man had a wife or kids. If his parents lived here in Nova Terra or if they were even alive. What were his hobbies? What motivated him in his daily life? Smitty had died after being swept into Cuss's world, just like Debra Gosling and too many before her. It weighed on him.

He turned his back on the mayhem and walked slowly up the lane toward the damaged cart, scanning the ground as he walked, looking for his gun.

"There it is," said Ygo. Cuss's lens highlighted the weapon, partially buried under dirt near the damaged cart. Picking it up by the grip, he blew off a residue as fine as talcum powder, and then he shook it, spilling dirt from the barrel. After a quick inspection, he concluded that until he cleaned and test-fired it, he didn't even want to cycle the slide, fearing that the fine grit would do permanent damage. He thumbed the selector to safety and returned it to his holster under his jacket.

Seeking a place to sit, he moved to the damaged cart and pushed on it until it toppled. The cart bounced about before settling on its tires. In the driver's seat, he took inventory of his injuries.

His ears were ringing like a church carillon calling the faithful to service. One knee was sore, and at first he thought it was damage from the blast. Then he remembered breaking Albrecht's face with it and it felt better. He inspected his hand where the cart tire had smacked it, saw a welt developing on the back, and flexed it into a fist. The hand wasn't broken, and he wouldn't let a bruise slow him down.

Satisfied with the state of his health, he called Darlena Washington.

"We'll take it from here," she told Cuss. "We're headed to Johansson's right now."

"Swing by and pick me up."

"There's only room for two in the cart."

"Then send another."

"You've been through a lot, Marshal. Get medical attention and then some rest." She ended the call.

Cuss felt his fury surge. His first impulse was to call her back and demand a ride to the salvage yard. But he'd learned long ago to be self-reliant. After taking some calming breaths, he got out of the cart and walked around it for a quick inspection. None of the tires were flat, a miraculous result given the violence of the explosion. But a front strut was bowed, the cowl was a twisted mess, the windshield was blown out, and the roof was bent back on itself.

There was a chance it would still run.

Back in the driver's seat, he waved a hand in front of the dash bubble, but the cart didn't respond. "What's the issue?" he asked Ygo.

"You're not an approved driver."

"So make me one."

"The police systems are hardened. It will take me a few."

Cuss motioned to the cop who'd given him the tie loop. "I need to drive this to meet up with Detective Washington. Can you activate it for me?"

She viewed the damaged vehicle with a skeptical eye. "Is it drivable?"

"I could take your cart instead."

She shook her head. "Not a chance." Leaning in, she waved a hand in front of the driver's bubble. When it glowed, she made a quick motion with her fingers. "There you go." She started to walk away but reversed course and said to the bubble, "Add driver." After a swipe, she told Cuss, "Wave your badge in front of it."

Cuss pulled his badge wallet from his inside coat pocket and held the star over the bubble. It chimed, and she said, "You're registered, so you can restart it later."

With the road ahead blocked, he lifted the front of the cart, carried it around so it aimed toward the tram tracks, climbed in, and engaged the drive. The vehicle made a dreadful grating sound, and the suspension was stiff and misaligned on the side with the damaged strut, causing the cart to shudder as it moved. But it drove.

Two cop carts, lights flashing and sirens wailing, squeezed past him as he started along the road, scouting the sides for an opening in the rocks wide enough for the cart to drive through. He was halfway to the tram tracks when he saw one he thought might work.

Moving slowly through the opening, he found himself on uneven terrain with jutting ridges, craters big enough to swallow the cart, and a scatter of rocks ranging from pebbles to boulders, all covered by a powdery grit. The enormous cavern wall—looming, craggy, shrouded in shadows—rose high to his right, suddenly dominant even though he was only ten meters closer to it.

He crept forward through the challenging topography, the cart bucking and squealing in protest. It took him ten minutes to reach a point parallel to the growing cluster of cops. He continued on, backtracking once when he found himself trapped with no way forward. But eventually he traveled a path onto the road on the other side of the crime scene. Back on smooth ground, he accelerated, making for Johansson's Ship Salvage as fast as his screeching, shuddering ride would move.

He was most of the way there when Ygo said, "Slow down. Threat at your ten."

Cuss's lens zoomed in on a point ahead and to the left. He could just make out the top of a person's head behind a low rise.

"Let me guess," said Cuss, swerving the cart to a halt and jumping out. "That's the mechanic."

"Bundee. I'd say the odds are good."

Cuss started to draw his gun and then remembered he

couldn't use it. "Come out, Bundee," he called. "You're under arrest. If I have to come in for you, I won't be gentle."

From his experience, people who weren't career criminals could be intimidated by the threat of violence, surrendering to avoid pain. Then again, if Bundee was smart enough to realize he was going down for murdering a police officer, then he'd probably fight to the end.

When a rock the size of a grapefruit came hurtling Cuss's way, he had his answer. He moved behind a boulder, lamenting that his gun was out of commission. Fortunately, he had physical talents as an alternative.

Cuss had been raised in Daytona Beach, Florida, where he'd attended Seabreeze High School. He'd played shortstop on their baseball team, thrown javelin and discus for their track team, and had been captain of their wrestling team. He'd continued with baseball at the intramural level while attending the University of Florida in Gainesville. Though it had been a while, that background had provided him a skillset he could draw upon for this particular situation.

Cuss poked through the rubble on the ground, gathering four egg-sized rocks, holding three in his left hand while readying one to throw in his right. On Earth, he would have chosen round stones worn smooth over eons by rain and wind and flowing water. But those kinds of rocks didn't exist on the Moon. These were jagged and rough, created during blasting and excavation of the vast underground cavern.

Peeking around the edge of his rock shield, he

estimated that Bundee was about thirty meters away. He picked out a series of mounds and ridges as waypoints, waiting for the man to make his second throw. When he did, Cuss reacted.

Moving around in front of the boulder, Cuss kept one foot on the ground while placing the other foot at waist height against the rock behind him, a brace against the "equal and opposite reaction" recoil he expected in the lunar gravity. The distance was typical of a shortstop's throw to first base, and he winged a rock, aiming for a surface near Bundee, hoping for a lucky ricochet.

His rock whistled across the distance, hitting the surface with a sharp crack, and rebounding in Bundee's general direction. The shape of the stone skewed the carom, and he didn't come close to hitting the man. But he expected Bundee to be surprised by the threat and to hunker down in response.

Cuss pushed off the rock and propelled himself forward to a ledge about ten meters closer to Bundee, stumbling once on an unseen outcropping, catching himself before he spilled. When he reached the relative safety of his next stop, he threw another stone. This time he thought the ricochet was good enough that it might have presented a threat, though if Bundee were smart, he'd be crawling to a different hiding spot.

Bundee couldn't present a danger to Cuss without showing himself. But since the man remained hidden, Cuss continued to bound toward him. He changed his angle of approach on the next dash to obscure his location and threw from just eight meters out. Bundee still didn't show himself, and Cuss finished his rush, turning the corner to find the man cowering in a crevice.

Bundee rose to make his last stand, his fists clenched in front of him, wrists upward, dancing about like a bare-knuckle boxer from the eighteenth century. Cuss watched for a moment and then stepped forward, feinted, and popped him in the throat, pulling the punch to avoid splintering the hyoid bone and risk killing the man.

Gasping and gagging, Bundee put a hand against an outcropping and propped himself up while doing his best to continue resisting.

Cuss sought to end it and flipped through his options. Punching him in the throat a second time could very well kill the guy. Hitting him in the head could damage Cuss's hand, elbow, or foot. Breaking his knee meant that moving him afterward would be a hassle. So he put the man down by kicking him in the balls.

"Nice work, Marshal," said Ygo as Cuss grabbed a handful of the writhing man's hair, drawing him to his feet and leading him back to the cart.

"I warned you," Cuss said as he pulled Bundee along, bent at the waist, coughing between groans. "This was your choice." Approaching the cart, he said aloud, "I need to cuff you somehow," a cue for Ygo to offer ideas about how to secure the guy.

"There's storage under the seats. Check there."

Cuss found tie loops on the driver's side of the cart and used them to bind Bundee's hands and feet. Lifting the man by his overalls, he plopped him into the passenger seat. After examining his handiwork, he laced several ties together and tied Bundee to the seat.

Climbing in next to him, Cuss resumed the trek to Johansson's, grilling his prisoner as they bounced along. He ignored legal protocols for questioning suspects, knowing better but letting his impatience influence his behavior. "You killed a cop. From this point forward, your life is going to be miserable. Brutal. Tell me who commissioned the *Yankee Spirit*, and maybe I can make things easier for you."

Bundee started crying. "It was Gustav," he blubbered.

"Gustav bought the *Yankee Spirit*?"

"No," he wailed. "He planted the bomb. I didn't even know he was going to do it."

Cuss could believe that Gustav Albrecht planted the bomb, but there was no way Bundee was ignorant of the fact. "Tell me about the ship and I'll ask the judge for leniency." He could ask the judge for anything, but it wouldn't make a difference to the outcome. Bundee didn't need to know that.

Bundee sat quietly for several moments. "I don't know who it was for. Gustav stole parts, and I combined them with our inventory to build it. It was just another job. Nothing made it different or more special than any other order. Anders was the one who dealt with the client." After a sullen silence, he perked up. "I saw the guy when he came to pick it up, if that helps."

"Can he pick him out?" asked Ygo. He co-opted the dash projector to show the images of five men in a simulated lineup.

Cuss asked Bundee which man he'd seen.

Bundee tried to lean forward but his straps stopped him. He pointed with his chin. "That's him. The first guy."

"Which one. Him?" Cuss deliberately pointed to the last guy.

"No. The first one on the left."

"That's the so-called pilot who chased Agnes Ming up to the farm," said Ygo.

"Do you know a name?" Cuss asked aloud.

"I have no idea." Bundee sniffled, shaking his head. "Ask Anders Johansson."

"It's Rex Luskin," said Ygo. "I've been able to track him from Trenton, New Jersey, to Armstrong, to Lagrange. After chasing Ming, he rode a personal craft out of Hermes and vanished. He's working for someone, though. He's not the mastermind type."

Cuss felt his face flush. This was the second reference to Trenton in the last hour. And he was growing immensely frustrated hearing about perpetrators who vanished.

Chapter 14

C uss was pondering the Trenton, New Jersey, connection when his attention was drawn to a grouping of spaceships in the salvage yard ahead, a half-dozen craft ranging from ten to more than twenty-five meters tall, framed by thirty-meter cranes on either side. The huge cavern wall curved around behind the vessels, a dark backdrop dwarfing them. The display of gleaming technology juxtaposed with primitive stone created a striking image.

As he drove the cart into the parking lot, however, his sense of wonder was dashed by the mounds of junk piled everywhere. It started at the base of an unkempt building and spilled across the lot, like a hoarder who'd filled the inside of his house and was now filling his yard.

There were four police carts parked among the piles, with another pulling in from the frontage road. He could see cops walking the low grav shuffle around the exterior of the building, moving cautiously as if searching for something. Others gathered near the structure's main entrance, clustered under a dented blue sign with orange lettering that branded the establishment as *Johansson's Ship Salvage.*

The squealing of his cart drew the attention of the group. Even though it had some semblance to one of their own, the vehicle's damaged condition and unfamiliar occupants caused two of the cops to rest their hands on their sidearms as they stared in his direction.

Cuss pulled out his badge wallet yet again, held it up, and shouted, "I'm Marshal Abbott! I'm with Detective Washington!"

"The hell you are!" Darlena yelled back, separating herself from the others and loping his way. "What the hell are you doing here, Marshal?" she demanded. "I suggested very strongly that you stay away." Darlena's partner, Hobby Bronson, followed behind her, his scowl deepening as he approached.

Cuss waited unperturbed, and when Darlena reached the cart, he changed her tune. "This is Benjamin Bigelow. He goes by Bundee. He's a mechanic here at the salvage yard and is one of Smitty's killers. The other is in custody back at the crime scene."

"I never meant to hurt anyone," cried Bundee. "It was Gustav Albrecht. I told him…"

Cuss reached over and silenced Bundee with an open-handed swat to the back of his head. Then he continued with Darlena. "I wonder if you might take charge of him? Put him through the system?"

"You're giving him to us?"

Hobby didn't wait for Cuss to answer, instead grabbing Bundee by the collar and yanking hard to pull him from the cart. The ties Cuss had used to lash Bundee into the seat pulled back, and it took Hobby a minute to figure out the issue. He fished out a knife and cut the man loose.

"I have him!" yelled Hobby as he dragged Bundee,

hands and feet still bound, toward the cluster of cops.

"I'm giving him to *you*," said Cuss. "Whether you put your partner's name on the arrest report is your call. I do ask that you include my name somewhere in the body of the report."

She shook her head. "No one does this. What's your game?"

It's exactly what he'd done for her a year ago, but he chose not to mention it. The truth was that the feed from Cuss's lens, edited by Ygo to remove any questionable acts, created a record for the director of the Marshals Service. Cuss could be generous without compromising his own career.

"My game is that I want free access inside the building and across the grounds. I'll stay out of your way, but don't let your people hassle me or throw up hurdles. We still have the murder of a cop on Lagrange to solve, not to mention the kidnappings and murders of those folks with wires in their necks. I'm hoping to find some answers here."

She looked at him for a long moment. "Give me a minute to smooth things with Hobby."

Cuss got out and stretched while Darlena spoke with her partner, who wouldn't look in Cuss's direction. Then she motioned one of the patrol cops out from the group and led her over to where Cuss was standing, briefing her as they walked.

"This is Beata. She'll be your escort. Right now we can defend exigent circumstances to pursue suspects and to stop imminent threats. Wait for the probable cause warrant before straying too far in the search, or you'll threaten our case in court. I expect we'll have official approval to look everywhere in the next ten or twenty minutes. Within the hour for sure."

"Do you have Johansson in custody?"

"We do. We're transporting him right now."

"I need to question him."

She glanced over at Hobby and then turned back to Cuss. "Meet me at the station tomorrow morning first thing. We'll question him together and then visit Lewiston-Mark."

A controlled interrogation, the kind with a defense lawyer and recorded by a suite of sensors, would make it impossible to play fast and loose with procedure. But he didn't see an alternative. This time he was the one who looked over at Hobby. "Sure. If you could make it just the two of us, I'd appreciate it."

"Then be there at eight." She turned away and rejoined her group across the lot.

Cuss smiled at Beata, a middle-aged woman with an angular face, thin as a rail, dressed in the same uniform as the other street cops. She had a nervous giggle, giving a quick laugh in response to everything he said. And she was full of energy. Where some people wiggled their foot or fidgeted with their hands, Beata hopped, pushing off with her toes to rise a foot in the air, over and over.

He didn't know what he was looking for, so he couldn't ask her to show him. He started toward the building. "Let's look around inside."

With a laugh, Beata followed.

The front door of the shop fed to a service desk, the

top a rectangle of worn metal smudged with grease and cluttered with a display of tools for sale. The grimy wall behind the desk was brightened with old posters from parts manufacturers: Nelson Oxygen Moderators, Stream Hatch Fittings, Dynama Fuel Pods. They weren't hung in a careful manner, instead appearing to be hastily mounted as afterthoughts, perhaps a freebie found packed along with a delivery, plopped in the nearest open wall space, affixed with whatever was handy at the moment.

A racy calendar from years ago—skimpily clad women posing suggestively with tools—had been broken apart, with pictures from the different months lined up in a row below the posters. When Cuss realized the all-but-naked women were actually girls, likely twelve or thirteen years old, it deepened his already intense dislike for Anders Johansson.

Leading Beata past the service desk, he found that the shop opened up into a warehouse. Spaceship parts and pieces were everywhere, from big to small, well-worn to almost new, some on the floor gathered in piles, others seemingly dropped where a worker had been standing when they were done with them. Hand tools, power tools, and old fabrication machines were scattered among the junk. The place smelled of lubricant and solvent and burnt metal, honey to a rocketeer but harsh and caustic to Cuss.

The warehouse had a high ceiling, Cuss guessed ten meters tall, with industrial shelving units against three of the walls, staged platforms that rose to the rafters. Each level was piled high, a jumble of stuff with no apparent order. Tilting his head back and looking up at the mess,

Cuss wondered how anyone working there knew what they had or where to find it even if they did.

The back wall held a huge hangar door, with an overhead rail crane running from it back across the shop floor. The core of a Paulson drive hung suspended from the chains of the crane, poised over the lower stage of a small spacecraft sitting in the middle of the workspace, either the old drive being removed or perhaps a replacement ready to go in.

All of it was interesting. None of it told Cuss anything useful about the *Yankee Spirit*.

Twirling in place, he zeroed in on his objective, Johansson's private office, or so he presumed. One of the storage units on a side wall was missing a lower shelf, and a door was fitted into the open space. The door was open. Light spilled through it out onto the shop floor.

As he approached the office, he peeked through the door and saw two men inside, one in street clothes and the other in a patrol uniform, poking around, talking in earnest. The men saw him and turned his way. The one in street clothes had a detective's badge draped from the chest pocket of his sport coat.

"Could you introduce me?" he asked Beata.

She led the way into the office. Cuss stayed close. "Gentleman, this is Marshal Abbott. He's here working with Detective Washington. She says he's part of our team and asks that we give him every consideration." She looked back at Cuss and nodded.

The office was small, the four of them crowding the space. A battered faux-wood desk sat at the rear, a hard-back chair behind it and two more in front, none of them matching. The wall to the left held rickety bookshelves overflowing with personal trinkets. On the right, more child-porn calendar pictures were on display. A well-worn rug had some blue showing along the edges, but was mostly grayish-brown from embedded dirt and grease.

Cuss shook hands with Detective Prentice and Officer Rosenbach, both in their forties, both serious about their work. They made good eye contact and had firm grips, which Cuss took as a positive sign.

"You were there when Shellback got it?" asked Prentice.

Cuss paused, and Ygo said, "That's Smitty. Smitty Shellback"

"I was. He was acting as my partner, doing everything right, helping with an investigation when he got caught by a booby trap. He was a good man."

There was a moment of silence, a tribute to the fallen. Then Cuss made his pitch. "Johansson built a ship here last month that was also booby-trapped, one that killed a cop on Hermes just days after it left this shop."

Their demeanor showed interest. Concern. Cuss pressed on. "Whoever bought it from Johansson is also a cop killer. I'm anxious to learn who it is."

He could see them hesitate. "We have Smitty's killers in custody. Anything I find here will add nails to their coffins as well."

Prentice and Rosenbach turned away from Cuss and whispered. As they turned back, Prentice said, "How can we help?"

"Have you found any records?"

He shook his head. "Johansson doesn't seem to be a hard-copy kind of guy." He waved his hand over the desk near where the chair tucked in, and a display came alive. "Can you access this?"

Cuss moved around him and studied the image. It was a standard welcome screen seeking credentials before revealing information. Cuss waved and tapped to see what would happen.

"I can't get past this without Johansson's cooperation," said Ygo.

"Damn it, I can't," Cuss said aloud. He scanned the walls. "Did you find a safe?"

"Not in here," said Prentice. "There could be one somewhere out there, but it's going to take serious effort to find it given all the shit they have piled everywhere."

Officer Rosenbach chimed in. "We've searched the desk drawers, looked behind the pictures, checked under the rug, probed the ceiling, and scanned the junk on the shelves. There's not much in here. Nothing useful, anyway."

Cuss's lens had a penetrating function that could see shallow anomalies in otherwise uniform surfaces. He scanned the walls, floor, and ceiling as he looked around but saw nothing that would give him pause. He thanked the men and excused himself after that.

As Cuss moved out into the shop, Ygo said, "We have three in custody, and at least one of them has the answer. Tomorrow's interrogation will be key."

After making a circuit around the outside of the

building, Cuss asked Beata for a lift to the nearest tram station. From there, he rode a tram through the tunnel to Port Collins.

. . .

As Cuss moved down the concourse, he passed the entrance to Gallo's Bistro, an overpriced restaurant chain found in spaceports and airports across the worlds. The adverts for the chain bragged of their travelers' amenities, and the sign posted in front of this one gave him an idea. He sent a message to Hatha.

"I'm stuck here in Armstrong and am about to have dinner. Care to join me?"

She answered just as he reached the *Nelly Marie*. "Love to! See you in forty minutes?"

"Perfect," he replied, more excited than he'd anticipated. "Let's start with a drink."

He was humming to himself as he closed the ship's hatch. "Hatha's coming to dinner!" he called to Ygo as he climbed to the third level to get ready. Ygo already knew, of course, but it felt good to say it out loud.

He considered shaving, but two days' growth was his signature look, and he decided Hatha should see him in all his glory. In the shower, his mood switched from joyous to melancholy, driven by the mental image of Smitty Shellback's broken body. He thought of the wasted life, of the desperate, futile attempt to save the young man. It sobered him.

He raised the temperature of the water and soaped

himself a second time, seeking to cleanse himself of the burdens he carried within, feelings of guilt and responsibility, emotions that weighed on his spirits. As he dried himself, he used the cloth to push his disquiet inward, seeking to suppress it, bury it, keep it at bay until it resurfaced at some future time unbidden.

In his bedroom, he sorted through his shirts, first considering plain and simple, but then eyeing the louder choices. After scolding himself to act his age, he succumbed to his desire and donned his Rocket Stars T-shirt. He'd seen the raucous band four years earlier at a theater venue in Apollo, the newest of Lagrange's tube cities, loved the show, and wore the souvenir shirt on special occasions, times when he felt like celebrating.

Climbing down to the second level, he pulled the dining table from its cubby and set it up on the floor. Scanning the contents of the refrigerator, he wavered between a burrito and a hamburger and solved his indecision by choosing a pizza with the works. After placing it in the warming oven, he popped the top of a Franco's Amber Ale, sat at the table, and activated Being There, a tool that provided holographic visits with others who had a compatible system, which was just about everyone at that point in time.

He was five minutes early and was pleased that her system connected, the signal strong. A table and chair emerged across from him, melding with his own setup to appear as one. Her chair was empty.

He could see most of her kitchen behind the chair. It had a larger footprint than he would have guessed, with top-of-the-line appliances, high-end cabinets, and elegant stone countertops. A spray of cut flowers sat in an artsy vase on the edge of the counter, positioned so they would be over her right shoulder when she sat. Either she came from money, or Nature's Nook Café was doing very well, because it all looked expensive.

He'd just opened his second beer when she slid into her chair ten minutes late, grinning, clearly happy. She took a swig from a bottle of beer she was carrying, never breaking eye contact as she sipped.

The idealized memory he'd nurtured of her paled in comparison to the beauty in front of him. Her hair was a more natural-looking reddish blonde, the orange color gone. Her cheeks had a fresh radiance, like she'd just scrubbed her face. She wore minimal makeup. The dazzle in her eyes enhanced her smile. Her dimples were his favorite feature, adorable bows on a beautifully wrapped gift.

She was wearing a lemon-colored blouse that complemented her natural coloring. It clung to her body, a second skin of satin material, showing off every curve and valley.

She spoke the first words. "Are you staring at my breasts?"

He lifted his eyes to meet hers. "I am so not sorry."

They both laughed and sipped their beers together.

Her dog, Pibbs, barked for attention, and she picked him up and introduced him. Cuss saw a small mutt with a strong shih tzu influence. She prattled on about him for a minute or two, telling dog stories. An anxious chatter. He listened, letting her get her nervous energy out, enjoying her spirit.

"How's the case going?" she asked when she put Pibbs down.

They hadn't really talked at length about anything, and he didn't want this to be their first deep discussion. So he kept it brief, moving the conversation to the personalities involved.

"A crew is kidnapping old, wealthy people and using technology to steal their money. I'm making headway on identifying them but haven't cracked it yet. The detectives here in Armstrong are antagonistic toward the Marshals Service and aren't as cooperative as they could be." He told her about Darlena and Hobby, painting Darlena as somewhat sympathetic and helpful, and Hobby as a complete asshole. "Tomorrow Darlena and I interrogate a key suspect, and then we're supposed to serve a warrant together at Lewiston-Mark. It's an important day, and I hope her cooperative attitude continues."

"I've taken Nanny to the Lewiston-Mark office on Luna Deck a few times. She invests with them because of their personal touch, which isn't the best logic for choosing an investment firm. But hell, it's her money."

Nanny was what Hatha called her grandmother, a term of endearment carried over from her childhood. It caused Cuss to ask, "Hatha is an unusual name. Is there a story behind it?"

Hatha smirked. "My given name is Hiawatha. I pronounced it as Hatha when I was like three years old and it stuck."

Cuss's brow creased. "Isn't Hiawatha a man? An Indian chief or something?"

Hatha sipped her beer. "My dad is an idiot. I love him but he's not the sharpest knife in the drawer. He claims I'm one-sixteenth Mohawk. I got myself tested when I was a teen, and it turns out I'm one-sixty-fourth Native American, and it's a mix of tribes. Anyway, my mom had a rough delivery when I was born. My dad took charge when it came to filling out the birth record. Even though they'd agreed on Hailie as my name, he decided to celebrate my misremembered heritage based on the misremembered story of Pocahontas, thinking that Hiawatha was the Indian girl who helped the settlers. My mom was livid, but not enough to change it afterward. I was self-conscious about it when I was younger. But now I kind of like it."

He laughed. She aroused him so much he became crass, immediately regretting it. "I'd love to explore your heritage."

She gave a demure smile and changed the subject. "I'm starving and am going to grab my meal. Excuse me for a moment."

She stood and walked behind her chair into the kitchen. He could see her clearly. Her blouse hung down just past her butt. Her legs were bare. Slim. Fit. He couldn't see any sign of shorts. He wondered if she wore anything more than panties underneath. His eyes were riveted on the lower hem of the blouse, hoping the fabric would bounce or ripple to reveal the secret. He couldn't stop staring.

Her back to him, she removed a large bowl of salad from the refrigerator, pulled out silverware from a drawer, then opened an overhead cabinet and reached up high for a plate. Her blouse rode up when she stretched. He discovered that she wasn't wearing anything underneath. Her bottom was breathtakingly beautiful.

She returned to the table, her blouse back down covering everything but her legs. She sat.

"That's the show for tonight, Marshal Abbott. You may close your mouth and fetch your food." She placed the plate under the salad bowl, revealing it as a prop all along. She sat back and waited for him to get his pizza.

While they ate, Hatha told the story of how she'd quit the Community Patrol force and opened Nature's Nook at the prompting of Nanny, who was worried about her granddaughter's safety. Nanny was apparently loaded, because she funded the eatery, a fun but not so profitable enterprise. Its breakfast and lunch focus gave Hatha plenty of time off, time she could spend with her grandmother.

"To make money, I'd need to be open for dinner, and I'd need more than six tables. But then I'd always be working." She looked into the distance, her eyes unfocused as though she were imagining it. She shook her head. "It would suck everything else out of my day."

Cuss opened up about his early life, telling her about working as a cop in Tallahassee, Florida. For some reason, perhaps because of the harrowing events of the day, he talked about an event he rarely mentioned before knowing someone really well, about how a deranged killer had murdered his wife, taking her from him when he was twenty-eight years old. "It was three days shy of our first anniversary. We'd talked about starting a family the night before."

"Oh, Cuss," Hatha stretched a hand across the table to comfort him. But even Being There's lifelike capabilities couldn't bridge the sixty-five thousand kilometers between Lagrange and the Moon. He reached out a hand anyway to acknowledge her act of sympathy.

"I moved to Lagrange to escape the memories," he continued. "I lucked into a detective slot and buried myself in my work."

In his first months on the job, he'd arrested a mugger whose most recent victim happened to be Michael Belnick, then an assembly representative from Apollo, visiting Hermes on government business. A few years later, he'd captured a man who postured as an assassin. The man proved to be psychotic, imagining his reality, believing an outside force was giving him orders.

"The guy had pictures of Michael Belnick, at that point the mayor of Apollo, on his apartment wall with a target drawn on the face. When Belnick was elected governor of Lagrange, he asked me if I wanted to be a marshal. When I said 'yes,' he led the charge to get me appointed."

She told him about her art. She'd been making pottery for years, submitted the occasional piece to juried shows, and had won a few ribbons. She pointed a thumb over her shoulder. "I made the vase holding the flowers." Then she held up her salad bowl and turned it so he could see the scene of a bear standing in a stream, salmon jumping nearby. "This, too."

They chatted for hours, sharing, laughing, teasing, drinking. Toward the end she adopted a serious demeanor.

"Don't invest too much in me, Cuss." She explained that she was seeing a few men on a casual basis. "I obviously like you, but something is broken in me. I don't think it's that I'm overly picky or waiting for the right man. I love having men in my life. But in the end I prefer to be single. I like the freedom." Her nose wrinkled, like she'd smelled a foul odor. "And Stan Shevchenko is not on my short list. I don't find him remotely attractive, and I wish he'd get the hint and move on."

He stopped himself from saying, "You sound like a female version of me." Instead, he said, "I saw Stan the Man here in Armstrong. It took me a minute to recognize him because he was out of place, in a different city on a different world. I'm still wondering what he's up to."

After a few minutes more, she said goodbye with, "I can't wait to see you in person."

Cuss slept fitfully that night, cursing God because, like a magnet, he'd been created with two poles. The positive side attracted beautiful women, accomplished and capable females eager to be in his company. The negative side attracted death. Horrifying tragedies, one after the next, that battered his psyche and tortured his soul.

Chapter 15

C uss was up early the next morning, and over breakfast, he touched base with Juan.

"How's it going?" he asked.

"You were supposed to get me access to the wire-and-chip assembly from Agnes Ming so the electronics guy could see if he could use it as a trace. He can't start without it. I looked into getting it through my own channels, but it's just like I predicted. Everyone is dragging their feet while they cover their asses, and I don't have the authority to take responsibility on my own."

"I did that," said Ygo. He sounded defensive. "Hold on."

"I started the process," Cuss told Juan. "Give me a sec while I see what the problem is." He put Juan on hold.

"It's stuck at the coroner's office" said Ygo. "She wants you to pick it up personally since you're the one taking the responsibility."

"Can you get around it?"

"Probably. But by the time I work through it all, you'll be back there anyway."

"Get started in case things drag out here." He paused. "Thanks, Ygo."

Cuss returned to Juan. "It's waiting for me to pick up at the coroner's office. I'm not sure if I can free it before I get back. I'll do my best." Then, "You were going to show pictures of Moore, Wallingford, and that pilot, Rex Luskin, around the flight decks."

"Yeah. As it turns out, with a passenger and cargo port for each of four cities, times four shifts in a twenty-four-hour day, times two sets of shifts to fill a week, it takes sixty-four interview visits to catch everyone, and that's if no one is out sick. So I've split it up. I'm covering Hermes, and I have a detective friend on Apollo who's covering there. My commander reached out to the commanders of Athena and Demeter to recruit detectives to cover those cities. So far we're about a third of the way along. I'm studying the reports as they come in to make sure I feel comfortable with everyone's efforts. Nothing has popped yet. I'll let you know when it's done."

"You continue to impress me, Juan. Keep me in the loop."

"Oh, and a last bit of news. I'm being promoted to the Terra Deck station when I get a new partner next week."

"Wow, congratulations! The mayor must be coming around. Who's the lucky detective?"

"Wanda Piccolo. She's a transfer from Demeter. I don't know much about her and am choosing not to review her file in advance. Instead of going in with a bunch of preconceived ideas, I'm going to meet her first and form an opinion based on my observations and our actual interactions. It's sort of an experiment. After I know her a bit, then I'll research her background, and hopefully then the information will have context."

"Let's get this case resolved so you two can start your

new partnership with a clean slate."

. . .

Cuss arrived at the detectives bullpen at eight hundred
sharp. Darlena was waiting for him.

She stood. "Hobby gets here at nine. That gives you
an hour to interview Johansson before we start, but no
more. I'll watch from outside." She started them walking.
"Hobby and I are going to talk to the three assholes one
after the other, and you are welcome to watch. If you have
any questions along the way, wait until we're done. Don't
send any questions in while we're working them. It fucks
with my rhythm. You can guess how Hobby would
respond."

They reached a hallway door. She stopped and turned
to him. "Johansson's been marinating in there for a few
hours." She motioned to more doors farther along. "So
have Gustav and Bundee. We didn't let them sleep much
last night. Didn't feed them either. They've had some water.
Their cells have a toilet. We made them shower to minimize
the stink." She paused. "You want to grab a coffee before
you go in?"

"Thanks. No."

She resumed her list. "We insisted they get different
lawyers. Otherwise, the lawyer would hear the questions for
the first asshole and have a heads-up when we moved on
to the next." She rubbed her neck. "You can't offer them
food or drink to motivate them. I want to save that for our
turn."

"Everything will be on the record?"

She nodded. "The three lawyers have communicated rights and procedures to them. We have that locked down."

"Are we still doing Lewiston-Mark today?"

"Yup, but realistically, it will be closer to thirteen hundred before I can break free. Hobby and I will take an hour with each interview. After, during lunch, he and I will talk through what we've learned and formulate a strategy for the afternoon. He'll take over the afternoon questioning while you and I go execute the warrant."

"Are there any deals on the table?"

"Definitely not for those two assholes." She indicated the rooms holding Bundee and Gustav Albrecht. "It's possible Johansson may get cut some slack if we need his testimony to bury those two *and* if his involvement proves to be after the fact. But don't mention it to him. That's for Hobby and me to offer."

Cuss nodded. "Okay. I'm ready."

She opened the door. He entered the same style of interrogation room he'd been in a hundred times before.

Johansson was a solidly built man, late fifties, with shaggy dirty-blond hair and a shaggy dirty-blond beard. He wore an orange prisoner's jumpsuit. His hands, secured to the table in front of him, were stained with grease, his fingernails lined with grime.

Cuss ignored him, taking a seat and instead focusing on the lawyer, a weaselly-looking person in a yellow-and-orange outfit.

The lawyer began bitching. "My client hasn't slept, been fed, or been given water. That constitutes inhumane treatment, outright torture."

Cuss didn't interrupt as the lawyer ranted about Johansson's innocence, the illegal behavior of the police force, how they'd sue for mistreatment, for harassment, for defamation. Cuss nodded like a bobblehead. When the lawyer started on the third iteration of complaints, Cuss spoke for the first time. "I'm Marshal Abbott. I don't work for this department. I'm not responsible for your client's treatment. I'm not here to talk about the murder of Smitty Shellback."

The lawyer sat back and stared at Cuss for a long moment. "Then why are you here?"

"And I'm not here to talk about the organized theft of rocket parts from Port Collins."

Johansson and the lawyer looked at each other, then looked back at Cuss.

"I'm here to talk about the *Yankee Spirit*."

"What's that?"

"Your client knows."

"But I don't."

"It's a ship built at Johansson's Ship Salvage last month, one used to transport kidnap victims from Nova Terra to Lagrange. The ship had a booby trap that killed a Lagrange police officer when the bomb exploded."

"So you say."

"That means that even if your client is found innocent of all charges here in Armstrong, he will be extradited to Hermes where it will start all over again. But now he'll be away from home, away from his loved ones, away from everything he knows. And we have the goods on him.

Yankee Spirit's pilot is ready to testify that your client installed the bomb when building the ship. That puts Mr. Johansson on the line for murder. For killing yet another cop."

"That's bullshit," yelled Johansson. "Complete nonsense. I didn't put a bomb on anything."

The lawyer rested a hand on Johansson's arm, quieting him. "I'd need to see proof of your allegations before we'd even consider discussing it here. I don't know of any kidnappings. Or bombs on a spaceship. Or an officer's death on Lagrange. It's all just words at this point."

Cuss pressed on. "Though the pilot is cooperating, it's not him we're after. And if Mr. Johansson didn't plant the bomb, then I'm not interested in him either. I don't care that he's a thief. But if he didn't plant it, then who did? Perhaps it was the person who purchased the ship. The one who commissioned the build."

"Obviously," said the lawyer.

"Yet the pilot says it's Johansson."

"He's lying!" yelled Johansson, spit flying as he shouted.

"I'm here to offer your client a deal. If he doesn't take it, then I go next door and offer it to Bundee. If *he* doesn't take it, then I go two doors down and offer it to Gustav Albrecht. First one to accept wins. The others are fucked."

"You're talking in riddles," said the lawyer.

"Tell me who purchased the *Yankee Spirit*. Who did your client deal with? Where did the payment originate? If your client is just a shipbuilder, then the charges get reduced to accessory."

"There are no charges. None I've seen anyway. And if charges are coming and we deal, he has to be free and clear. None of this reduced-charges bullshit."

"I understand." Cuss stood. "Let me go see if Bundee or Gustav will tell me."

Johansson laughed. "They don't know."

The lawyer glared at Johansson. "Jesus, Anders. Shut the fuck up."

Cuss sat back down. "I'll leave you two alone to conference. Check the news feeds. Everything I just said was discussed by the governor of Lagrange and mayor of Hermes in a public news conference two days ago. Dozens of news stories have documented the details. The only thing you won't find is a summary of charges for your client. But after viewing the feeds, it won't be hard to figure that part out."

"He'll kill me if I tell you."

"Goddamn it, Anders," shouted the lawyer. "I'm two seconds away from resigning. What part of 'shut up' is too difficult to understand?" Then to Cuss, "Has this deal been signed off by the Hermes prosecutor, or are you freelancing?"

"I'm not going to jump through those hurdles until I know there's a bargain to be had. Confirm your client knows the name, and I'll bring the municipal attorney into the loop to negotiate a deal."

"If you've been misrepresenting any of this, it puts your case at risk. You know that, right?"

Cuss stared at him and waited.

"Give us a minute." The lawyer held up Legal Block, a

device that cast an electronic privacy shield. The shield was unbreakable by anything on the civilian market. No defense agencies on any world had the means. There were occasional rumors that an intelligence agency from a country on Earth had secreted a back door into the system they could use in moments of national security, but that had never been publicly confirmed. And the information garnered that way would be inadmissible in any court.

But Ygo had figured out how to decode sensor reflections to hear the words spoken. And Cuss's priority was learning who killed Debra Gosling, Agnes Ming, Kaycee Gibbons, and likely Robert Moore and Franklin Wallingford. He didn't care if Ygo's eavesdropping compromised his ability to testify about a theft ring. And if Johansson was involved with Smitty Shellback's murder, Darlena would make sure he paid.

"It's Yuri Melnikov," said Ygo. A pause. "Police records tag him as leading a mid-level crime organization out of Trenton, New Jersey."

It took every ounce of Cuss's patience to wait for the lawyer-client conference to end. With the name in hand, it didn't matter to him what they decided.

Eventually, the lawyer lowered Legal Block and faced Cuss. "We will consider offers from your prosecutor. But tell whoever it is to be serious or don't bother."

Cuss stood and tapped on the door. "You got it."

Outside, he met Darlena, who was exiting an observation room across the hall. He began with a lie. "I'm going to reach out to the municipal attorney on Hermes to see about a deal, so I won't be observing your interviews."

Then the truth. "When the time comes, I'll make myself available to testify about Smitty Shellback. Nail them, Darlena. Make them pay."

Darlena nodded.

"Call when you're on your way to Lewiston-Mark. I'll meet you there."

She nodded again.

. . .

Cuss sat at a sidewalk table outside Westside Café on Colby Corner, killing time until Darlena finished her interrogations. He sipped an imported Sumatran blend while he waited, each delicious cup as expensive as a meal but worth it to avoid the bitter mud the locals called coffee. And while he sipped, he watched the entryway to Lewiston-Mark Corporate Headquarters, an impressive building across the street that also housed their tech center, the organization the warrant permitted them to search.

Colby Corner was actually a bustling city square filled with pedestrians and ringed by the headquarters and home offices of a number of mega-corporations. A few of the buildings in the square were constructed of hewn gray stone and had façades filled with windows, the distinctive styling indicative of a building constructed in the last ten years. But they were draped with the same olive-green vines as every other structure in Armstrong, muting the progress in architectural design and new building materials.

Bright signage trumpeted the names of the businesses occupying the buildings. Around the square, Cuss saw signs for an entertainment company, a marketing firm, a food and beverage company, an interworld logistics outfit, and a mining and minerals conglomerate. Most signs were electronic displays, some streaming press releases touting the company's latest accomplishments and newest offerings, others hawking company products: drink this, watch that, buy our goods. Lewiston-Mark was the most subdued of the group, with a clean, elegant display that did nothing more than state their name.

As Cuss watched the entryway, he mulled the facts he knew and things he suspected, and always reached the same conclusion. Someone at Lewiston-Mark had assembled a list of their rich clients who had an old-style wire authentication device, and either gave or sold the list to Yuri Melnikov.

With so many remote employees in a modern workforce, it wasn't at all certain that the list creator reported to work at the building across the square. Nor was it likely that the data the person used to assemble the list resided on equipment housed in the building. But warrants were served on people and locations. This was the place to start.

As Cuss drained his cup, he considered that Trenton, New Jersey, was the epicenter of the murderous enterprise. Too many suspects had that connection. Not only did Yuri Melnikov hail from Trenton, but so did crime partner Stan Shevchenko, ferret-faced Factory production head Roscoe Antonov, and spacecraft pilot Rex Luskin.

Ygo had been working overtime to locate Melnikov, an immensely difficult proposition given the vastness of the search area.

"Still no luck?" Cuss asked.

"I won't say that he's vanished, because I know how much the phrase frustrates you. But I can't locate him on Earth, Lagrange, or Nova Terra."

"Maybe we should take a different approach and focus on his last-known activities. Whatever he was up to when he disappeared might provide clues to where he is now."

Since finishing his interview with Anders Johansson that morning, Cuss had been monitoring the Lewiston-Mark entryway, with Ygo identifying employees who passed through, checking to see if any of them had a Trenton connection. Similar to Juan showing pictures at the Lagrange city ports, this was basic police work. A long shot at best. But even in a world of advanced technology, stirring the pot to see what happened remained an important component in solving difficult cases.

There hadn't been a lot of foot traffic in or out of the building since he'd arrived. But as noon approached, that changed. Employees started spilling out for lunch, some alone, some in groups. Ygo identified the people as they appeared, performing snap background checks to determine their position with the company and their hometowns. Most of the employees proved to be native Nova Terrans, with Earth immigrants a distant second, a result that Cuss hadn't expected but in retrospect made a certain sense.

The outflow waned. Minutes passed. And then a man came out alone. Fiftyish. Dressed in muted colors, not the bright attire so popular in the city. And with casual styling, like he was planning on cleaning his closet or sweeping the porch rather than going to work in a corporate office.

"Here we go," said Ygo. "Peter Sobol. Born in Detroit but moved to Trenton when he was two years old. Let's see. He's listed in the company directory as a systems security specialist."

"That sounds like someone who could assemble the list."

"Winner, winner, chicken dinner, to quote my dear old dad."

"You haven't mentioned Pops in a while. How's he doing?" Cuss watched Sobol walk to a corner kiosk and get in line.

"Still driving Mom crazy while she returns the favor."

Cuss smiled. "If this is our guy, I want him for kidnapping and murder. And we need a copy of his list."

"The warrant lets us dig through their systems to search for it. But unless we have the company's cooperation, it will take a lot of time and effort. And before we get very far, they'll be challenging the search in court."

"Any ideas for getting ahead of that?"

"Throw a scare into Peter Sobol, something so threatening it causes him to confess."

"If he's working for killers, it's hard to imagine that we could scare him more than what they would do to him if he talked."

Sobol reached the front of the line, bought a sandwich and a drink, and returned to the building.

A chime informed Cuss that he was receiving a call. It was Darlena.

"Hey, Cuss. The chief wants Hobby and me front and center at a news conference at thirteen thirty. Cop killers get the media worked up, and they're clamoring for details."

"Understood. Good luck." Cuss could hear the disappointment in his voice. "Call when you're done."

His brain churned as he decided what to do with the time. "Who's the biggest Lewiston-Mark honcho living here in Nova Terra?"

"Gerard Mark is the president and CEO," said Ygo. "He lives in Springrock, a suburb of Armstrong."

"Mark as in Lewiston-Mark?"

"The very one."

"Is he here at the building?"

A pause. "He's at his home. Has been all day."

Cuss stood and began to lope toward the Colby Corner tram station. "How long does it take to get there?"

"Twenty-five minutes. Take the southbound for three stops to Franklin, then transfer to the eastbound to Springrock."

"Tell me if Mark leaves."

"The warrant doesn't cover his home."

"I know. But if we can't scare Sobol, maybe we can throw enough worry into old man Gerard that he cuts through the crap and gets us the list and its creator." Cuss reached the station and queued up for the next car. "Is he an old man, or is he the son or something?"

"His dad founded the company with Lewiston, but Gerard is seventy-two, so both I guess, maybe older more than old."

Cuss got off the tram at the Franklin station, and as he

waited for his connection, he studied the eastbound map. "Springrock is the end of the line," he commented to Ygo. "A place you travel to but not one you pass through."

"A key to exclusivity."

Fifteen minutes later, when the tram pulled into the Springrock station, Cuss saw homes that were huge by Nova Terra standards. "Exclusivity indeed," he muttered.

The station was exquisite. Quiet. Constructed of faux wood to look like an old red barn that had been refurbished into a quaint tram stop, no doubt an expensive illusion to create. And it wasn't covered in vines, presumably so the building could be seen and enjoyed.

Inside the station, the flora draped on the walls wasn't the drab olive-green vines found everywhere else in Nova Terra. Instead, it was the gorgeous greenery common on Lagrange. A bot was trimming the plants, fussing like a barber who sought to clip the last stray hair before calling it done.

The floor of the exit ramp displayed a series of tile mandalas, painstakingly constructed, striking to look at, seemingly too special to walk on, though the two women who had exited the tram with Cuss did so without hesitation. The railings and fixtures along the way were brass, clear of smudges, the light dancing off their polished surfaces.

The ramp fed out to a well-maintained parking lot. A dozen upscale carts awaited, new vehicles with plush seating and expensive trim. The women stepped into separate carts and scooted away, privileged passengers on the way to their mansions.

"Uh-oh," said Ygo at the same time Cuss saw the issue.

The carts exited through a gate, the only way out. A guard, a youngish man in uniform, sat in a booth that coordinated with the tram station building, waving the ladies through while watching Cuss, an interloper among the chosen. The guard waited patiently. Cuss approached.

"May I help you?" asked the guard. His long blond hair and soft, tanned face made him look more like a beach bum than a sentry.

Cuss showed his credentials. The guard seemed unimpressed, waiting for Cuss to state his business.

"I'd like to walk around the neighborhood. I'm thinking of moving out here and want to get a feel for it."

"Do you have an appointment?"

"To walk around?"

"Yes, sir. The whole town is private property. Streets, parks, schools, shopping, sidewalks, all of it. Everyone, including detectives, either needs an appointment, is accompanied by a resident, or has a warrant to enter."

"I'm a marshal. And I've come packing." He showed the warrant. The guard flipped his hair out of his eyes and read it.

"This is for the Lewiston-Mark Tech Center." He pointed back toward the tram station. "Take the westbound to Franklin Station, then the northbound to Colby Corner."

Cuss felt his frustration building. "Gerard Mark works from home. By extension, that makes his house part of the tech center."

"I'm no lawyer, Marshal. I just know that my one job is to keep everyone out who isn't invited. Would you wait while I call Mr. Mark and ask if you may visit?"

Cuss gritted his teeth, angry at the guard, angry at the situation, annoyed that Ygo hadn't foreseen it and made appropriate accommodations. He ran through scenarios in his head and decided it would be best if he was the one to make contact, especially given his false claim about the extension of the search warrant.

"I'll call. Wait right here." Being sarcastic to the guard wouldn't help, but it made him feel better. Cuss withdrew to a far corner of the parking lot. "Go ahead and connect me," he said to Ygo.

After most of a minute, a handsome man, well preserved for his seventy-two years, clean-shaven, kind face, hair gray at the temples, appeared in Cuss's lens display. "How may I help you, Marshal Abbott?"

To encourage a response, Ygo had labeled the call as urgent and had included Cuss's name and title.

"Sir, I have a situation involving kidnapping and murder. I believe an employee of Lewiston-Mark is using company resources to orchestrate the crime, killing your clients. I'm at the Springrock tram station right now, here to speak with you about it. Would you allow me to enter the town and meet you at your home?"

"Good lord, Marshal. Well, if you are coming to question me, then I should contact my attorney."

Cuss's heart sank. Nothing about this visit was progressing as he'd envisioned. "By all means, contact your attorney. Tell him or her that I have a warrant to enter the tech center, a warrant already signed by a judge, giving me and a team of local detectives authority to search all

Lewiston-Mark systems to find a name and a list." He paused for dramatic effect. "In spite of our best efforts at discretion, the news media will likely learn about it. Somehow they always do." Another pause. "Or you and I could sit down and figure out a way to avoid all that. We wouldn't even have to execute the warrant if you could help us with the name and list."

"Who's the person, and what's this list?"

"I'm sorry, sir, but I'm done talking to you from a parking lot. Invite me to the house and let's discuss this in person. I'll be at the guard station for another five minutes, and then I return to Colby Corner to execute the warrant." He ended the call.

Heart thumping, he walked back to the guard station. The guard eyed him, eyebrows raised, asking silently about the outcome.

Cuss shrugged, as if to reply, "We'll see."

A full minute passed. Then another. Then Cuss heard a chime, and the guard answered. Behind Cuss, a cart pulled out from a parking slot and headed in his direction.

"The cart will bring you to the Mark estate," said the guard. "Enjoy your visit."

Cuss sank into the sumptuous seat, still too frustrated to feel triumph at the victory. The gate lifted. The cart scooted through and started up the street. He heard a faint whine overhead, leaned out, and looked up. A small drone was pacing the cart, whirring its presence as it tracked him to his destination.

The roadway had a smooth, clean surface. The homes were mansions in size and styling, tightly packed on small but beautiful yards, green lawns filled with trees, shrubs, and flowers. In spite of the time and expense spent creating the beautiful setting, no one was out enjoying it other than a handful of bots tending to maintenance.

The cart turned onto a cul-de-sac. The Mark home sat at the end, a monument to wealth and taste. It was constructed from brick-size stones painted a rusty red, with multiple gables sectioning the front of the house to create an impressive architectural presence. The steep, tiled roof completed the structure, making the home look similar to an elegant mansion on Earth, though with no wind, rain, or snow anywhere in Nova Terra, the rooftop peaks were purely an aesthetic feature.

The cart pulled up the short drive and swung around a circle at the top, stopping in front of a front porch with white columns and a rocking chair. The oversized door was made of dark wood slabs, with brass hinges and a heavy ring knocker.

As Cuss stepped from the cart, the door opened. Gerard Mark, a tall, slim man, stood in the opening.

"My attorney is on the way," were his first words.

"I understand," said Cuss, staying with the cart, waiting for an invitation into the home. "If you'll give me a few minutes, I think you'll see that I am trying to solve something you also want solved. That I am not a threat to you or Lewiston-Mark, but here for the opposite reason, to identify those responsible for a heinous crime without swirling you or your company into the vortex."

Gerard Mark looked at Cuss, taking his measure.

Cuss removed his badge wallet and held it out for the

man to see, stepping forward so it was easier to view.

Gerard glanced at it but didn't study it. "You have a gun under your coat, I suppose."

"Yes, sir."

A pause. "Come in, Detective. Now you have me curious."

Cuss withheld the urge to say, "Marshal."

The foyer was as impressive as the exterior. Wood floors, old carpets, antique furniture, crystal chandelier, a grand staircase. Gerard led Cuss down a short hallway and into a white kitchen, passing through it to a breakfast nook set into a large floor-to-ceiling bay window. He motioned to a chair at a round oak table.

"Would you like coffee? Water?"

"I'll have coffee if you are, but please don't go to any trouble."

"It's no trouble, Marshal," he said, this time getting the title correct. He poured from a carafe into two hearty ceramic mugs and brought them over. "There's cream and sugar on the table."

Gerard took a colorful cloth napkin from a basket in the center of the table and rested his coffee mug on it.

Seeing that, Cuss did the same. Then he again removed his badge wallet, peeled a projector disk the size of a coin off the back, set it on the table, and used it to open a display they both could see. "I'd like to show you some disturbing pictures." The first was of Agnes Ming lying face down in the soybean fields on the farm on Hermes. Gerard grimaced. Cuss then showed Kaycee Gibbons lying behind a hedge next to the fertilizer plant in the industrial district of Armstrong.

"Goodness, Marshal. I've seen enough. How does this involve my company?"

Cuss showed him a picture of the wire sticking out from Gibbons' neck.

Gerard leaned forward to look. "What's that?"

"We have two dead and two more missing. They all have one of these identification implants, devices connected to Lewiston-Mark systems to give them secure control of their funds. A criminal outfit has kidnapped these people, somehow connected to their accounts through this device, and has drained their funds, funds entrusted to your company. When the accounts are empty, they kill them."

Gerard was in a daze, trying to comprehend what he was seeing and hearing.

"We know you have nothing to do with this. But we believe one of your employees has assembled a list of wealthy people who use this device and has given it to a criminal enterprise."

"Who? Who would do this?"

"That's the thing. We don't know. It's why we are coming with a warrant rather than simply arresting the guilty party. We need to search your systems to find whoever it is before anyone else gets hurt. And we need a copy of the list because, at any moment, the next person on it could be taken and killed."

"My God." Gerard paled as he slumped in his chair.

"Would you be willing to ask one of your staff to hunt for it now? Get me the name and a copy of the list. It saves your company the intrusion. And most important, it saves lives."

Gerard didn't hesitate. With a swoop of his hand, a different kind of display popped up in front of him, positioned at an oblique angle to Cuss. "Chuck, are you there?"

"Yes, sir," said Chuck.

"It seems one of our staff is using Sissy to run an illegal enterprise. Who is our most skilled ops tech? Someone who can search out this person based on vague parameters?"

"That's vague, indeed, sir. Heather Frierson is remarkably skilled. So is Tawny Gustavo. If I knew what this was about, I could direct you better."

"Are either of them working today?"

"I was in a meeting with Heather twenty minutes ago, so I know she's around."

"Thanks, Chuck. I'll explain later." He refreshed the display and asked it for a list of account verification devices spanning from ten to forty years ago. He scrolled up and down through the results. "There." He jabbed at an image and then adjusted the display so Cuss could see.

It showed the same wire and chip implant Cuss had seen at the autopsy of Agnes Ming. The page identified it as a Semident 318 and included a list of specifications, special features, and instructions for installation in the human body.

"I remember it now," said Gerard. "We stopped recommending them almost thirty years ago, though. The technology got simpler and less invasive."

He refreshed the display yet again. "Heather, are you

there?"

A woman who looked like she was twenty years old appeared. Hair in braids. Dark eye makeup that ran onto her forehead and over to her temples. Gaudy red lips. Metal loops implanted in her chin like a pop-art goatee. Cuss didn't find the look appealing but appreciated that each generation sought to separate themselves from those before it.

"Hi, Gerard. How are you?"

"Hi, Heather. I'm well, thanks. Could you help with something very urgent? Very confidential."

"Hold, please." She moved her hands, Cuss assumed to close whatever she had been working on. She stood and shut her office door. "Yes, sir. How may I help?"

"I fear someone has used Sissy to identify those of our clients who use a Semident 318 for account verification. Can you probe to find who has been performing inquiries using that term?"

"Say that again. Semi…"

"Semident 318. It's a legacy device for identity authentication and account access, four or five generations before Waveform technology hit the market."

"And you want to know who's been asking about it?"

"Yes. It's really old tech. I can't imagine there'll be much activity to sift through."

"How long ago did they do this?"

Gerard looked at Cuss, who said, "I'm guessing six months, but go back a full year to be safe."

Gerard relayed the information to Heather.

"One of our own employees?"

"We believe so. Does it matter?"

"One of our own can hide their work in sophisticated ways."

Heather snugged a neural interface cap onto her head and started chanting to the Lewiston-Mark system, apparently called Sissy, using technical jargon, issuing strings of commands that caused it to react.

After a few moments, she stopped and rubbed her neck. "A simple search shows no activity in the last year, which doesn't surprise me. Let me look for someone who searched for the term and then swept after themselves." She chanted some more, then announced her failure. "Nothing."

"How would *you* hide this search if you didn't want anyone to know?" Gerard asked.

"After I swept, I'd remove the echoes, sweep again, then feather any ripples."

Cuss hadn't a clue what she was talking about, but Gerard either did or accepted his ignorance.

"And how could someone find out about your search after you did all that?"

"They couldn't." She bit her lip, causing her chin rings to clink together. Her eyes brightened. "Sissy would be clean, but they couldn't clean Cordy."

Her singsong chanting resumed, now with finger swooping included.

"Cordy is our company AI," explained Gerard.

She stopped and threw her arms over her head, a grin on her face. "She shoots. She scores!" Then she dropped her arms and leaned in on the display. "Oh, shit." She moved her hands frantically for a good twenty seconds. Cuss watched in fascination. "It's Peter Sobol. He set a loop trap designed to inform him if anyone came looking. He knows I snagged him. Sorry."

Cuss stood, adrenaline flooding his veins. "I need to go in case he runs. Send me a copy of the list and we're done. Because of your cooperation, we won't be executing the warrant." He started moving and then stopped. "It's essential that you document everything as evidence. Lock it down as tight as you can. He may not have kidnapped and murdered anyone directly, but he's just as guilty."

He was halfway to the door when he turned back again. "Gerard, get your security team to protect Heather. Do it now, and keep them with her until the police arrive. It hadn't occurred to me that there could be danger to her, but until we have the guy in custody, I fear it's a possibility."

Outside, he cursed the unhurried pace of the cart and the tram, taking comfort in the fact that they wouldn't move any faster for Peter Sobol.

Chapter 16

Yuri Melnikov, floating near his desk chair in his Corridor 62 office, eyed Stan Shevchenko and Roscoe Antonov. They'd just returned from Armstrong and had come to give their report.

"Roscoe bought us ten days," said Stan, holding on to a cabinet to stop his drift. "Even that was a challenge."

"Oh?" Yuri looked at Roscoe.

"Stan and I measured everything. Checked tolerances. Compared specs. The company did an excellent job with fabrication and construction. The only issue I could find is that they bolted the sift plates to the frame instead of welding them. They did it to make maintenance cheaper and easier for us. I insisted they follow our specs. It buys us ten days while they fix it, but six months from now during the maintenance cycle, we'll need to cut the plates out and grind off the welds. It will be an expensive and time-consuming hassle." Roscoe shook his head. "They couldn't understand why I'd want that but I insisted. I think they suspect that something is off."

"But we got the ten days?"

"We did," confirmed Stan.

"Good job, Roscoe. I knew you could do it. You can get back to work while Stan and I figure out how to use that time to our advantage."

Yuri watched while Roscoe floated to the exit. When the door shut, he turned to Stan. "I'd hoped we were done, but the only way I can see getting the last three million is from someone on the list. And given the time frame, it needs to be someone local."

"That's risky as hell, boss. The Lagrange patrol is all over this."

"I'm not happy about it. But the choices are to walk away and lose our hard work, or cash out one last account and finish the job. I'm open to ideas if you can see another way."

Stan shrugged and shook his head.

"I've identified two good candidates, a man and a woman. Both have solid profiles: they live alone, no pets, reasonably mobile, no children living in the cities, healthy account balances."

"How much do they weigh?"

"The man is as fat as Roscoe. The woman is frail, less than a hundred pounds on Earth."

"Grandkids?"

"The man has two grandchildren living somewhere in Lagrange. The woman has one."

"With the heat on us, that's the big worry."

"I agree." Yuri let the silence develop.

"How far from a utility entrance?

"The man is half a block closer, but it's less than two blocks for both."

"I'll take the old lady, then," said Stan. "I'll probably be able to hide her in a pack and carry her. I'd need a crate for him."

"I figured you'd choose her. Her name is Francesca Sophia. She lives in Elmore Manor, apartment twenty-four. That's on Strip S-11 on Hermes' Luna Deck."

Chapter 17

C uss found himself pacing as the *Nelly Marie* made the return trip to Hermes.

The Armstrong police had cornered Peter Sobol in the industrial district outside Armstrong, with Port Collins his only way off-world. After they'd locked down the spaceport, it became a waiting game, one that could stretch out for hours and possibly days.

Cuss had been helping as they searched the district, the noose tightening, when Ygo reported an important discovery: prior to Yuri Melnikov's mysterious disappearance, his activities had included meetings in Trenton, New Jersey, with Stan Shevchenko and Roscoe Antonov, and arranging to travel from there to Lagrange. That led to deeper questions about Roscoe's involvement in the crime spree, and *that* led to questions about the Factory, a place neither Cuss nor Ygo had considered when searching for Robert Moore, Franklin Wallingford, or the pilot Rex Luskin.

"How did we look past it for so long?" he asked as he paced, furious with himself for missing something so obvious. He'd decided to leave Sobol's capture in the capable hands of the Armstrong police while he and Ygo raced back to correct the oversight.

"I am truly mortified," said Ygo.

Ygo's distress made Cuss wish he hadn't said "we" in his rant. "To be fair to us, it's been less than a week since this whole thing started, and we've been in reaction mode from the beginning. There hasn't been much time to sit back and think about anything."

"Still, it's inexcusable."

The Factory was a huge facility hovering a short distance from the tube cities. It was a chaotic place with moving machinery, molten rock, and hazardous chemicals. Because of the danger, it was highly automated, run by specialized robots and a small crew of human workers. And just the way a workshop in the backyard might be overlooked in the first pass when a home is searched, the Factory was a detached facility off to the side, an outbuilding in the largest sense, something separate that the eye subconsciously erased because it marred the view.

Which made it the perfect place to hide things.

Sensors had shown Rex Luskin riding a Skeeter out of the Hermes passenger port after killing Agnes Ming. They'd assumed he'd met up with a larger ship and escaped. But personal craft could easily reach the Factory. In fact, that's how most workers and visitors got out there.

A chime signaled. Cuss saw Darlena was calling. He stopped his pacing.

"We have Peter Sobol in custody," she announced.

"Congratulations! Hopefully, he won't get bail."

"He doesn't get a hearing until tomorrow. We'll have to see."

"Is Heather Frierson safe?"

"We'll watch her for a few more days, but there's

nothing to indicate that she's in danger."

"I hope not." When Darlena didn't speak, Cuss continued. "Was she able to find anything that linked Sobol and the list to Yuri Melnikov?"

"Not that I've heard. I know she tried."

"Damn. Did Gerard Mark at least have her document Sobol's involvement?"

"He did. And to his credit, Mark's lawyers were all over him about potential blowback to the company. They fear lawsuits for restitution of funds, wrongful death, negligence, stuff like that. But in the end, he was more interested in punishing the bad guy than protecting his own ass."

"Society needs more people like him."

"Speaking of good deeds, we'll need you to testify. Between Sobol and Smitty Shellback's killers, it will take a chunk of your time."

"Trust me, it will be my pleasure."

They spoke for another minute, and then she closed the call.

Cuss blew out through pursed lips, his frustrations mounting. Without evidence showing that Sobol gave the list to Yuri Melnikov, then Sobol could simply deny it ever happened. The link between the two men would be circumstantial. And that would complicate convicting him of accessory to murder.

"Do you think you could find how Sobol got the list to Yuri?" Cuss asked Ygo.

"Not likely. There are just too many ways it could happen, many of them low-tech. It could be something as simple as him handing Melnikov a piece of paper. I'll do my best, though."

Slumping into the pilot's seat, Cuss took a folded sheet from his pocket and counted names. The original list that Sobol had created included one hundred fifty-three people who had at least two million common invested with Lewiston-Mark and who had a Semident 318 implant they still used for authentication.

Ygo had sifted through it, keeping those who fit certain requirements: they lived alone, lived on either Nova Terra or Lagrange, and were still breathing. Agnes Ming and Kaycee Gibbons had been removed. Others had died from natural causes. Most on the original list resided on Earth.

The shortened list had thirty-eight people, including Robert Moore and Franklin Wallingford, leaving thirty-six potential targets.

"How far have you gotten in checking up on them?"

"I'm almost done. I've been able to locate everyone but Anton Agyemang. He lives in Aldrin and dropped from sight two days after Kaycee Gibbons. My instincts are that he's another victim, but I haven't finished checking the possibilities. I'll let you know."

With time to kill, Cuss called Hatha. No answer. He owed himself sleep but was too wired to rest. So, he burned through his energy with an intense workout, three bouts of Street Fighting Full Contact, where he scrapped against a projected opponent controlled by Ygo. It was a no-holds-barred fighting game, a realistic visual and tactile interaction that honed his practical skills, both offensive and defensive, while working every part of his body.

As always, Ygo slapped and punched and kicked him to near submission, forcing Cuss to fight with everything he had. When Ygo felt Cuss had earned it, he backed off enough to let him win in the end. Cuss was aware that Ygo allowed him to take the victory. But Ygo hadn't made it easy, requiring him to employ a broad range of skills, practice different moves, and exercise all the muscle groups before receiving the reward.

As the *Nelly Marie* neared Lagrange, Cuss looked at the Factory through a viewport and then switched to the huge display in front of the pilot's seat so he could study it with Ygo.

At one level, the Factory, a floating cylinder covered with sheets of iridescent photovoltaic material, looked like a small version of a tube city, similar to how some toolsheds were constructed to look like miniature versions of the house they sat behind. It was two kilometers long and half a kilometer across. A big difference, however, was that the Factory had a maw at one end that ate asteroids. One was being slowly consumed as they watched.

"Giant jaws are taking bites out of the end inside the Factory," said Ygo, "chewing the asteroid chunks into manageable pieces, and swallowing those into a massive thermochemical digester."

The view switched to a side view of the Factory. A seam along its length was slowly feeding out a sheet of material like a printer fed out paper. "The equipment inside forms the digested asteroid into huge sheets of condensate composite, readying it for use in construction."

"How big is that?" asked Cuss of the material growing out from the seam.

"It creates kilometer-wide sheets, curved into sections that will form a cylinder. When they've made enough pieces, bots fuse them together."

"It looks like a toy."

"It does, but when you approach it, you'll see that it's huge. And the challenge is that the inside is a massive hive. The structure isn't organized into understandable decks like the cities. It's a maze of industrial equipment on a huge scale. The number of places to hide a prisoner are as high as you can count. And while it's packed with hundreds of thousands of sensors, almost all of them are focused on the equipment so the staff can see what's happening and make sure it's operating correctly. That leaves lots of nooks and cubbies we can't see. And in that monster, what I'm calling a nook could fit ten *Nelly Maries* with room to spare."

"We need a guide. Roscoe must have a boss we could talk to."

"Oh, lots of bosses. He works for a corporation, after all. Most of them are on Earth, though. Here on site, Roscoe Antonov is head of production. He has an equal, Jada Lorenz, who is head of planning. Their immediate boss is Rhonda Kilkenny, who is Factory manager. Both Lorenz and Kilkenny are desk jockeys, though. They spend their days in an office in Apollo."

"Let's start with the Factory manager. She should be able to identify a guide who can lead us around." He had a thought. "Will we need a warrant?"

"No. The Factory itself is owned by the Lagrange

Compact, so wandering through it is like wandering through one of the cities. The corporation that runs the place, Stratus Interworld Partners, does so under contract from the Compact, so in the end, they work for us."

"Would you reach out to the manager and get an appointment? I'll contact Juan and have him meet us there."

"Do you want to meet her at her office or at the Factory?"

"Let's start at her office. If Roscoe is up to his eyeballs in this like I suspect, there's no point in tipping him off any earlier than necessary."

As the *Nelly Marie* lined up for landing in Hermes' passenger port, Cuss felt his exhaustion catch up with him. "Would you mind taking her in? I'm going to hit the sack. We'll start fresh in the morning."

. . .

The next morning, as Cuss stepped from the pod onto Apollo's Deck 2, he enjoyed the sunrise illusion overhead. It promised to be another beautiful day in the city, one he was starting with Juan over breakfast so they could catch up and plan before their meeting with Factory manager Rhonda Kilkenny.

The pedestrian thoroughfare was uncrowded at this hour, permitting him to enjoy the sights. Apollo had been completed twenty years after Hermes, and the most obvious difference was that vegetation was much less prevalent here. Few of the buildings were covered in the foliage found in the other tube cities, a controversial decision, as much a battle of tradition as technology. The city required fewer plantings because it had been built with redundant, distributed oxygen generators, next-generation units that had the full confidence of the engineers, even in emergency situations including shell breach and power loss.

And with the buildings uncovered, their features became more important to the view. Though they were still constructed of dyed condensate composite, Apollo's building façades included moldings, flutings, sills, columns, and other decorations to add interest and further differentiate one structure from the next.

Up ahead, though, the Stratus building had few such embellishments, as if it were the last unoccupied building in the project, chosen by the company the way cooks will choose the imperfect serving from a dish for themselves.

Cuss was the first to arrive, and when he turned to look for Juan, he saw the man approaching from behind, a smile on his face. They shook hands as they greeted each other, then Cuss tilted his head toward Aunt Meg's Diner situated diagonally from the Stratus building. "Sound good?"

Inside, they took a booth with red pleated cushions and a white laminate tabletop under a window that looked out onto the pedestrian thoroughfare. The retro look continued with a counter in the center that ran the length of the diner, topped with the same white laminate. A row of pedestal seats lined up in front of the counter, chairs covered in red pleated fabric perched atop shiny poles with chrome footrests.

Behind the counter, the cook worked away, his metal

spatula singing as he scooped and flipped eggs and hash browns and pancakes and bacon and sausage. The smells created by the maestro working his cooktop made Cuss's mouth water.

A waitress in her twenties, cute, friendly, dressed in a white outfit that could have doubled as a nurses uniform, approached with two mugs and a carafe. "Coffee, gentlemen?"

Famished, Cuss ordered the Hungry Diner's breakfast, which included some of everything on the griddle plus grits. Juan was less ambitious, sticking with an omelet and toast.

As they sipped their coffee, Cuss lamented their oversight of the Factory.

"I was thinking that the mayor even rubbed my nose in it," said Juan, looking into the distance. "Remember when we were at the farm looking at Agnes Ming in the soybeans, and she threatened me by saying she'd have me patrolling the Factory if I didn't toe the line? Maybe that's why I put it out of my head."

"What made her come around and support your move to Terra Deck?"

"I don't know if she had anything to do with it. I need a partner, there's an opening on Terra, my clearance rate is strong, and you upped my profile by picking Debra and me for this case."

"Well congrats, whatever the reason." Cuss lifted his mug to toast the occasion and sipped.

"So what's our play with Stratus?" asked Juan.

"Have you ever been inside the Factory?"

"No. You?"

"No. We need to go out and poke around, see if we can find Moore and Franklin, or even indications that they've been there. But from what I hear, someone needs to guide us. I'm told it's big, confusing, and dangerous if you don't know what you're doing."

As they ate, Cuss brought Juan up to date on his trip to Nova Terra, including the death of Smitty Shellback, that Anders Johansson had revealed Yuri Melnikov's name during interrogation, and that Peter Sobol was responsible for the list of targets, but linking him to the kidnappings remained a challenge. "When I learned that Yuri and Roscoe Antonov were hometown buddies, that they'd been seen hanging out together, and that Roscoe oversaw operations at the Factory, it came together. Now I'm anxious to confirm what my instincts are screaming."

Juan checked the time and took a last sip. "Let's go find out."

Chapter 18

F actory manager Rhonda Kilkenny welcomed Cuss and Juan to her office on the eighth floor of the Stratus building. She was a friendly person, professional in her demeanor, with a powerful build, the kind that required regular visits to a gym. Her office was all business, with institutional furniture and minimal personal effects, as if she'd settled into temporary digs years ago and simply never bothered to make it her own.

A small meeting table sat next to her desk with two guest chairs tucked beneath. She motioned to it. "Please, Detectives, get comfortable." She dragged her desk chair over, asking, "I understand you have questions about the Factory?"

"We do," said Cuss. "Is it Roscoe Antonov who runs it for Stratus?"

"He's the head of production. Why do you ask?"

"What kind of employee is he?"

"Good. Solid. Gets the job done, which is most important. Works well with others both above and below him in the org chart. Moderately ambitious but not the hardest charger. Never been in trouble with the law. He wouldn't have his job otherwise. Why, did he do something?"

"How about recently? Has his attitude changed? His

work ethic? Anything like that?"

She paused to think, pressing her lips together as she did so. "He went through a funk for a few months a while back. He had this plan to recover precious metals from the condensate slurry—silver, gold, platinum. It was a good idea, but Corporate said no. I agreed with him that they were leaving money on the table. Told my boss we should do it. But we've recently started production for Hera, the fifth city of Lagrange, and Corporate doesn't want to do anything that could risk changing our condensate characteristics or production volumes even a little bit. We have a difficult deadline over the next four years, and anything that takes our eye off the ball is a nonstarter. It was all explained to him, but he sulked. Why, what did he do?"

"What was he doing in Nova Terra yesterday?"

"Yesterday? I'll be honest with you. At his level, I don't follow his schedule that closely." She tapped the table, and when a display appeared, one only she could see, she commanded, "Show me Roscoe's calendar." A pause. "He was on vacation the last two days." She looked at Cuss. "Apparently he went to the Moon. Did he do something there?"

Cuss looked at Juan before continuing. "We suspect that some unsavory characters might be using the Factory as a base to conduct illegal activities. We're planning to search it to see if that's true. But if we ask Roscoe to help us, we need to know he's clean. I mean, if he works over there and our hunch is correct, it seems like he would know. The last thing we want is to ask the fox for a tour of the henhouse."

Rhonda laughed. It seemed genuine to Cuss. "I've worked with Roscoe for six years, and I can't see him involved in anything illegal. He has a gentle nature. He follows company rules. Hell, he could have said he was going to Nova Terra on business, and I would have believed him. The company would have paid for it. But he took vacation. Does that sound like an unsavory character? What kind of business are these people running?"

"Could people hide out there without Roscoe knowing?"

"In the Factory? The inside is huge and chaotic. You could hide a dozen criminal enterprises in there without any of us knowing. The shell is a cylinder that's two kilometers long and half a kilometer across. And it's stuffed with huge machines that can eat an asteroid and spit out a perfect sheet of condensate, hour after hour, day after day. The Factory doesn't spin, so it's weightless inside. And it's harsh and nasty." She tugged on an earlobe, thinking. "The shell isn't pressurized, which means they'd have to wear a suit when they move about out there. How big is this operation?"

"How do your employees manage?" asked Juan.

"What do you mean?"

"How do they work in a dangerous place with no air or gravity?"

"Oh. There are sixty-four office corridors spread inside the structure, habitable spaces that are insulated, pressurized, and temperature regulated. Places to meet, work, eat, whatever you might need. You don't need a suit if you're in one of those. They also serve as rally points if people need to get to safety for some reason."

"Are all of them occupied?"

"Heavens no. They were full when the Factory was being built and are well used during the occasional maintenance shutdown. But most of them sit empty during regular production."

"Is that how you're running now?" asked Cuss.

She nodded. "That's right."

"Could we shut down the plant before we started searching? Reduce the danger to those involved?"

"Whew." She sat back. "It takes three months to get the plant started up and lined out after a shutdown, so we only do it when we have no choice. That alone costs over seven million common to pay for human labor, additives, specialized equipment, skilled bots. If it happens when a sheet is being rolled, we lose the whole sheet, magnifying the loss. Corporate would be calling on everyone with influence to block the move. And if you did succeed in shutting it down, they'd be screaming even louder to get the startup operation underway as soon as possible."

The answer frustrated Cuss because it made the deaths sound like inconveniences more than criminal outrages. A question of profit and loss.

"Can you see inside the corridors from here?"

"Certainly." She flicked her hand and said, "Give us a brief tour of Corridor 1 at the Factory."

A display opened, hovering above the table, positioned so they all could see. The view was from the end of a hallway, a miniature version in full dimension, as if a person holding a holoview was conducting the tour for them.

They could see a branch in the hall to the left but not on the right. Straight ahead, the hall had five doors down its length on the left, sturdy portals spaced equally along the way. The right side of the hall was a solid wall colored an off-white. Repeating geometric figures—a square, a circle, a triangle—were attached to it in an artistic fashion, perhaps installed during construction as a form of inexpensive decoration. Or maybe an employee put them up one day when they were bored, hoping to give the place some visual interest. There was a sixth door at the very end of the hall, facing them, also closed.

The floor had a gray industrial covering, the nap too short to be called carpeting, perhaps best described as matting. A drop ceiling overhead allowed easy access to the pipes, wires, and ducts above while hiding them in the interim.

The tour began with a look to the left. The branch in the hallway turned out to be a changing room. The back of the room had seven tall cubbies in a row, five holding spacesuits, the other two empty, revealing the hooks used to hold the suits in place. The spacesuits looked similar to the grav suits Cuss and Juan had worn up to the farm, though these included gloves and a flex helmet as part of their assembly.

One side of the changing room had benches in front of storage lockers. The lockers were separated into two groups along the wall, split by a door labeled *Toilet*. The other side held two cleansing boxes designed for use in zero gravity, with a mirror on the wall between them.

"Do those empty hooks mean someone is wearing those suits now?" asked Cuss.

"I believe so." She paused. "I suppose they could be draped over a chair in someone's office. Or maybe out for cleaning or repair. I guess we'd have to ask Roscoe or someone over there to be sure."

"Is this live or a simulation?" asked Juan.

"It's live. This is what's happening right now."

The tour returned to the hallway, and they moved down to the first door on the left. The image seemed to melt through the door to provide a view of a small office on the other side. It had the same floor covering and drop ceiling as the hallway. There were closed cabinets along one wall, and a large discussion board with writing and doodles filling another. The image of the back of the office where a desk might be was blurred, making it impossible for them to discern what was there.

"That means somebody is sitting at the desk," said Rhonda. "Probably Marta; I think this is her office. The system won't show a person without first making an announcement and then waiting a minimum of one minute before unblurring. After the announcement, the occupant can request an additional four minutes. It's company policy. No one wants to be spied on."

"Could you override it? Command it to show us anyway?"

"I've never tried, and honestly, I don't want to. It would break trust."

Cuss let it go. The tour continued.

No one was in the next four offices. Two had writing

on the discussion boards and personal effects stuck to the desks, suggesting the occupants were out and perhaps explaining the missing spacesuits. The other two had a vacant feel, with no evidence of occupation or use at all.

At the end of the hall, the view melted through the door to show a bigger office with blue carpet instead of the gray matting. It had pictures on the wall and extras like a meeting table similar to the one they sat at now. Cuss could tell that the desk in back was larger, even with the blur.

"This is Roscoe's office, so that's probably him. Do you want to meet him?"

"Can you talk to him while we watch?" asked Cuss.

"No, the system will show him everyone who's here in the room with me."

"Let it go, then. We'd like to meet him in person for our first encounter."

After that, they toured Corridors 2 through 4 where they saw an identical layout, though only Corridor 2 had employees occupying the offices.

Rhonda sat back and looked at them. "Is that enough to get the gist?"

"We'd like to look at all of them," said Cuss. "See if any are inhabited by non-Stratus employees."

"Yikes." She checked the time. "That will take close to ninety minutes. I hadn't budgeted that long for our meeting."

"I could show you later," Ygo told Cuss. "But if we include Juan, he'll have questions."

"Could you set us up in a spare office, and we'll go through it ourselves?" asked Cuss as the tour of Corridor 5 began.

"Tell you what. You stay here and watch. I have to touch base with my assistant, and I'll do that in his office. I should be back in twenty minutes or so." She stood. "Does that sound okay?"

"Perfect," said Cuss, eyes focused on the show.

After Rhonda left, they continued to watch.

"By the way," said Juan. "I'm almost finished with questioning staff at the ports. So far the only positive responses have come from two people working Hermes' passenger port. When I showed them pictures of Rex Luskin, both replied with something along the lines of, 'He looks familiar.' But they didn't know where or when they might have seen him. The detectives in the other cities came up dry as well."

Cuss shrugged. "It was worth a try."

They watched what looked like a repeating loop of empty corridors and began picking out something distinctive in each one that confirmed it was unique: the arrangement of suits in the cubbies, a scuff on the wall, a tear in the hallway matting, a name tag stuck to a door.

Fighting boredom, they played the "there's something different" game until they reached Corridor 33, and then the display went dark. They sat up in their chairs.

Corridor 34 was also dark. Not as though lights were off, but like no signal was coming through.

"I can't tell what the problem is," said Ygo. "It could be equipment failure, a bad circuit, a broken connection…"

"I wonder if someone disconnected a link on purpose?" said Cuss aloud.

"Could be," said Juan. "Rhonda might know what's going on."

"Yes," said Ygo. "It could be deliberate as well."

The tour had reached Corridor 51 when Rhonda returned. All of them had been dark since Corridor 33. "Sorry, that took much longer than I'd expected." She saw that the display was blank. "You're done already?"

They told her the problem.

"Now *I* want to go over and see what's going on."

Cuss sat back in his chair as he mulled options, then looked at Juan. "How about if we invite Roscoe over here, and I'll have a long chat with him. While he's occupied, you lead a team over to the Factory to see what you can see."

Juan nodded. "I can do that. I'll get a few patrol officers for backup."

"Maybe reach out to your new partner. Sorry, I forget her name."

"Wanda Piccolo." Juan bit his lip as he thought, then nodded. "That's a good idea. Let me call her and see if she's available." He stood up and looked at Rhonda. "Is there someplace private?"

"Sure, follow me."

Cuss called to Rhonda as she led Juan out, "Please come back after you show him. I have more questions." When they were gone, Cuss asked Ygo. "What do you think?"

"They'll need an employee over there to show them around. But we don't want civilians out front. Juan will need to be careful how he handles that."

Rhonda returned, and as she retook her seat, Cuss

asked her, "We need someone who knows the equipment to help Juan. Someone who can tell us what's causing the signal loss and if it's deliberate sabotage or a legitimate equipment issue."

"George Hall is our comms lead. The sensor suite is part of his portfolio."

"Is he a supervisor? We need someone hands-on who really knows the tech."

"He's both. He was hands-on until last year and then got promoted. We always call him when there's an issue of this sort. He has a real can-do attitude."

"Good. You offered to join us as well, but I'm hesitant to include more civilians than necessary on this first pass. Does George know his way around?"

She nodded. "Better than I do. When he was commissioning the sensors after installation, he had to visit every corner of the Factory to review the work."

"I'm going to ask that you stay here, then. Think of a reason why Roscoe needs to come over to see you. Once Juan confirms his timing, you can call and make sure Roscoe is over here."

"Will I actually be meeting with him?"

"No, I'll intercept him on the flight deck and talk to him privately."

. . .

Ivan Kosmin had just climbed into the Sprite utility spacecraft on the Factory's small flight deck when he realized he needed to pee. Stan Shevchenko had departed in the van a few minutes earlier to fetch the rich lady from Hermes. Ivan's job was to fly the utility craft to Apollo and bring back the doctor, the one who would expose the old bird's money wire buried in her neck.

With pressure building on his bladder, he checked the time and concluded that even if he used five minutes to take off his suit and five more to put it back on, he could still stay mostly on schedule. And that way he wouldn't have to squirm on the short flight over to Apollo.

Pushing off the vehicle, he floated to the ready room airlock and the bathroom inside. He stepped out of the suit, glad no one was there to judge him, especially Yuri Melnikov. Ever since Rex Luskin had paid the ultimate price for fucking up with Agnes Ming, Ivan had been walking on eggshells.

To Ivan's credit, he'd been praised for his success in snatching Robert Moore from Armstrong and transporting him here to the Factory. And this was his third trip fetching the doctor, the previous two without incident. But when the penalty for a mistake was being tossed into a Factory feed port, it made him second guess everything he did.

Down to his street clothes, he floated into the bathroom stall and hooked his feet into the stirrups to keep himself stationary. As he unbuttoned his pants, his gun floated out of his pocket, a semiautomatic with nanostructured honeycomb construction, fitted grip, and smart activation. It was the weapon he used to persuade the doctor to behave. He grabbed the gun out of the air before it could become contaminated with other people's toilet germs. Twirling it once around his index finger, he shoved it back into his pants pocket.

He peed into the vacuum hose, and when he was done, he used the suction to toy with his dick, wondering if he had time to rub one out. Thoughts of Rex and the feed port dampened his ardor, and he fastened up and exited the stall.

A man was there, stepping into a spacesuit.

"Hi," said the stranger, a short, stocky, friendly chap with a smile under his mustache. He had one hand on the overhead stabilizing bar, a length of pipe put there so people could orient themselves and pull themselves about.

"Hello," said Ivan, avoiding eye contact. He floated to his own suit and started to dress.

"You're with Trenton Consulting out in Corridor Sixty-two, right? How's the project going?"

"We're making good progress," Ivan said cautiously, pushing his feet into the suit, cursing himself for his bad luck.

"I'm George, by the way." The man stuck out his hand to shake. "George Hall."

"Rex Luskin," said Ivan, using the only name he could think of in the moment that wasn't his own. "Good to meet you."

They both worked on suiting up for a minute. Then George said, "Hey, are your feeds working out in Sixty-two? We've had reports of problems with some of the corridors."

"Feeds?" Ivan didn't know what he was talking about and struggled to get the suit on so he could end the conversation.

"Yeah. Can you get sensor data from the plant on your

displays? See camera video? All that?"

"I'm an assistant, mostly a courier who gets what they need. I don't do any of the things you mention."

George went quiet for a moment as he pulled his suit up over his hips but then perked up. "Any chance you've seen people out your way who don't belong? We've had reports of a crew squatting somewhere out in the Factory, using it as a home base for illegal activity."

The question made Ivan desperate to finish dressing. He yanked hard on the suit to get it up over his hips, the sudden motion jogging his gun loose. It floated lazily in the air between them.

"What's that?" George froze in place, staring at the weapon.

"It's nothing." Ivan lurched for it, but weightlessness and the spacesuit hanging off his lower torso made his movements awkward. The gun bounced from his palm before he could close his grip, and it caromed off the ceiling. Luck was on his side, though. It rebounded in his direction, and this time he snagged it.

"You aren't a contractor," said George, his tone making it an accusation. The man locked eyes with Ivan, then turned toward the door, the movement causing his hand to slip from the overhead bar. He swam frantically, trying to reach it to regain leverage.

"Stop," Ivan barked, pointing the gun to add threat to his command. "Don't move."

George ignored him. With a lunge, he stretched and snagged the bar. Yanking hard, he sent himself zipping toward the exit.

"Stop!" Ivan yelled it this time. He couldn't let the man leave, but there was no way he could reach him in time to prevent his escape.

With seconds to act, he used the only option he could see in the moment. He pulled the trigger. While his gun was a beauty, it didn't have options like drop or stun. It was a traditional weapon, a simple tool, the kind that propelled bullets with an explosive charge.

Ivan's hand kicked as the gun barked a sharp report. A small hole appeared in the side of George's abdomen. Blood squirted out at the moment of impact, and then it began to flow, a red splotch spreading across his shirt. The man cried out and gripped the wound, his face a mask of fear and shock. Blood oozed through his fingers.

Feeling he had no choice, Ivan shot him a second time in the chest. George stopped all movement and went slack. The impact of the bullet started the lifeless body in a slow spin, his arms spreading out as he drifted.

Viewing his handiwork, Ivan panicked. Yuri and Stan would be furious. He couldn't let them find out. Ever.

The blood that squirted out at the moment of impact now drifted in the air. Ivan floated over to the bathroom, grabbed a huge wad of tissue, and waved it about, trying to collect as much of the gore as he could. After a hurried effort, he moved to the body and pressed tissue on the wounds themselves before they could add to the mess.

Flipping himself over, he hooked his feet through the bar to give himself stability while leaving his hands free and started the task of wrestling George the rest of the way into the suit. It was hard enough getting himself into one, and he'd expected it to be all but impossible to do so for a dead person. But George already had his legs inside and the suit pulled up to his hips. The weightless environment made it relatively easy to move him about to complete the task.

Ivan made a last attempt at gathering drops with a wad of tissue. Then he focused on dressing himself.

He needed to dispose of the body before anyone came, before Yuri or Stan learned what he'd done. His first thought was to stuff the body in the toilet stall, but he realized it would be discovered in no time, bringing swarms of police to the Factory.

Then he considered throwing it into the feed port. There, the body would be carried along in a tumble of asteroid dust to a molten pool of rock that would erase the corpse forever. But it was a long trip from the flight deck back to the port, creating too much opportunity for discovery. And getting close to the huge machinery made him anxious. Even scared.

So he decided to toss George into the vastness of space. The body would continue to exist that way, floating forever in the void. But the odds of someone finding it were not much different from someone finding a particular grain of sand hidden along the coastline of Florida. He'd take those odds and sleep well.

With suits on, Ivan put an arm around George and, like escorting a drunken buddy, floated him on to the flight deck and over to the utility vehicle. The craft, a brown tube, looked like a big cigar lying on its side. The end of the ship where the ash would be held the main thruster, a black nozzle shaped like a lampshade. Around the body of the vehicle were a dozen more nozzles, small stabilizing thrusters the size of champagne flutes. Like a car, the viewport at the front looked something like a windshield, though with no air in space, there was no wind to deflect. Also like a car, the craft had a door on each side.

He opened the passenger door and guided George into the seat. Then he hand-walked himself over the top of the vessel, climbed in the driver's side, and secured himself with the seat's safety harness.

"Open the bay door," he commanded the pilot's console, his heart pounding. Through the front viewport, he watched a corrugated door twenty-five meters across roll up onto an overhead spool. Too flimsy to maintain pressure, its purpose was to keep people and things from drifting off the flight deck and into space.

When there was enough clearance, he pushed on the joystick, and the craft edged forward. Piloting manually, he guided the craft off the flight deck and away from the Factory and the cities, as if he were in a boat leaving harbor and heading out into open waters. He flew along for a full minute. Then, while the craft coasted, he leaned over the body, opened the passenger door, and pushed George out.

After closing the door, he let the ship take over, commanding, "Take me to the Apollo passenger port." The small thrusters fired in sequence to turn the craft around, and then the rear thruster fired to start him toward his destination. George Hall continued floating in the other direction, drifting off into the solar system where he would orbit the sun for millennia.

With that done, Ivan exhaled a sigh of relief and put

the incident out of his mind, concentrating on the task of retrieving the doctor. The display in front of him said he was twenty minutes behind schedule. "I've been that late even when I didn't need to dump a body," he said aloud, using the sound of his voice to further calm his nerves.

As he zipped past the Factory on his way to Apollo, the bay door was again closed. So he didn't see that he'd been lucky enough to miss Roscoe Antonov, who was prepping a Skeeter to fly to Hermes for an in-person meeting with his boss, Rhonda Kilkenny.

Chapter 19

The boarding team that Juan had organized met with Cuss in a rally room at the rear of Hermes' flight deck. They floated in a group, holding on to stabilizing bars to keep themselves oriented, talking quietly among themselves. Everyone but Cuss wore a bright-blue spacesuit with the words *Community Patrol* printed in large white letters across the back and a gold badge embroidered over the heart in front. Their flex helmets, attached to the back of their suits at the neck, were off their heads and hovering behind them.

Juan had found four patrol officers to help, and Wanda Piccolo had flown over from Demeter. Juan introduced her to Cuss, who was dressed in his own uniform: black pants, a blue collared shirt, and a gray blazer.

Because she wore a suit, all he could see of Wanda was her head. He guessed she was about his age. She wasn't feminine in a traditional sense. No makeup, no jewelry, eyebrows fuller than most women's, her hair styled in a short fade. But her features were soft, her eyes bright, her warmth genuine. She had the kind of smile that hinted that she knew things about him. Secrets she'd keep in confidence.

"Hello, Cuss," she said, shaking his hand. She had a firm grip and made good eye contact. "Nice to meet you."

"I hear that you and Juan are to be partners."

"It becomes official next week, but I'm excited to get started early, especially if it means bringing kidnappers and murderers to justice."

"With that attitude, you and Juan will make a powerful team."

Ygo spoke. "Roscoe just left the Factory. He'll be here in twelve minutes."

They had arranged for Roscoe come to Hermes rather than Apollo for what he thought was a special meeting with Rhonda Kilkenny. It made it easier to coordinate the different parts of the operation.

Cuss moved back and raised his voice. "Okay, everyone." He waited for the chatter to cease. "The man I'm questioning has left the Factory and is on his way here. So in a few moments, you'll board the bus and lie low. After I move him off the flight deck, you'll fly to the Factory. Your mission has two tasks. One is to protect George Hall. He'll be waiting for you when you arrive. Make sure no harm comes to him as he works to restore sensor links. We don't know that he'll be in any danger. But we don't know why the links are down, either."

He paused to let them digest his words before continuing. "The second task is to look for people or things that don't belong. We think a crew is operating out of the Factory, kidnapping people, performing surgery on them, holding them prisoner. Keep alert for anything that looks like a prison cell or a makeshift medical facility. Anything that seems out of place."

He motioned to Juan. "Detective Luisa is your team

leader and will give final assignments. We're told that it's dangerous to move about over there, so work in pairs and look out for each other. Be smart. Don't take risks. Don't venture off where you don't understand."

One of the officers raised a hand. "Should we confront suspects? Arrest them? Just observe?"

"Call for reinforcements if you find something that sends your antenna up. Detain them if you can do it without putting yourself in danger. We may pull you early depending on how the questioning goes here. So stay in contact and follow Juan's lead."

"Five minutes," said Ygo.

Cuss signaled he was done with a wave. "Good luck, everyone." He followed them out and watched them float over to the bus, an unmarked box-like craft big enough to hold a dozen people plus equipment.

Then he switched his attention to the airlock. Roscoe was riding a Skeeter, so Cuss anticipated he would land in the small airlock on the left side of the flight deck. Cuss drifted over to the shuttle ramp near there and waited.

Like its larger cousin, the small airlock was two muscular gray metal doors positioned at each end of a tunnel. The doors were rigged so only one door could be open at a time, ensuring that the life-giving air on the flight deck remained trapped inside, preventing it from rushing out into the void.

As Cuss mentally prepared to confront Roscoe, motors whirred, air hissed, and the inner door of the airlock slid open. Like the curtain opening on a stage play, it pulled back to reveal a shuttle down from Luna Deck. He watched a mechanism hook the shuttle and pull it over to the loading platform for passenger debarkation. The airlock door slid closed with a hiss.

It cycled again, this time revealing two small utility vehicles from one of the other cities. They sputtered forward and parked in the zone on the flight deck reserved for small craft. The airlock door closed.

It cycled again, this time revealing a fat man on a Skeeter, the spacecraft equivalent of a motorcycle.

"There he is," said Ygo.

Roscoe rode over to small-craft parking, shut down the Skeeter, and removed his space suit, draping it over the machine. He turned, pushed off from an upright post at the corner of the parking area, and floated like a parade balloon toward the door where Cuss waited.

Cuss had been considering two possible locations for his interview with Roscoe and didn't like either. One was an interrogation room at a Community Patrol station. But he worried that the formal setting would cause the man to demand a lawyer, and that would muck up the works, ensuring Cuss didn't learn anything.

The other was on board the *Nelly Marie* for a private interview. He could use the seclusion to push boundaries in ways he couldn't in a public setting, to color outside the lines. But he didn't want the slime bag anywhere near his living quarters, so he nixed the idea.

As the man approached, Cuss chose a new plan. He'd use the rally room at the back of the flight deck, the one the group had just vacated.

"Excuse me," he said to Roscoe as the man

approached the door.

Roscoe, lost in thought, turned his head to look but didn't seem to register the interaction.

Cuss retrieved his badge wallet from his inside coat pocket and held it out. "I'm Marshal Abbott. I need a word with you."

Roscoe froze, but in the weightless environment, he kept drifting forward. He thumped into the wall, and Cuss reached out a hand to steady him.

"Let's go where we can talk in private."

Cuss could see Roscoe's initial confusion turn to understanding and then panic. It showed in his face, in his eyes, in the movement of his hands.

Pointing with his chin, Cuss continued. "See on the back wall the words *Rally Point* in black lettering? Go through that door. Ignore the warnings about alarms. Wait in the hallway, and I'll meet you there in five minutes. I'll be taking a different route to get there in case your accomplices are watching."

Roscoe finally succeeded in mustering a response. He started with indignation. "What are you talking about? I'm not going anywhere but to see my boss."

Cuss gave him a cold stare. "Your partners are unforgiving, Roscoe Antonov. If Yuri Melnikov hears that you are cooperating with the Marshals Service, he will kill you."

Roscoe turned red, hesitated, and then rephrased his earlier response. "I don't know what you're talking about." Adding, "I'm not going to talk to you, because I have nothing to say."

"You don't understand. I'll make him think you're cooperating. I'll leak it to him in a believable way. You'll be dead by the weekend." He paused to let the threat fester, but not so long that Roscoe could muster his emotions yet again. "Now go through that door and wait. I'll come around the other side. This is the last time we'll talk in public. The longer you protest, the more dangerous this conversation becomes for you."

"What about the meeting with my boss? She's expecting me."

"I'll take care of it. Now go."

Leaving Roscoe on the flight deck, Cuss passed through the door and into a hallway. He stayed near the wall as the group from the shuttle made their way to the passenger loading zone, speaking to Ygo as they drifted past. "How can I get around to that rally room from the far side? That room where the farmers change clothes?"

"He's still standing there. Like he's confused."

"I'd say more like in shock. Don't worry, he'll go." Cuss spoke with greater confidence than he felt.

"The farmers' prep area is to your left. At the end of the hall, take the door that says *Restricted Access.*" Ygo's tone changed. "He's moving toward the rally room."

Relieved at the news, Cuss floated left down the hall to meet Roscoe.

He'd guessed it would be fairly easy to get around to the farmers' prep area, the place where he'd encountered Beckman Thicke in his search for Agnes Ming. But he'd guessed wrong. Ygo had him zigging and zagging through doors, down hallways, and across rooms.

As he made his way, Cuss thought about how best to approach Roscoe. "So we know they're a group from Trenton, New Jersey. They've collected millions common from seniors. They're using the Factory as their home base."

"Go left," said Ygo. "Through the third door."

"But why the Factory? There are more people with those wires living in the northeastern United States than Lagrange and Nova Terra combined. They could have stayed home, stayed with their friends and family, and done the same thing." Cuss reached out to open a door.

"No, the next one," said Ygo. "With the red sign."

Cuss shifted down one and passed through. "And why did Roscoe and Stan visit a metal fabrication company in Armstrong? At their own expense, no less."

"Turn left at the branch."

"What kinds of things do they make at that shop?"

Ygo paused his instructions. "The firm is Pine Industrial Fabrication. They make equipment based on customer drawings and specifications. They specialize in big stuff. Industrial-sized manufacturing and processing equipment."

"Which makes sense for the Factory," said Cuss. "Could that be what the money is for? Specialized industrial equipment? But what would a crime crew from Trenton want with that?"

Finally reaching the farmers' prep room, he floated through the changing area, past the orange grav suits, and paused before the door leading into the hallway with the rally rooms. "Could they spend millions on that sort of thing?"

"Oh, tens of millions. When I say big equipment, I mean really big."

"Yuri and Stan wouldn't be huddling out at the Factory, far from their home turf, unless whatever they were doing required that they be out there. It's got to be something that makes them more money than what they're spending. A lot more." Cuss shook his head. "Could it be sabotage? Maybe they demand a ransom with the threat of ruining production?"

"But they wouldn't need specialized equipment for that. A bomb would be faster, easier, and much, much cheaper. And bombs fit their profile."

Cuss opened the door and called down to Roscoe, "Stay right there. It'll be just a minute." He closed it again and called Darlena in Armstrong. After a short delay, she answered.

"Hi, Darlena. I need a big favor."

"Yes?" She sounded hesitant. Careful.

"A company in Armstrong's industrial district, Pine Fabrication, is building a big piece of equipment that's to be used here in Lagrange's Factory. Their contact here is a guy named Roscoe Antonov. Would you be able to swing by and learn what they're building? What's its purpose? I'm also curious to know when it's going to be completed, and how much it costs."

"That's it?"

"Pretty much. I have a lead on Kaycee Gibbons' murderers, and this could be a key piece of evidence. If it breaks, I'll be sure to pass the credit back your way."

A pause, like she was weighing the pros and cons. "I can do that. I'll send what I learn later today."

"Thanks, Darlena."

Cuss started moving again, passing through the door into the hallway. He floated past the door to the first rally room, then past the door to the utility room that Beckman Thicke claimed was really a rally room for the rich and connected. When he reached the door to the rally room nearest the flight deck, he said, "This way," to Roscoe and entered.

Inside, Roscoe grabbed a vertical stabilizing bar and hugged it like a stripper about to start her pole dance. His face was pinched with fear and worry.

"Okay, Roscoe. I know you're part of a crime crew from New Jersey. I know you're building equipment in Armstrong to put in the Factory. Big stuff. Stuff that costs millions common."

As Cuss went through the summary, it sparked connections in his brain that brought it all together for him. "I know you're going to use it to pull out the gold and silver from the rock, metals Corporate told you to leave alone. You're going to steal it for yourself."

Roscoe gasped.

"And you've kidnapped and killed five people to fund your crime spree." Cuss was including Anton Agyemang in the count, the fellow from Aldrin who'd dropped from sight two days after Kaycee Gibbons. Though they hadn't found him or his body yet, Ygo had become convinced he was another victim.

Roscoe frowned, pulling his head back with his chin

down, shaking his head. "What are you talking about? We didn't kidnap anyone, let alone kill them."

"What are *you* talking about?" Cuss got aggressive, putting his face closer to Roscoe's. "The body count stands at five rich seniors plus two cops. You're fucked from here to Mars and back." Cuss studied him, letting the man's nervousness fester. "Have you ever been alone? Like really alone? Solitary is the worst torture. You can't begin to imagine. Living in a tiny box. No sun. No stars. No plants or trees. Stale air. No friends or family. No books. No vids. Day after day after long, long day. Your food delivered by a machine. Hell would be a vacation compared to what's ahead for you."

Roscoe started to cry. "I helped design a machine. It hasn't even been installed yet, so there is no crime. Not yet." He stopped to wipe his face on a sleeve. "You're making shit up about dead people just to scare me."

"How is the equipment being paid for? Where are you getting millions and millions common?"

"That's not my part," he blubbered. "Yuri is the money guy. I'm the technical person."

"Your money guy is as cold blooded as they come. And no jury is going to believe you didn't have a part in it. Do you think they'll believe that people were dying all around you but you didn't know? I know *I* don't believe it."

"I *didn't* know. I still think you're making it up." He curled into a weeping ball. "He threatened me. He forced me to cooperate."

Cuss let out a *pfft* of disbelief.

"Please," begged Roscoe in a plaintive voice. "You

have to believe me."

Ygo spoke. "Do you think we can turn him? Let him go back and gather evidence? We'll need proof to prosecute Yuri and his crew, just like we do with Peter Sobol."

Roscoe was floating in the air, hugging himself, bathing in misery.

"Stay here," Cuss said to the man.

He floated into the hall, shut the door, and spoke to Ygo. "If Yuri or Stan gets a whiff of his disloyalty, they'll kill him and run."

"Where can they run where we can't catch them? Roscoe is guilty, but I don't think he's behind the murders. If they've disposed of the bodies, if they're gone, it makes a murder conviction iffy. We need hard evidence, as much as we can get so there's no question about who did what."

"What about Robert Moore and Franklin Wallingford? If they're still alive, we have to rescue them."

"The way their necks get butchered, they last four or five days tops. They're both dead at this point. But if they are alive, Roscoe could be our best hope for finding them."

"We could flood the Factory with searchers. Tear the place apart."

"What if they're imprisoned on a spacecraft, and their accounts are being sucked dry from orbit around the Moon or Earth? And who's doing the surgery? That person can't go free. My point is that the unknowns are huge, and we need a guide to figure it out."

"How long do we give him?"

"That's a tough call. I would hope just a day or two."

"And what do I offer him to do this?"

"We'd need the municipal attorney involved to make a legitimate offer. It would take too long. I say fake it."

"I'm not liking this. Jesus, Ygo. What if someone else gets hurt or dies because I tried to be a hero?"

Ygo didn't answer.

Cuss turned to the door. "God help me if this goes wrong."

Inside, he grabbed Roscoe by the hair and slapped him. "Stop feeling sorry for yourself and listen up. You're at a fork in the road. I'm offering you a lifeline. Your one chance to save yourself."

"What?"

"I'm going to let you go back. Live your life. Act normal."

Roscoe's forehead creased in confusion.

"But you'll need to wear a spot."

Roscoe's look changed from confusion to fear. "Oh, hell no. They'll kill me for sure."

"They'll never know. It's invisible and undetectable."

"No. No. No." He shook his head emphatically.

"And you're going to have to earn your innocence. Nose around. Look for prisoners and a medical room. Talk to Yuri and Stan and get them to admit what they've done. That you didn't know anything about the kidnappings and murders."

"How am I going to do that?"

"You got yourself into it. You figure a way out. Until you prove otherwise, you're a cop killer. A kidnapper. A thief. A murderer. You'll sit with them at trial and share their fate."

Roscoe started to weep again. "I should kill myself now."

"From what I hear, there are lots of ways to do that over there." He moved back to the door. "It will take me a few minutes to get a spot ready. Stay here until I get back. Do *not* leave."

Cuss made his way out to the flight deck, pushed off the back wall, and sailed above the deck to the *Nelly Marie*. As he flew, he reached out to Juan. "I've recruited Roscoe as a double agent. I'm sending him over in about fifteen minutes to gather evidence. Unless you have something breaking, collect your crew and come back."

"Nothing's going on over here. George is a no-show, and there's no one around to ask about him. It's been a complete bust."

"I wonder if he got the time wrong?" Cuss's thoughts were swirling with his plans for Roscoe, so he didn't dwell on it.

In the *Nelly Marie*, he rummaged around in his supply cabinet looking for the box of spots. As he did, he fretted about leaving two people as prisoner while he played long odds on an evidence-gathering gambit. It weighed on him.

After locating the box and pulling out an envelope containing the surveillance device, he launched himself back across the flight deck toward the rally room. As he traveled, he asked Ygo, "Would you reach out to Gerard Mark and see if he'll tell us about the Moore and Franklin accounts? I'm anxious to learn if trades are still being executed and curious about how much was taken."

Back with Roscoe, he fished out a bit of clear, sticky

plastic the size of a sesame seed from the envelope, studied the man's face, and stuck the spot next to a mole toward the end of his eyebrow near his right temple. He stood back to view his handiwork. The spot was invisible.

"Have a look," said Ygo, directing the spot's feed through Cuss's lens.

Cuss saw himself looking at Roscoe and nodded. "Good."

As Cuss led Roscoe out of the rally room, he restated his instructions. "You are to go back and gather evidence. Look around. Engage Yuri and Stan in conversation. Get them to admit to the killings. To admit they planted the bomb that killed a cop. You need to either find physical evidence or get them to say it in words. They may have a couple of prisoners over there right now. Two men, ninety-five years old. If you find out where they are, that will go a long way toward mitigating your circumstances."

Roscoe looked as dejected as a person could be.

"And get out of your funk. If they ask what's wrong, why you're acting different, it means they're suspicious."

"Should I go see my boss before I go back?"

"It's Rhonda Kilkenny, right? I'll let her know you're helping us with something very important and that she needs to stand back for a few days. Now get to work."

From a distance, he watched Roscoe suit up and ride his Skeeter into the airlock. While he waited for Juan to return, he watched through Roscoe's spot as the man flew across open space back to the Factory.

Ygo interrupted his spying to report what he'd learned from Gerard Mark. "After a period of intense liquidation activity, both Franklin's and Moore's accounts have gone quiet. No transactions in the past few days for either of them. In total, just over twenty-three million common was transferred to the Grand Cayman Bank in Utopia."

"So they're dead."

"That's my conclusion."

"I feel better now about waiting for Roscoe."

"So do I."

Chapter 20

Stan Shevchenko approached the door to apartment 24 at Elmore Manor, looking up and down the upscale hallway to make sure he was alone. The door was a sturdy six-panel, solid-oak number, stained dark, with heavy brass latches that boasted of the security and protection it provided. When he heard the door chime signaling his presence, he announced, "Flowers for Francesca Sophia."

He'd bought a spring mix bouquet from the florist kiosk a block down on the pedestrian thoroughfare, figuring everyone had a few favorites among the selection of blossoms. But Francesca wouldn't see him or them in her doorview image because of the data mask, a device he wore like a necklace that disrupted the feeds from any sensors pointed in his direction. Still, he needed the flowers in case a neighbor walked by.

He waited, counting the seconds, willing her to open the door.

Finally she responded. "How come I can't see you?"

"I don't know, ma'am. I'm holding them up. Can you see them now?"

A long pause. "No. This is very odd. Who are they from?"

"The card says, 'From your loving grandchild.'"

"From Hatha?"

Stan felt his cheeks burn when he heard the name. He replayed the sound in his mind to be sure that's what she'd said. He weighed the odds of two women with such an unusual name.

Could it be true that Hatha was the old lady's granddaughter? The woman who'd spurned him. Who did it so coldly, publicly, casually? Like he was something she'd wipe off the bottom of her shoe?

"Yes, that's the signature at the bottom of the card. Hatha."

He felt a swirl of emotions, a cocktail of anger, self-pity, and indignation. Bitterness he hadn't realized he'd been repressing. Then in a manic swing, his resentment switched to delight. He contemplated the joy of revenge and found himself excited by the opportunity to lash out at the bitch, to make her suffer for the disdain she'd pissed all over him.

Hurting Grandma would be perfectly satisfying because Hatha would feel the old lady's pain in her heart, magnified a hundredfold because she'd be impotent to do anything about it.

"But it's not my birthday," said Grandma.

"I'm just the delivery person, and I have a dozen more stops. If you like, I can leave them here on the floor."

"That would be nice."

"Would you please say, 'Leave the flowers in the hallway' for my record? My boss will fire me if she thinks I did it because I was being lazy." He thought the improvisation made his act more believable. He'd long thought he had the creative spark to be an actor.

"You may leave the flowers in the hallway. Thank you for the delivery."

"Perfect. Enjoy, ma'am."

Stan set the vase on the carpet in front of the door, a good meter out so she would have to come outside to collect it. Then he hopped down the hallway past a couple of neighbors' doors and waited.

With distance from his data mask, Grandma's doorview would resolve. She'd see the flowers on the carpet and that the hallway near her door was clear.

He became anxious as he waited. A neighbor passing by at this moment would ruin the plan. The door opened and Grandma stepped out. He began moving toward her with a bounce in his step. Like this was a place he belonged.

"Hi, neighbor! Would you like some help with that?"

The old woman had been bending forward to retrieve the vase but stood up at the sound of his voice. "Are you new here?" she asked, her forehead creasing. She wore a house dress over a frail body. Her skin was translucent. Her wispy hair a salt-and-pepper gray. Stan put her at ninety-five pounds on Earth soaking wet, which made her about sixteen pounds here on Luna Deck.

"Just moved in." He gave her a broad smile. "Here, let me help." He stooped, picked up the vase with one hand, and held it out to her. When she reached to take it, he grabbed the front of her house dress and carried her through the open door into the apartment. As the door shut behind him, he tossed the vase and used the hand to cover her mouth. The last thing he wanted was for her to activate the apartment's security system.

Her struggles were feeble. In no time he had her turned so her back was pressed against his front, making her easy to control. With one hand cupping her face, he used the other to peel a medi-patch off his belt, one he'd placed there for rapid access. He slapped the sticky side to her neck and began counting to ten. She went slack when he reached eight. He let her slump to the ground.

He exhaled. The hard part was done.

Taking off his sport coat, he unshouldered the neatly folded backpack it was hiding. He unfurled the pack, spreading it out on the floor next to Grandma as he thought about how to bend her so she'd fit inside. Nature had already determined that the fetal position—rounded spine, tucked chin, knees bent, limbs drawn into the abdomen—was optimal for humans, minimizing size while allowing the person to breathe. He went with that, positioning Grandma like a baby in the womb.

It was a bit of a chore to pull the pack up around her. He wanted to be sure her head was up when he carried her so she wouldn't suffocate along the way. When he was satisfied, he closed the pack and hefted it onto his back, this time with his sport coat beneath the backpack.

He checked the hall using the doorview, then exited the apartment, closing the door behind him. As he moved down to the pedestrian thoroughfare, he began to remove his clear medical gloves but changed his mind. He'd wait until he was back at the Factory to do so.

. . .

Cuss returned to the *Nelly Marie*, thinking he'd spend the afternoon watching Roscoe while he contemplated his next steps. He felt a sense of accomplishment at discovering the motivation behind the whole affair—recovering precious metals—because it gave the case structure, one he could use to put the rest of it into context. It prompted him to think about what else must have happened to get to this point. And that helped with understanding new bits as they came to the fore.

But as he watched, he grew frustrated. Roscoe wasn't doing much of anything, mostly sitting at his desk, staring at the back wall. After watching him for a while, his exasperation growing, he asked Ygo, "Would you send him this message? 'Get moving. Find the medical room. Talk to your partners. Or accept the consequences.' Send it like it came from Rhonda so it doesn't stand out if someone else sees his display."

A chime alerted him to a call. It was Hatha.

"Hi, Cuss. I keep hoping I'll bump into you at the park when I walk Pibbs."

"Sorry. Things have been hectic."

"I'd like to see you. Would you have time to get together?"

His heart leapt. "How about later this afternoon on the *Nelly Marie* for a drink or two?" He didn't want to travel her direction because he'd lose that time watching Roscoe.

"Do you live there?"

"Yup. It's my home. Like living on a boat in a marina."

"Sounds fun. And private."

He smiled. "See you in a bit."

Even though Peanut, the ship's bot, kept the place tidy, Cuss moved through the levels anyway, straightening up, making sure it was ready for her first impressions. In his bedroom, he felt a burst of optimism and changed the bedsheets, choosing his blue cotton set because they felt so good on the skin. He shaved and showered and then faced the perennial challenge of deciding what to wear.

After shuffling through his shirt collection, he went with his green Ski Vail T-shirt. It was getting long in the tooth, showing frays around the bottom hem and one sleeve, and the words and logo on the back were fading. But it was a lucky shirt. A celebratory garment. As he pulled it over his head, he thought of the gorgeous Becky Hostetter and that amazing weekend in Colorado almost a decade ago. As far as he was concerned, he'd call on the shirt's magical powers until if fell off him from excess wear.

"How do I look?" he asked Ygo when he was done.

"Like an overeager teenager, including the speck of food on his front tooth."

Cuss studied his smile in the bedroom mirror and couldn't see the errant bit.

"Got ya," laughed Ygo.

Cuss shook his head with a wry smile. Ygo's timing was impeccable, and he fell for his pranks more often than not.

He continued to watch Roscoe with one eye during this time. The man had finally started moving about, but he remained in his own corridor. He hadn't ventured out or made contact with Yuri or Stan, something necessary if he were to fulfill his mission.

"Has he seen my message?"

"It's been sent, but he hasn't looked. He's in a funk and wasting our time."

Cuss drifted down to the pilot's level to wait for Hatha. After watching Roscoe do nothing for a while longer, he brainstormed with Ygo. "How about if we send some microdrones over to nose around?"

"We'd be limited to the Scepters. Everything else flies through air. And while the Scepters are small, the glow from their thrusters makes them visible."

"Let's think about it. They obviously won't work for surveillance in a corridor. But if it's as chaotic over there as we've heard, they might be able to fly in the equipment area without being observed. And is it that bad if they're seen? Maybe Corporate sent them for a legitimate reason."

He watched Roscoe get snacks from a cabinet in his office, return to his desk, and start eating.

"Did we ever find out what happened to that George guy? Why wasn't he there at the meet?"

"George Hall. I checked with Rhonda Kilkenny, and she confirmed that she'd told him the correct time and place. He not only acknowledged her message but sent her a confirmation that he was on his way. He's not responding to calls from her. I can't locate him either."

"That doesn't sound good."

"I fear the worst."

"And you can't track him in the record?"

"The people who designed the Factory's sensor suite had a production focus to the exclusion of all else. The industrial equipment is heavily monitored with multiple redundancies. The human spaces not so much."

"Jesus, Ygo. We can't keep letting people die while we figure this out." He chewed a thumbnail, his moral compass in crisis mode. "Does the company have a tech bot they could send over? Let it fix the corridor feeds and maybe poke around? Roscoe isn't living up to his end of the bargain. He can cook in hell with the rest of them as far as I'm concerned."

"I'll work with Rhonda to see what she can recommend."

He fretted some more. "Where does George live? Is he married? Have a partner?"

After a short pause, Ygo reported, "He lives here in Hermes. Homewood Villa on Deck 9 with his wife and daughter."

Cuss thought for a moment, then reached out to Juan, who responded right away.

"Hey, Juan. George Hall assured Rhonda Kilkenny that he would meet you. He even sent a confirmation to her that he was on his way. Could you visit his wife and see if she knows anything? Has he been in contact? If not, is that unusual for him? See what you can learn about his routine and where he might be. If he's missing and in trouble, we may need to go looking for him, even if it screws up our case against Yuri and Stan."

"I'm about to meet with the captain up here on Terra Deck. Realistically it will be a couple of hours before I can get there. Is that okay?"

"Do what you can. Maybe send a colleague if the delay stretches out."

He was about to close the call when he had a thought. "Let's meet with Roscoe first thing tomorrow morning. I want to know the best ways to dispose of a body in the Factory. If he can narrow it to a few places, maybe we should get a judge to shut everything down and have the crime scene crew look for evidence."

Juan tilted his head in a kind of shrug. "Remember Rhonda and her Corporate timelines? Shutting down the Factory would piss off some really powerful forces. If we came up dry, we'd both be looking for jobs."

"I know. But can we just sit by while an innocent dies?"

"Of course not. But we need something solid that supports the move. It has to be more than a feeling that someone might be in danger. It sucks to say, but that's the reality."

"Yeah. Shit. Let me know what the wife says."

Cuss closed the connection, unhappy with their choices, knowing Juan was right. Shutting down such a massive operation wasn't something that would be taken lightly. The business and political power structure would demand big results in return for action so drastic. If they didn't save a life and find direct evidence of murder, even Governor Belnick might not be able to save them. Hell, he may even side against them.

Cuss spoke to Ygo. "Maybe Roscoe can suggest places to look for evidence that can be screened while the plant is still running. Would you see if a medical examiner can join us tomorrow morning to vet Roscoe's ideas and give us a sense of what might work and what won't?"

He was watching Roscoe stuff his face when a deep dinging sound signaled a presence at the ship's hatch. Using his lens, he confirmed it was Hatha.

Cuss cracked the hatch and let Hatha in. Unlike the door to a home, the hatch was an oval-shaped piece of alloy, strengthened with ribbing, that swung open and closed on stout articulated hinges. Before acknowledging her, he took a moment to confirm that when he closed the hatch, the half-dozen pistons around its circumference plunged into receiving cylinders built into the ship's walls, the procedure creating a barrier able to withstand the absolute cold in the vacuum of space and the intense heat and pressure during atmospheric reentry to Earth.

With the cycle complete, he turned to greet her. She all but attacked him, wrapping her arms around him, squeezing him, kissing him on the lips. He hugged her back as they floated together on the pilot's level, glorying in her taste, lost in her fragrance, giving his best in return.

When they finally came up for air, she asked, "Show me around?" Her dimples made the request irresistible.

In spite of his witty banter along the way, she didn't seem overly engaged in the tour. His last stop was the bedroom. She took in the music posters and then studied the pictures of his family. After surveying the place, she caught his eye. "Can I be honest?"

"By all means." He studied her hovering in front of him, her face earnest, almost pensive. Her red-blonde hair was floating up around her head, giving it added volume, an unplanned look he found endearing. She wore a crop top that revealed a flat, firm stomach, with a tiny hole in the skin near her bellybutton, a piercing for jewelry. He wondered if she'd removed the adornment just for him, or if she'd abandoned it at an earlier point in her life. Either way, he felt an overwhelming urge to kiss the spot. She wore form-fitting pants that hid her legs but hugged her perfect bottom. He wanted to kiss that as well.

"I'm not a fan of making love in zero-g. You need gravity to help whoever's on top. You push up and then fall back, up and back. Mother nature knew what she was doing. But like we are now, if you push up, you keep going. It's awkward."

Cuss heard a whimper emerge from the back of his throat. "I have a butt band," he squeaked. Constructed using the same concept as an oversized slingshot, this was an elastic strap that attached to either side of the bed with a pocket in the middle that snugged the butt, providing the rebound she described. Created for the missionary position in a weightless environment, they were a hassle to use, requiring a certain desperation on the part of the lovers.

She crinkled her nose to convey her dislike for the contraption. "Would you be willing to go to my place? Or maybe we could just postpone until another time."

"Or we could go for a cruise."

The *Nelly Marie*'s systems powered up. Ygo was taking them out for a spin to give the ship the gravity she desired. When she heard the noise, she raised an eyebrow.

"The ship's AI is taking us out for a ride. The acceleration will give us gravity. What's your preference: Earth, Moon, or something in between?"

"I want you on top, so it's your call." Her face was

dead serious. Like she was discussing the news of the day. "I enjoy being taken. Move me around, have your way, but don't hurt me. Be motivated by your desire for me, not by some Neanderthal attitudes about women. Insistent but gentle." She gave him a half-smile. "Would that be something that interests you?"

Cuss had a lot of experience with women. Life had been extremely generous to him in that regard. But he'd never met a casual lover who had such a business-like approach to sex. It was a first, and the novelty heightened his hunger even more.

"Goddamn, Hatha." He took her in his arms and pressed his lips to hers. As the Paulson drives ignited, the ship's movements caused them to drift to the floor. The craft started its acceleration, and as he spoke to her, he spoke to Ygo, "I think Luna grav would be perfect."

And it was.

Afterward, they lay naked on top of the bed cover, the blue sheets unused beneath them.

Hatha spoke first. "Thank you, sir. May I have another?"

Cuss laughed, loving her irreverent attitude. "You may. But I don't take meds to help my performance, so you'll need to wait a bit."

He got up, filled a glass with water, drank some, topped it off, and brought the glass to her. She sat up to drink and handed it back to him. She watched as he returned it to its cubby. "Holy shit, Cuss. It's intimidating when the guy is more beautiful than me."

"Stop. You're a perfect ten, the operative word being

'perfect.'" He slumped down next to her, laid her back, propped himself up on an elbow, and began running the fingertips of his free hand over her body. He pressed harder than a tickle, but not by much, enjoying the sensation, studying her form as his hand moved up and down.

She closed her eyes. "You listen well. I really enjoyed that."

He didn't say anything, continuing to explore.

"You surprised me, though. Somehow I expected that once you had the green light, the first thing you'd do was put it in my mouth."

"Is that what you wanted?"

"No. I wanted exactly what I asked for. What you did." She opened her eyes and lifted her head. "Still, you seem different."

"I'm not that different. I was thinking I'd do the mouth thing in round two."

This time she was the one to laugh. "I'll do it for you. I don't mind."

He let the silence develop. Then asked, "Tell me something about yourself."

"Like what?"

"I don't know. Have you ever been married?"

"No. I don't see the point unless we're having kids. Nanny keeps telling me that my biological clock is ticking and I need to get serious. But the doctors tell me I have a good decade with today's medicine. I'm in no hurry."

"Tell me about Nanny."

"Let's see. She's my mom's mother. Very Italian. She dotes on me, her only grandchild. I've adored her since I was a kid. She was strong in body and spirit back then, but she's in her nineties now, and that has slowed her down. She'd been talking about moving to a low-grav home for a while, and when I joined the Community Patrol here, she used that as an excuse to move up here from Seattle. She ended up on Luna Deck, not far from Nature's Nook Café. That way I'm nearby if she needs me."

"What about her husband?"

"Gramps? He passed thirty years ago. I don't really remember him." She bit her lip, like she was thinking. "Would you like to meet her? She's with me in the park every afternoon. We walk Pibbs together."

"I'd love to."

She lifted her head and met his gaze. "It would require you actually showing up."

"I will. I want to. But this case has me wrapped up. People are dying, and I can't figure out how to stop it." He thought about telling her the details but decided it would kill the mood.

Instead, he leaned over and began kissing her body, his lips following his fingers up and down. For the first time, she took control, pushing him over and doing the mouth thing. When she had him ready, she pulled him back and they started their second round of lovemaking.

Afterward, he dozed. When he awoke, he was alone.

Chapter 21

Yuri Melnikov huddled with Stan in his office in Corridor 62. Together they watched a display showing the doctor operating on Francesca Sophia, Hatha's grandmother, in a makeshift operating room at the far end of the hall. When the Semident 318 account verification appliance came alive, Yuri made a test transaction, and then nodded to Stan, signaling to him that the link was good.

"Top off the saline feed, and Ivan will take you back," Yuri called to the doctor.

As the doctor filled the reservoir with clear liquid, Stan said to Yuri, "Ivan knows to toss the dear doctor into the feed port. Any second thoughts?"

Yuri, who was paging through the woman's financials, shook his head. "No. The tide is turning. This idea was always a longshot, but it seemed so...romantic in the craziest way. Travel into space and harvest asteroid gold. When Roscoe pitched it, I had to give it a try."

"So we're calling it quits?"

"Between Roscoe's change of behavior, strangers nosing about, and that damned police investigation, I think the quits is being called on us." He moved the balance of Grandma's cash account to the Grand Cayman Bank in Utopia. He looked up from the display. "When Ivan's done with the doctor, I want you two to load the woman into the van and park it outside the Factory near where the sheet is being formed, under it as best you can. She'll be close enough that I can maintain access to her funds. But if they come looking, they'll never find her. And they won't catch us scrambling to hide her." He shrugged. "It means we'll lose her faster, lose some of her money. But better safe than sorry."

"How much is she worth?"

Yuri scanned the display. "A better question is, how much can we collect before she dies? I'd guestimate around four to five million, depending on how much time we get."

"So we could go back to Trenton with thirty-two million common?"

"Now I wish we hadn't paid that deposit." Yuri got a wistful look. "But space gold. What an outrageous idea!"

Stan watched Yuri execute another trade. "What should we do with Roscoe?"

"When you get back from positioning the van, I'll call him down here and we'll have him help us clean the place. We need to vacuum, spray, scrub, wipe. Deep clean everything. Fold up the operating table, pull up the floor mats, collect whatever's come in contact with any of our guests, and toss it all into the feed port. And then we'll toss Roscoe."

"What will you tell his folks?"

"That he died a hero."

. . .

Hearing the shower running, Cuss climbed out of bed and

peeked in to confirm it was Hatha. He lamented that the stall was too small for two people at once and returned to bed to wait his turn. He used the time to page through his messages, where he found a confirmation from Shawna Lewis, the medical examiner who'd found the wire in Agnes Ming's neck. She was available to meet tomorrow morning and asked for the time and location.

"Tell her we'll meet at the Stratus building at nine," he said to Ygo, "so if anyone is watching Roscoe, it won't set off alarms." He looked up. "Any news from Juan?"

"He's on his way to George Hall's house as we speak. I'll send him the particulars for tomorrow's meeting when I send them to Shawna."

He also found a message from Darlena Washington confirming what he'd already guessed: Pine Fabrication was building a unit to pull gold, platinum, and silver from the condensate slurry. The equipment would be ready for delivery in just over a week at a cost of forty million common. Ten million had been paid in advance, with the balance pending.

Cuss whistled at the price tag. Now he understood the need to rob so many rich people.

And he found a message from the Marshals Service reminding him that he had a week left for his annual gun qualification. He'd already taken two extensions and knew a third was difficult to secure. He grumbled about the hassle but then had a thought.

Hatha came back to the bedroom, beautifully naked. He watched her get into her bra and panties, and when she was covered, asked, "I need to go through my required gun qual in the next few days. Would you be interested in tagging along?" Since she'd been a Community Patrol officer in her past life, she'd been through the qualification process herself. In his experience, people who were proficient shooters enjoyed the opportunity to practice their skill.

"I have to work tomorrow morning." She pulled her top over her head. "Do you have time now? Let's shoot and then have dinner. Highest score picks the restaurant. Lowest score pays."

"You're on."

Ygo landed the *Nelly Marie* back on Hermes' flight deck while Cuss was in the shower. As he dried off, he thought about the enthusiasm of Hatha's response to shooting guns and her willingness to place a bet. The detective in him concluded that she was likely a good shot. He was pretty good himself and would easily qualify. His competitive spirit took hold. He was determined to beat her and win the wager.

While he dressed, he asked her, "Luna or Terra?"

It was an important question because the higher the gravity, the more challenging it was to shoot with accuracy. When a gun fires, gravity causes the bullet to drop. If you fired a gun with the barrel perfectly level to the ground and dropped a book at the same instant, they both would land together, though the bullet would travel thousands of meters before doing so. This assumed, of course, that the ground was level, there were no imperfections in the bullet's shape that would skew its path as it tore through the air, and there was no wind to push it one way or another.

Marksmen must account for gravity's pull when sighting a shot, forcing them to guess how far above the bullseye to aim to account for the drop. It's a computation based on distance to the target, the speed of the bullet, and the strength of gravity pulling the bullet downward.

Shooting in zero-g was easiest, because the gunner didn't need to adjust for gravity at all when aiming. Just point and shoot. Luna gravity was next, since the bullet would reach all but the most distant targets before the feeble gravity had a chance to play a role in the bullet's trajectory. Earth gravity was the hardest by far, its significant pull requiring the shooter to use skill and experience to adjust, even for targets at intermediate distances.

"Doesn't matter to me," she responded.

It wasn't the answer he wanted to hear. Someone who didn't care was someone who either expected to lose so was indifferent to the choice, or was so skilled they expected to win no matter what.

"Let's go with Luna." In the end, he made the choice to save time. It was an extra twenty minutes up to Terra Deck and another twenty back. He had a busy morning tomorrow and was already operating in sleep-deficit mode.

Though he carried a Tosic 325 Hybrid on the job, he dug out his service pistol, a traditional gun like the one Ivan Kosmin had used to kill George Hall. The Marshals Service required that he qualify with his service piece, a somewhat controversial policy but a policy nevertheless.

They took the shuttle up to Luna Deck and rode a pod

to Skidman's Sports Club, a place Hatha recommended near the Community Patrol station. The front lobby was small, with most of the building's space reserved for shooting lanes in back. The walls on either side of the entryway were tribute walls, with targets on display showing hits clustered around the bullseye and pictures of shooters holding various weapons and trophies. Names and dates and other pertinent information were listed for each exhibit.

A middle-aged man stood behind a counter at the rear of the lobby. The style and coloring of his clothes, the buzz haircut, the weathered face, the muscled frame with inked arms, all screamed ex-military. The counter itself was a glass case filled with an array of firearms for shooters to rent. Through the glass wall behind the proprietor, Cuss could see a dozen shooting lanes. About a third were occupied, the patrons creating a muffled popping as they fired their weapons.

"Hi, Hatha," said the counter man.

Cuss's heart sank. This wasn't starting out well.

"Hi, Skip," she said with a smile. "My friend is doing his annual qual, so he'll need a complete set with full doc. I'll shoot a set as well, but I won't need formal documentation." She looked at the pistols in the display case, some sleek and modern, some well-used. Some made of modern composite materials, others of more classic metals. After scanning the selection a few times, she pointed at a beautiful blued-steel pistol with a twelve-centimeter competition barrel and an anatomical grip engraved with intricate filigree. "I'll use the Encore."

Skip shifted his gaze to Cuss. "Did you bet?'

Sensing he'd been suckered, Cuss nodded. "Dinner."

Skip winked. "Hell, you win either way." He recorded Cuss's credentials as part of the formal qualification procedure, raising an eyebrow at the interworld marshal badge. When he was done, he jerked a thumb over his shoulder. "You have lanes eight and nine. Lane eight is set up for documenting the qual. The target sequence is set on both lanes to follow Marshals Service specs." He turned to Hatha. "Where are you going for dinner?" He asked the question like she'd already won.

"I'm in the mood for Italian, so probably Antonio's."

"Nice." Then to Cuss, "She must like you, because she's letting you off easy."

Cuss wasn't ready to concede the bet. After inspecting his weapon, he squared up in his lane and relaxed into his stance, forcing his frontal lobe to overcome the distractions of his reptilian brain, trusting his muscle memory. He felt jittery at the beginning and willed his heart to slow, calming himself with rhythmic breathing, taking his time, eventually settling into his zone.

He shot his best qualification round since becoming a marshal, logging a ninety-three out of a hundred based on a Marshals Service algorithm that normalized the raw points into a simple percentage. His previous best score had been a ninety-one. He needed better than an eighty-two to qualify in Luna gravity.

Hatha shot a ninety-seven and seemed disappointed in her performance.

. . .

Antonio's was a mid-priced restaurant with white tablecloths and cloth napkins, real candles as part of the table centerpiece, and a menu promising generous portions of traditional Italian fare. They got a booth, and Cuss ordered what he always did at Italian places: chicken parmigiana with linguini and extra marinara sauce. Hatha got the pumpkin ravioli with sage butter sauce.

While they picked at bread and waited for the meal, Cuss raised his glass of chianti. "A toast to the champ." They clicked glasses and sipped. "There has to be a story behind your skill. Care to share?"

She looked into the distance as she formed her thoughts. "My dad was a hobby farmer. We had a few goats and chickens, and four acres of corn and tomatoes, lettuce and squash, carrots and cucumbers and beans and watermelon and on and on. Way more than we could eat. We had a farm stand I helped run in the summers. Our neighbors loved us because Dad was generous with the overflow. Anyway, he believed a farmer's daughter should know her way around a gun."

"Where was this?"

"Near East Olympia in Washington State, about a hundred kilometers south of Seattle. He bought me a twenty-two rifle. A Fredricks lever action with a lacquered walnut stock. I used to set up rows of vegetables that had gone too far to eat and plink at them. He noticed my interest and aptitude and enrolled me in a gun club. They had competitions for kids. I flourished." She formed a wistful smile. "When I was thirteen and my hormones were in control, I had a crush on a guy who shot pistols, Gary Jenrry. I switched from rifles, hoping we'd cross paths and he'd notice me."

"Did he?"

She shook her head. "It took him so long to come around that by the time he was interested, I no longer was. But I'd become hooked on competitions. I was a natural with pistols and that helped keep my interest. I continued shooting and competing through high school. The coaches and parents involved tended to have a heavy military and law enforcement background. It influenced my thought process as I got older."

Their food arrived. Cuss let the server grate a generous helping of parmesan cheese on his meal and took a bite. It was delicious. He steered her back to her story. "So how do you get from there to Community Patrol in Lagrange?"

"After I graduated from college, I worked a series of jobs, trying to find a passion. Gramps had left Nanny in great financial shape, and she was happy to support me while I tried to find myself. Let's see." She bit her lip as she thought. "I worked as a fitness instructor, then for a catering outfit, then I managed a community farm, then ran the front of house at an upscale seafood restaurant."

She shook her head. "I love food service, but the hours are ridiculous. Anyway, when Nanny started making noises about wanting to move to a low-grav situation, I looked into different options for her. I came across an article about how Lagrange was in the process of growing its population, and among the opportunities were openings for cops. I'd taken some criminal justice courses in college, and that combined with my shooting awards and score on the screening exam apparently made me a desirable candidate. They admitted me to the patrol academy on my first try. The rest, as they say, is history."

She'd finished her story but then added, "The funny thing is that it was my shooting skills that attracted their attention. But in the four years I served, I never shot my gun. Hell, I only ever pulled it from my holster twice."

"How is it we never crossed paths?"

They talked through their timelines and assignments during her time of service, thought it possible they were in the same auditorium a time or two for big events, but agreed that it wasn't an unreasonable outcome that they'd never met.

"When Nanny followed me up, she bought me Nature's Nook so I could get back to food service. She was happy to cover the loss so I didn't need to work the crazy hours. I recognize that I'm lucky. Privileged. But I don't feel bad about it."

"No reason you should."

"Enough about me. Tell me about your case. I'm interested."

Seeing her in a new light, Cuss took her through it. "You're not going to believe this. Or maybe you will. Stan Shevchenko is a target of the investigation."

"No shit." She sat back in her chair. "I could feel the slime on him. But our interactions were never anything more than me serving him at the café, and him being hot for my body." She peered at him across the table. "Kind of like you." She dimpled. "I'm glad to know my instincts are still good."

Cuss felt his cheeks redden. He resumed the story. "So this is complicated. You know the Factory, the small cylinder floating near the cities?" He used finger quotes when saying the word "small."

She nodded.

"It's really a huge machine that eats asteroids and spits out the material used to build the city tubes and everything inside. It turns out the asteroids have bits of gold and silver and such mixed in with the rock. Stan, working with these other guys, Yuri and Roscoe, has this scheme to install equipment that recovers the precious metals for themselves. They're funding it by kidnapping rich, old people and taking their money."

"What does being elderly have to do with being rich?"

Cuss nodded, understanding the confusion. "So thirty years ago, Lewiston-Mark offered this security system for big investors where they put an authentication wire just beneath the skin in a customer's neck. It made their accounts perfectly secure, offering peace of mind to those who felt they needed it. This crew is kidnapping the folks who still use the wire—all elderly because new tech came along to replace it. They've figure out a way to link in through that wire, co-opt control, and drain the accounts."

Since they were eating, Cuss skipped the part where they sliced along the neck to dig out the wire.

"How much have they taken?"

"Somewhere around forty million common."

She shook her head in amazement. "With that kind of

cash, why don't they just keep the money and skip the metal harvesting?"

Cuss shrugged. It was a good question. "Greed, I guess. The metals are worth way more."

"How come you haven't arrested them?"

"It's the classic law enforcement dilemma. We know what they're doing, but we aren't in a position to prove it in court. The folks they've abducted are all dead, and presumably their bodies are long gone, chewed up with the rock. They use a data mask that hides their presence when they're committing their crimes, so we can't document that it's them doing the kidnapping. We even know that one of their underlings blew up the ship they used to transport some of the victims, and it killed a cop. A good one."

"That's when you ended up in Mercy Hospital."

"That's right. We can prove the underling had been in the ship, giving him the opportunity. But we can't tie him to the explosives or prove he set the charge. We can't show any reasonable motive, other than speculation that he was ordered to do it. And we aren't even sure where he is at the moment, so we haven't had a chance to sweat him. It's frustrating beyond measure."

"It seems like you could prove that the abducted people were kept a certain place. They'd leave biological markers."

"I think that's our best option. But that place is likely out at the Factory. Tomorrow I meet with the medical examiner and the plant operations guy to learn the likelihood of gathering evidence without shutting down the equipment, which apparently is all but impossible. And the place is huge. Think that a crime scene crew would need five or six hours to process a place the size of my bedroom. The Factory is, I don't know, millions of times larger. We need to focus our efforts before starting crime teams over there. And even if we can prove they were once there, it still presents a challenge for the municipal attorney to turn that into a murder conviction."

"So you're waiting for them to do it again so you can catch them in the act."

"I hope it doesn't come to that."

"Hi, Marshal."

Cuss looked up to see Sarah Janowicz, a reporter for the Star Record, one of the more credible news outlets on Lagrange, standing at the edge of their table. In her late thirties, she had coiffed hair, a commanding voice, and a curvy body dressed in fashionable clothes. Overly white teeth dominated her smile, their luminous glow distracting from an otherwise pleasant face.

"You promised us fast action," said the interloper.

"Jesus, Sarah. I'm having dinner. Show a little class." Cuss and Sarah went way back. At different times, he'd used her. She'd used him. They'd used each other.

"Who's your friend?" Sarah gave Hatha the up and down.

"Sarah," said Cuss, making no effort to hide his annoyance. "I'll be at my ship in ninety minutes. If you leave now and meet me there, *without* anyone else, I'll give you ten minutes."

She smiled and gave a fingertip wave. "Toodles."

"Sorry about that," he said as Sarah walked away.

"She's right, though. We should have results by now. I'm guessing the director will be calling me because Governor Belnick is calling him."

"What are you going to tell her?"

"Not sure. There are two basic plays. I give her carefully selected tidbits. Or I promise her an exclusive if she gives me more time. The first one is good if I'm trying to manipulate someone. Say, flush them out because I believe they're ego driven. I can tease them through the media. But in this case, I know who the assholes are. Teasing would just send them into hiding. So likely a promise of future access if she cuts me some slack."

"Is she good in bed?"

He sat back and folded his arms across his chest. "None of your business."

"It's just that she seems more like a taker than a giver."

He shook his head and relaxed his position. "You keep impressing me. She and I had a fling a few years back, but it ran its course after a couple of months. And during the period when we were enjoying each other's company, she was definitely taking more than giving. Not only in sex but using the relationship to milk me for information."

"Why didn't you tell her to go to hell?"

"I did, after I got control of my libido. When I'd thrown her over the side, she decided to strike a more equitable arrangement. She helps me on occasion. I help her back. We get along much better now that sex isn't part of the equation."

Hatha toyed with her food. "I guess this means you won't be coming to my place after dinner."

"If that was an invitation, thank you. Make the offer when things aren't so crazy, and I'll be there in a heartbeat. But we both have an early day tomorrow. I need my head fully in the game right now." He told her about George Hall and his concern for the man's well-being. "I'm torn trying to figure out what I should be doing to ensure his safety."

They dawdled over coffee, talking about trivial topics. Being silly. Enjoying each other's company. Making each other laugh.

Outside the restaurant, they strolled to the pod station and waited in line together. After a lingering kiss on the loading platform, they took separate pods, going in different directions.

As the pod carried him toward the shuttle station, his mind returned to work. "Hey, Ygo. What did Juan learn?"

"George Hall's wife is worried, but not panicked. George sometimes goes to the bars after work. He usually calls, but not always. And he doesn't always check his messages, sometimes waiting until he's on his way home."

"So by the time we're certain there's an issue, it's going to be too late to catch anyone in the act."

"Based on his reliability at work, we know there's an issue. But what that is, and what to do about it, are the open questions."

"Any thoughts on what I should say to Sarah?"

"Maybe misdirect her. Use her to make Yuri and Stan think they're still operating under the radar."

Cuss rubbed his neck, thinking. "Not bad. She'll be pissed off when she learns that I've used her."

"Make it up to her on the back end."

"Was that a double entendre, or is my head in the gutter?"

Ygo laughed but didn't comment.

Cuss changed direction. "How's Mannan doing? I'm thinking I should check in." Girish Mannan was the director of the Marshals Service. Ygo handled communication with him most of the time, keeping him in the loop, documenting what they'd done, informing him of their next steps. But it was politic for Cuss to reach out when things were heating up. Better he make the call rather than answering one from a harried boss.

"He asked a lot of questions with my last report, which means he's feeling pressure. It might be good for him to hear your voice. Let him know we have it under control so he's comfortable going to bat for us."

"So lie to him the same way I'll lie to Sarah?"

While Cuss was purposely being a smart-ass, Ygo corrected him anyway. "Mislead Sarah. Let Mannan draw conclusions that make him feel comfortable."

Chapter 22

As Cuss floated across the flight deck, he saw the *Kelly Sue*, a sister ship to the *Nelly Marie*, docked among the mid-sized craft. And that meant that Miles Burton was in town, the asshole marshal who'd aggravated Darlena Washington in Armstrong about sharing credit on a case. Cuss wanted to speak with him about his attitude, but he wasn't in the mood to do so tonight.

Instead, he turned his attention to Sarah Janowicz, who floated outside the *Nelly Marie*, holding onto the ladder that led up to the hatch, waiting for him. He didn't invite her inside. "You have ten minutes, Sarah. And before we start, I'm not happy about you barging in on my dinner."

"She's a cutie, Cuss. Sorry if I blocked you from getting laid."

Her behavior frustrated him, but he wasn't going to let her button-pushing rile him. "Now you have nine minutes."

"How did someone so cute become such a hard-ass? Okay, how close are you to catching Debra Gosling's killer?"

"We've narrowed it down to a few suspects and are moving with deliberate speed to ensure we have a solid case that will make those responsible pay for their crimes to the full extent of the law."

"Is Community Patrol supporting you? Leading the investigation?"

"As always, we are an integrated team cooperating to protect the citizens. It's not about who gets the credit but how fast we can solve the crime and deliver justice."

"We're hearing reports about kidnappings of seniors. Have you been brought in on those cases?"

"We've had a couple of families reach out, concerned about their loved ones. But to call those kidnappings at this point is a jump in logic. Let's see how the cases develop."

"Should people be worried for their own safety?"

"No."

"Are the same criminals responsible for all of it?"

"We've tracked the suspects to their home base in Trenton, New Jersey. We're setting up surveillance in their local haunts down there, waiting for them to surface. It's just a matter of time."

Sarah smirked. "Cuss, I'll print that if it'll help. But you'll owe me big time if I do."

"What are you talking about?"

"If it were true, you'd never tell me. So you're using me. It hurts."

"Oh, stop. Off the record?"

"Not for what you've said up to this point. That's fair game. But yes from this point forward."

"Agreed. I want to keep them where they are. So I'm asking you to help me make their home, Trenton, a place they want to avoid. It will give us time to make the case."

"Give me an exclusive afterward?"

"I'll give you first crack and save a few tidbits, but I'm

sure the politicians will make it a public news conference."

"I'll take it."

"So how've you been?" At one level he still liked her. She had her moments.

"Lookin' for love. You have any plans for tonight?"

He gave her a wry smile. "For the Trenton thing, if you would make it a 'sources say' rather than a direct attribution, it will play better to the bad guys."

"Sure, Cuss." She gave him a long look. Like she was weighing asking again. She looked away. "You take care."

Inside the *Nelly Marie*, he floated up to his bedroom and put on a dress shirt so he'd look professional. "Time to pay the piper," he said to Ygo. He placed a call to Girish Mannan and was informed the director would call back in about twenty minutes.

Girish called back in fifteen, and Cuss took him through it. Then, "I'm thinking of raiding the Factory tomorrow afternoon, after we have a sense of what success looks like and can organize the people and equipment."

"What do you need from me?" Girish Mannan was in his early sixties, with hair graying at the temples of a round face, his brown complexion reflecting his Indian heritage. He looked tired, the creases near his eyes speaking to the life-and-death decisions he made on a daily basis.

"We'll need the cities to turn out dozens of patrol officers for the search, crime scene techs for analysis, detectives to lead the different teams, transport ships to get people there and back. It'll be a real production. And we could come up empty, Girish. I'll do my best. I won't start without a reasonable sense of success. I'll be as cautious as

I can justify. But it could happen."

"Why not a smaller effort? Target your best options?"

"We're searching something the size of a small city. If we take it too slow, they can play a shell game on us, moving whatever their hiding over here while we're searching over there, destroying evidence at their leisure while we search through locations in order. At a practical level, we will have a list of priorities, hit several of them at a time, move through them as fast as we can. But even a focused effort will be big. How big depends on how the planning meeting goes tomorrow."

"This is my classic dilemma," said Girish. "They're screaming for a solution but will hesitate when they hear the cost. I'll let the governor know what's in the works and ask him to appoint a lead. I'll forward a name when I get it."

"Thanks."

"How are you doing otherwise? How are you and Ygo getting along?"

Cuss wanted to say, "He's listening." Girish should know better. Cuss chose to play it straight. "Ygo is the best partner I could ever have. We're an inseparable pair. It would be hard for me to continue in this job without having him there to watch my back. I'm guessing he'd say the same about me."

"That's good to hear. No one is planning any moves. I wanted to provide an opportunity for feedback if you thought a different arrangement would let you be more effective. It's called management."

"Understood."

After an awkward moment, Mannan said, "I'll let you know the governor's decision. Good hunting." He closed the call.

As Cuss removed his dress shirt, he said to Ygo, "We should have a municipal attorney at the meeting as well. I know we don't have the evidence they need for a conviction. Not yet. But in the end it's their call, not ours. We need guidance on what to concentrate on, what to avoid, what they consider a minimum threshold, all of it."

"I'll shake the tree and see who falls out."

Cuss tucked both sides of the blue bedsheets under the mattress so he wouldn't float away as he slept, and then climbed into bed. Closing his eyes, he said, "Thanks for everything, Ygo. I know I treat you like an assistant sometimes. I want you to know I really appreciate it. I value your help."

"As long as it's for the job, I don't mind. No task too big. No task too small."

"I meant what I said about having you as a partner. We're a great team."

He was asleep before Ygo had a chance to respond.

. . .

A chime sounded, rousing Cuss. Juan was calling. Cuss checked the time. He'd been asleep three hours.

"Hey, Juan," he said, his voice groggy. "What's up?"

"Melanie Hall, George's wife, is in a panic. He's way overdue."

"Shit," said Cuss. "Shit, shit, shit."

"I've checked the population tracking system. He doesn't show in any of the cities."

"I hate to say it, but let's pull everyone out of bed and have our morning meeting now."

"Still meet at Stratus?"

"Jesus. I haven't thought it through. Let's get everyone up and moving and decide the location on the fly." As Cuss dressed, he asked Ygo, "Have you had a chance to contact the municipal attorney's office?"

"We have Hermes' MA himself, Reggie Tolson, serving as liaison."

"I've worked with Reggie before. Somehow I missed that he'd landed the MA slot."

"Mayor Florence appointed him almost a year ago."

"The thing I like about him is that he's a problem solver. I've worked with assistant MAs who will spend a meeting covering their ass, telling you why something won't work but never explaining what we need to do to solve their problem. He gets right to it. Would you pull him out of bed and get him moving?"

"I'll get Shawna moving as well."

"Thanks." Yawning, Cuss floated over to a drawer and looked through his stim patches. "What do you think?"

"Bring an S and an X. Get by on coffee for as long as you can before using one. That should give you forty-plus hours from where you are now."

The S patches provided a standard stimulant; the X patches were the extra strength. He'd use the S for twelve hours, and then the X for twelve more. If he didn't start until he was ready to drop, he could go two more days without sleep. But given that he was starting in a sleep-deprived state, he'd be a mess when he came down.

He'd been churning over an idea and decided to go with it. "Is there someone we can sub in for Roscoe? After watching him sit on his ass all day, I'd rather let him sink with the rest of them. There were three other staff members housed in his corridor and more in the next one. I'll bet one of them knows the plant as well as he does."

"Roscoe Antonov's title is head of production. On the org chart near him is a production supervisor, production engineer, and production coordinator. Honestly, they all sound like they could have something to contribute."

"Then let's bring in all three. Could you organize their names, titles, and addresses into a message and send it to Juan?"

"Done."

Cuss called Juan. "I just sent you three names with addresses. People who work for Roscoe. He's been so worthless, let's let him sink with his partners and use these three in his place. Could you dispatch patrol officers to bring them to the meeting? Stress that these are not arrests. Ask the officers to tell them there was an emergency incident at the Factory and their expertise is needed to address it. Treat them kindly, gently, but get them there."

"I can do that."

"If any show resistance, link them through to me, and I'll answer their questions."

"Where did we decide to meet?"

"I'm going to say the Stratus building because it's possible these three may need information that will require a company secure link to access. It saves us from having to move the party if it turns out that's true. I'll reach out to Rhonda Kilkenny to get approval and a room."

After he closed the link, he said, "Oh, shit, Ygo. We need logistics in on the planning. We can't launch until we have the people and ships. Did Mannan get the governor to appoint a lead?"

"He hasn't sent a name, but it's only been a few hours. I'll call MFOD for guidance." Ygo pronounced it emm-fod, which was the Marshals Field Operations Desk, a central clearinghouse with staff available around the clock to coordinate field actions for marshals in real time.

While Ygo worked on that, Cuss called Rhonda Kilkenny, who didn't answer. Instead of leaving a message as requested, he used a law enforcement tool that overrode the request, forcing her device to continue an incessant chime until she responded. He finished dressing while he waited for it to pull her out of her sleep.

"What!" she snapped. "This better be good."

"Good morning, Rhonda. This is Marshal Cuss Abbott." He explained the situation and named the staff members they'd identified. "Will these three from your company know what Roscoe knows?"

"That and a lot more."

"Would you give us permission to use a room in your building that seats a dozen people? One where your staff will have access to whatever tools they'll need to help us plan?"

She paused. "Go to the second floor, room 202. If you could send an attendance list, I'll alert security." Another pause. "Should I be there?"

"We're trying to keep the information compartmentalized. So unless there's something you can offer that one of these three can't, then no."

"I probably can't. Tell you what. I'll go in and hang out in my office. Call me down if you need me."

"You got it." Cuss's stomach rumbled. "Does Stratus have a food service contract? Would you be willing to get us coffee and water? Maybe even breakfast?"

"We do and I will."

As he floated across the flight deck to catch a shuttle over to Apollo, he thought it likely that participants would be staggering in over the next hour. Rather than wait for the group, he'd pick their brains as they showed up and integrate it all when he had a full picture.

A chime alerted him to a call from Louis Triolo.

"He's the production engineer with Stratus," said Ygo. "One of the three employees you invited to the meeting."

"What does he want?"

"A lawyer."

"Oh, for God's sake." Cuss answered. "This is Marshal Abbott."

"Are you the one who ordered my arrest?" asked Louis without introducing himself.

"Is this Louis Triolo, production engineer for Stratus?"

"I want a lawyer."

"Then you'll have one. I'll ask the officer with you to arrest you for accessory to murder and book you at the station. Your lawyer can meet you there."

"What!" screamed Louis. "That's insane!"

"Or you can stop being an asshole and help us out. Rhonda Kilkenny says you're an expert who has information we need for an emergency situation. You can save lives."

"What are you talking about?"

"You'll get a free breakfast."

"Free?"

"One hundred percent. Coffee, juice, eggs, toast, the works."

"Why didn't you say so before?"

Chapter 23

Cuss was the third person to arrive at the Stratus meeting room. He introduced himself to production supervisor Robb Zeigler, and production coordinator Joseline "Jelly" Quinn, both of whom were already seated at the conference table. A food service bot was unloading a cart onto a sideboard cabinet. Cuss felt confident Louis Triolo would be happy, because Rhonda had provided them with a selection of breads and muffins, scrambled eggs, hash browns, breakfast meats, hot and dry cereals, the works.

His prediction proved accurate. Louis walked in as the bot was finishing and immediately began loading a plate. He was so wrapped up in the food that Jelly Quinn was the one who introduced him to Cuss. Louis plopped a full plate down on the table and returned for extras he couldn't carry on his first trip.

As Cuss chatted with Jelly, Juan arrived, introduced himself to the Stratus employees, grabbed a coffee, looked at Cuss, and tilted his head toward the door. Cuss joined him in the hall.

"What's the plan?" asked Juan.

"My thought was to ask the Stratus crew for guidance on where Yuri and Stan are holed up, and where the best places might be to dispose of a body. Then ask the ME for input on where they want to focus the crime team efforts. Next, we'll have the MA discuss legal thresholds, dos and don'ts, and whatnot. Then ask whoever shows up from the governor's office for guidance on personnel and transport."

"Okay, thanks. I just wanted to have a sense of where we're headed so I can look competent. Especially if a senior officer will be here from the governor's office."

"Why don't you lead the discussion with the ME and MA?"

"Really? Thanks!"

As they spoke, Deputy Chief of Community Patrol Golda Kaetzel strode around the corner.

The upper leadership structure for Community Patrol was mostly linear. There was one captain on each deck who reported to a commander. There was one commander for each city who reported to the deputy chief. Commanders also coordinated with their city's mayor. There was one deputy chief for all of Lagrange who coordinated with the four commanders and four mayors and who reported to the colonel. There was one colonel who reported to the governor. Confusing the structure was the chief of detectives, one for each city. Confusing because although they held the title of chief, they reported to their city's commander.

Getting the deputy chief at the meeting meant the effort was being taken very seriously by the governor and colonel. Both Cuss and Juan felt their stomachs clench. The game was on.

"Good morning, gentlemen," said Golda, shaking

Cuss's hand with a firm grip, making good eye contact as she did so. She was surprisingly young: early forties, small frame, brunette hair up in a tight bun. She was dressed in a clean uniform and looked well put together for being pulled from her bed forty minutes earlier. "You're the roamer? I'm pretty sure we've met before."

He didn't think so, because he found her attractive, which meant he would have remembered her, but he didn't say any of that. Instead, he simply nodded.

Juan shook her hand next and spoke formally. "Hello. I'm Detective Juan Luisa from Hermes' Terra Deck."

"Good to meet you, Detective." She looked at his cup. "Is there more coffee?"

They moved into the conference room. Golda grabbed coffee and a muffin, and they sat.

Cuss got the group started, first addressing the deputy chief. "Reps from the municipal attorney's office and the medical examiner's office are due any minute."

He turned to the Stratus employees. "Thank you for coming at this ungodly hour. Rhonda Kilkenny knows you're here helping us. She fully supports this effort and is hanging out in her office if you feel the need for her input or direction."

The three looked at each other, confusion evident in their expressions.

"What I'm about to tell you is classified and very disturbing. It has to do with abduction and murder in the Factory. About criminals who are there now, using it as their base of operations."

Jelly inhaled with a gasp. Robb folded his arms across

his chest and frowned. Louis layered strips of bacon on toast as he worked to assemble a multilayered breakfast sandwich.

"If you feel frightened or overwhelmed, let us know and we'll get you the assistance you need."

"Go for it," said Louis, who had spread scrambled eggs over the bacon and was now adding a layer of cheese.

Cuss began. "We believe criminals from Trenton, New Jersey, have a base of operations somewhere in the Factory. We think they set the bomb that killed one of our officers, Debra Gosling. We believe they have kidnapped at least two people and performed medical procedures on them over there. And we think they have disposed of the bodies somewhere in the plant."

Jelly pushed her food toward the center of the table. Louis took a bite of his sandwich.

"We asked you here to brainstorm with us."

Shawna Lewis from the ME's office entered the room and Cuss stopped. "Hi, Shawna. You know Juan and Deputy Chief Golda Kaetzel." He motioned in order with his hand. "This is Robb Zeigler, Jelly Quinn, and Louis Triolo, who work for Stratus Corp. Grab some breakfast and a seat. We're just getting started."

Back to the three. "The Factory is huge, and the resources we have to search it are limited. We've asked you here to help guide us. We'd like you to think like criminals and tell us the best places to hide, and the best way to dispose of a body."

"Can I interrupt?" asked Robb Zeigler, holding a hand up high as if he were a student in a classroom.

When Cuss imagined what a production supervisor might look like, he envisioned Robb: late thirties, serious, meticulous, geeky. His shirt looked huge because his body was so lean, his big head balancing on an oversized collar. "I want you to. What's up?"

"There's a small group from a company called Trenton Consulting out in Corridor Sixty-two. I have no idea what they're supposed to be working on, and Roscoe Antonov, my boss, told me to leave them be, that he was working with them on a special assignment. But you said Trenton, New Jersey. Plus, we've been having sensor issues with the corridors out that way. I'm just wondering if they're someone to talk to?"

Cuss looked at Juan, who raised his eyebrows.

"That was easy," said Ygo.

"What do you know about Trenton Consulting?" Cuss asked Louis.

Louis, his mouth full, shrugged and shook his head.

Cuss turned to ask the same of Jelly, but she spoke first. "One of them, a guy named Ivan, chatted me up one time in the ready room."

Jelly reminded Cuss of the girl in grade school with the pigtails, button nose with freckles, and apples for cheeks. Now in her late twenties, she was tallish, slim, modern hair, a little awkward, not really cute or pretty but with a look that could grow on you as you got to know her.

"Ivan Kosmin?" asked Juan.

"Don't know his last name." She shivered and hugged herself. "He seemed kind of creepy. Now I'm really weirded out."

"I've loaded his picture," Ygo told Cuss.

Cuss took out his badge wallet, peeled the projector disk off the back, set it on the table, and had it project a display they all could see. Is showed a picture of Ivan Kosmin, sullen, swarthy, disheveled. "Is this him?"

Jelly looked away, nodding. "That's him."

He switched the display to a picture of Rex Luskin, the one they'd been calling the pilot. "Have any of you seen him?"

"I might have," said Robb. "Maybe ten days ago coming out of the ready room. He was wearing a spacesuit, though. I could only see his face through the visor, so I'm not a hundred percent."

"Have any of you seen George Hall today?" asked Juan. "Or I guess it would be yesterday."

The three looked at each other, shaking their heads.

"Where's the ready room?" asked Cuss.

"Off the flight deck," said Jelly. "I can show you?"

Cuss nodded.

She tapped the table and spoke to the company AI. At that point, Reggie Tolson, municipal attorney, arrived. Introductions were made, food was plated, and attention returned to Jelly.

A holoview display hovered over the table, a larger version of the one Cuss and Juan had viewed in Rhonda Kilkenny's office when they'd toured the corridors. It showed the Factory floating in space, a half-eaten asteroid sticking out the end.

"Is this a model, or is it showing what's actually happening now?" asked Golda.

"This is live," said Jelly.

"Actually, the image updates with a ninety-second delay on this system," corrected Louis, speaking in the officious tone of an engineer. He was at the sideboard pouring cream into his coffee. "So it's really a minute and a half old."

"Anyway," said Jelly, apparently used to Louis's quirks, "the cylindrical shell you see here is approximately two kilometers long and half a kilometer in diameter."

As Louis inhaled to speak, Jelly shut him down. "I said approximately, Louis."

Louis shrugged.

"The sheet you see being produced is *approximately* a kilometer wide and *about* five meters thick." She spoke with one eye on Louis, ready to head him off if he made a move to interrupt.

"The end of the cylinder opposite the asteroid ingress is where a small flight deck and associated facilities are located." The image swooped around the cylinder to the other end, the asteroid now blocked from view by the Factory itself. "It's large enough to handle midsized transports, and there's room to squeeze two of them in on the deck at once. But deliveries of really big items are unloaded at one of the city's cargo ports and tugged over."

The view melted through the corrugated door shielding the flight deck. Inside was open space for the larger ships Jelly had mentioned. None were present at the moment. Off to the side was a grouping of small spacecraft, ranging in size from single-person Skeeters up to vehicles capable of carrying six or eight people plus a small load of cargo.

"Three of these belong to Trenton Consulting." She zoomed in and used a pointer function to show them. "This Skeeter, this Sprite utility craft, and this Frontier van are theirs." The Trenton Consulting craft were a mix of colors and styling, like they'd been leased or purchased locally from whatever was available at the moment.

"So all your craft are either white or blue and have Stratus logos clearly displayed on them," observed Juan.

Louis studied the display and nodded his approval. "That's correct."

Cuss understood this was important information to internalize because things could get crazy when they mobilized. They could well be finding themselves making snap decisions in hectic conditions.

The view swiveled across the deck to show an airlock door along the far wall. They zoomed toward it, and the image melted through and into the ready room, a combination locker room and waiting lounge. The lounge, the portion to the right, didn't have seats because with no gravity, there was no need to take a load off your feet. Instead, a row of loops along the back wall was available for occupants to thread their arms through, preventing them from drifting if they wanted to daydream or snooze while waiting.

Stabilizing poles and overhead bars were placed down the middle to help with navigation through the lounge to the changing area to the left. The view panned to show a suite of lockers on one wall, a row of a dozen spacesuit cubbies along the back, and on the other wall, a washing station with mirrors and a door to a bathroom. About half the cubbies in the back held suits. The other half were empty.

"I was getting into my suit when that guy, Ivan, came through the airlock from the flight deck and started yacking," said Jelly. "I talked with him for about three minutes while I finished suiting up, and then I was out of there."

Juan said, "I was scheduled to meet George Hall yesterday on the flight deck. He confirmed with Rhonda that he'd be there. Would he have used this room? Or is it more likely that he'd come through the plant already dressed in his suit?"

"Company policy is to keep clear of the flight deck while waiting," said Robb.

"It's a safety thing," added Louis. "It's dangerous to be out there when craft are on the move."

Jelly finished. "So it's likely he'd been waiting here in the ready room."

"Can you show us the vid feeds for the room?" asked Juan. "I was supposed to meet late morning, so start at eight and roll forward to noon?"

"No problem," said Jelly. She spoke to the AI, and the recording began playing. "All the people are blurred, though. Employees have the right to privacy, and the corporation is required to provide it. Also, this is a changing area, so even without employee rights, it would still be blurred."

The recording played at high speed, and it was apparent that different people passed through. But the blurring was effective, making the result useless.

"Those three spacesuits in the cubbies to the left were never touched," said Ygo. "They all have forward-facing cameras. Ask them to show the record stream from one of those."

Cuss asked.

Jelly seemed flummoxed and turned to Robb. "Are the cameras even on when no one is wearing the suit?"

Robb frowned and spoke to the AI interface in an attempt to access the camera feeds. He had no luck. "I don't think they are."

Louis let out a huff of disgust. "They're passive arrays. They're always on." He began working the AI, speaking rhythmically, like a quiet chant, having it parse data, separate signals, and cast the result to the display. "You wanted to start from eight yesterday morning?" He chanted some more.

A view of the locker area from the perspective of the cubbies showed on the display. After it zipped forward for a bit, Louis slowed it to show a sequence that included Stratus employees arriving for work, including Roscoe Antonov, George Hall, and Jelly, Robb, and Louis.

The view sped up again and then slowed when Ivan Kosmin entered the locker room, stepped out of his spacesuit, and went into the bathroom.

"That's the guy," Jelly said to the group. Then to Robb, "The employees will be ballistic when they learn that suit video isn't blurred."

George Hall floated into the locker area and began suiting up. Ivan exited the bathroom stall. They could see the two men chatting, but there was no sound, giving an otherworldly cast to the action.

Then in a chilling sequence, Ivan fumbled his gun, George made an effort to escape, and Ivan shot him. Blood squirted from the wound and floated in the air. Then Ivan shot him again.

Jelly screamed and began crying. Robb turned white. Louis said, "Whoa," and played the sequence a second time.

Cuss looked from Juan to Deputy Chief Golda Kaetzel, ME Shawna Lewis, and MA Reggie Tolson. All were focused on the vid, jaws slack, watching the tragedy repeat. Cuss had been worried that he couldn't deliver proof, that some of them might leave the meeting feeling he'd robbed them of sleep for no good reason.

He didn't feel that way anymore.

When Jelly put her head down and continued sobbing, Golda Kaetzel moved around the table, whispered to her as she rubbed her back, and then helped her stand and led her out of the room.

Louis worked for several minutes and then showed the scene a third time from George Hall's perspective through his suit camera. He played the vid stream until the man was jettisoned from the craft by Ivan. The scene from George's suit from that point onward showed a brilliant field of stars rotating ever so slowly. After watching it for a few moments more, Louis closed the image.

Cuss spoke to calm everyone and get them back on track. "We'll send search parties out to recover him for the family." Then to Shawna Lewis, "With that as evidence, will you even need to process the room?"

"Absolutely. We'll match the blood splatter on the vid with collection points off the floor, walls, and ceiling. It will confirm that the vid is real. That the murder happened as we just saw."

Cuss turned to Robb and Louis. "How are you guys doing? You need a break?"

Robb, who was as white as a sheet, shrugged as if to say, "Keep going."

Louis nodded, agreeing with Robb.

Shawna asked, "How do people get from the ready room to their offices? Since people come and go without suits, there must be a passageway?"

Louis took them through it, explaining the idea of sixty-four office corridors positioned around the Factory, built to provide life support to workers and visitors. "The corridors are organized in groups of four, meaning four of them are linked together by these long travel tubes."

He worked the display to show a schematic of four corridors spaced along the inside wall of the Factory, connected in a long sequence by a smaller tube. He zoomed the view out to show that sixteen groupings of four corridors were spaced evenly around the Factory's outer wall.

"The travel tube is two meters in diameter, so it's plenty big enough for two people to float past each other as they move from one corridor to the next, but not so big that people hang out in them. We can move within any group of four linked corridors without suits and have to suit up to travel to a different group of four." He zoomed the display. "Corridors one through four are different in that not only are they linked together, but their travel tube also connects to the ready room. So that's why you see people coming and going from there without suits."

Cuss asked, "Can you give us a tour of the plant, Louis? Help us get familiar with the inner workings of the industrial equipment?"

"Absolutely." Louis spoke to the AI, and the image shifted to a wonderland of black and gray shapes. Big containers—boxes, cylinders, cones, spheres—were stacked and joined and assembled in an intricate network, one grouping linked to the next by ramps and tubes in an intricate configuration to create a Rube Goldberg–like manufacturing facility that filled much of the space inside the vast cylinder.

Louis was in his element. "These containers house different processing units, each a step that transforms chunks of an asteroid into a perfect sheet of condensate."

Just as he got into his zone, Jelly and Golda returned. Jelly looked reasonably composed as she retook her seat.

Louis continued. "This entire process can be thought of as three steps: rock crushing, slurry preparation, and sheet extrusion." He droned on for a good ten minutes, describing details of the steps, pointing out the machines associated with each, explaining how they functioned. "Everything needs to be inside its own enclosure and connected by sealed conveyors, because with no gravity, bits of dust and goop would eventually float into the open spaces. This way we keep everything contained."

"So suppose I had a bag of trash," said Cuss. "I wanted

to put it into the plant and have it get eaten up and turned into product. Some place where it would disappear and be gone forever. Are there access points where I could do that?"

Louis sat back and manipulated the image, thinking about the question.

"Maybe start near Corridor Sixty-two," said Juan. "Can you point that out for us and think about the equipment near there?"

Louis zoomed to a place about halfway back into the depths of the Factory and began tracing through the containers and tubes located there.

"Wouldn't it be loud and scary approaching the equipment?" asked Reggie Tolson.

"Actually, just the opposite," said Jelly, speaking in a softer tone than before. "It's air that carries sound and the machine vibrations we hear and feel, but there's no air in the Factory. So you could be floating a meter above some huge piece of equipment that would be deafening on Earth, that would shake your bones and send you running. But out there, with utter chaos all around you, you're floating in serenity. You can't hear anything, and the only way you'd feel it is if you were touching the floor or a piece of equipment. You might see the rattling and shaking in the housings, but the quiet lulls some people into a false sense of security. We have to train visitors to be on their guard because of it."

As she spoke, Corridor 62's airlock opened. A person wearing a spacesuit floated out. He turned and pulled something after him. It took Cuss a moment to recognize it as a fat man in street clothes. The man had a strip of dark hair around his mouth and down his chin.

"That looks like Roscoe," said Louis, his voice and posture showing emotion for the first time.

Cuss agreed.

Roscoe floated with arms and legs outstretched, like he was lying on a bed. Without air, the man should have been panicking, waving his arms, swinging his legs, fighting to return to the airlock. But he remained inert, which meant he was unconscious, or worse.

Jelly and Robb both gasped.

The man in the suit pushed off against the corridor wall, floating with Roscoe in his grip, moving him over to a huge tube connecting two pieces of the Factory. The enormity of the equipment became apparent when the two men together were dwarfed by the size of the pipe.

"Can you get a view through the visor. Who's the person in the suit?"

Louis worked on the display while the suited man fiddled with a round plate fixed to the surface of the tube. The image zoomed closer but not enough to identify the individual through the visor. "The sensors I'm using are designed for panoramic views. This is the best I can get."

The suited man pulled open the round plate, a hatch of some sort. He maneuvered Roscoe through the opening like he was putting out the day's trash, throwing him away. With Roscoe inside the tube, the man in the suit closed the hatch and floated back toward the airlock.

Jelly screamed. Everyone else sat in shocked silence.

"This is real time?" asked Golda.

"A minute and a half delayed," said Louis.

"We need to act *now*," said the deputy chief.

Louis chanted to the AI. An alarm horn blared, and a red light on the wall began to flash.

"My God, Louis," said Robb, staring at the image floating over the table. "What have you done?"

"He shut down the plant," said Jelly. "Holy hell, Louis. You are in the deepest shit anyone has ever been."

"Roscoe's body is on its way to the slurry tank." Louis spoke with conviction. "A real person. Someone we know. I stopped him from being processed into condensate. You really think we should just sit back and let that happen?"

"Can you play that sequence again from a different angle?" asked Shawna, a medical examiner in search of evidence.

Before Louis could respond, the door to the conference room opened. Rhonda Kilkenny stuck her head in, her face red, balled in fury. "Who did that?"

Jelly and Robb looked at Louis, who was pale from fear.

Rhonda pointed at him. "You're fired!" Then she looked at the other two. "You all are finished, effective immediately." She looked around the table. "I'm going to need this room back. You can't believe the shit storm that's about to unfold." She stormed away before any of them had a chance to respond.

Cuss barely heard her because Ygo was talking to him. "If you can get over there, I can guide you to that point."

He rose from his chair. "C'mon, Juan. We need to get moving." He turned to Golda. "We could use a dozen officers and a couple of transports, right now. The more of them that are detectives, the better. We'll meet them on Hermes' flight deck."

Golda, who was speaking urgently to someone they couldn't see, nodded to him, held up a finger, and then lifted her head, "Thirty minutes." She resumed her private discussion.

As Cuss moved with Juan toward the exit, he said to Reggie and Shawna, "We'll catch up with you when we have them in custody."

He paused at the door and looked into the room. "Louis, I know my saying it isn't worth much right now, but you did a good thing. Really good." He looked at Jelly and Robb. "You all did."

Chapter 24

Twenty-five minutes later, Cuss and Juan exited the Community Patrol emergency shuttle onto Hermes' flight deck, both still in their street clothes. Pushing off the side of the vessel, they floated over to a group of ten officers gathered near the muscular gray doors of the large airlock. Already dressed in blue spacesuits, their flex helmets hovering behind their heads, four detectives and six patrol officers were deep in discussion. Near them, a white patrol bus was being prepped for launch.

Deputy Chief Kaetzel arrived just after Cuss and Juan. "We stopped at ten because we were worried about tripping over each other and losing time in coordination. Do you want me to round up more?"

Cuss looked at Juan, who shrugged. "Maybe round up a second wave of six or eight and have them wait here. We may not use them, but it will be good to know that if we need backup fast, we have someone to call on."

She nodded and turned away, speaking quietly.

"My suit is in the *Nelly Marie*," said Cuss, motioning toward his ship.

"We keep extras on the bus," said Juan. Then to the group, "Everyone load up. We'll brief you on the trip over."

They scrambled aboard the bus, a boxy ship designed to carry thirty-two people plus a driver between the cities.

Inside, the layout looked more like a traditional airplane than a bus. Seats were arranged four across with an aisle down the middle. Small oval windows on each side aligned with rows. The seats reclined to accommodate thrust, had deep cushions to support the entire body, and included safety straps to secure passengers. Oxygen masks were hidden overhead, ready for release in case of emergency. Displays at each seat permitted officers to access resources they might need during the short flights.

One of the patrol officers strapped into the pilot's seat, activated the navigation systems, and chatted to the deck crew as he worked through the prelaunch warmup. The others distributed themselves through the bus, all taking aisle seats. The pilot received permission to proceed and called, "Hold tight," to Juan and Cuss, who were floating in the aisle, wriggling into their suits.

As the bus floated forward into the airlock, Cuss divided the officers into three groups: two groups of three with one detective and two patrol officers, and a group of four with two detectives and two patrol officers. Pointing, he made assignments. "You three will cover the flight deck and ready room. No one leaves. Period. Take anyone you find into custody and hold them here on the bus. We'll work out who's who later. The ready room is a crime scene, so be careful in there. Preserve it once you know it's clear."

The bus launched into space as he pointed to the next group. The gentle acceleration allowed him to remain standing, but it required that he hold tight to one of the loops hanging from the craft's ceiling. "You three will clear Corridors 1 through 4, and then move onto 5 through 8."

He explained how corridors were connected by travel tubes. "Keep going until we tell you to stop. Pick a room as a holding space and put anyone you find in there."

He turned to the group of four. "You'll come with us to Corridor Sixty-two. It contains evidence we'll need to identify and protect. We expect to find some sort of medical operating room, offices where they conduct their business, and God knows what else. Maybe even a body or two. Everyone we see gets taken into custody. We saw a perp dump someone into the machines, and Juan and I will try to find the body."

"I've loaded pictures and briefs to their seat displays and their suits," said Ygo.

"Everyone enable the display in front of your seat." Cuss waited while they did so. "These four are our primary targets: Yuri Melnikov, Stan Shevchenko, Ivan Kosmin, and Rex Luskin. I've sent their pictures and bios to your suit systems as well. Everyone familiarize yourself. These guys have weapons. Ivan used a pistol to shoot and kill a civilian yesterday. So take care. Your safety comes first."

He prompted Ygo as he continued. "Here's a diagram of the inside of the Factory." He paused for a few seconds while Ygo scrambled to create and project the image. Using it, Cuss talked through the organization of corridors and travel tubes, the flight deck and ready room, the location of Corridors 60 through 64, and the hatch one of them had used to dispose of the body.

At the speed the bus was traveling, the journey across open space to the Factory took fifteen minutes, and Cuss used every moment to brief them. As they approached the corrugated door to the flight deck and the pilot triggered it to open, Juan called out, "Weapons check, everyone. There won't be time to fumble about inside. And seal your helmets. We're about to lose air."

The bus filled with the sounds of clicks and snaps as the group readied their weapons—special issues designed to accommodate gloved hands—returning them to the holster-like pockets on the outside of their suits, ready for rapid access. The bus edged its way inside, and magnetics secured it firmly to the flight deck. The corrugated door rolled closed behind them as the pilot shut down the navigation system. The bus had front and back doors. After the pilot confirmed everyone was suited and ready, both doors opened and they exited.

. . .

When the alarm horn blared and red lights began flashing, Yuri and Stan were in Yuri's office in Corridor 62. Yuri put a hand on the wall. The vibration he was accustomed to feeling from the operation of the plant was diminishing, as if the massive facility were shutting down. His desire to wrap things up flipped into overdrive.

"Ivan," he called to their comrade working in a neighboring office. "Stan and I are going to take the Sprite to check on the woman and then head over to Apollo. Finish dumping the mats, then take the Skeeter and meet us at Hopkins Pub on Luna Deck at noon. Those mats are covered in evidence, so be sure to dispose of them before you follow."

Stan was already suited, his helmet hovering behind his head. Yuri donned his spacesuit in record time, talking to Stan as he dressed. "I don't know if this alarm has anything to do with us. But at a minimum, it means people will be coming through to address whatever issue set if off. We'll rally at the pub and plan our trip home from there."

They secured their helmets, and then Yuri closed up the electronic box he used to communicate with the authentication wire in Nanny's neck and tucked it under an arm. "Let's move," he said through the suit's comm.

They squeezed into the airlock together. After it cycled, they slipped outside, looking cautiously in every direction, searching for people responding to the alarm. Seeing no one, they pushed off, Yuri in the lead, making their way through the plant. They floated in tandem, pulling and pushing along the same route they'd taken dozens of times before. But they moved with a new sense of urgency, traveling faster than normal. Much faster.

Pausing at the edge of the flight deck, they hid behind a structural plate located at the rear of the landing area and peeked around its edge, surveying the scene. The deck was clear of people. Nothing seemed out of place. They moved in front of the plate, pushed off, and zipped to the Sprite, scrambling inside with Yuri at the controls.

Yuri enabled the navigation display and warmed the engine, readying the craft for departure. As the ship came alive, he signaled the corrugated door to open. They watched impatiently through the front viewport as the gate scrolled up onto the overhead spool. The moment there was sufficient clearance for their ship, he edged the joystick forward, moving them off the flight deck and out into open space. When they were clear of the structure, he signaled the corrugated door to close.

The Factory's front face was a dark gray disk, huge, imposing, free of bolts or welds or other imperfections that would mar the smooth surface. The Sprite rose in front of it, stabilizing thrusters spurting and hissing as they responded to Yuri's joystick manipulations, the only other sounds being their breathing and the thumping of their hearts in their suits. When the craft cleared the rim of the cylinder, Yuri edged the small ship forward over the Factory's curved exterior, traveling just meters above the iridescent photovoltaic cover that gave power to everything inside.

Looming in front of them like a cresting wave frozen in place, the condensate sheet produced by the Factory—the very reason for its existence—curled up and over, a massive wall protruding out of the seam along the cylinder's exterior. The huge overhang of material dwarfed their ship, an impossible shape avoiding collapse because it floated stress free in a weightless environment.

When the Sprite moved under the condensate sheet, Yuri felt like he was entering a cave, material looming over them like a cavern ceiling. The nav detected the Frontier van holding Nanny before either of them saw it, and Yuri guided the Sprite forward until they drew alongside it.

"I'm going to look," Yuri said to Stan, his desire for the woman's wealth driving him to take an uncharacteristic risk. He fastened a tether to a loop on his suit designed for that purpose, opened the door, and slid out, fighting vertigo but determined to assess her viability, to gauge how much time he had to harvest her treasure.

Peering through the window of the van, he studied the woman. She lay unmoving, strapped face down on the rear seat, a tube trailing from a bag of clear liquid feeding into her arm. Her skin color was pink. Her torso rose and fell with each breath. He saw nothing that would justify towing the craft back to the flight deck, a necessary step before they could enter the pressurized environment supporting her survival. Concluding that she was doing as well as could be expected, he tugged on the tether and pulled himself back to the Sprite.

Again in the pilot's seat, Yuri opened the electronic box he'd carried from Corridor 62, established a link through the woman's authentication wire, and spent ten minutes moving cash from recently completed sell orders out to the Grand Cayman Bank. "She looks good. I think she'll last another couple of days easy. But I'm not sure how far away we can get and still have this link work."

Ten minutes turned into twenty as he unloaded blocks of stock in a new wave of sell orders. "The way she's structured her account, these sales take twenty-four hours to complete. If I can't establish a link from Apollo, we'll have to swing back here tomorrow to move the cash."

When he'd done what he could, he closed up the electronic box, turned the Sprite around, and guided it back the way they'd come. As they approached the mouth of the cavern, Stan pointed through the viewport and shouted, "Stop! Whoa! Back up!"

A boxy vehicle, lights flashing, with Community Patrol

logos on the outside, approached the Factory from the direction of the cities.

Yuri jerked back on the joystick, returning the Sprite to the cover of the condensate sheet. Hiding there, they waited, uncertain whether they'd been seen, guessing how long to wait before the police vehicle was on the other side of the corrugated door and their systems shut down.

"We need to warn Ivan," said Stan.

"If we broadcast, they'll hear us," said Yuri, realizing that things had gone awry much faster than he had anticipated.

"He's going to shit when he sees them."

"He's resourceful as hell. He'll make it out. We'll see him at the pub."

They waited until they were sure the police bus was docked and the corrugated door was closed. Then they waited some more.

"We should go out the other end," said Stan. "It just seems prudent."

Yuri agreed. He piloted them beneath the length of the condensate sheet, where they exited above the half-eaten asteroid. He aimed the craft for Apollo and engaged the main drive.

. . .

Ivan's mood changed from upbeat to angry when Yuri called to say they were leaving but that he should stay behind and handle the mats. "They treat me like I'm disposable," he muttered to himself, wondering what had triggered the alarm as he pulled the covering from the floor in the operating room with increasingly aggressive tugs. "I've done more to make this work than those two combined."

Moving as fast as he could, he rolled the mats into three tubes, each as tall as he was, and hustled them over to the airlock, standing them upright inside the airlock chamber. He felt anxious, uneasy. As he wriggled into his spacesuit, he paused to move his pistol from his pants to an outside suit pocket.

Securing the flex helmet over his head, he squeezed into the airlock with the rolls of floor covering and started the cycle. The indicator above the external door was red, and he chewed on his lower lip as he waited for the process to complete. When the indictor light flashed green, he opened the outside door and pushed the mats out ahead of him.

"Goddamn it to hell!" he shouted, venting his anger at Stan and Yuri when the mats unfurled in front of the airlock door, scrolls opening like oversized royal proclamations. "Fucking fuck!" Steaming mad, he worked to corral the wayward sheets but stopped when he saw people in bright-blue suits in the distance, cops for sure, floating through the plant in his direction.

Fighting panic, he ducked behind the open mats, using them as shields as he cast about for a place to hide. His first thought was to return to the airlock and use the travel tube to sneak past and get on the other side of them. But if they had people inside working their way through the corridors in his direction, they'd have him cornered.

From outside the airlock, the corridor looked like a long rectangular conduit encased in a gray plastic material, its cross section as large as a mobile home, the kind found in trailer parks on Earth. The corridor system ran along the Factory's cylinder wall, snaking in both directions for as far as he could see.

He nudged the nearest floor mat so it moved between him and the approaching officers, and when he was fully shielded, he pulled himself up and over the rectangular structure. On the other side, he found himself in a gap that had a forest of sturdy metal brackets holding the corridor to the wall. The gap was a couple of meters wide, and the brackets were well spaced, leaving plenty of room for him to move about.

He didn't wait to learn if they'd seen him. Instead, he pulled himself toward the flight deck in the space behind the corridor, taking care to keep the structure between him and the blue suits at all times.

In just a few tugs, he reached a travel tube connecting this length of corridor with the next. Though it was a much smaller diameter than the rectangular conduit, it still provided sufficient cover for him to continue his trek. When he felt he'd left the blue suits far enough behind that they no longer presented an immediate threat, he abandoned the gap and made a beeline for the flight deck and the waiting Skeeter.

He slowed when he neared the landing area, approaching cautiously. He knew the patrol officers must have taken a ship to reach the Factory, and that some of them likely remained behind, stationed near the craft. His worry was confirmed when he peeked from behind a thick support beam to see two people in bright-blue suits patrolling the flight deck. He pulled back into his hiding spot and waited, racking his brain for a plan.

Chapter 25

Hatha entered her apartment with Pibbs in tow, returning from the pup's early-morning constitutional. Humming as she changed for work, she couldn't deny her feelings of optimism, even joy. She was at the start of a new relationship, that magic time when the guy had no faults, when everything about him and their situation seemed perfect. And this one was sexy as hell, the hottest man she'd been with in recent memory.

She moved into the kitchen and poured a coffee, a new blend from South America that she was considering for Nature's Nook. As she sipped, she reviewed her weekly purchase sheets, double-checking what she'd ordered for coffee beans. The last thing a café needed was to run out of its more popular brews.

Pibbs wandered into the kitchen with his favorite toy—a furry yellow duck—and placed it in the middle of the floor. Wagging his tail, he sat behind it and looked up at her. She glanced at the time and frowned. Nanny, who looked after Pibbs when Hatha was at work, should have checked in by now to wish them both a good morning. She'd overslept before. She was in her nineties, after all. But it was rare.

Hatha lived four doors down from Nanny, another indulgence her generous grandmother provided. Needing to stay on schedule, Hatha called her. When Nanny didn't answer, she upped the urgency of the communication, causing the chime to amplify. Nanny still didn't answer.

Frowning, she told a confused Pibbs, "Wait here, sweetie. I have to go wake Nanny."

Hatha was still thinking about the café's purchase order when she rang the bell. Nanny's door was programmed to recognize her, and when no one answered, she entered.

"Rise and shine!" she sang. "It's me!"

When she saw fresh cut flowers scattered on the floor with a vase lying beside them, adrenaline poured through her veins. Her heart pumping, she hurried through the rooms of the apartment—two bedrooms, two bathrooms, a combination living and dining area, and a kitchen— calling, "Nanny?" over and over.

She wasn't there.

By definition, if Nanny wasn't in the apartment, she had used the door to leave. Hatha accessed the doorview record, started watching from when they'd come home from the park together the afternoon before, and played it forward at high speed, looking for when her grandmother had left. She stopped and backed up on the timeline when she saw the door open. Playing it forward, she watched and listened.

The image of whoever was outside talking to Nanny was diffuse and shapeless. She'd never seen anything like it. The blur claimed to be delivering flowers from Hatha herself. The voice sounded familiar, but she couldn't place it. Nanny stepped out into the hallway, where she disappeared into a blur. The blur moved back inside the apartment, and six minutes later, it exited. Nanny was gone.

Hatha felt a tingle as she remembered Cuss talking about criminals hiding out in the Factory, crooks who used a data mask to kidnap seniors and rob them. Replaying that conversation in her head, she placed the voice. It was Stan!

Her mind crowded with a growing list of things she needed to do. Call Cuss. Call emergency services. Take care of Pibbs. Get her gun and go after the asshole.

But like muscle memory, her training overcame her impulses and guided her thoughts. She started by moving to her own apartment to preserve the scene in case there were clues to Nanny's fate that a crime scene investigator might uncover. Then she placed a call to Cuss, sending it with maximum urgency. "C'mon," she muttered, her stomach twisting in knots, waiting for him to respond. When he didn't answer, she left a quick message. "Stan took Nanny. I need your help."

Realizing that Stan must have passed by her apartment twice, coming and going during the kidnapping, she watched her own doorview record at the time of the incident to see if she could catch him in the act. His image was blurred on her display as well.

She watched it a second time with one eye while calling the city's emergency services desk. After she reported the incident and asked for help, the dispatcher told her, "Stay in your apartment in case the perpetrator is still in the area. Officers are on the way."

Hustling into her bedroom, she changed from her work dress into jeans and a T-shirt. She called Cuss again, and while she waited for him to answer, she opened her closet and swept the clothes hanging from the rod, pushing them to the left, giving her access to the gun safe built into the side wall on the right. Cuss didn't answer, and she repeated her message, this time the desperation in her voice reflecting her fear and frustration.

Inside the gun safe were three pistols and a dozen boxes of ammunition. One gun was a hybrid like Cuss's, with the same selection of stop, drop, and kill. One was the weapon she used most often for target practice, with its longer barrel and performance sight.

She selected the third, a Duluth Adapton, a pistol with a small profile that fired traditional 9mm rounds. She chose it for its flex grip and trigger guard, designed to accommodate shooters who were both barehanded and gloved. She loaded two clips with eight rounds of SSPs: Stop Safe Performance. The bullet entered the body, expanded to provide maximum stopping power, and did not exit, ensuring safety to anyone on the far side of the target. Sliding a clip into the gun, she chambered a round, snugged the pistol into a custom holster, and clipped it inside the waistband of her pants at the small of her back. She put the other clip in her pocket.

Hurrying out to the kitchen, she filled the dog's water and food bowls while she called Annie Uprose, a neighbor and friend who agreed to stop in and check on Pibbs. Giving the pup a quick rub on his head, she stepped into the hallway, where she encountered two patrol officers responding to her emergency.

"This way," she said. She led them to Nanny's door,

opened it, and stood back. "I'm her granddaughter and live four doors down. You can see from the flowers and vase on the ground that something is wrong. Watch the doorview record and you'll see that someone using a data mask abducted her. I walked through the apartment looking for her, then exited and haven't been inside since."

"Please stay out here, miss," said the older of the two. "We'll look around and talk to you in a minute."

As soon as they were inside Nanny's apartment, Hatha departed, hurrying down the hall. She made her way out to the pedestrian thoroughfare and ran in long, low-grav strides to the shuttle station. Though it was four kilometers away, she could move faster on foot than she could in the sedate pods. Her conditioning made it easy to sustain the pace in the low gravity. The greater challenge was threading her way through the unyielding crowds.

She called Cuss a third time while waiting for the shuttle. This time she left a more detailed message. "Stan has taken Nanny. I'm on my way to the Factory to rescue her. I could use some backup."

She fretted during the shuttle ride, wringing her hands, willing it to move faster. After an interminable ten minutes, it landed in Hermes' passenger port. As it was being towed into position at the passenger loading platform, she saw a group of Community Patrol officers gathered on the flight deck. Freddy Lerwicki, a long-time admirer, was among them.

She was the first person out of the shuttle, where she pulled herself down the gangway and out to where Freddy stood, wondering if she could persuade him to back her up.

"What's going on?" she asked as way of starting the conversation.

"A hotshot roamer is raiding the Factory," said Freddy, looking her up and down. "He's even wrangled the deputy chief into it." He tilted his head toward Golda Kaetzel when he said that. "We're the second string, standing by in case they need backup."

"What's their objective?" Her heart leapt. It meant Cuss was already on the case.

"I guess they saw a guy get tossed into the works and are going to rescue him and bring in the assholes responsible."

"Did you hear about a new kidnapping? An elderly woman?"

His eyebrows scrunched. "Wait. Say that again?"

Hatha just shrugged, said her goodbyes, and made for small-craft parking. Weaving her way through the vehicles, she reached Nanny's Scape Skimmer, a six-person luxury spacecraft she and her grandmother used for flitting between the cities. Another of Nanny's indulgences, it was high-end transportation for the rare occasions that the elderly woman wanted to travel in comfort to see a show or eat at a restaurant in Athena, Demeter, or Apollo.

The craft had big doors for easy access. Hatha opened the pilot's side door, reached in, and pulled out her spacesuit from the back seat. As she climbed into the lightly armored suit, yet more extravagance from a worried grandmother, she moved her gun to its holster-like side pocket, turning her body as she did so to conceal the act.

After sealing the helmet, she climbed into the pilot's

seat, enabled the nav, and warmed the engine. As soon as the craft was ready, she edged it forward and positioned herself in line for launch. Tapping her fingers in nervous impatience, she waited her turn at the airlock, trying to formulate a plan. But with so many unknowns, all she could think to do was show up and play it by ear.

Once in space, she pushed the small craft hard, making it to the Factory in just under ten minutes. Having never been there before, she didn't know the protocol. She approached from the asteroid side, couldn't see a ship's entryway, and called to the deck master for guidance. An AI voice responded, directing her to the other end of the cylinder. The corrugated door on that side was the clue she sought. Her nav displayed options for the door, and she signaled for it to open.

The broad door lifted to expose a flight deck. She advanced into the bay, landed, and as the craft shut down, the big door closed behind her. She exited the skimmer, and two patrol officers in bright-blue spacesuits started yelling at her, waving their guns, commanding her to raise her hands.

"It's just me," she called to them.

. . .

Ivan Kosmin watched the flight deck from behind the support beam, struggling to keep his anxiety in check. There were blue suits everywhere, squeezing him in a pincer movement, compelling him to watch both his front and rear. And since he hadn't taken the time to recharge his suit's oxygen generator in a couple of days, he needed to find a habitable place at some point to replenish his diminishing stores.

He didn't think things could get worse. And then his suit beeped, his display now confirming he had just two hours of air remaining, forcing his hand. The emotional pressure caused his brain to swirl, and he cursed Stan and Yuri for leaving him in such an impossible situation.

His first impulse was to shoot his way out. But with two cops drifting over the flight deck, widely separated, probing here and there, the odds were against him. And even if he could take both out, he'd need to defend against others in the area, cops he couldn't see at the moment while he readied the Skeeter for launch.

He looked back into the plant and searched for a place to hide while he recharged his generator. He thought Corridor 2 might be his best option. But when a blue suit exited from its airlock, joined moments later by another, it eliminated that option from consideration. His anxiety drifted toward panic.

Returning his attention forward, he finally caught a break. The corrugated door lifted, a private skimmer flew in, and a civilian got out. With the newcomer's craft hot and unsecured, he could steal it and be ready for departure in seconds. And the two cops patrolling the flight deck were moving toward it, putting themselves next to each other with their backs to him. He worked through the choreography in his head, thinking he might be able to pull it off.

Again looking into the plant, the count had grown to

three blue suits floating outside the Corridor 2 airlock.

Ahead on the flight deck, the cops were shoulder to shoulder, pointing their guns at the interloper, their attention fully focused on their target. It was like shooting fish in a barrel. He couldn't miss.

Acting on impulse, he pushed hard off the beam and flew toward them like a homing missile, his legs straight behind him, head up, one arm outstretched, his gun in front. He fired once and missed. He fired again, and the cop on the right flexed backward, like he'd been hit in the kidney with a baseball bat. Shifting aim, Ivan fired at the second cop and missed again.

Then the interloper, in an impressive move, drew a weapon from nowhere and fired a shot right at him. He felt a thump, but before his mind could register it as a hit, his world went dark. There was no fourth shot.

. . .

When the patrol officers moved toward Hatha, their guns pointing at her chest, shouting at her to comply, she hooked a foot under the skimmer to keep from drifting and raised her hands high. She waited for them to get close enough to see inside her helmet, believing that being a pretty woman would play in her favor.

"My name is Hatha," she said as they approached. "I'm with Marshal Cuss Abbott. Give him a call. He'll vouch for me."

The officers were just a few meters away from her when behind them, Hatha saw a man flying across the flight deck, bearing down on them, an arm extended, gun in hand.

"Behind you!" she yelled. "Danger!"

The officers didn't react, like they didn't trust her, like "behind you" was the oldest suckers gambit in the books.

She saw a muzzle flash. Saw it again. And then the officer to her left flexed as a bullet hit him in the back, a ghastly "ohh" escaping his lips.

Reacting, she snapped her weapon from her side holster and fired between the two officers, hitting the man, killing him.

The officer to her right, thinking Hatha had just shot his partner, pulled his trigger, then pulled it again, shooting her twice in the chest at point-blank range.

. . .

Cuss led Juan and the team of four officers through the Factory toward Corridor 62.

"Keep going," said Ygo. "You're almost there."

Cuss thought that at one level, the internals of the Factory looked like what they'd seen in the conference room display. But at another, it was completely different. Specifically in size. The equipment was huge. The things that had appeared as neat geometric shapes in the conference room were as big as ten-story buildings. The *Nelly Marie* could fit inside the pipes connecting the boxes with room to spare. The flow of equipment climbed, split, descended, and split again, filling the space with a wonderland of confusion. He couldn't imagine how the designers thought such a jumble made sense. Yet here it was. And apparently it worked quite well.

Still some distance away, he saw loose sheets of dark material floating near an airlock, empty billboards that blocked the view but had nothing to say.

"The airlock near those mats leads to Corridor Sixty-two," said Ygo. "Travel tubes link Corridor Sixty in a series up through Corridor Sixty-four."

"What are these things?" asked Cuss as they approached the floating banners.

Juan put his gloved hand on one. "They look like floor covering. I wonder if they're scrubbing the crime scene."

"They're floor mats from a room in Corridor Sixty-two," confirmed Ygo. "They should be preserved and examined for evidence."

Cuss gestured toward the airlock and spoke to the two detectives and two patrol officers who were part of their team. "We think this is their hideout. This corridor is linked by travel tubes to three more just like it. Treat them like a crime scene. Sweep the entire length for perps and victims, and then do it again to identify where the medical examiner should concentrate their efforts. Juan and I are going to search for the body we saw being stuffed into the pipe."

The group split, with Cuss and Juan heading to the manhole cover on the side of a huge pipe. Ygo helped Cuss figure out how to open it. Inside was a chamber filled with a cloud of fine powder, some of which proceeded to leak out into the space around them.

Using a light on his suit, Cuss probed in both directions, even leaning inside to look up and down the pipe. But it was like using headlights in heavy fog. The powder scattered the beam, reflecting light back, limiting how far he could see. He thought about climbing in, but feared being hurt by something he didn't understand. Frustrated, he closed the cover. "Let's get someone from Stratus out here to tell us what's safe."

"Code red! Code red! Shots fired. Officer down." The voice was shouting, breathless, disembodied. "Need ambulance and backup. Now!"

"Where are you?" Juan yelled.

"Landing deck!" said the voice. "Heller is hit. Hurt bad. Two civilians are down."

Cuss and Juan reacted, pushing off the pipe, flying through the plant, moving at a reckless speed toward the scene of the shooting. The other four on their team had already cycled inside the corridor through the airlock and would need to cycle back out before they could join the response.

"Are you alone?" called Cuss. In his mind, he was thinking "two civilians" meant two Stratus employees. Combined with the loss of George Hall, the company was experiencing a bloodbath. "Can you get Heller on the bus and take him in?"

"Working on it," came the reply.

Chapter 26

From his lounge chair in the hold of the *Nelly Marie*, Ygo accessed the flight deck sensors and surveyed the carnage, expecting to give Cuss information he could use to direct the response from afar. The injured officer, Paya Heller, had been shot in the back. Ygo linked to the man's suit sensors and learned that he was in shock, bleeding profusely, losing air through the hole in his suit, and needing medical attention in minutes if he was to survive. Paya's best chance was evacuation to Hermes for immediate medical intervention.

Ygo next scanned one of the civilians and learned it was Ivan Kosmin. He was dead, with no chance of resuscitation.

Shifting his focus to the second civilian, he swallowed hard when he realized it was Hatha. A scan confirmed she was severely wounded, clinging to life with devastating injuries. He wailed in horror, wishing he didn't have to be the one to tell Cuss, but knowing he must.

Pausing to curse God, he wondered if there ever would be a day in his difficult existence where he might share in some of life's rewards, where he could bask in the comfort and joy lauded in song. Then he reached out to his friend and partner. "Cuss, one of the civilians shot on the flight deck is Hatha. It's bad. We need to get her help *now*."

As he spoke, Ygo scanned Hatha's recent actions, hoping to learn why she was there. Her voice messages to Cuss told most of the story.

. . .

"What!?" screamed Cuss as he led Juan in a scramble through the Factory. "What are you talking about?"

"Stan kidnapped Nanny and brought her to the Factory," said Ygo. "Hatha flew in to rescue her."

"What?" Cuss said louder, his brain refusing to hear or comprehend, his helmet comms distracting him with the chatter of officers responding to the crisis.

"Nanny's name is Francesca Sophia. She's on the list of those living in Lagrange who have a wire implant. Stan kidnapped her yesterday, and Hatha believes he brought her here. She came to rescue her and was caught in the crossfire when Ivan Kosmin tried to shoot his way off the flight deck."

"How badly is she hurt?" Cuss's heart pounded as he digested Ygo's message. He motioned for Juan to take the lead so he could focus on Hatha's situation.

"Two bullets point blank to the chest. They've moved her onto the bus and are attaching a resuscitation rig now."

"Hold on, babe," Cuss called out, even though she couldn't hear him. "I'm coming."

Forty seconds later they reached the flight deck and learned that Hatha, Ivan, and Paya Heller were already on the bus along with a half-dozen cops. The pilot, hurrying through the launch sequence, paused in his preparations, opened the door of a mini airlock into the craft, and let Cuss and Juan aboard.

Cuss pulled himself down the aisle, moving around a clutch of officers tending to Heller as he scrambled to reach Hatha. He found her strapped to a gurney toward the back, lifeless, helmet off, head lolling, suit pulled open. Two officers were huddled over her, adjusting tubes and wires connecting her to an electronic box the size of a travel suitcase. The wounds in her chest and the volume of blood on her clothes told the story. It never occurred to him that her shooter was sitting mere feet away.

He crouched next to her head and whispered encouragement, doing his best to stay out of the way of the team working on her survival.

"How long before we land?" he asked, willing modern medicine to keep her alive, to make her whole again. When no one answered, he asked again, louder, "How long?"

"Twelve minutes," said Ygo.

Cuss moved her hair off her forehead with an index finger, battling anguish and fear and fury and dread. Her face was deathly pale, the only signs of life coming from the sounds of the rig keeping her alive.

He held her hand during the return trip, alternating between studying her angelic face and staring out the viewport, the whole time working to compartmentalize his worry and redirect his anger. He told her over and over that if she could just hang on for the next few minutes, long enough to get to the specialized medical equipment available in Hermes, then she'd be okay.

And the moment he had her safe, he would end this.

He would find Stan and Yuri and make them pay.

"Don't let them leave, Ygo," he told his partner. "Whatever it takes, just keep them here."

As he juggled a thousand thoughts, a new one added to his turmoil, it too requiring some urgency. "Would you find someone to look after Pibbs? Make sure he's okay?"

. . .

Yuri Melnikov fretted on the flight over to Apollo, reviewing his mistakes, his bad assumptions, his misread of events, cycling through it in his head over and over. With each iteration, he grew more hopeful that he could make it home with millions in the bank, that it would all work out in the end. Stan sat next to him, deep in thought, likely working through his own analysis of the situation.

When they reached Apollo and passed through the small airlock, cops didn't descend on them. It raised his optimism. It meant they still had time.

He guided the Sprite to small-craft parking, shut down its systems, and they climbed out. Hovering next to the vehicle, he and Stan pulled off their spacesuits and stowed them inside. As they did, Yuri saw a couple of cops patrolling the flight deck, something atypical for the cities.

"Give me your gun," he told Stan. He wasn't sure how things would play out but knew that if there was a confrontation, he wanted to be armed.

"What are you going to do?" Stan wrapped both his hands around the weapon to hide it as he delivered it to Yuri.

"We may need to get creative about our ride home." Stan had given him the gun in a belt holster. Yuri clipped it inside his pants at the small of his back and adjusted his shirt to cover it.

"How creative?"

"Which gives us a better chance?" asked Yuri as he scanned the vessels around them, seeing a dozen ships capable of reaching Earth, modern vessels that didn't require specialized skills to pilot. "Hiding for a few weeks to let the heat die down, or making a run for it now? Maybe we should grab a ship before they have a chance to box us in."

"What about Ivan?"

"He's resourceful. He can find his own way."

Stan studied the ships on the flight deck along with Yuri. "How would this work?"

"Let's go shopping. See what we have for options."

They floated among the ships, searching for one they could steal, acting as though they belonged. Yuri sought an unoccupied vessel, one they could board and fly away as if they owned it. But as he worked through the steps, he acknowledged that was an unrealistic goal. It required gaining unauthorized entry to a vessel, overcoming the craft's internal security to enable pilot functions, and persuading the deck master to let them depart as if everything were normal.

"Do you know how to spoof a ship's security systems?"

Stan shook his head. "That's one of the reasons I hired Rex Luskin."

"I don't either," admitted Yuri, fighting annoyance because Stan was provoking him by throwing Luskin in his face, as if killing him had been a mistake.

"But we do know how to persuade someone to do that for us."

"A gun to the head is a persuasive argument," agreed Yuri, taking comfort that he and Stan were on the same page.

.   .   .

The bus landed on Hermes, and Cuss hurried off to give the medical teams room to work, climbing out of his suit while he waited. Two medics floated Hatha out of the bus strapped to a stretcher, her face the same ashen color as the sheet covering her body. The resuscitation rig, carried by a third medic, gave a quiet *ker-thump* once a second.

As Cuss followed the team toward the hospital, Ygo crowed, "I found them! They're on Apollo's flight deck."

"What are they doing?"

"Wandering among the ships, like they're looking for one to steal."

"Keep them there." Cuss hesitated, but just for a moment, wanting desperately to stay with Hatha but needing to pursue Yuri and Stan. He pushed off the bus and made for small-craft parking. "Don't let them leave."

"Where are you going?" Juan called after him.

At first Cuss remained silent, wanting the freedom to take his revenge, to dispense his own justice unfettered by the scrutiny of others. But then he realized he didn't have a craft to get there.

"C'mon," he called to Juan, making a "come here" motion with his hand. "Stan and Yuri are over in Apollo. How fast can you get us there?"

Community Patrol kept a variety of craft at the ready. "This way," said Juan, leading Cuss to the fleet. They climbed into a four-seater with a pressurized cabin so they didn't need suits. As he fired it up, Juan asked, "What do you know?"

"I have intel that they're casing Apollo's flight deck. Like they're looking for a ship to steal."

"Have you called for backup?"

"It's covered," he lied. "Just get us there as fast as you can."

During the short hop between cities, Ygo fed him updates on Hatha's progress. In a lull, he checked his messages and found her pleas for help. It added to his emotional burden. If he'd listened to them earlier, she would be safe, not clinging to life in intensive care.

. . .

Governor Michael Belnick boarded the shuttle on Luna Deck for the short hop down to Apollo's passenger port, thinking about the shit storm that was compelling him to act. A private ship was being readied to transport him to Earth. There he was to meet with Stratus Interworld Partners' board of directors, whose members were his largest campaign donors by a good measure.

The board couldn't understand why his Community

Patrol had caused the Factory to shut down. The cost of the fuckup was astronomical. They were furious and had summoned him to explain in person.

It was an ego play on their part. By forcing him to heel, they were demonstrating their power over him. He didn't like it, not one bit, but was wise enough to know that was how life worked. No matter what your title or position, there was always someone higher up the food chain.

Over the protest of his senior advisors, he'd decided to travel alone so they couldn't witness his humiliation. When he arrived, he would act contrite and apologize profusely, maybe even bow a few times.

But in the end, heads would have to roll to mollify the board. To avoid it being his, he'd have to offer another. The Marshals Service seemed like a scapegoat they might accept. To make it work, he'd have to sacrifice someone big. Someone he cared for. He shrugged at the thought, acknowledging that while he'd hate himself in the moment, it was how a politician survived.

. . .

"Check this one out," said Stan.

"The ship or the woman?" asked Yuri, being clever in spite of the circumstances.

The ship was a sleek cruiser, a cream-colored job with red and blue details at the bottom, squatting on four bent legs like an oversized insect preparing to jump. Its full-height hatch, large viewports all around, and exterior finish polished to a sheen all screamed luxury. In a commercial configuration, it could easily hold twenty passengers within its spacious hull. But Yuri guessed it seated just six or eight people in sumptuous recliners.

Floating toward it was a woman, mid-thirties, petite. She wore a crisp white pilot's uniform with epaulets on the shoulders and a couple of service stripes on her sleeves. A matching cap sat at a rakish angle on her head. Light brown hair spilled over her shoulders.

She waved a hand in front of the access panel next to the hatch, a barely visible square positioned just below the name of the vessel, *Stratus Regal*, written in blue script. The hatch disappeared inward. She followed it into the ship.

Yuri was intrigued. Not only was the ship a beauty, but it was sitting at the front of the queue, the position awarded to craft being prepped for launch. As they watched, a fuel truck operator disconnected a nozzle from the *Stratus Regal*'s fill port, coiled and stowed the hose, and drove away, a sure sign it was being readied for departure.

Yuri led Stan over to the far side of the flight deck, across the way from the shuttle and its loading platform filled with passengers. They hovered in front of a honeycomb of storage bins, a wall filled with six-sided cells, sturdy compartments about as wide and deep as Yuri was tall. They chose a spot where they could see the vessel through a gap between two other craft.

"I wish we had another gun," lamented Yuri.

"I do, too," said Stan, his eye on the ship. "Are you thinking this is the one?"

"I like what I'm seeing." He glanced over his shoulder at the shelves behind them, taking in the breadth of items stored there. "We should change into maintenance uniforms so we can move around without drawing attention."

While Stan watched the ship, Yuri moved along a row of the cubbies, shifting the contents about, poking around for something that would fit the bill. He found all manner of equipment and supplies used to service ships: tools, meters, containers of fluids, wires and cables, hoses, cleaning materials, a host of machines and devices of unknown purpose. But nothing like uniforms.

"We have movement," called Stan.

Yuri rejoined him to see a food service cart pull up in front of the *Stratus Regal*. A man climbed out and rapped his knuckles on the hull next to the open hatch as if he were knocking on a door. The pilot appeared in the opening, the man chatted her up, they laughed a few times, and then he got down to business, shifting three hard-shelled crates from his cart onto the ship. He followed them inside.

Yuri watched with rapt attention, gauging the interplay, seeking an opening he could exploit. Deep in thought, he didn't notice a maintenance man approaching them from behind, a working stiff who seemed in a hurry.

"This is a restricted area," said the man as he muscled an air blower out from a storage cell. "It's safer for you over in the passenger section." He moved off to do his business, not waiting to see if they complied.

The food service man exited the ship, stacked the now-empty crates on the back of the cart, and drove away.

Feeling pressure to act, Yuri committed. "That ship is a winner." He turned back to the storage cells and resumed his search. "Help me look. We need something that disguises our clothes, that buys us time to approach and board without drawing attention." He pawed through a jumble of ribbon cables, wondering if draping one across his shoulders would make him look like a tech worker. But they were all too long, making them unwieldy.

Stan discovered a cubby with welding equipment. Among the items was a welder's jacket, a heavy dark canvas top designed to protect clothing from the shower of sparks. He handed it to Yuri, who ran his hands over the material, appraising it. "This will work. Is there one for you?"

"Don't see one, but I see safety hats." Both plopped yellow plastic helmets on their heads.

The best they could come up with for Stan was a splotchy catch cloth that he draped over his shoulders like a shawl. It wasn't something a worker would normally do, but it muted his street clothes, and it wasn't so odd as to attract attention from casual observers.

Ready to go for it, Yuri hesitated. A man, an executive—tall, distinguished, early sixties, graying hair, tailored suit—approached the ship and called inside. The pilot appeared in the hatch, all smiles. She welcomed him aboard.

"Let's go before it gets crowded," said Yuri, pushing off and floating toward the craft. When they reached the hatch, Yuri checked to make sure Stan was behind him and then entered the ship.

He saw the luxury he expected. Plush gray carpet. Wood accents and gold trim everywhere. Extra-wide aisle between two rows of four oversized acceleration couches, each covered in generous amounts of brown faux leather, with wide armrests, adjustable footrests, and retractable tables.

There was an open area at the back where people could congregate. That's where the man and woman hovered.

Brandishing his gun, Yuri addressed their captives. "Remain calm and no one will get hurt." To the pilot, "You are going to fly us to Earth. What remains of your prelaunch preparations?"

She looked back at him, her face pale, her chin quivering. She didn't answer, Yuri guessed more from fear than defiance. The man put an arm around her in a protective fashion.

Yuri let the gun point down toward the carpet to temper the threat. "What needs to happen before we can launch?" he asked again.

"It's okay, Kel," the man said to her. "They're here for me, not you. Tell him what you need to do before launch."

"My whole preflight checklist."

Stan, who was looking through the items in the food galley, pulled a paring knife off a magnetic holder on the wall and waved it at the pilot. "Your name is Kel?"

"Kelly," she said softly.

"Kelly, let's go up to the cockpit and see how fast you can get through your list." Approaching the pair, Stan held the knife toward them but with the tip pointing upward. He moved it side to side in a rapid motion, a signal to separate. "Your passenger is correct. I won't hurt you if you behave."

To underscore Stan's message, Yuri moved next to him and pointed the gun at the man.

The cockpit was up one level. Stan grasped the woman by the upper arm, pulled her away from her protector, and moved her to the ladder on the wall behind them. She pulled herself up into the cockpit. Stan followed.

As Stan and Kelly moved up to the cockpit, Yuri held his arm straight out, pointing the gun, locking eyes with the man. He called to Stan. "If she moves too slow or signals anyone, cut her face." The man gasped, and Yuri told him in a quiet voice, "She won't be harmed if she cooperates. Neither will you. Now it's your turn. Moving slowly, I want you to grab the ladder with both hands. Don't climb it. Just hold it tight."

The executive moved to the ladder and wrapped his hands around the outside rails, about halfway up between the passenger level and the cockpit. His feet floated out behind him, as though flying through the air.

Yuri approached the man and pressed the gun into his ribs so he could feel its menace. "Give me your ID."

The man reached inside his coat, pulled out a black wallet from the inside pocket, and held it out. Yuri snatched it from him and backed away. "Let's see what we have for a bargaining chip."

"You don't know who I am?" the man asked, his voice incredulous.

"I'm about to find out." Yuri flipped open the wallet, looked at the ID, looked at the man, then looked back at the ID. "Holy shit, Stan. We have the governor."

"Governor of what?" Stan called down from the cockpit.

"The governor of Lagrange."

He heard a thump outside the ship, then a man called to them.

"Stan! Yuri!"

The voice was deep, commanding. He tried to place it but couldn't.

"You're surrounded," the man continued. "It's over. Come out now. Both of you."

Yuri moved to close the hatch, but it didn't respond to his commands.

Chapter 27

Ygo directed Cuss as he scrambled out of the Community Patrol ship. "It's the white cruiser in queue near the airlock."

Looking toward the front of the flight deck, Cuss's lens highlighted the *Stratus Regal*. Shifting his legs up against the patrol ship, he pushed off hard, arms stretched out in front, flying through the air like Superman, leaving Juan to catch up.

"There are two hostages on board with Yuri and Stan," Ygo told him as he soared above the deck. "Kelly Estero, the pilot, and Michael Belnick, the governor."

"Belnick? Really?"

"Yup."

The news should have influenced the evolution of his response strategy. But instead, his mind dwelled on the dearth of evidence that would prove Yuri and Stan were killers, hard facts that would convince a jury beyond doubt that both were guilty of multiple murders. It could mean that the families of the seniors might not see justice. That Hatha's injuries would go unavenged.

So instead of the dispassionate mindset expected of a marshal on a case, he found himself seething, vowing to hold Stan and Yuri accountable, right here, right now. It required him to ignore his inner voice. To willfully override its urgent call for caution, for procedure, for due process. He did that by nurturing his anger, feeding it, cultivating it like a gardener tending to his prize orchids.

As he drew closer to the *Stratus Regal*, he wondered how the two had gained access to the opulent craft. As he pondered the circumstances, his thoughts were interrupted by Ygo, who spoke in a rush. "Shoot the hatch access panel so they can't close the door. Do it now!"

Cuss acted, accepting Ygo's urgency without question. Drawing his Tosic 325 Hybrid in a smooth motion, he thumbed the selector as his arm swung up, moving it forward from safety, through stop, arriving at dead, the selection delivering the largest punch. As he leveled the weapon, he pressed the selector inward, disabling the requirement for contact with human skin before the projectile would dump its charge.

Shooting while in motion was an order of magnitude more difficult than doing so from a fixed position. It required his arm to be moving, sweeping through an arc to track the target while he drew a bead. With the gun out in front of him, arm straight, finger tightening on the trigger, he exploited an advantage he would never consider using when performing his gun qual, when competing against Hatha. He let Ygo help.

Through his lens, Ygo zeroed in on the small access panel from among the features and facets on the exterior of the craft, highlighting it for Cuss. Like a heads-up display in a warcraft, Ygo used color and sound and haptic corrections to help Cuss fine-tune his aim. When the target was acquired and success seemed certain, Cuss exhaled, waited for his heart to beat, and then squeezed the trigger. The projectile exploded from the barrel and tore through the air, traveling over the flight deck in an instant, hitting the access panel dead center with a shower of sparks at the same time the gun's explosive percussion reached his ears.

Closing on the *Stratus Regal* at a reckless speed, he executed an airborne flip in the final moments so his legs were out front to absorb the impact. He landed on the side of the craft as if he'd jumped from a ledge, shouting as he rebounded from his crouch. "Stan! Yuri!"

Craning his neck, he could make out shadowy figures through the hatch but couldn't distinguish who was who. Realizing his position made him a target, he kicked the air in a fruitless effort to pull himself out of the line of fire. Feeling exposed, he turned to bravado. "You're surrounded. It's over. Come out now. Both of you." Then he spoke to Ygo. "Can you show me?"

Working behind the scenes, Ygo had already established links to the *Stratus Regal*'s internal sensors. Transmitting the image to Cuss's lens, he was able to reveal the inside of the craft: an image of Yuri hustling Governor Belnick toward the hatch, an arm around his neck.

When Yuri reached the hatch, he held Belnick in front of him like a shield, his gun pressed to the man's temple. "We will be leaving *now*," called Yuri, wiggling the gun as if to highlight the stakes. "Hustle to make that happen, or lose your governor."

Cuss found himself drifting away from the ship, seemingly in deference to Yuri. But he kept his gun pointed at the hatch. At them. He wasn't going to let Yuri and Stan leave, with or without the governor. He wasn't going to chase them to Earth. He wasn't going to give them a chance to hurt anyone else.

He needed a solution. A way to stop them in their tracks. His calculus didn't consider his career. It didn't weigh the repercussions of any action. He simply distilled his options down to the best one that would achieve his goal in the moment. When he had a solution, he acted.

He shot Belnick in the stomach.

With an "oof," the governor doubled over, bending reflexively as the projectile dumped its charge into his gut. Belnick's movement exposed Yuri's head. Cuss was ready, shooting a second time and hitting Yuri in the face just below his right eye. Yuri's head snapped back, his yellow safety helmet flipping off his head, his arms splaying wide. The force of impact pushed Yuri into the ship, his backward arch thrusting Belnick out from the hatch. Lifeless, the governor drifted above the flight deck.

Cuss grabbed Belnick by the leg and pulled, using him as leverage to move himself through the ship's hatch. Once inside, he shot Yuri again, this time in the gut, ensuring he would not be a factor as the drama unfolded. Then he called up to the cockpit. "Stan, it's over! You've lost your partner and your hostage."

Stan appeared in the accessway at the top of the ladder. Like Yuri, he held Kelly in front of him as a shield, the point of the knife against her neck, a drop of blood oozing out where the tip pressed against her flesh. He looked from Cuss to Yuri and back. "Is he dead?"

"Of course he is. And you will be, too, if you hurt her.

Let her go *now* and you can live. Maybe even win at trial. But force my hand, and I end it by ending you." Gun leveled at the two, Cuss tilted his head toward Yuri, floating in the air like he was asleep. "Do you think I'm bluffing?"

"Cuss," Juan called from outside the ship. "What have you done, man? You need to stop this now."

"Don't come in here, Juan. Don't become part of it." Then to Stan, "I don't have time to negotiate. Toss the knife or die. Five, four, three…"

Stan let the count get to one before tossing the knife and pushing Kelly away from him. Cuss responded with a double tap, a shot to Stan's chest followed immediately by another to his forehead.

. . .

As Stan drifted backward into the cockpit, Kelly pulled herself over to Cuss, clasped her arms around him, and wailed, releasing her pent-up fear and panic, thanking him for saving her. Her legs began to drift back, and she wrapped them around his waist to maintain contact. He hugged her in return, burying his face in her neck, letting the fury and grief he'd bottled up inside spill out in a final dump of emotion.

While they shared the moment, Juan entered the craft with a half-dozen Community Patrol officers. "C'mon, pal," he said to Cuss, pulling Kelly off him. "I need your weapon."

Cuss held it out, not making eye contact as he did.

Juan took it from him and passed it off to one of the

DOUG J. COOPER

officers. "You need to go with these guys. I'll see you at the station. Then to Kelly, "Ma'am, we'll need a formal statement. A witness account."

Cuss let himself be led up to Terra Deck for questioning.

. . .

Cuss sat alone in an interview room, an off-white box at the Community Patrol station, eyes closed, completely exhausted. Like he'd climbed a mountain. Or run a marathon.

"Hatha is responding well to the vitalizer," said Ygo, referring to a medical device that embraced patients in a womb-like environment as it stimulated the body to repair itself. "She's stable, though still unconscious. Oh, and Belnick is awake, sore as hell, but singing your praise. Now that they know you didn't kill him, you should be out pretty quick."

"Pretty quick" turned out to be another hour and a half, a torturous time because Cuss wanted to be at Hatha's side.

Finally, Juan entered the room. "Sorry for the wait. We have to follow procedure when there's a gun discharge in the city."

Cuss nodded, aware of the rules, glad he'd maintained enough presence of mind to thumb his gun's selector forward, pushing it from dead to drop before shooting the governor.

"We've documented most of it from sensor data but

need an incident summary from you to complete the report."

"I prepared it while I was waiting," said Cuss. "I'm sending it now." In truth, Ygo had written it up, relaying it the moment Cuss announced he had done so.

Policy was for Cuss to sit through an extended interview after that. He cooperated as an AI examiner, following an exhaustive script, took him through the incident step by step, circling back to confirm everything, continuing until the facts were established with no inconsistencies or gray areas. Cuss let Ygo feed him the answers so he could be complete, avoid contradictions, and get through the interview as quickly as possible.

From there he raced to the hospital, took up residence in Hatha's room, and watched her as she lay inert in a medically induced coma. A spiderweb of tubes and ducts and wires were connected to her arms and chest. More ran up her nose and down her throat.

"She got lucky," said Ygo as Cuss took in the sight. "Nanny had purchased a suit for her with the same protective plate over the chest that Community Patrol suits have. That extravagance saved her life."

Even with the protective plate, though, the surgical robot still needed three hours to repair the damage to her cardiovascular soft tissue. After that it was up to Hatha and her will to live.

While he waited for her to surface, he and Ygo completed additional reports destined for the Marshals Service. And he closely monitored developments at the Factory, doing so remotely because he'd been ordered to stay away.

One of the earliest reveals was the identity of Hatha's shooter. Ygo delivered the news and Cuss reacted badly. "Shot by a cop? What the fuck, Ygo?"

At Cuss's insistence, Ygo showed him the sensor feeds from the incident. Together they watched Ivan Kosmin fly above the landing deck, shooting officer Paya Heller in the back as he approached him. Then in rapid sequence, Hatha drew her weapon and, in an incredible feat of skill, shot Ivan out of the air. Jake Hamilton then shot Hatha point blank in the chest.

"Jake thought it was Hatha who'd shot Paya, that she was about to kill him, and he reacted to save himself."

At an intellectual level, Cuss could understand the man's actions. During life-and-death situations, officers were forced to make snap decisions with incomplete and often incorrect information. He'd made his own share of mistakes in the fog of war. Yet his personal involvement in this case made him see Jake's behavior as careless, irresponsible, unacceptable. "Is he going to pay?"

"A review board will decide. He could get anything from a reprimand to charges of attempted murder. My guess is that he'll lose his job, and the MA will spend most of a year threatening criminal charges, punishing him with the uncertainty. When public interest has waned, the MA will decide not to prosecute."

Cuss let out a "pfft" of disgust.

Later, they received electrifying news: searchers had found Nanny's body.

"She was in the back seat of a van," reported Ygo. "It

took so long to locate her because the craft was parked outside the shell of the Factory under the condensate sheet. She'd been dead for half a day by the time they found her. Stan's and Yuri's biologicals are all over the vessel. All over her. It makes the case for the MA. He's pressing first degree murder charges for both of them. Add the evidence of the electronic box the two used to connect to the authentication wire and steal the money; it was covered by Yuri's markers. Plus, they discovered a spacesuit that had Roscoe Antonov's blood on the outside and Stan's biologicals inside. There's lots more evidence being collected and processed, so the case will just get tighter. Suffice it to say both will die in prison."

Then more bad news: investigators couldn't find Roscoe's body anywhere in the pipe.

"They think it's because the shutdown took too long," said Ygo. "It gave his body time to reach the smelter. And he wasn't alone. A forensic team combined the data from all the sensors that see that feed port and enhanced the result. They were able to determine that Roscoe, Robert Moore, Franklin Wallingford, and that missing pilot, Rex Luskin, were tossed into the pipe. There's at least one more body they've tentatively identified as Dr. Gall Parrack. They think he's the guy who performed the surgery to expose the wires."

While Cuss took it all in, Ygo added, "They also found a paper printout in Yuri's pocket, the list of rich seniors created by Peter Sobol. For all his genius, the idiot had handwritten at the top of the page, 'Yuri, as agreed - Peter.' It cinches the charges against him, and the DA in Nova

Terra is taking full advantage of it." Another pause. "And they've recovered George Hall from space. Ivan Kosmin's biologicals are all over the body, though he's no longer alive to answer for the crime."

. . .

Two long days later, the doctors disconnected Hatha from the machines and brought her out of her coma. It took most of an hour for her awareness to return, for her thought processes to stabilize.

"What happened?" she asked in a daze.

Holding her hand, Cuss provided details of the shootout and the subsequent arrests.

"How's Nanny?" she asked when he didn't mention her.

Hatha swooned when she heard the news, crying, then going silent, eventually asking to be left alone so she could process the loss. The next morning she made an announcement. "I'm going home."

She reasoned that she had weeks of physical recovery ahead of her, months of psychological healing on top of that. She would return to her childhood home in East Olympia, Washington, to grieve with her parents. They would nurse her back to health.

. . .

Cuss exited the pod station and crossed the pedestrian thoroughfare, making his way to the governor's mansion.

Michael Belnick had invited him to lunch so he could personally thank him for ending the most heinous crime spree in Lagrange's history. And, of course, for rescuing him from Stan and Yuri.

Located just outside the city center, the mansion sat at the top of an artificial hill, a small rise that added to its splendor. The building, made from condensate formed to look like weathered limestone blocks, had a massive front portico supported by Ionic columns. There were sculptured embellishments around the windows and ledges, a slate roof, and a gold dome topped by the red, yellow, and green flag of Lagrange, all trumpeting the majesty of the place and the people inside.

Yet with all the formality, the land around the mansion doubled as a park, with the grounds and a portion of the building open to the public. In front were lush gardens sectioned by hedges and enhanced with cascading water features. Swathes of grass continued around the sides and back for picnics and community gatherings. There were even a handful of specimen trees here and there, adding a certain stateliness to the setting.

Cuss climbed the broad limestone steps to the mansion, weaving through tourists posing for pictures, filming vids, chatting among themselves. The stairs fed onto an open plaza where crowds gathered to enjoy the panorama and regal ambiance.

He paused to take in the view, feeling empty from Hatha's recent decision: she would spend the summer in East Olympia running the family farm stand while she contemplated her future.

"Marshal? This way."

Cuss turned to find a member of the governor's guard—an elite unit of Community Patrol—calling for his attention. Dressed in glittering finery and acting with grand ceremony, the guard ushered him into a great hall that looked like an art museum. Marble steps, marble columns, marble floor, opulent light fixtures, paintings in ornate frames on the walls, statues of Greek gods in the far corners. An appointment secretary greeted him and led him up more stairs and into a much smaller room: a library filled with old books, lots of paneling, and a table set for three.

The other occupant was a woman, mid-thirties, petite, very pretty, dressed for a special occasion. She looked familiar.

"Cuss Abbott? I'm Kelly Estero. Remember me?"

Levers clicked. "You're the pilot."

She beamed, a thousand watts of beauty. "Good for you, Marshal."

She approached him, standing close, acting shy. "Thank you for saving my life." She blushed and shifted her gaze to the floor.

Before Cuss could respond, Governor Belnick swept into the room, saw Cuss, and put a hand on his stomach where the bullet had hit. "Jesus, Cuss. That hurt like hell. I woke up on a gurney being rushed to the hospital. And from the way everyone was acting, I thought I was dying." He looked at Kelly and smiled. "Turns out it was just a bruise and a burn mark. I'll take that any day if it saves lives. Especially my own."

Cuss gave a weak smile. "My gun lets me choose

between stop, drop, or dead. I needed the reflex from you so I could get to Yuri. You experienced the drop option. Sorry about that."

"No need to apologize. And what an experience it was." Belnick gave a genuine laugh as he motioned to the table loaded with food. He held Kelly's chair as she sat.

"I don't know if Kelly told you, but her dad is Manny Estero, the chair of the board of directors for Stratus Interworld Partners. She was about to deliver me to him so he could chew my ass off. He blamed the Marshals Service for the Factory shutdown and was zeroing in on you in particular. I was on my way to Earth to defend you and the Service. But now that you've saved his daughter, we're both in the clear." Belnick raised his wine glass. "If that's not reason to celebrate, I don't know what is."

"He was on his way to Earth to throw you to the wolves," said Ygo. "Oh, and Kelly's hot for you, but I'm guessing you knew that."

They sat to a sumptuous feast. Cuss enjoyed the meal and the company. Belnick had an easy way about him, telling wonderful stories, keeping things light, showing why people voted for him. He made Cuss feel comfortable, listening when Cuss spoke, like he genuinely cared, like he enjoyed his company.

Kelly was charming as well. She allowed that being a pilot for Stratus was a low-stress job that let her travel the worlds in style, with lots of free time to enjoy the sights wherever she landed. Cuss found his head turned by her charms.

When the dishes were cleared and they were enjoying

coffee, Cuss thanked Belnick for having faith in him. "I'm grateful for your continued support. We all are at the Marshals Service."

He almost choked on his words mid-sentence, though. Under the table, Kelly's foot was riding up his leg.

Also by Doug J. Cooper

The Crystal Series

The Crystal Series is four books of action and suspense involving AI, spies, romance, and battles in space!

Crystal Deception (Book 1)
Crystal Conquest (Book 2)
Crystal Rebellion (Book 3)
Crystal Escape (Book 4)

Readers' Praise for The Crystal Series (Amazon Reviews):

★★★★★ "Characters that feel like real people, who behave in ways that make sense and you can empathize with."

★★★★★ "It has all the features of Anne McCaffrey 's Dragon Riders of Pern series. Strong characters, sentient improbability and interesting plots."

★★★★★ "Nicely done hard sci-fi. I am a fan of this kind of story line so it sucked me right in."

★★★★★ "A tale of intrigue, action, a touch of romance and heartbreak."

For info and purchases, visit: crystalseries.com

Free Story!

Crystal Horizon – Prequel to the Crystal Series

The Crystal Series is four full-length books where the emergence of self-aware AI and alien first contact occur at the same time.

Sample this popular space opera for free by downloading Crystal Horizon, the prequel.

In book 1 of the series, Crystal Deception, Cheryl is captain of the military space cruiser Alliance, and Sid is a covert warrior for the Defense Specialists Agency. We learn that the two have a shared history, and in particular, a romantic relationship that has somehow gone awry.

In the prequel, we get their backstory. We join Sid and Cheryl on the day they first meet, and experience that shared history with them.

Crystal Horizon is offered free to newsletter subscribers.

For more about the Crystal Series and to obtain this free book, please visit: crystalseries.com

Made in the USA
Monee, IL
22 May 2023

34313210R00213